"Blankets and whiskey," called Jesse's rescuer as he stepped onto the deck.

The crisp edge to his deep baritone sent the men gathered around them scrambling to obey.

Here was no common sailor, she thought as he bent to lay her down. She blinked, trying to see past her momentary blindness to the man who had braved the icy water to save her.

His image came to her in pieces. Impossibly wide shoulders and a corded neck. Hair slicked wetly back from ruggedly chiseled features. Dark brows slashing above even darker eyes that stared at her intently. He looked . . . familiar.

"Th—thank you," she stammered.

"My pleasure." A crooked smile split his lips, his teeth a white blur against his tanned face.

Recognition burst inside her like a bolt of lightning, and Jesse groaned with the stunning force of it.

'Twas her worst nightmare come to life. . . .

Alexander Sommerville!

Dear Reader,

August brings us another batch of great titles!

In *The Seduction of Deanna* by Maura Seger, the next book in the BELLE HAVEN series, Deanna Marlowe is a woman torn between family loyalty and her passion for Edward Nash.

Sir Alexander Sommerville is determined to restore his family's good name, yet the daughter of his worst enemy, Lady Jesselynn, becomes an obstacle to his plans in *Knight's Honor* by Suzanne Barclay, the story of the third Sommerville brother.

Deborah Simmons gives us *Silent Heart,* the story of Dominique Morineau, a woman forced to leave her home in the midst of the French revolution, only to have a silent stranger once more draw her into the fray.

And rounding out this month is *Aurelia* by Andrea Parnell, a swashbuckling adventure of a young woman who enlists the aid of a hardened sea captain to help find her grandfather's pirate treasure.

A month of four rough-and-tumble Westerns is on tap for September. We'll be featuring some of today's hottest authors, including Pat Tracy and Mary McBride, so don't miss a single title. Watch for them wherever Harlequin Historicals are sold.

Sincerely,

Tracy Farrell
Senior Editor

Knight's Honor

SUZANNE BARCLAY

Harlequin Books

TORONTO • NEW YORK • LONDON
AMSTERDAM • PARIS • SYDNEY • HAMBURG
STOCKHOLM • ATHENS • TOKYO • MILAN
MADRID • WARSAW • BUDAPEST • AUCKLAND

Harlequin Historicals first edition August 1993

ISBN 0-373-28784-4

KNIGHT'S HONOR

SUZANNE BARCLAY

has been an avid reader since she was very young; her mother claims Suzanne could read and recite "The Night Before Christmas" on her first birthday! Not surprisingly, history was her favorite subject in school and historical novels are her number-one reading choice. The house she shares with her husband and their two dogs is set in fifty-five acres of New York State's wine-growing region. When she's not writing, the author makes fine furniture and carpets in miniature.

To all those brave men who, centuries ago, set out to conquer the uncharted seas in boats no larger than my living room—and about as sturdy as a wooden bowl.

Prologue

London, May 1358

It was long past the supper hour, dark and drizzling steadily, when Parlan Graham rode triumphantly into the courtyard of his uncle's London house. Smugness oozing from every pore of his handsome face, he dismounted and tossed the reins to the gaunt young serf who had shuffled out from the shadows.

"Good eve, capt'n," the groom said in a low, servile whine. The sight of the wet head bent in deference and the tattered clothes that hung from the boy's thin shoulders brought a mirthless smile to Parlan's lips. Uncle Edmund neither spared the whip nor spent a penny more than was absolutely necessary to care for his peasants.

A sensible, thrifty practice, Parlan reckoned—one he would continue when he was master here. On that happy thought, he skimmed the stone-and-wood manor house with a possessive eye. 'Twas as sleek and well groomed as a prosperous Italian banker. Tiny compared to Harte Court, Edmund Harcourt's castle a day's ride to the north, but a jewel nonetheless. A ripe plum about to fall into Parlan's lap along with the other juicy fruit on Uncle Edmund's tree.

"Do not unsaddle my horse," Parlan tossed over his shoulder as he mounted the steps. "I will not be long."

Gaining the entryway, Parlan grabbed a hovering servant by the scruff of the neck. "Find Hugh for me, and be quick about it," he snarled, shoving the terrified woman on her way. While he waited for his cousin, Parlan admired the ancestral portraits of hard-eyed Harcourt males lining the whitewashed walls.

Though he was no closer than a sixth cousin, Parlan felt a stirring in his blood each time he beheld these men whose ruthless pursuit of wealth had added to the Harcourt fortune with each succeeding generation. That fever burned so brightly in Edmund it had earned him the title England's greediest man.

Just then Edmund rounded the carved wooden screen that separated the entryway from the great hall, resplendent as usual in a surcoat of green velvet that strained to accommodate his big, burly body. The obscene quantity of gold chain hanging from his neck and the large gems winking from every fat finger made Parlan's mouth water, his palms itch. When they were his, he'd wear as much to the court of his native Scotland—for the sheer pleasure of watching men who had once ignored him fall over themselves trying to gain his notice.

"Parlan, my boy, you are well come!" Edmund roared. Black hair shot with silver framed a puffy face, florid from drink. In his wake, he dragged a buxom blond girl.

Blanche, Edmund's fifth wife. Or was it his sixth? Parlan had lost track of the number of times his uncle had remarried in the vain attempt to get a more suitable heir than Hugh, his only son. Either Edmund had incredibly bad luck, or something had gone wrong with his seed after he'd impregnated his first wife with the twins, Hugh and Jesselynn, twenty years ago.

"I'd visit with you, but my new mare wants servicing," Edmund announced. Blanche gasped and turned purple, but his wide hand on her arm prevented her from bolting. His stubbled jowls aquiver, he laughed at her struggles. "You are welcome to stay if you like. This should not take long," Edmund added as he pulled her up the stairwell to the sleeping chambers.

"Disgusting." Jesselynn Harcourt stalked around the screen, her brother trailing behind. "Men are greedy, disgusting animals, and Edmund the worst." She spotted Parlan and stopped, her nose wrinkling with loathing. "Well, nearly the worst."

"Hush, Jesse, you'll hurt Parlan's feelings," Hugh murmured.

"He has none." She tossed her head, green eyes flashing.

"Good eve, Hugh. Jesselynn." Parlan bowed low, ignoring her outburst. When she was his wife, she'd rue the times she'd snubbed him. Aye, he'd enjoy taming his hot-tempered cousin.

The twins were alike in looks if not in temperament, their thickly lashed green eyes, pale skin and slender builds making them look like young lads. Jesse played on this, dressing like an indigent squire in baggy hose and a loose green tunic that hid her shape entirely. Her curly red hair was ruthlessly pulled back from her face so only the braid that rode her spine to her hips marked her as female.

Parlan would see she wore gowns when she was his wife.

"Hugh, please do not go out tonight," Jesselynn was saying. One hand anxiously gripped her brother's arm.

Hugh smiled fondly and patted her hand, but his gaze locked with Parlan's, eyes bright with excitement and the trace of fear that marked him as a novice at this game of intrigue. "Parlan and I have something we must do. And, nay, you can not come," he added gently. This inbred softness of Hugh's had made Edmund decide his son was not man enough to succeed him, not strong enough to control the reins of the Harcourts' vast empire.

'Twas a gap Parlan planned to fill personally.

"So you said the last time you went off, and the time before that." Jesse scowled fiercely at Parlan. "What have you coaxed Hugh into? Where do you two go week after week?"

"I beg you have patience," Hugh pleaded. "Soon things will be different for us, but I can tell you no more than that." Releasing her hand, he nudged her toward the stairwell. "Go up to your room where you belong."

"Belong! You know I do not belong here . . . or anywhere. 'Tis because I am female you will not take me," she snapped, stamping her foot and whirling to fly up the stairs in a typical burst of anger. "If you get yourself into trouble, do not come to me for help," her voice floated down to them.

"Poor Jesse," Hugh said. "She finds it hard being a woman."

Parlan snorted. "'Twas a mistake to give in to her pleas and teach her to ride and wield a sword like a man. Now she thinks she can do everything a man does—even ride about the countryside helping the peasants cheat Edmund of his due." She'd not do that when she was his wife. "What she needs is a husband to curb her and lesson that foul temper out of her." *Me.*

"Knowing my sister, she already regrets her hasty words, and if she is prickly, 'tis Edmund's abuse that has made her so," Hugh said defensively. Then he sighed. "Beneath her tough husk, she is really gentle and caring as any woman. I agree she needs a husband, but not one who would beat her. One who cares for her enough to see beneath her exterior. One who is patient enough to heal her scars. Though she'll not get any husband if Edmund has his way. He's said she is not womanly enough to wed, when the truth is he'd not part with a penny to dower her."

"Uncle Edmund may be convinced to change his mind," Parlan said silkily, thinking of his own plans.

Hugh shrugged. "It matters not. Part of my reason for undertaking this scheme of ours is so I will have the means to set up a household for Jesse and myself out from under Edmund's thumb. Speaking of which, 'tis time we were away." Slipping on the cloak he had draped over his arm, he started for the outer door. "I spoke with King Edward earlier. He will send his man down to meet us at the docks at midnight."

"Excellent. My crew stands ready to sail on the tide."

Hugh smiled and rubbed his hands together. "Once the king's man sees the counterfeit coins we had made and listens to the false evidence we fed to Tyneham's merchants, his majesty will have no choice but to hang Geoffrey Sommerville for treason. In payment for uncovering this heinous crime of the earl's," Hugh rattled on, obviously carried away by his enthusiasm, "I will demand the one thing that has obsessed yet eluded Edmund's greedy grasp—Geoffrey Sommerville's earldom. Then Edmund will see I am worthy of being his heir."

Parlan smiled, too, as they descended the stairs to the courtyard, but it was his own triumph he contemplated.

"Again, my thanks for your help with this scheme." Hugh gazed up at Parlan with the sickening adoration of a faithful pup. "I will see you amply rewarded, I swear."

"Oh, I will have my reward," Parlan said archly. Only this foolish boy stood between him and Edmund's estates. Parlan planned to have the Sommervilles take care of that for him. Since they had been feuding with the Harcourts over the earl-dom of Winchester for three centuries, 'twould not seem strange when Hugh perished in this scheme to get their title.

Parlan would offer to wed Jesselynn. Edmund's agreement was assured. 'Twould be his only hope of having his precious fortune pass to one of his blood—namely their child. And since a wife's property belonged to her husband...Parlan would have it all.

Chapter One

Jesselynn stood in her bedchamber, her nose pressed to the mullioned windowpanes. Already regretting her outburst, she hoped to catch Hugh before he left and call down an apology. But the sight of her brother emerging into the rain-slicked courtyard at Parlan's side sent a shaft of pain through her, sharp and quick as a thrust from the knife belted to her waist.

Jealousy—she hated herself for feeling it. 'Twas as useless an emotion as yearning for things that could not be... like happiness, or a place to live that was not more prison than home, a place where she belonged.

Do not care that Hugh prefers Parlan's company to yours, she warned herself, but 'twas useless. Since their mother's death in childbed when they were seven, Hugh had been all Jesse had. That she would eventually have to share him with the woman he wed had dimly occurred to her. That she should lose Hugh's friendship to a man she despised was unbearable.

Jesse reached for the window latch, not wanting Hugh to ride off with her harsh words between them, but the way the two men stood, shoulders hunched against the rain, heads bent together in a circle of misty torchlight, fairly reeked of conspiracy.

Sweet Mary! Hugh looked so small and vulnerable with the muscular Parlan towering over him that she was suddenly afraid. Whatever they were about, Jesse could not let Hugh go off alone with Parlan. Though Hugh seemed blinded to Parlan's faults, she knew firsthand that their cousin was capable of great evil.

She had to follow them.

Heart thudding, Jesse whipped around. Hers was a Spartan room, the walls devoid of hangings, the only furnishings a single chair, a narrow, curtainless bed and the clothes trunk that sat at its foot. Wrenching up the lid, she cast aside her other two sets of boy's garments, dragged out her chain mail and sword. There were no woman's things within, and certainly no furs or jewelry. She despised the luxury Edmund wallowed in, knowing it was paid for by the sweat and the blood of downtrodden peasants and those nobles who fell into his web.

Jesse snatched the cloak off the foot of her bed where she had dropped it on returning from the forest and ran out the door. Tomorrow she was due back in the glade to help the villeins with this project she'd coaxed them into, but she'd not sleep tonight until she knew Hugh was safe.

Edmund's voice coming from the entry stopped her on the stairs. "So, John Grimsby can not repay the money I loaned him?"

Jesse's stomach clenched. 'Twas a scene so often played out she knew exactly what was coming.

"Nay, m'lord." Though the tone was low and the voice rougher than usual, Jesselynn realized the speaker was Sir Ralph Thurlow, castellan of the Harcourts' largest holding, Ravenshead Keep, and chief of Edmund's vassals.

"Excellent," Edmund exclaimed. Jesse could see him rubbing his thick hands together. Hands whose effectiveness at dealing pain she knew only too well. "Grimsby's sire refused to sell me his mill and water rights. With him dead of the Black Death, 'twas only a matter of waiting for the son to make a mistake."

"Not a mistake, surely. Young John lost so many people to the plague there were not enough to work the land, and—"

"His loss is my gain. Would that I could visit a plague on every bastard who stands between me and what I want. Throw Grimsby out of the keep and take control of that mill."

Sir Ralph coughed. "He has a wife and four small children."

"Are you growing soft, Ralph?" Edmund snarled.

"Nay," he answered quickly, with a trace of fear. Even a knight long in his service knew better than to cross Edmund.

Jesse's whole body shook with revulsion, and she bit her lip to keep from crying out in horror and frustration. Surely 'twas a sickness for a man who owned more land than he could ride over in a lifetime and more gold than he could ever use to constantly hunger for more. Worse still was knowing there was nothing she could do to stop him.

"If Grimsby resists, kill him, and put the woman and children to work in the mill," Edmund said with relish.

'Twas the last straw. Jesse was down the stairs before she even realized she was moving. She dashed across the entryway and skidded to a halt before the two startled men. "Nay, you can not!" she shouted, one hand on her sword hilt.

Edmund snorted, green eyes glittering with annoyance. "Take her below and lock her in a cell," Edmund growled at the two hard-faced mercenaries who flanked him.

"Nay!" Ducking under the guard's outstretched hand, Jesse darted out the doorway and down the stairs. Desperation lent wings to her feet as she streaked across the slick courtyard and through the open gate out to the city road. Behind her she heard the heavy thud of pursuit. With a burst of speed, she darted into a side alley.

After a while, Jesse thought she spotted Parlan and Hugh riding through the crowd up ahead. Lucky for her, the bustle of the London traffic had forced them to ride slowly, she thought as she settled in to follow the duo—with one eye over her own shoulder, on the lookout for Edmund's thugs. She did not feel nearly as confident when their trail led first to London's squalid docks and thence out across the dark harbor to *The Salamander,* Parlan's ship.

Sweet Mary, but she hated the water, she thought, shivering as she crouched in the shadows of the forecastle. The inky sea reminded her too forcefully of the lightless cell Edmund shoved her into whenever he caught her helping his peasants defy him.

She was about to go in search of Hugh, when he appeared on deck to welcome a richly dressed stranger.

"I'm Lord Robert Peverell," the portly old man said. "King Edward has sent me to investigate these charges you would bring against the Sommervilles."

Sommervilles! Jesse all but fell over trying to get closer.

"You are well come," Hugh said pleasantly. "A cabin has been prepared where we may sit and talk in comfort. I expect we will reach Tyneham by tomorrow night."

"Sensible men to not venture from shore at night," Lord Robert grumbled. A sentiment Jesse heartily shared. "Can we not wait until dawn?"

"The longer we delay the greater the risk that Geoffrey Sommerville will somehow learn we are on to his counterfeiting scheme and destroy the evidence I am taking you to see."

Lord Robert grunted in reluctant agreement and allowed himself to be escorted from the deck.

What was going on? Curiosity goaded Jesse to follow, confront Hugh and demand the answers. But no sooner had she begun to crawl from hiding than Parlan stepped into view, a lantern in one hand. Even in that dim light, she saw the greed glittering in his eyes. His thin lips twisted into an evil smile that sent shivers of apprehension racing down her spine.

Sweet Mary! Parlan *was* up to no good.

As he turned and walked away, Jesse slumped back, boneless, against a coil of rope. What should she do? Too often she'd been accused of acting without thinking. She could not afford to act hastily this time: the scent of danger was so strong she could almost taste it. Her first impulse was to find Hugh.

And tell him what? That she trusted not Parlan's smile? That she had seen Parlan commit a deed so foul she knew he was capable of great cruelty? Nay, dear as he was to her, Hugh might not see Parlan's rape of a young girl as proof their cousin was evil. Men and women viewed things very differently when it came to how women were treated.

Jesse sighed and decided to bide her time. Slinking forward, she ducked beneath one of the overturned rowboats that offered shelter from the cold wind and the spray. Her cloak wrapped securely around her, she settled down to sleep. 'Twas no worse than the lean-tos she had fashioned when harking about the woods, but with the chain mail biting into her skin, she resigned herself to a restless night.

It was not physical discomfort that preyed on her, nay 'twas thoughts of the Sommervilles. Their name rang through her head like the tolling of a warning bell. Much as she applauded Hugh's efforts to bring them to justice, she was afraid for him. Unlike the Harcourts, the Sommervilles were a close-knit family. What threatened one threatened them all, as she well knew from time she'd spent at Wilton Castle two years ago with Ruarke Sommerville and Gabrielle, his wife.

'Twas not by choice that she had sheltered there. A fall from her horse had cracked her head and stolen her memories. Gabrielle had nursed her back to health and given her a place in the household. The Sommervilles had treated her kindly enough—all but one—yet if they learned Hugh was on to this scheme, they would stop at nothing to silence him.

Jesse's restive mind drifted to the middle Sommerville son—Alexander. Dark eyes and a sizzling temper that had struck sparks from hers the instant they had met. Shivering, she wrapped the cloak tighter around her and wished herself in the woods with a dozen wolves ringing her camp. Aye, even that would be preferable to seeing Alexander Sommerville again.

Tyneham Cliffs were sheer and impregnable, plummeting down hundreds of feet to meet the sea that foamed at its rocky base. Awesome, had been Alexander Sommerville's first thought when he'd sailed into the bay this morn and beheld the towering rock walls. The keep perched on the rim of the cliffs had belonged to his family for generations, but Alex had lived at sea since the age of fourteen, and this was his first visit to Tyneham. In truth, 'twas no idle visit.

"Thank you for coming, Alex," Gareth said from behind him. The strain in his older brother's voice was evident.

Alex raked a hand through his long, dark-blond hair and turned away from the view of the churning bay, conscious that the unseen currents swirling through the room were deeper and more turbulent than the sea. "Your message sounded urgent." He crossed his arms over his chest and braced his legs as he did at sea when he expected to ride out a storm.

Both men had inherited their sire's height and wide shoulders, but Alex was built more leanly, his high cheekbones and straight nose a bit more chiseled. That he had their grandsire's stubbornness and hot temper were reflected in his square jaw and the fire that never quite left his midnight eyes, Gareth thought. His gaze fell on the thin scar that cut across Alex's tanned throat. "Aye, 'tis urgent. Papa asked me to come here to Tyneham to attend the wedding of Sir Neil, who was castellan here, and to investigate the murder of one of his knights—presumably by smugglers. I never dreamed I'd uncover a plot against us."

"A plot?" Alex straightened instantly.

"Aye. A Harcourt plot." Alex's horror grew as he listened to Gareth relate what he had overheard while investigating the caves the smugglers were suspected of using. "There were no smugglers. The ship the villagers had seen each week brought Hugh Harcourt. I became trapped in the caves and overheard him discussing his plans to frame Papa and me for counterfeiting."

"Counterfeiting?" Alex's eyes widened; his blood ran colder still. "'Tis a treasonable offense. Punishable by hanging."

Gareth nodded. "The coins were made by the goldsmith's apprentice, Charles Beck, half brother to Walter, the man Ruarke ran out of Wilton Castle for stealing from him."

"Damn." Alex knew their younger brother had wanted to hang Walter Beck, but Gabrielle had pleaded for mercy. "If Walter is involved in this, too, Ruarke will wish he had killed the man."

"'Twas Walter who convinced four of the local merchants to pass the false coins to their customers. The merchants were there, and I can name them, for all the good it will do us." Gareth exhaled sharply. "There was a masked man with Hugh. He claimed to be me and said that Papa was behind this scheme."

"And the merchants believed him?" At Gareth's nod, Alex groaned. "So even if we brought them in for questioning, they'd point a guilty finger at you and Papa." At Gareth's nod, Alex squeezed his eyes shut. Nay! Not his precious family!

Geoffrey, his scholarly father, and Catherine, his gentle mother. Ruarke, the youngest, whose warrior ways hid a soft heart. Gabrielle and their two baby daughters who would never have a chance at life if Harcourt succeeded. And Gareth, who had lived through hell married to Emilie and with her death a few months ago was finally free. Nay. He could not let that happen. "We have to capture Hugh and force the truth from his lying lips," Alex said grimly. Teeth grinding, he began to pace.

Gareth watched his brother prowl the room like a rangy bronze cat, restless as the seas he sailed. Only a few yards separated him from the brother he'd always admired for his quick wit and sense of honor, but it might well have been miles. 'Twas a woman who had come between them. *Emilie*. God curse her for the lies that had nearly caused him to kill Alex.

"When do you expect his ship to return?" Alex asked.

"They have been coming every Monday, but after the merchants had left the cave, Hugh told the masked man he was not waiting for Monday next to roll around, he was returning to London straight away to tell the king."

"Who will send someone to investigate." Alex locked his clenched fists together to keep from smashing something. "We will be waiting for them!"

"I'd feel more assured of our success if Ruarke were here."

Alex scowled at his brother. Even knowing 'twas his own fitness to lead that Gareth questioned did not lessen the sting. "There was not time to wait for him. I made port three days ago, and arrived at Ransford yesterday to find your message. Knowing I could reach you quickest by sea, I sent word to Ruarke and Papa, rounded up as many of my sailors as I could and sailed here. *The Sommerville Star* is anchored some two miles down the coast; aboard are eighty men-at-arms from Ransford."

Gareth nodded. "I didn't mean to sound ungrateful for your presence here, Alex, but..."

"Seeing me brings back the guilt." Shoving a hand through his hair, Alex drew in a cleansing breath and crossed to Gareth. "Let it go," he said, taking his brother's shoulders.

Gareth tensed, his eyes dropping to the scar that shone white against Alex's tanned throat. "I can't."

"Given the terrible lies Emilie had fed you, you had every reason to seek revenge." Alex's voice was low, charged.

"God, I nearly killed you. My own brother." Such agony.

Alex felt it, fought to absolve his brother. "Nay. Your blade barely broke my skin," he insisted. He gripped Gareth tighter, his heart going out to him.

"I lost control and attacked you like a madman."

"Mad! Bah. Your temper is nothing to the one I inherited from our mother's sire," Alex reminded him.

"Aye, Roger de Rivers's rages were something to behold," Gareth allowed. "At least you do not foam at the mouth as he used to," he added with a ghost of a smile that gave Alex hope they could mend the rift. "But you never hurt anyone."

If you only knew. Now it was Alex who could not meet Gareth's gaze. Bowing his head, he mumbled, "My temper has been a trial to me all my life. I have vowed not to lose it again."

Gareth's snort brought Alex's head up. "That I'd like to see."

"Aye." Alex grinned ruefully, pleased by his brother's answering smile. In him, love of family ran even deeper than it did in his two brothers, and it nearly killed him to have this friction between them. "Bevan tells me I should scrub the decks to work my anger off. Have you any suggestions?" he asked the most patient of the Sommervilles.

"I usually walk away or count to twenty." Gareth's smile dimmed. "Would that I had counted to one hundred that day Emilie's lies sent me after you."

Alex sighed in exasperation. "When we were boys there were countless times I had to beg your pardon for starting a fight. Now *I* forgive *you*. Please forgive yourself."

"I'd speak of it no more." Gareth went to the desk and poured himself a cup of wine, downing it in one long swallow.

Damn, he was stubborn. Alex joined Gareth, but the wine did not ease the tightness in his throat or gut. "True, it was a blow to my pride when Emilie tossed me aside for you." He ignored Gareth's warning growl. "But I feel I should apologize for having met the witch in the first place." He pasted on the crooked smile that so often hid unhappiness. "Had I not, you would have been spared two hellish years of marriage to her."

"Alex! Will you stop."

"Not until I've convinced you—"

"Stop meddling! I hate it when you stick your nose into my affairs," Gareth grumbled.

"Papa always said I had a talent for charming people into doing things they did not know they wanted to do." He strove for his usual light, lazy tone, but missed by a ship's length.

"Then you should have joined him at court as he'd wanted you to instead of running off to sea and breaking his heart," Gareth snapped, setting his cup down with undue force.

Alex winced. "Does he still speak of that?" Alex asked, suddenly concerned.

"From time to time." Gareth eyed his brother's bleak expression and sighed. Beneath his teasing and mockery, Alex was the healer of the family. He could not see a needy creature without trying to cure its ills or an unjust situation without trying to right its wrongs. "Excuse my hasty tongue."

"Only if you will forgive yourself for—"

"Damn! You are the most infuriating, stubborn—"

"I have been told that before," Alex quipped, shoving the pain of having disappointed his sire back behind a grin.

Gareth was not fooled for a moment. He was one of the few who saw the sensitive man beneath the roguish mask Alex wore. And, too, he had sat up with his brother the night before Alex had announced to their parents that he was going to sea. The decision had not been easily or lightly made.

"I'm not suited to be a warrior like Ruarke," Alex had said as he paced their chamber that night. "Nor am I a man of the land like you. The sea seems to suit me. Aye, I feel at home there, and I need the challenge of besting it."

To curb his restlessness, Gareth thought. And it had. Until Emilie had come into their lives. Alex claimed only his pride had been wounded by Emilie's decision to wed Gareth, but he had been different ever since the episode. Quieter. Almost...lonely.

Gareth's expression was so strained Alex feared he was dwelling on their confrontation again. "How do you plan to capture Hugh?" he asked by way of diversion.

"What? Oh... I thought you could hide your ship in one of the inlets until Harcourt's ship enters the cove. My force will wait on the beach, while you sail in to block the entrance and cut off their escape route to the open sea."

"Agreed," Alex said at once. Ironic that it had taken their enemy's evil scheme to bring them back together again. He added a few embellishments of his own to Gareth's plan, then poured himself a cup of wine and dropped into a chair. "So, tell me about the wench?" he drawled, thinking of the woman he had found in his brother's bed when he'd arrived this morn.

Gareth bristled. "Arianna is not a wench."

"All women are wenches," Alex said lazily.

"She is the woman I intend to wed."

"What?" Alex bolted from the chair, his eyes wide. "After the time Emilie put you through, I did not expect you to rush into another marriage."

Gareth did not even wince over Emilie's name. "Papa reminded me that it's my duty to provide the Sommervilles with an heir. I had agreed to let him choose my next wife, but then I came here and, er, something came up."

"And I can guess what it was," Alex said with a lewd wink. "She's a tempting morsel."

"You will not speak of her so!"

Alex blinked. He had been fortunate to avoid love all these years, but he recognized the signs in a Sommerville. 'Twas said Sommerville males fell in love only once, but they fell hard and fast. "Does she love you?"

"Aye." Defensively.

"Is she the daughter of some visiting lord?"

"Nay. She is the granddaughter of Tyneham's goldsmith."

"The one who made the false coins?" Alex exclaimed.

"Nay," Gareth shot back. "'Twas the apprentice who made them. Arianna's family had no idea what he'd been up to."

"Ah, well. In any case, what will Papa say to the heir and future earl wedding a burgher?"

"She is the only woman I will have."

Alex started to differ, then laughed. "You are as protective of her as Ruarke is of Gaby. It must be love."

"Your time will come," Gareth predicted darkly.

Alex shook his head. Still laughing, he took a sip of wine and choked on it. "Never. I'm wedded to the sea."

"I admit it is hard to picture you settling down with just one woman when you are used to having your pick of dozens."

Somehow Alex kept his smile in place, though he no longer felt like laughing. Aye, he'd enjoyed many women in his time, but none of them had truly touched him.

"Does your Arianna have a sister?" Alex asked abruptly.

"Nay, and we've work to do," Gareth said stiffly.

"Aye." Alex stood. "'Tis high time we did something about ending this cursed feud." Before he turned to stalk to the window, his eyes blazed with a fervor Gareth knew well.

"Alex!" he cried, chasing after his brother, catching him by the arm and spinning him around.

The ruthless determination glittering in Alex's eyes sent Gareth back a step. When he'd challenged Alex over Emilie's lies, his brother had shrugged and refused to fight; now Alex looked ready to take on an army. It was the hint of desperation shadowing those dark eyes so like his own that struck terror in Gareth's heart, made him forget all about guilt and discord. "Alex, what are you planning?" He seized Alex by the shoulders, shook him far harder than Alex had him earlier.

"To end the feud. No matter what it takes."

After her sleepless night, Jesse slept the day away. When she crawled from hiding the next night they were in sight of land. Was this Tyneham? The sheer cliffs and deserted beaches they drifted past looked rocky and inhospitable. The black clouds overhead and the thick bank of fog lurking just off the coast hinted at bad weather to come.

"The tide turns. Make ready the boats." Parlan. No torches had been lit, but she tucked her face deeper into her cowl.

"Ah. This is it, then." Hugh sounded excited and scared.

"Aye. I wish I were going with you, but it would not do for Sir Robert and any of the merchants to see me without the mask."

Jesse puzzled over that strange statement as Parlan ordered the rowboats lowered. Under cover of darkness, she sneaked down the swinging rope ladder, determined to keep track of Hugh.

Hers was the last of the three boats to land. She saw Hugh already on shore as the hull of her craft scraped on the rocky beach. The men had just started to climb out when battle cries split the air, ringing off the rocky cliffs as men poured onto the beach and cut off all means of escape but the sea.

"Beware! Ambush!" Hugh screamed. The sailors fumbled for their weapons, dropping their torches onto the wet sand. Most hissed out, adding to the confusion.

"Back to the ship!" a man shouted. Beneath her, the boat heaved as two men jumped in and pulled furiously on the oars.

"We can not leave Hugh," Jesse cried, but the men ignored her. Clutching the side of the boat, she struggled to make sense of the figures writhing in combat on the beach. Dimly she saw the other two boats being launched, but could not find Hugh.

"*Dieu*, we are lost!" cried one of the men in her boat.

Jesse whipped around just as a huge ship burst from the gray wall of fog. Sails flapping like the wings of a giant predator, it swooped down on Jesse's boat, cutting between it and the safety of *The Salamander,* running on a collision course that would surely slice the tiny boat in two.

Her companions screamed and jumped, swamping the boat and tossing Jesse into the choppy bay. Seawater filled her mouth and nose as the waves closed over her with terrible finality. Down, down the inky black swirl pulled her. She clawed at the water, lungs burning, searching frantically for the way out.

Suddenly something snagged the neck of her tunic and wrenched her upward. Air. Blessed air. Jesse coughed and gagged, her limbs struggling feebly against the water.

"Be still, or I'll let you go again," growled a deep voice.

Though it killed her to relax in a man's grip, Jesse slumped against the hard, muscular chest. By force of will alone, she remained limp as he pulled her with him through the water.

Whoever he was, he was strong. He slung her over his shoulder and climbed the swaying rope ladder as lithely and quickly as though she weighed nothing in her wet clothes and chain mail. At the top, they were met by men bearing torches.

She squeezed her eyes shut against the sudden light.

"Blankets and whiskey," called her rescuer, laying her on the deck. The crisp edge to his baritone sent men scrambling to obey. She blinked, trying to see past her momentary blindness to the man who had braved the icy water to save her.

His image came in pieces. Impossibly wide shoulders and a corded neck. Hair slicked back from rugged features. Dark brows slashing above black eyes that stared intently. He looked . . .

"By all that's holy—you!" he exclaimed, his teeth a white blur against his tanned face.

Recognition burst inside her like a bolt of lightning.

Alexander Sommerville.

Chapter Two

Jesselynn Harcourt.

Alex's lean, callused fingers curled into fists, imitating the tension that tightened his gut. The treacherous Edmund Harcourt's daughter, here. Damn. As though he did not already have enough problems.

It had been two years since he'd seen her, but Alex knew that oval face with its fragile bones and full, sensual mouth, recalled only too well that her fragile appearance was deceiving. Seawater darkened her rebellious red hair, smoothing it back from a face gone white as marble, but when it dried, it would be every bit as wild and unruly as she would be once she'd regained her breath—and her spitting temper.

Alex groaned inwardly in disappointment. In the darkness, he had mistaken the slim, red-haired figure for Hugh.

Hugh. Surging to his feet, Alex wheeled on his captain. "Bevan, this is not Hugh Harcourt. See if you can locate him."

Jesse seized the moment, leaping to her feet and darting toward the rail with no conscious thought as to what she'd do when she got there. But she'd forgotten how fast Alex was.

"I think not," he grated in her ear at the same second those hard arms that had so recently saved her scooped her up around the waist and mashed her against a lean hip.

Alex had expected resistance, but he got more than he'd bargained for from the half-drowned girl. She thrashed wildly, kicking and swearing a blue streak a sailor would envy.

Two years ago some spark in her could make him see red in a flaming instant. It seemed that had not changed. But his

tactics had. He would not let her goad him into losing control. *One*, he began. *Two.* "Cease this—" *three* "—ere I beat
you," Alex said in a strangled voice, battling rising anger as
much as her thrashing under his arm.

"Do it then," she snarled and sank her teeth into his hand.

Alex stopped counting and started cursing. He applied his
thumb and forefinger to the hinge of her jaw with just enough
pressure to open her mouth. "Have it your way," he growled,
and relaxed his grip on her struggling body. She tumbled to the
deck.

Welling tears magnified the green of her eyes and pricked his
conscience. Alex grabbed her by the upper arms and set her on
her feet. He nearly started to apologize, then outrage chased
the pain from her expression, bringing her little chin up and
out a mile. How could he have forgotten her spunk? he
thought, smiling in rueful appreciation.

"Laugh at me, you bastard!" she hissed. He caught the
fierce gleam in her angry eyes as she lunged.

"Enough!" he bellowed, neatly avoiding her flailing fists.
"What in holy hell do you think you'd do if you did manage
to jump overboard?" The hostility crackling from her rivaled
the lightning now streaking across the dark sky. "You can not
swim," he coldly reminded her.

"Better dead than your prisoner," she shot back.

Alex drew in a deep, calming breath, then released it on an
exasperated groan. "You are many things, Jesselynn." Fiery.
Impetuous. Stubborn. "But not stupid. You no more want to
kill yourself than . . ." *Than I want you to,* only he could not
give her that much power over him. "You are my prisoner.
Comport yourself with some dignity."

That spur to her pride drained some of the fight from the
slender but surprisingly well-muscled arms he still held. The
fury in her face softened just a bit. 'Twas the most he could
expect, he supposed.

"Ellis," he shouted over his shoulder.

"Here." Expression bright and eager as ever, the squire
popped around his left side, a post he had held for nearly a
year now.

"Take *Lady* Jesselynn to my cabin and lock her within."
Alex said in English. His sailors and soldiers had not mas-

tered the Norman French of the nobility, and he'd have all know he'd hold her under lock and key while he went after Hugh.

Ellis's mouth gaped and brown eyes widened with equal parts awe and disbelief. "That's a lady?"

Alex suppressed the bubbling laughter that would have set off his indignant prisoner again. "Aye." He sent a warning glance her way. "If you attack my squire, I'll see you in chains."

"I'd prefer to remain on deck," Jesselynn said tightly.

"I'm a little pressed for time right now," he drawled, "and could not give you a proper tour of the ship." Beneath her loose tunic, Alex had felt the metal links of chain mail. A woman in chain mail? 'Twas an abomination!

Jesse quivered. Not from fear, though he towered over her, large and overwhelmingly masculine in the confines of the small ship. She had weathered Edmund's intimidation. Nay, 'twas loathing. Alex's smugness, the mocking light in his eyes as he released his hold on her and turned her over to his squire, that made her belly churn with hate. Letting it show in her eyes, she took a quick step back, brushed off her arms to remove the feel of his hands, then whirled and stalked after the squire.

Unruly as ever, Alex thought, taking in the proud line of her stiff little body. Even wet and ashen with anger, she was lovelier than his memories of her. Hauntingly so. Aye, she haunted him, tempted him, but she was a Harcourt and he a Sommerville. There could be nothing between them except what had been there years ago—a clash of wills so hot it had singed them both.

"Alex." Bevan MacLean's thick burr tore Alex's eyes from the retreating figure. "There's still no sign of Hugh, but we're comin' about on his ship now."

Grateful for the diversion, Alex followed *The Sommerville Star*'s captain to the aftercastle. It was constructed in two tiers, the lower one sheltering the cog's helmsman from the elements while he plied the rudder that steered the ship. The upper gallery provided an unobstructed view of the whole ship.

From here, Alex and the grizzled Scots captain watched *The Star* close the distance to Harcourt's ship. "Bloody hell, that's

Hugh there at the side rail. Have the archers stand ready to let go a volley on my signal," Alex roared above the rush of wind.

"It'll be a very near thing," Bevan commented, gauging the distance to the fog as Alex's order was relayed to the archers in the forecastle.

Damn. Alex pounded the rail. "I should have had you make directly for the ship, but I was so sure Hugh was in that boat."

Bevan shrugged, one hand rubbing his big belly. "It wouldna matter but fer the bloody fog. It's comin' in faster than even I figured. If Harcourt reaches it afore we catch him, he stands a good chance o' slippin' away." Bevan eyed the triangular lateen sails billowing overhead and ordered the lines tightened. "We need ta coax every bit o' speed we can out o' our lady."

Despite their circumstances, Alex smiled faintly at Bevan's reference to the ship. At nearly fifty, Bevan's wiry hair was more gray than red, his broad face seamed by wind and sun. To the Scot, *The Star* was indeed a lady, and he lavished on her the love he'd have given a wife if he'd had one. Bevan had captained her for ten years. First under James Sommerville, Alex's uncle, dead these past seven years, then under Alex. As his bachelor uncle's heir, Alex had inherited four ships and Bevan to captain the pride of that small trading fleet.

Between them, James and Bevan had taught Alex all he knew about the sea, and she'd become as much his mistress as theirs. When he had left court at the age of fourteen, Alex had found the sea a welcome change from the boredom of gossip and silly intrigues, an irresistible challenge. Even at twenty and seven, the sea continued to test and excite him. Ever changing, ever dangerous, the sea was more mysterious, more alluring than any of the women Alex had known . . . and had held his interest far longer.

The incident with Emilie had changed that, somehow, made him less content with life at sea. The birth of Ruarke and Gaby's daughter Cat eight months later had given Alex a focus for these yearnings. One look into her pansy-purple eyes, one smile from her rosebud mouth and Alex had fallen in love. He wanted a child of his own. Unfortunately, he still did not want a wife.

Beside him, Bevan stirred, leaning forward to add his brawn to *The Star*. Reflexively Alex strained with him, gripping the rail as he urged the ship on, but the wind was light and capricious. The enemy vessel continued to run before them, dangling just out of range of his archers, her sails silhouetted against the curtain of gray fog that would soon swallow her up and reduce *The Star*'s chances of catching her to naught.

Alex knew just how thick that fog was, for *The Star* had hidden in it while waiting for Harcourt and his men to row ashore. Even if he and Bevan had been familiar with this particular stretch of coast, which they were not, tracking a ship in the fog at night was risky business.

"Damn!" Bevan cried, striking the rail with a balled fist as Harcourt's ship slipped from sight—bow first, then the rest, like a hand slowly vanishing inside a gray glove.

"We're not giving up," Alex ground out, eyes fierce. "Fetch me the Portolan Charts and the wind rose."

"Aye, that's the spirit." Bevan bared his teeth, eagerly taking up the challenge. "We'll send the sharpest eyes aloft and put two men on the sounding lines."

Nodding, Alex turned toward shore. By the light of the rekindled torches, he made out Gareth's tall form standing at the water's edge. Even at this distance, he could feel his brother's frustration. They could not afford to fail. "I'll get Hugh!" Alex called through cupped hands.

But the fog was even thicker than Alex had remembered. From atop the aftercastle, he could scarce make out the mast a few yards away. The disembodied voices of the men calling out the depth of the water they traveled drifted eerily over the ship. Sailors went about their tasks in tense silence, their thoughts and prayers with the lookouts above straining to catch a glimpse of the enemy vessel—or some hint of imminent danger.

His gut tight with apprehension, Alex pored over the Portolan Charts—text and scale drawings of the coast. Until the drawing up of these charts, ships had been forced to sail close to the shore or risk becoming lost in the vastness of the seas. Still, there was no foolproof way to know the location of every submerged rock and shoal that might tear into *The Star*'s belly and send them all to a watery grave.

Judging from the charts that they would be coming up on a point of land in a mile or so, he immediately relayed a new heading to the helmsman. It was critical to make the course correction early, because the cogs responded slowly.

As *The Star* swung, the lookout called, "Ahoy, ship to port!"

Alex caught a fleeting glimpse of a large, dark shape a quarter mile ahead in the shifting fog. *Harcourt.* Who else would be desperate enough to sail so close to shore? Alex's pulse leaped. "Come about," he ordered, then heard a sound that struck terror into the heart of every seaman.

Surf breaking over rocks. The steady, deadly crash and suck came from the landward side of the ship. But how far away?

"Lookout. Can you see the rocks?"

"Nay, but I hear the waves on them. Th-they sound close by."

Damn. Legs braced against the pitch of the ship, both hands buried in his sun-bleached hair, Alex strained for some glimpse of the rocks. His blood boiled with the frustrated desire to capture Hugh, but his mind, weaned on a hundred other dangerous situations, was cool, calculating.

Harcourt's ship lay somewhere between them and the rocks. Either Harcourt knew these waters like his own black soul, or he did not care what happened to his men and his ship. Given the Harcourts' reputation for greed, it was likely the latter. But Alex could not change his sense of duty and honor any more than he could change the color of his eyes.

"Hard to starboard," he called down to the helmsman.

"Of all the bloody luck," Jesse raged, pacing the confines of the tiny cabin she'd been locked into. The shouts she had heard reverberating off the cliff walls when Hugh was attacked must have been the Sommerville battle cry.

Somehow the cursed Sommervilles had discovered Hugh was on to their scheme and was bringing Lord Robert Peverell to expose their crime and see them punished.

Had Hugh managed to escape? She had seen his boat making for *The Salamander,* but 'twas possible Alex had run him down, too. At the thought of Hugh in Sommerville hands, a cold sweat broke out on her already chilled body. Nor was

Hugh the only one in danger. Though Alex was a weak womanizer, she was his prisoner.

A Sommerville would not torture a woman; they were soft where females were concerned, Jesse knew from her time at Wilton. But given his reputation, Alex would likely delight in relieving his enemy of her virginity. Not because he desired Jesse as a woman, but merely to prove his mastery over her.

Jesse shuddered, the thought of Alexander rutting on her worse than any torture ever devised. She stopped pacing immediately and started searching for a way out of her prison.

Luxury. It was the first thing that struck her when she took a good look around. Small the cabin might be, but richly appointed, from the blue velvet hangings on the wide bunk built into one wall to the intricately carved desk nearby. Her lip curled at the vulgar display. So, he was greedy for things as well as for women. How many of his men had he worked to death to pay for these worthless trappings? Almost, she could imagine his lean, tanned body stretched out on the rumpled sheets, entwined with the white, fleshy limbs of some woman he wanted to impress.

A tremor of disgust moving through her, Jesse turned away quickly. Pushing aside the blue velvet that covered the wall beside the bunk, she was surprised to find an oriel complete with window seat covered in blue velvet and trimmed with gold tassels. Tassels! Of all the frivolous, wasteful . . .

She glanced out the mullioned window and saw naught but dense fog. Her first thought was to break the window and jump, but the urge died aborning. Alex's words about killing herself came back to haunt her. Even if she had known how to swim, in what direction lay the land? And how far away?

Damn. She left the window and bent to rummage through the cupboard beneath the bunk, unearthing an extra blanket and a chest containing needle and thread, rolls of parchment, a pen and jar of ink. He probably composed love poems for his whores, she scoffed and moved on to the trunk beside the door.

It was locked. Jesse growled in frustration, pounded the lock with her fist, then kicked it. "Ouch! Damn." She hopped on one foot, massaging her throbbing toes through the soft leather of her boot. Casting the trunk a scathing glance, she limped to the desk and found it bolted to the floor. The single drawer yielded a skin of wine, two metal cups and an eating knife.

Jesse sat back, smiling for the first time in hours as she ran her thumb over the sharp little blade. She even excused the exorbitance of the gem-encrusted hilt sparkling in the candle-light. As a weapon, the knife was not much, but as a tool . . . She scurried across the rough plank floor and attacked the latch.

Suddenly a key grated in the other side, and the door was flung open, sending her stumbling back to hide behind it.

"Bloody hell!" roared a familiar voice.

Jesse held her breath and prayed.

He muttered another oath that drew her reluctant admiration for creativity, then slammed the door shut and wheeled on her. "Leaving?" His casual tone was at odds with his blazing eyes.

"Just try to stop me," Jesse snarled. Holding the knife before her, she was poised to spring the moment he moved.

Alex cocked one mocking brow at her and smiled, making no move to unsheathe his sword. The arrogance, the sheer masculine superiority radiating from him drove Jesse past the boiling point. *Underestimate her, would he*? She leaped at him, aiming her thin blade at the vulnerable hollow on his throat.

Quicker than the eye could follow, he grabbed her up, lifted her off the ground and spun. Before she could draw breath, she found herself sprawled on the bunk, his large body pressing her smaller one into the straw mattress.

His thumb and forefinger gripped her right wrist, securing it painlessly above her head yet somehow rendering her hand useless so he could pluck the knife from her. He shifted slightly, his face so close she could see the salt that had dried on his brows and long lashes, a subtle reminder of her rescue. The intensity of his gaze was anything but subtle.

It stripped everything away but this moment and the awe-some strength of the body poised over hers. Leashed power held in check so she did not bear his full, crushing weight, yet the feel of him was indelibly imprinted on her. Deep inside her, a primitive fear stirred. She was vulnerable to him. No matter the defensive moves Hugh had taught her, she was powerless.

Jesse squeezed her eyes shut on a whimper and twisted beneath him. "Please," she whispered, she who never begged for anything, yet stark terror swept away her pride.

"I have never ravished a woman," he rasped in her ear. "And never think I'd start with one who dresses as a man."

Jesse went still, startled by his swift strike. Typically, anger followed, driving out panic and reason. As she redoubled her efforts to escape him, she rashly cried, "You are not man enough—"

Alex gritted his teeth as her challenge grated along tautly stretched nerves. She was his enemy, his prisoner, his to do with as he wished. His lower body stirred, inflamed by thoughts of making her pay...for past taunts, for past wrongs inflicted on his family by hers, for Hugh's present scheme.

'Twould be only a moment's work to strip her and bury himself between her thrashing legs. He had wanted her from the first moment he had laid eyes on her. Now he had the excuse of revenge to ease his conscience.

Alex shuddered as a primitive, red-hot wash of lust tore at the very fiber of his inbred honor. As though sensing his intent, she turned her head. Her green eyes locked with his, widening with dawning horror as she realized what she had goaded him to. Her vulnerability reached past his fury to touch the gentle core of him. Groaning, he leaped off her and stood by the bed, chest heaving, muscles trembling with the effort of pulling back from the edge of madness.

A muscle twitched in his cheek as he glared at her. "Do you know how close you are to getting that which you fear most?"

"Do it, then, and be damned," she snapped. Though the leaden taste of dread filled her mouth.

He spat an oath so vile it made her blink. "You pass all bounds of reason!" he roared, a vein throbbing at his temple.

Jesse steeled herself, then noticed he seemed to be muttering to himself. Strange. "What are you doing?" she asked when he did not hit her. "What are you waiting for?"

"I am counting," he rasped, face flushed.

"Counting what?"

"Reasons why I should not give you exactly what—" He shuddered. "To cool my temper."

She blinked, clearly amazed. "Does it help."

The question surprised Alex nearly as much as the realization that his anger was easing. "Aye." He took another deep breath. "Aye." He even remembered he'd come here for information, not a fight. "Where is your brother headed?"

"Even if I knew, I'd not tell you," she said warily.

"I expected as much, but I will find him—with or without your help—and stop him from ruining my family."

"Kill him, you mean."

Alex cocked his head, his dark eyes probing hers for answers she refused to give. "Nay, 'tis not his death I want. I'd have him tell the truth about—"

"Truth. Hah! Lies, more like. Lies to clear your name of counterfeiting," she snarled.

Alex's features hardened, as though he'd suddenly turned to stone. Inside him, whatever measure of softness he had felt for this beautiful, rebellious girl did the same. "I had wondered if you were party to your brother's schemes," he said, icy and low. "I should have remembered that the same greedy, treacherous blood flows in your veins."

"Greedy!" Jesse reached instinctively for the sword she'd lost in the water. Her hand came up empty and clenched into a fist she longed to plow into his chin. "Curse you, Sommerville. And all your damned family."

"We were indeed cursed the day the first Harcourt was born."

"Bastard!"

"Hellcat!" Alex watched her through lowered lids, admiring her courage if nothing else. Idly his gaze dropped to the front of her tunic, confirming what he'd noted when he had had her pinned beneath him. She still bound her breasts, denying even that sign of her sex. And the anger continued to sizzle between them like lightning on a hot summer night. "You may call me anything you like," he said, knowing where to aim his bolts. "But at least *my* sire values me, is proud to call me son. What does Edmund Harcourt call you? Son? Or daughter?"

Jesse recoiled as though he had slapped her.

"And you have it wrong." The softness of his voice was at odds with the barely suppressed anger evident in his tense body. "'Tis Hugh who minted the false gold florins."

"Why would he do such a thing?" she asked, frowning.

Her confusion almost convinced him she was not involved in this. Almost. "Jesselynn, I am surprised. You are not usually so dense in the head. By the king's own order, counterfeiting is a treasonable crime. If Hugh frames the Sommervilles for treason, he can claim our properties and the earldom as his reward."

"Hugh does not care about your title," she said stoutly.

"But your dear sire does. And Hugh could use the earldom to convince Edmund he'd make a suitable heir."

Jesse started. How could a Sommerville know so much about her family? It could not be true, was her next thought. Edmund was capable of such villainy, but not Hugh. Yet even as she stared up into Alexander's hard, searching gaze, Jesse recalled Hugh's cryptic words, *Things will be different.*

Stubbornly Jesse shook the words away. Hugh could not do such a thing. She would not believe it. Eyes narrowing, she said, "Set me ashore at the first town we come to, and I will not tell my brother you held me."

Alex threw back his head and laughed, the harsh echo filling the tiny cabin. "I hope your brother learns you are here." His calculating smile reminded Jesse that Gabrielle had once accused Alex of being a master at shifting people and events to suit himself. Well, he'd not use her to lure Hugh to his doom.

Suiting thought to action, Jesse leaped off the bunk and darted toward the door. He caught her before she'd taken two steps and tossed her back where she had begun. "I will not stay here." She scrambled to her knees. "I will not let you use me against my brother."

"You have no choice," Alex said cheerfully.

Jesse nibbled on her salty lips. There must be something she could do to delay Alex and give Hugh a chance to escape. But what? Surreptitiously she eyed her captor as he watched her, wondering how she might manipulate *him*. Given his weakness for women, could he be turned from his purpose for the chance to dally with one? Could she bring herself to lie with a man?

A slow, mocking smile drew Alex's mouth up at one corner. *He knew what she had been thinking.*

Jesse's cheeks burned, but she lifted her chin. "If I had a weapon, I would carve off that which you prize so highly."

"Nay. Like all women, you wonder what it would be like to lie with me. To kiss my lips, to feel my touch on your—"

"'Tis hell being even this close to you, you—"

"Little liar," he said softly, surely.

"Leave me." Her fingers curved into claws with which to scratch out his eyes did he come any closer.

"As my *lady* bids." He swept her a mocking bow. The ship shifted suddenly, and he whipped his gaze to the small window.

"What?" Jesse craned to see out but could tell nothing.

"The wind rises. Soon the fog will lift, and we will be able to follow your brother's ship."

"Not Hugh's ship," she said angrily. "'Tis Parlan's."

"Parlan Graham?" he asked so furiously she recoiled.

"A-aye."

"Dammit. I should have known he'd be involved in this scheme." A muscle twitched in his cheek as he clenched his jaw. "This makes the chase doubly worth the while," he muttered, scowling darkly. Then he stirred, shook himself. "There is a storm brewing and I'll be needed on deck." Reaching up, he pinched out the candle, plunging the cabin into total darkness.

"Nay. Do not put out the light."

"I'd not risk setting us afire in the storm. Surely the girl who faced me with an eating knife is not afraid of the dark."

She was, but she would die ere she admitted a weakness to any man, least of all to him. Yet when the door closed behind him and the key grated in the lock, her heart nearly stopped. 'Twas worse even than when Edmund had locked her away. This time there would be no Hugh to sneak in and set her free.

Chapter Three

Alex sought Bevan at the rail of the aftercastle the moment he gained the deck. "You will not guess what ship we chase," he said in a tight voice. "'Tis *The Salamander*."

"Parlan Graham's ship," the captain spat.

For a long minute, neither of them spoke, both carried back seven years to another night when *The Star* and *The Salamander* had shared a corner of the sea off Winchelsea. Then James had stood on *The Star*'s deck and Colin Graham, Parlan's sire, had captained *The Salamander*. The two men had been part of King Edward III's fleet arrayed against the Spanish.

Only it had been a Scots arrow that had cut James down at the height of the battle of *Les Espagnols sur Mer*. An arrow shot from Colin Graham's ship by Parlan himself, so James's crew had sworn. Lacking proof, Alex had been forced to let his beloved uncle's death go unavenged. But it was not forgotten or forgiven. Nay, Alex would dearly love to make Parlan pay.

"What are ye thinkin'?" Bevan asked, eyeing the way his young lord clenched the rail, gaze savagely narrowed.

"Of revenge." Alex savored the word, let it linger on his tongue. "Parlan must be involved in Hugh's scheme. The king would not complain if we brought Harcourt and Graham to justice over the counterfeiting," he reasoned grimly.

"Aye. But I'm not sure we'll catch him in this."

"We'll stay as close as we can. If he keeps on as he is, his ship will not survive undamaged. Blakeney is the nearest port where he can put in for repairs, we'll catch him there. Then will we see how greatly Hugh values his dear sister."

"Aye. We'll make fer Blakeney," Bevan agreed. "When Hugh hears ye've got her, he'll fall o'er himself clearin' Lord Geoffrey and Gareth ta get her back."

Alex dragged a weary hand through his hair. "We've no guarantee of that. Harcourts have no honor." He had grown up believing so, and recent developments only deepened his hatred for the ancient enemy that had plagued his family for years.

"But she's his sister."

"And Edmund is sire to both of them." That said it all.

"Ye think she's in this, too, even though she's a lady?"

"Do not be fooled by her sex. She's as handy with a knife and sword as any man, and twice as devious as any other *lady*."

Bevan frowned at his young lord's vehemence. Alex used to enjoy the scores of women who chased after him, attracted by his handsome face, muscular body and the aura of danger that clung to him like a second skin. But ever since that business with his brother's woman, Bevan had sensed a change in him. A wariness where women were concerned and a restlessness the sea no longer seemed to satisfy. "Not all women are like Lady Emilie."

"Bevan," Alex warned, sick of being lectured on the subject by everyone from his captain to Gabrielle.

"I dinna see why ye were interested in the likes o' Lady Emilie ta begin wi'. 'Twas clear the lady had weddin' on her mind. Men like ye and me and yer Uncle James ha' no business marryin'—wed ta the sea, we are, if ye catch my drift."

"No doubt you are right." Alex tilted his head and looked at the clouds. His life resembled the shifting gray mass, the way no longer as clear to him as it had once been. And Jesselynn's arrival only complicated matters. He had thought of her more than once since the night her true identity had been revealed and she'd sneaked away from Wilton. Always with a sense of something unfinished between them.

"What do ye plan ta do wi' Lady Jesselynn?"

"Use her to get Hugh," Alex said flatly.

"Ye best tread carefully, she's a highborn lady," Bevan muttered. "After that last battle, King Edward forbid the Sommervilles and the Harcourts ta fight."

Alex raised one mocking brow, yet there was no humor in his expression. "Did I say I'd fight with her?"

Bevan grunted and rubbed his jowls. "But she'll be ruined when 'tis known she was held aboard yer ship. No man'll ha' her to wife. She'll ha' ta take the veil."

"No convent would take a vixen like her. Besides, her future is no concern of mine. Saving my family is."

The implacable ruthlessness in Alex's dark eyes did not startle Bevan. Of all people, he knew his young lord's lazy smile hid a core of pure steel. But abuse a woman? True Alex had been called heartless by more than one sent on her way when passion had cooled, but for all his unruly temper and reputation as a rogue, Alex was not cruel. "I dunno, lad. I've a bad feelin' about this business."

"That," Alex said darkly, "makes two of us."

Hours later Alex approached his cabin with caution, the ache in his hand a reminder of the reception he might receive. Wet and exhausted from fighting the storm, he was in no mood for any more of her games. With the seas calmer and the wind falling, all he wanted was to tumble into bed and sleep till morn.

He started in surprise when the spill of light from his candle illuminated her body sprawled on the floor, fingers white where they gripped the leg of the desk, eyes shut.

"Jesselynn. Let loose the desk," he growled, tensed to repel an ambush. She whimpered when he tried to pry her fingers free, but did not open her eyes.

"Jesu." Thumping the candle he carried down on the desk, he knelt beside her and tried to peel the bloodless fingers of her right hand away from the wood. His touch gentled when he saw the deep grooves pressed into her flesh. "What is wrong with you?"

She shivered and grabbed convulsively for his left hand, snagging the middle two fingers and squeezing so hard he yelped.

"Let go!" He tried to shake her off; she clung tighter than a barnacle. Short of breaking her hand, he could not get free.

"Ah, hell." Sagging back on his heels, he sighed heavily.

For the first time since entering the cabin, he took a good look at her. What he saw made his gut cramp with unexpected sympathy. If anything, she looked worse than when he had fished her from the water. Her gray face and scrunched-up eyes worried him more than the ugly bruise on her forehead. She looked small and utterly terrified—like a child caught in a nightmare.

What nightmares haunt you? he wondered, then cursed himself for caring. Harcourts deserved to suffer. Steeling himself against her wiles, he reached for her shoulder. Her bones felt so fragile beneath his large hand that he instantly gentled his grip. "Jesselynn." He shook her ever so carefully. "Wake up."

Her eyes flickered open, but their glazed look increased his concern. "Please, don't throw me into the hole again, Edmund." Her voice was barely a whisper.

"No one is going to throw you anywhere," he said in the soft voice he used with baby Cat.

"I—I won't steal any more grain," she said as though he had not spoken, her gaze focused on some horror from her past.

Why would she steal grain? Did Edmund starve her? It fit with Alex's image of the man. Yet he did not want to feel anything for Jesselynn...certainly not pity. Nay, he wanted to go on distrusting her, so he shrugged away the tender feelings, fought to ignore her trembling mouth and dazed expression. "Let go of the desk and I'll put you to bed."

"Hugh?" she murmured.

"Nay, I—"

"Oh, Hugh. I knew you'd come for me. You are the only one who is ever kind to me." She threw herself into his arms.

Caught off balance, Alex fell over. Instinctively he twisted to spare her his weight. They landed in a heap with Jesselynn on top, her arms locked in a stranglehold around his neck.

"Jesselynn," Alex choked out as he tried to pry her loose.

"Safe now," she mumbled. "So tired . . ." Her voice trailed off and, incredibly, she seemed to fall asleep on him. Yet her iron hold on him did not lessen one bit.

Alex bit off an angry curse and grabbed her wrists. But she was a tenacious little thing, and he saw no way to free himself without hurting her. That he could not do it made him curse the gentleness that warred constantly with his temper.

Blessedly someone knocked at the door to his cabin.

"Get in here quick!" he called.

The door opened and Bevan's frowning face appeared. "So," he muttered disapprovingly and started to pull the door closed.

"Goddammit, Bevan! Come back and help me." Alex thrashed his way into a sitting position with Jesselynn wound around him as securely as a skein of seaweed. "I am not trying to bed her. She thinks I'm her brother."

"Brother?" Bevan's grizzled brows flew up.

"Ah, hell, Bevan. She's having some kind of nightmare."

"How can she be asleep and still hang on ta ye like that?"

Alex closed his eyes and prayed for strength. "I do not know," he said, teeth clenched. "But I would appreciate your getting her the hell off before she strangles me."

Strangely enough it was Bevan's deep, patient voice that coaxed Jesselynn into relaxing her grip. And Bevan who picked her up and laid her gently on the bunk. Stranger still was the hollowness Alex felt when he no longer held her. Relief, he told himself. That was all it was. Relief and fatigue.

Bevan pursed his lips as he studied Jesselynn in the flickering candlelight. "Like a fairy sprite, she is, so pale and fragile. She does na look like a spy."

"A woman's looks can be deceiving. Especially hers," Alex added ominously, dragging himself from the floor.

"She needs a good wash and fresh clothes," Bevan grumbled.

"Bring me some water, and I'll see to her."

"'Tis na fittin'. We should ha' a woman ta tend her."

This from the man who, like most sailors, thought having a woman aboard ship was bad luck. "I'm too tired to have an impure thought, much less the strength to act on it," Alex stonily assured him. But a few moments later, when he had finally gotten rid of his captain and started to undress Jesselynn, Alex discovered that neither exhaustion nor the fact that she was a Harcourt made him immune to the lure of the soft curves hidden beneath her ugly boy's clothes.

* * *

Sleep left Jesse in slow stages—peeled away like the layers of an onion.

Warmth was the first sensation to penetrate. She was lying half on top of something warm and furry. The wolf skin that covered the hearth in her room at Harte Court. Snuggling closer, she hazily recalled the day she had killed the great beast. She had not wanted to harm it, but Edmund had come upon her and the huntsmen just as the hounds had cornered the wolf.

"Ah, a fine specimen," Edmund had cried, seeing the wounded wolf fight to keep the snapping hounds at bay. "Bring it back to Harte Court and we will amuse ourselves with a wolf baiting."

Unwilling to see such a noble beast suffer an ignoble death, Jesse had ridden in and dispatched it with a swift sword thrust. She'd taken no pride in the kill, for the hounds had already weakened the wolf. But it had pleased her to deprive Edmund of his sick entertainment. She had even cheated him of the satisfaction of seeing her cry when he beat her for disobeying.

To Jesse, the wolf had become a symbol of her rebellion against Edmund. What few tears of rage and humiliation she had shed in the past few years had flowed late at night and been soaked up by the wolf's thick, rough coat.

Jesse flexed her fingers, digging them into the fur as her cheek nuzzled it. A sigh of contentment escaped her lips.

The wolf growled back.

Jesse's eyes snapped open. In the dim light she saw that the pelt on which she lay was curly and golden brown. Beneath the swirls of hair was deeply bronzed skin. Dread iced Jesse's own flesh as she lifted her gaze. For the second time, it met and locked with the mocking stare of midnight eyes.

Alexander Sommerville.

Awareness rocked her more sharply than a lash from Edmund's whip. She was not in her room. She was aboard Alexander's ship...in Alexander's bunk.... "Sweet Mary!" she breathed. Her body went hot, then cold, then hot again. She tensed to leap out of bed, felt the hairy, muscular leg pressed against her smoother one and realized they were not wearing any clothes.

"Going somewhere, sweetling?" Alex drawled.

Sweetling? Jesse swallowed hard. What had happened between them? Her head ached and her body, too. Had he beaten her? Or worse, bedded her? Her stomach lurched. What she'd seen Parlan do to the cook's daughter had been terrible, but 'twas ten times worse to have been used by this rogue whilst she was unconscious and powerless to resist. "So, this is the secret of your success with women," she spat. "You drug them, then ravish them."

He arched one brow, amusement dancing in his eyes. "I have never had to force a woman in my life. If I wanted you, I'd need but a kiss to have your mind dizzy with desire, your body willing—nay begging—for more."

"Oh!" Jesse shrieked. Naked or no, she leaped out of bed, fists clenched to knock the insolent smile from his lips. A soft slithering at her knees distracted her, and she looked down to see the garment she wore settling about her. It was a shirt. His shirt. Revolted by the feel of the fine linen against her skin, she started to rip it off, then stopped, realizing she was nude beneath. Which meant he had removed her clothes.

Alex levered himself up on one elbow, intrigued by the play of emotions across her face. Outrage. Confusion. Embarrassment. She was as transparent as a clear mountain stream. But not nearly as cool, he amended as rage colored her pale cheeks.

"What did you do with my clothes? I will not wear these cursed *rich* clothes." She made it a curse.

In the past two years her beauty had blossomed to fulfill its earlier promise, but her instinctive reaction to any threat was still anger. Grudgingly he admitted he enjoyed her fire, found it a refreshing change from the women who had fawned over him from the time his voice had changed. Yet he slipped behind the familiar mask of mockery. "Why ever not, my lady?"

"I hate such things. I want something . . . rough."

"Rough? Surely not against such soft, creamy skin."

"Lecherous bastard."

"My desires run to . . . cleaner game."

Jesse flinched. She did not need to peer into a piece of polished metal to know she looked a fright, her skin grimy from salt, her hair unbraided and sticking out every which way like a nest of red snakes. "Good. Then you will leave me alone."

"But I have left you alone—so far," Alex taunted silkily. His implied threat brought a flicker of fear to her remarkable eyes, reminding him that a man's attentions seemed the one thing capable of frightening her. The vulnerability in her eyes drew on him again in the instant before they blazed with anger.

"I want my clothes, and I want to be set ashore."

"Where is Hugh bound?" he asked quietly, his eyes piercing.

Fists clenched, insides churning, Jesse studied her enemy. In the wash of early light, he looked unbearably handsome. Damn him. His sun-kissed hair hung wild and free to his shoulders; his eyes were alight with humor and intelligence, neither of which she was used to seeing in a man. The sheet rode low on his hips, revealing too much naked, bronzed skin for her liking.

Yet he drew her, reminded her not of a wolf, but of the lion King Edward kept in a cage. Jesse had been captivated by the magnificent tawny beast lazing with deceptive innocence in the sun when she knew perfectly well it was dangerous. Looking into Alex's dark eyes made her heart beat every bit as fast as looking into the lion's amber ones had.

Come touch me, you know you want to, he silently taunted. But well she remembered that when she had reached through the bars to stroke the lion's paw it had been quick to spring.

Jesse swallowed hard and shook free of his spell. Alex was no lion; he was soft, greedy for women. Despite the ease with which he had overpowered her physically, his wine-sogged brain could not match hers. Hope buoyed her flagging spirits. "Hugh returns to London," she said in answer to his earlier question.

"He'd not dare now that we are on to his scheme."

"'Tis your scheme," Jesse snapped, "not his."

"Indeed? Why would we counterfeit coins?"

"'Tis common knowledge the Sommervilles need money."

His smile faded. "Everyone does." The rents of most landowners were much less because so many of the villeins who worked the land had died of the Black Death. "But how would we profit from passing worthless coins in our own town?"

"What do you care what happens to the peasants?"

"Surely in the time you lived with Ruarke and Gaby you came to know that next to our own flesh and blood, we Sommervilles value our people's welfare. As so many of the nobles do not."

As Edmund did not. Jesse damned Alex for once again striking so close to the bone. She was ashamed of how cruelly Edmund treated the people who lived under his thumb, abusing them and starving them even in time of plenty. To a lesser degree, she blamed Hugh for not somehow rectifying matters. Realizing her brother had his own cross to bear, she had secretly done what she could to help the peasants.

"The coins are not of our doing," Alex said again.

Jesse threw herself into the argument. "Hugh has proof."

"Of his own making. Gareth overheard him discussing his vile plans with his henchmen."

"Gareth lies."

"Mind your tongue," Alex warned harshly, feeling his temper begin to heat. "Recall what happened last night."

"Are you going to count again?" she snapped, glaring at him.

Contempt? Alex caught himself before he blinked. No woman had ever looked at him with contempt. But then, Jesselynn did not want to be a woman. What would it take to awaken the softness she hid beneath her male garb and prickly manner? Speculation became frank appraisal as his eyes moved from her sulky mouth to the swell of her breasts pushing against his shirt and down to her bare calves and feet. Memory filled in the details from what he had dimly seen last night when he had hastily divested her of her clothes—including the strip of linen so cruelly used to bind her breasts. In the same breath, he checked himself. The situation was hazardous enough without lust to muddle his brain.

"Nay, not counting or torture," he said slowly, as though he had been considering it. "A man like me has other ways of getting information from a woman."

Jesse fought the urge to abandon pride and run, her skin prickling. "Y-you said you did not ravish women."

"I have already told you it would not come to that."

His confident, low-voiced words intensified the panic pounding through her veins, made the room seem smaller, made her feel weaker. "I'll fight no matter what you do," she vowed, backing away though there was no place to go.

He shrugged and tossed back the sheet, giving her a heart-stopping glimpse of his strong thighs and the linen that covered their apex. Gasping, she spun, grabbed the eating knife from the desk, then whirled back to face him as he came up behind her.

"I will not hurt—" he began.

She lunged. He dodged, grunting softly as she buried the blade in his left shoulder. Spitting a curse, he caught her with his right arm, snatched her off her feet. The breath left her lungs in a whoosh as she hit the wall, trapped by the hard, hot length of his body. "Vixen," he growled. Gone was the mockery. His eyes were black now as hell's gates.

Jesse shivered in his iron grip, too terrified to struggle. Sweet Mary but he moved swiftly for a big man.

"Look at me!" When she refused, he took her chin and forced her head up. The knife protruded obscenely from his flesh, a trickle of dark blood trailing down his bunched muscles. Yet he seemed scarcely to notice it as his eyes bored into hers.

Would he beat her or strangle her? He looked enraged enough to do either. Pride alone kept her from begging for mercy.

One. Two. Alex filled his lungs, exhaled slowly, conscious of her heart beating wildly in counterpoint to his. *Three.* She was terrified, and rightly so, yet she did not cringe. Grudging respect muted his anger. *Four.* "What am I going to do with you?"

"Counting again?" she snarled. "A *man* would beat me."

Alex got from five to twenty in a flash, and found his anger had miraculously evened out. "You were frightened and trying to protect yourself," he generously allowed.

"I was not frightened," she lied, head high.

Alex snorted. Only his lightning reflexes had diverted her thrust from his throat. 'Twas more sobering than the burning pain in his shoulder. A reminder that he should have expected such villainy from a Harcourt. Setting her on her feet, he put space between them but kept hold of her arm. "Take the knife from my shoulder and bandage the wound."

Her eyes widened, darted to the bloodied hilt. "Nay, I—"

"You will, or when I leave I will take away anything you might use to cover your nakedness. Aye, even the hangings."

"I know nothing of the healing arts."

"Liar. 'Twas the only skill you showed when at Wilton."

"I—I did not think you would remember."

"I remember everything about you." Quiet, yet intent.

She raised her eyes to his, which was a mistake. Her mind tumbled back to the first time she had seen him—hotly furious at her for ordering his hound from Gaby's hall. Aye, they riled each other, but he was more vitally alive than anyone she had ever known, as though a fire burned inside him. The part of her that feared the dark was oddly drawn to that light.

"Now, which is it to be?" he asked, breaking the spell. "Do I take the shirt, or do you tend my wound?"

He'd won this time, but she'd find a way to escape him. She had to... before she got scorched.

It lacked an hour to dawn when Hugh picked his way across *The Salamander*'s littered deck and tapped his cousin on the arm. "Now that the storm has abated, I'd have you set me ashore."

"Are you mad? We can not stop with Sommerville on our trail and repairs to be made." He'd lost six men overboard in the storm, but his concern was for the smashed tackle without which he could not tighten the shrouds.

Hugh thought it was Parlan's own fault for taking such risks, but he had other more pressing worries. "'Tis likely Gareth captured Charles. If he talks..." Though the apprentice had been told the Sommervilles were behind the counterfeiting, he could point the finger at Hugh for ordering the coins made.

Parlan snorted, all trace of the man who had encouraged Hugh's efforts over the past weeks obliterated by rage. "I knew I should have gone with you when you went ashore."

"There was nothing you could have done to prevent his capture," Hugh insisted. "I don't know how Gareth found out what we were about, but he was waiting on the beach when we landed.''

"I would have made certain that Charles Beck and Lord Robert did not fall into Sommerville hands."

"There were too many o' them," intruded a rough voice.

Frowning, Hugh turned on Walter. "I told you to wait below."

"I'm goin' after me brother," Walter Beck snarled.

"Charles may already have talked," Parlan said.

"Nay, he's tougher than he looks," Walter argued, his sharp brown eyes at odds with his slovenly appearance. "Besides, I know the Sommervilles from when I was Wilton's steward. They ask a lot of questions afore they stoop ta torturin'. If we get Charlie out quick, they won't get ta work on him."

All this talk of torture caused Parlan to reconsider. "We're in sight of land now, I could have someone row you ashore."

"Good." Walter started toward the small boats in the bow.

"Excuse my hasty words," Parlan said to Hugh. "I was concerned about my ship and crew."

Hugh nodded. "I only wish things had gone as planned."

"Never mind." Parlan smiled inwardly, thinking Hugh would die trying to rescue Charles. "The important thing is to get Charles away from the Sommervilles before he spills what he knows."

Hugh swallowed hard. "'Twill not be easy."

More like impossible. "If Charles talks, it'll be your neck stretched on the royal gallows. For myself, I'd rather be dead than face Edmund's censure or poor Jesselynn's pain."

"Aye." Hugh nodded glumly. "I'd have your word you'll look after Jesse should . . . should aught happen to me."

"Of course." Gravely. "I'll even promise to wed her."

"I do not know—" Hugh shifted uneasily.

"I'll not force her." *Edmund will do that*. Then he changed the subject. "I'll draw Alexander north. A sail to Scotland should keep him too busy to trouble you. Send word to me at Edinburgh when things are settled here."

"You are certain 'tis Alexander's ship."

"I know her lines as well as I know *The Salamander*'s."

"How can you be certain he'll follow you?"

"Because he and I have unfinished business. Aye, Alexander would trail me into hell if he thought he stood a chance of catching me." Something ugly moved through Parlan's eyes. "And hell is just where I intend to lead him."

Chapter Four

"Damn the man for being so confounding," Jesse muttered. She had curled up in the little window seat with the intention of searching for *The Salamander* as they sailed into Blakeney harbor that afternoon. But she did not really see the ships on the other side of the wavy glass. Her mind was on the events of the past day and night since she had been Alex's prisoner.

He confused her, and she did not like it. Or him. But her reasons were no longer as clear as they'd been the first time they'd met. Like the ships' images, her thinking rippled.

Though Alex still had a temper, he was much more controlled then he'd been two years ago. Twice he had pulled back from a fury hotter than the sun's. She admired that ability, mayhap even envied it, but his motives perplexed her. He was her enemy. He believed Hugh plotted against him, had even hinted she might be involved. Yet where she had expected hostility and abuse, she had been met with mocking smiles and a strength that imprisoned but did not wound, not even when she had stabbed him.

What was he then? Compassionate. The word crept into her mind on a soft whisper. Jesse tensed to resist. She wanted no man's pity, least of all her enemy's. But most terrifying of all was the insidious warmth that washed over her when he did something . . . nice. Aye, the greatest danger was within herself.

Footsteps outside the door brought her around so quickly she nearly tripped on the blanket she'd draped over Alex's shirt.

"I've brought you bread and ale, my lady," a thin voice called through the stout wood. The squire, Ellis, not Alex.

Jesse bolted for the bed, pulled the covers up to her neck before bidding him enter. She fluttered her lashes helplessly, in the manner of the stepmother before Blanche. It revolted her to act the simpering female, but she was desperate. Besides, stupid creatures that they were, men thrived on the notion that women were weak. Well, Alex would not find *her* so. "Oh, 'twas kind of you to remember me, alone here," she said faintly.

Ellis flushed to his blond roots. "I brought you food and drink." A gangly thirteen or so, with big hands and feet he had yet to grow into, he had a face so guilelessly appealing it pinched her to deceive him.

Jesse swallowed. "I fear what I need is fresh air."

"Oh." Ellis's big brown eyes widened with pity. "I'm so sorry. I know how awful it is to be locked away, b-but Alex said you weren't to go topside without his permission."

Jesse ignored both the squire's haunted look and the familiar way he handled his lord's name. Alex would give her no leeway at all. "Surely it would not hurt if I went for a moment," she said softly. "And he need not know—"

"Wheedling, Jesselynn?" Alex mocked from the doorway. "I wouldn't have thought you the sort." He lounged with one shoulder against the wooden frame, a smirk she longed to slap away curving his mouth. He looked the pirate, dressed in loose black breeches and a white linen shirt open at the throat. His wet hair and freshly scrubbed face made her all the more aware of her own disheveled state.

She looked adorable sitting there puffed up like an enraged vixen, but the soreness in his shoulder reminded him that *this* fox had sharp teeth. Tossing Ellis a key, he said, "Find my red surcoat and black hose, and take them to Bevan's cabin. I'll dress there. And Ellis," he added as the flustered boy knelt to the chest, "You had best learn to resist a woman's wiles."

"Wiles!" Jesse welcomed the anger to speed up the pulse that had faltered at seeing him. "I am not one of your whores."

"Then do not simper like one." Alex held up his hand to forestall her retort. Damn. He wanted to thrust his hands in her mane of wild red hair, press her trembling body against the ache in his and crush her grim little mouth beneath his until it softened for him and they were both senseless with desire. It was a struggle to master the desire jolting through him. "I'd not see you embarrass yourself before the lad," he said huskily.

Oh! Only biting her tongue allowed Jesse to keep it still until the squire had snatched the clothes from the chest and fled the oppressive tension hanging in the air. Then she hissed, "You are the rudest, most vile—"

"He's a good boy, and only fourteen. I'd not have you upset him," Alex said quietly.

"Me!" Jesse leaped from the bed and advanced on him, the blanket flowing out behind her like a war banner. She stopped a foot from him, hands on hips, eyes blazing. "I am shocked that anyone would trust you with a boy. He runs far more risk of being corrupted by you and your women you abuse—"

"Enough!" Alex growled. "Damn, but your temper is hotter than mine," he mused. "You had best take up counting when it flares. 'Tis a handy—"

"Give me a sword, and I will show you what I can do."

"Jesselynn." He shook his head sadly. "What ails you that you strike out at a simple word of kindness?"

"A pox on kindness. I want none of it."

Her flashing eyes and outthrust chin told him she believed the nonsense she spouted. Pity twisted his gut, but he knew she'd not want it did he offer it. Once he had found a hawk tangled in a fishing net. Weak from hunger and the struggle to free itself, it had nonetheless clawed him when he'd tried to help. Jesselynn was much like that hawk, he reflected, flexing his shoulder. Wild, wary and badly scarred. The need to undo the damage rose swiftly. Almost, he reached for her, then remembered her pain was none of his concern. Finding her brother was.

"Ah, Jesselynn, I would remain and trade barbs with you, but I must go ashore to learn where *The Salamander* has gone."

Hugh wasn't here. Sweet relief. "I'd go with you."

"I wager you would *like* to." The fine lines at his eyes crinkled with amusement. "But you'd run at the first chance."

"What if I gave my word I would not?" she pressed. A lie passed between enemies was not really a lie, was it?

His eyes swept over her as they had before, dark, intense, disconcerting. "I would not believe you."

Judged and found wanting. No matter the source, it still stung. "Because I am a Harcourt?" she asked, standing taller.

"That, and you are a woman," Alex goaded, reading, testing.

Like a flame to kindling, she flared, "So, like all men you believe the church teachings that women are sinful, deceitful creatures, incapable of honor, unworthy of respect."

Alex pursed his lips, having gotten even more than he had bargained for. "I hadn't really given the subject much thought." To him, women were…women. From the time he'd been old enough to appreciate the differences between male and female, he'd thought them delightful creatures, full of soft promise and dark mystery. But honor? Respect?

His mother and Gaby were proof women could be good, kind and honest. But at court and on his travels he had met women who lied and cheated to get what they wanted, even dishonored their wedding vows. On principle, he had avoided such creatures.

And then there was Emilie. A hard lesson that had left him with a bad taste in his mouth and a new wariness where women were concerned. "I find women endlessly entertaining," he said slowly, "but I'd not trust one."

"I am not like other women. *My* word is my bond." Jesse meant it. The smug cynicism glittering in his gaze challenged her, made her want to prove him wrong about her even though moments ago she *had* intended to lie. Aye, she'd have the satisfaction of his apology—*on his knees*.

The small, secret smile that lifted the corners of her mouth sent Alex's heart racing; like a gauntlet thrown down at his feet, it dared, provoked, excited him. On one level he knew he should resist. She was his hostage against Hugh's cooperation; he could ill afford to lose her. Still the chance to match wits with her was a powerful lure.

Looking deep into her green eyes, he acknowledged that men and women had been waging this battle for centuries, on many levels. For power. For passion. Even had their names not been Sommerville and Harcourt, they would have been natural adversaries in a struggle older than the feud.

"Well?" she demanded, arms crossed beneath her breasts so they pushed at the front of his shirt, the dark shadows at their crests clearly visible through the fine linen. "If I vow not to escape, will you take me with you off this bloody ship?"

What a shame, Alex thought, ignoring her question as his body tensed again in swift response. What a waste of a beautiful woman that she should deny what God made her. He deplored waste. 'Twas one of the reasons he avoided killing if he could. His reaction to her, the unwanted desire and the inconvenient regret, shook him. "Women do not make vows," he muttered.

And men are greedy idiots. She longed to slap the hauteur from his face, but for once restrained herself. "Why should they not? They have minds and hearts to pledge."

"What of honor?" he retorted, grudgingly admiring the way she stood toe to toe with him and stuck up for her beliefs. "A man—a knight—vows on his sacred honor. On what would you stake your vow?"

Jesse paused only a moment. "I believe God gives each of us honor. But since you think me devoid of such, I would swear on that which I hold dearest—my brother's immortal soul."

"First you must convince me he has one."

"Hugh is not like my...not like Edmund. You judge him without knowing him."

"I don't need to know an adder to stay clear of it."

"Hugh is not a snake. He's a man—a good man."

"Who plots to ruin my family," Alex growled.

"Nay!" she shouted. "'Tis a lie. A filthy Sommerville lie."

"A greedy Harcourt plot," Alex shouted back.

Jesse winced, then struck back. "Did you get that scar on your neck at the hands of a jealous husband? Gareth, mayhap?"

Her words rocked Alex swifter than a jab to the gut. Jesu, she slipped under his guard faster than anyone he knew. He'd forgotten she knew about Emilie. Gritting his teeth, he grabbed the door. "Emilie is dead, and now *you* judge without knowing."

"Wait!" Jesse snagged his arm. "I—I am sorry. I did not know." The words were rusty. "Would . . . would you take me ashore?"

Alex glared down at her determined face, appalled by his near loss of control. After the incident a year ago when he had come close to killing a man for beating Ellis, Alex had taken great care never to allow his temper free rein. "Why should I?"

"Because . . ." She cast about for some threat. "Because if you do not, I will break the window and swim ashore."

Alex regarded her narrowly. She would do it, though she could not swim. Anger cooled to ire as smugness glinted in her eyes. Damn her! The day had not come when he couldn't keep a woman in line, even one as willful as Jesselynn. Nor would she like his methods. "I'll want your pledge you'll not escape."

"I can go?" She looked startled, recovered quickly. "If you will return my clothes—"

"First the swearing." He drew his sword and bade her kneel. Her consternation when she realized she'd not only be vulnerable to him, but subservient, as well, nearly made him laugh. Clearing his throat, he said, "Repeat after me. I Jesselynn Harcourt do solemnly pledge . . ." On he rattled, adding every lofty clause and flowery phrase he could recall from the ponderous ceremonies King Edward was so fond of staging.

"The one about cherishing womankind does not apply," Jesse grumbled, switching her weight on her sore knees.

Does it not? The words that had come by rote took on new meaning as he turned them over. 'Twas unnatural for a woman to turn against her sex as Jesselynn had. But then, Edmund Harcourt was an unnatural parent. Recalling the gentle guidance of his own mother and father, Alex felt another unwelcome stab of pity. Small wonder she had turned out as she had, a female trying to push her way into the dominion of men where she didn't belong. Someone should make a proper woman of her.

A plan leaped into Alex's agile mind. Aye, and he'd make her pay for the cut she'd dealt him, as well, he thought. "Do you refuse a part of the swearing?"

"Nay." Grudgingly. "I vow to cherish women. Are we done?"

"All that remains is the sealing of the pledge." The sight of her leaning forward to press her lips to his blade put him in mind of something else entirely. Both of them had flushed faces when 'twas done, though he guessed their reasons differed.

Jesse leaped up, and their gazes locked, sharp green clashing with the relentless gleam of dark brown, each certain they had gained an advantage over the other.

The air was clear, soft with the promise of spring warmth when Jesse stepped on deck.

"Where did you get those clothes?" Alex demanded, cutting through a group of sailors to tower over her.

His scowl delighted her. "Mine were stiff with salt, so I borrowed these from Ellis." With a rag stuffed in each toe, his boots weren't a bad fit. Because the squire was thinner than she was, the hose were snug, the knee-length tunic a bit tight in the chest even with her breasts bound.

"I'd see you decently clothed ere you distract my men." Alex glowered at the sailors who ogled her legs.

Jesse dismissed them with a toss of the untidy braids she'd fashioned. "They are merely curious. None would be interested in an ugly witch like me."

Alex blinked. She did not search for a compliment. Nay, but she was blinded to her own beauty. Clearly the damage went deeper than he had thought. "We will find you a gown in town."

"Find one if you like, but I'll not wear it."

"Careful," he warned. "Remember your vow."

"Not to escape? I haven't—"

"To 'cherish women.'" He flashed that annoying grin of his.

"How can that part of the pledge apply when I am a woman?" she asked him through her teeth.

"That's exactly why it does." Without explaining, he herded her down the ladder and seated her in the rear of the boat. Jesse clung to the side, cursing her situation and her captor.

As though to mock her fear of the water, Alex stood in the front of the boat with his broad back to her, one foot propped on the prow. The boldness of the stance as he defied the swells that rocked the boat showed his arrogance, the corded muscles beneath his hose the unexpected strength of the man she'd thought weakened by soft living. Belatedly it occurred to her that she might have underestimated him. Why had she made that foolish pledge not to escape him?

Pride. Aye, he'd rubbed her nose in her pride with his casual attitude toward women. Better she had let the insult pass, let him think her like other women. Nay, she could no more have done that than she could have seduced him last night.

Looking up as the boat scraped bottom, she saw Alex vault lithely over the side into ankle-deep water. He watched her intently. If he expected her to bolt, he would be sadly mistaken, and she told him so with a lift of her chin.

He chuckled. Before she guessed his intent, he'd swung her into his arms and lifted her from the boat. "I—I can walk."

"I'd not have you get wet today."

"Put me down." She pounded his chest with her fist. It was like punching a rock wall. Pain radiated up her arm; his step didn't falter, nor did he even look at her. The wretch.

"Ah, here we are." He deposited her on the rocky beach, capturing her hand when she would have turned away. Frowning, he flexed her fingers, stroked the length of each.

Jesse shivered as the friction from his warm, callused skin sent tingles racing up her arm. "What are you doing?" she asked in a breathless voice that could not be hers.

"I guess no bones are broken," he murmured.

She snatched her hand free, struggling to subdue her runaway pulse. "Your . . . your chest is not that hard."

His grin said he knew she'd lied. "Lady Jesselynn and I will be back shortly," he told the sailors who'd rowed them in.

"You don't take them with you in case there's trouble?" Port towns were reputed to be rough, and too, Edmund never went anywhere without a cadre of mercenaries to guard him.

"There is no need. I am well-known in Blakeney." He took her arm. When she tried to tug it back, he reminded her of the pledge. "A woman requires an escort."

"Well, I don't. I've been walking unaided since I was one."

"I'm sure you have," he said smoothly. "But my knightly vows and your pledge require me to escort you."

Jesse blinked, her usually facile mind struggling to discern what went on behind that sly grin of his. "What game is this?"

"'Tis called chivalry." *And his guess was that she'd not like it.* "By your vow to me, you agreed to abide by its rules."

"I said no such thing."

"You agreed to cherish women. You are a woman. So you must hold yourself in esteem, Jesselynn . . . unless you've decided you can not fulfill the pledge."

At first she looked confused, as though hearing her name coupled with esteem was new to her. 'Twas hard to credit in one so wild and rebellious, but he was living proof that people hid much behind the masks they wore. He meant to have all her secrets before he let her go. Given what they were to each other, 'twas not the wisest or safest course of action, but then, a sailor was used to taking risks.

"I hate you." The words were ground out between Jesselynn's even white teeth.

"My lady." He gravely offered her his arm.

A tremor of fury so intense it nearly choked her swept through Jesse. With her eyes, she shot lethal green daggers into the dark, lazy pools of his. If he smiled . . . so help her, she would strangle him. He didn't, unfortunately, because her fingers itched to strike. Very reluctantly she set her hand on his arm. "I'd sooner touch a snake than you."

"I'll see if I can find you one."

Jesse kept her nails pared short, but there was enough length to them to draw a satisfactory wince from him as she dug her fingers into his muscular forearm.

"Ach, you wound me, m'lady," he mocked, eyes dancing.

"Not yet, but the day is not over."

"Nay, it is not." Lips twitching, Alex escorted her from the beach and up the worn stone steps to the town.

Everything about him from the teasing grin to the way he treated her like a delicate lady garbed in her finest court silks instead of a squire's ill-fitting woolens inflamed Jesse's raw nerves. Never had she met *anyone* as infuriating as Alexander Sommerville. And well he knew it—relished it. She seethed as he solicitously helped her around a puddle.

The town was old and small, with narrow, crooked streets bounded by mud-and-wattle homes that leaned against each other for support. The only spots of color were the signs of the sail maker, butcher, grocer and baker. Peddlers prowled the lanes crying their wares: ale and milk and fish and pastries. From the free-flowing gutters rose the stench of rotting garbage and night soil from the chamber pots that had been emptied into it.

Alex halted to let a cart laden with sheared wool clatter by, then he lifted Jesse over the clogged gutter and into the muddy, rutted street.

"I would not have you treat me thus," she said stiffly.

A brow quirked. "Courteously?"

"You know what I mean."

"Nay, in truth I do not, Jesselynn," he replied, serious for the moment. "You are like no woman I have ever known."

The intensity of his stare made Jesse's stomach tighten anew, but she squared her shoulders. "Nay, I am not." Proudly. "And I'd not have you call me Jesselynn."

"'Tis your name."

Edmund called her thus, and it fell from his lips like a curse. "I prefer Jesse."

"'Tis a man's name. Why do you not wish to be a woman?"

"I'd not be treated like one. Edmund despises anything that is weaker and smaller than he. Women are both," she said flatly.

Edmund was a bull of a man with a vicious temper, Alex recalled from having seen him two years ago. Edmund had first maneuvered the Sommervilles into fielding an army, then provoked Geoffrey into meeting him in single combat. The winner was to have gotten the contested earldom. Only the timely arrival of Gaby with proof of Harcourt's treachery had saved Alex's father.

Aye, Alex remembered well that encounter with Edmund. Inside him, something pulled tight at the thought of tiny Jesselynn at the mercy of that raving monster. "Not all men are like Edmund Harcourt, praise be to God."

"Amen," she echoed. "Still the quality of the man changes not a woman's lot." She knew he didn't understand. No man could.

Not even Hugh, who had humored her, teaching her to wield a weapon so she would be less vulnerable. Nay, none but another woman could know what it was like to be a victim with no recourse against a father or husband in the courts of man or in God's church. "'Tis the unfairness that hurts the most."

Alex nodded. His hatred of injustice had prompted him to take on more than one lost cause. Would she be the next? "Not all women are mistreated as you have been," he said quietly.

"Nay. The peasants are also their master's property and suffer from his whims."

"Is that why you stole the grain?" Alex asked slowly.

She paled and looked away. "I know nothing about any grain."

Alex let the lie pass. "I'm sorry your father mistreated you."

"Save your pity. What Edmund did made me strong."

"Gabrielle is not weak," he said, his pity growing.

"Nay. I will allow she is not."

"And she acts very much the woman." *As should you.* Suddenly it occurred to him that his plans for her could have the added benefit of teaching her to take pride in her femininity. She would fight him every step of the way, he thought, glancing down at her rebellious profile, but at least the day would not be dull. "Come, we have a distance to go."

Jesse paused as he passed the tavern she had supposed was their destination. "Are we going to ask after *The Salamander?*"

Alex shook his head and kept walking. He would have gone by a second tavern, but the innkeeper stepped outside just then.

"My Lord Alexander," the portly man cried, bowing low. "'Tis a pleasure to see you again." Apparently the patrons of the place thought so, too, because they poured out of the dark, smoky interior, greeting Alex with easy smiles and offers of everything from supplies for his ship to a bed for the night.

To Jesse's surprise, Alex did not talk down to these men as Hugh might; for all his good qualities, her twin enjoyed lording it over others. Nor did Alex cuff the townsfolk for daring to speak to a noble as Edmund did. Nay, Alex joked and spoke to them without irritation or condescension. And they obviously held him in such high esteem it was sickening.

Jesse was so startled to see lack of pretense where she had expected arrogance that it took her a moment to realize she had become separated from him and stood on the fringe of the group of laughing men. Over her shoulder, she spotted an alley a few steps away. Now was her chance to escape. But when she looked back, something in the tenseness of Alex's stance warned her that he knew very well where she was and what she was thinking.

Awareness shivered across Jesse's skin. *He expected her to make a break.* Aye, and break her pledge with the same mad, futile scramble for freedom. Then he'd hold that over her head when he caught her. And catch her he would, she thought, recalling how quickly he could move. Nor would these people, his friends, aid her. Suddenly she felt cold and alone.

Alex glanced over his shoulder and saw Jesselynn poised for flight. She looked so lost and unhappy that for one mad moment he wanted to let her go. 'Twas she who decided the matter, giving him a hard glare to let him know she'd not make her move—yet. Cheeky wench. He found he liked even that about her. He truly was going mad.

He was clever, Jesse grudgingly admitted as Alex bade the men farewell and led her down the street. For the moment he held her securely in check, caged by her own foolish vow. But she had not sharpened her own brain on the whetstone of Edmund's all these years for naught. All she had to do was stay calm and in control and she would win freedom—without violating her pledge.

Jesselynn had not tried to run away. Alex turned that over in his mind as they walked. He'd purposely given her an opening, but she had not taken it. 'Twas passing strange. Mayhap she but waited for a better opportunity.

He glanced down at the top of the red head that did not quite reach his shoulder and wondered what was going on inside it. Rebellion, no doubt. She was a complex mix of beauty and brains, fire and fear, strengths and weaknesses. Her vulnerability drew him as surely as did the challenge of taming her. Aye, she'd lead him a merry chase. And he relished it as he had not relished anything or anyone in recent memory.

Chapter Five

Jesse peered through the raised horizontal shutters of the shop. Inside, a woman looked up from her sewing. "What are we doing here?" Jesse asked warily. Before Alex could reply, the woman launched herself out the door.

"Oh, m'lord Alex. We've nay see ye in ever so long." She dropped him a low curtsy, then bobbed up to catch his hand. "Ye are well come." She kissed Alex's knuckles.

"Here now, Meggie, there's no need of that." He flushed beneath his tan.

"I owe ye that an' more," she insisted. She was plump and pretty, with wide blue eyes that looked at Alex with sickening adoration and flaxen braids that bounced against her ample breasts as she tugged Alex forward. "Come in. Let me fetch ye a cup o' ale and make ye more comfortable."

He shot Jesse an apologetic glance. Which she countered with a narrowed one. She had been right, he was a heartless rogue. "By all means, bed your whore. 'Tis no concern of mine."

"Jesselynn," he warned, just as two small children tumbled over the threshold and grabbed him by the knees.

"Up, up!" demanded the girl, a blond cherub of three or so, stretching out her grubby hands.

"I knowed him longest," cried the boy of four or five. He was thinner with dark hair and eyes.

Oh, God. They were Alex's bastard children. "I will wait outside," Jesse managed.

"Nay, you're the reason we've come here," Alex replied. Deftly swinging a child up in each arm, he somehow managed to nudge Jesse into the shop ahead of him.

After the sunny street, it seemed dark and cold inside. A shiver of foreboding iced Jesse's skin. *Why had he brought her to this place?*

"Meggie, this is Lady Jesselynn."

The girl bobbed a curtsy, her gaze open and friendly.

"We've come about some clothes for her," Alex explained to Meggie, but his watchful eyes never left Jesse's face.

"I will not wear a gown," Jesse declared.

"Remember your vow," Alex cautioned, but the rest of his sermon went unspoken as the curtains at the back of the shop parted and a man gimped out.

"M'lord." The man balanced his weight on a single crutch. The left leg of his breeches was empty from about the knee down.

"George. What kind of greeting is that for an old shipmate?" Alex gave Jesse an odd smile, thrust the little girl at her and moved to take George's free hand.

Jesse felt all thumbs as she struggled to keep a grip on the child. She had shied away from contact with children because she knew she would never have any. The girl's weight and the feel of the chunky arms felt strange around her neck, confining. "Er, what is your name?" she asked awkwardly, wishing someone would take the child before she dropped it.

"Annie," the child mumbled around the finger she'd stuck in her mouth. "I don't know ye . . . an' I gotta wee."

"A wee what?"

"Too late," Annie said sadly.

A wet warmth gushed down the front of Jesse. "Oh, no—"

"Nay, Annie!" Meggie cried. "I'm that sorry, m'lady. She does this when she gets excited."

"Aye, so she does." Alex winked at Jesse.

"You did that on purpose. I'll not wear a gown even if these clothes are wet," Jesse snapped, his grin firing her fury.

"Remember to count," Alex advised pleasantly.

"Counting be damned—even if I knew how. Take her!" demanded Jesse, holding the child away from her body.

"Ouch. Ye pinched me." Annie wiggled and started to sob.

"I—I'm sorry." Instantly contrite, Jesse hugged the soggy Annie and patted her back, all the while shooting daggers at Alex over the child's head. "There, there, 'tis not your fault Lord Alexander is a snake."

"A snake?" Annie ceased crying. "Nay, Lord Alex is a man... like ye."

Jesse groaned, already afraid of where this could lead. "I am not a man," she said firmly.

"Course, ye aren't." Meggie reached for her daughter, but Annie dodged her mother's hands and planted both of hers on Jesse's chest, bound flat by linen wrappings.

"Ye are a man," the child insisted. "See... no boobies."

Alex threw back his head and roared with laughter.

Meggie looked from Alex to Jesse and shook her head. "Always said there was no understandin' the nobles," she said to no one in particular as she relieved Jesse of the wet child.

"Lady Jesselynn, er, lost her clothing in an accident at sea," Alex choked out, wiping the tears from his eyes with the back of his hand. "I was hoping you might have some clothes already made in your shop—woman's clothes suitable for—"

"Nay!" Jesse stamped her foot and turned to flee, but Alex grabbed her around the waist before she'd gone two steps, bringing her face-to-face with the little boy he still held.

"One, two, three," Alex prompted.

The boy said, "Ye stink. Ye'll ha' ta change yer clothes."

Alex watched the rage darken her eyes as Jesselynn realized she was cornered, forced to wear a gown. He had his revenge, but the dish tasted flat. Her gentleness when she'd soothed Annie had surprised Alex. The sight of her holding Annie had caused an odd stirring in his chest. The last female to affect that part of his body rather than something lower down had been baby Cat. And what he felt for Jesselynn was not unclelike. He sensed the game was changing again, getting away from him. "Go along with Meggie," he said huskily, "and see what she has—"

"I won't wear a gown and I won't stay here a minute longer to be humiliated by your whore and your bastards," Jesse hissed.

"Whot's a bas... a baster?" Annie asked.

Jesse's face went hot with shame. Damn. She wished the child hadn't heard that. She'd always maintained that a child was not responsible for the actions of its parents. Mayhap to distance herself from Edmund and his destructive greed.

"Meggie is me wife," George said stiffly into the tense silence. "An' John and Annie our legal get."

"I will teach you to count," Alex softly offered.

Jesse closed her eyes and moaned quietly.

"Lord Alex is a good man," Meggie mumbled around the pins she held in her mouth. She turned up the hem in the yellow tunic Jesse had on and plied her needle. "'Tis a good fit," she observed, gauging the slender line of Jesse's waist and hips.

Jesse stared stonily into the fire crackling in the tiny hearth of George and Meggie's chamber above their shop. Her body was as rigid as her vow not to speak to any of these people. They were his friends; they had witnessed her disgrace, and they were helping him to clothe her in the hated woman's garb.

"Ye were right about me bein' a prostitute," Meggie said with a sigh. "There were ten of us in me family, and I was the oldest. Me da sold me ta Master Will, the tavern keeper, when I was twelve. I served food an' ale in the common room downstairs, an' when the place closed, I made extra money upstairs."

"Hateful! A boy would not be sold like that."

"Dunno. There are some men who prefer boys."

"For what? Never mind." Jesse dismissed that nonsense with a wave of her hand. "Men are all such greedy creatures!"

"Greedy? Nay, me da bought a cow wi' the money, so as me younger brothers 'n' sisters could ha' milk."

"Oh." Jesse gave serious thought to learning how to count. "Still, it must have been terrible for you."

"'Tweren't so bad. Master Will didn't hold wi' the customers beatin' his girls, an' he let us keep a bit o' whot we got." She bit off the thread with her teeth and patted the garment into place. "Besides, that's where I met Lord Alex."

Jesse stiffened slightly, unsure why her heart suddenly dropped. "You . . . he bedded you."

"Aye. Once." Her long sigh went through Jesse like a lance. "He likes women, that much is plain. He was kind ta me, and—"

"Could we get on with this?" Jesse snapped, shivering despite the fire. Damn. She didn't want to hear any of this.

Meggie drew the sleeveless green surcoat over Jesse's head, twitching it so the fine woolen garment skimmed the hips and fell straight to the ground. The armholes were open to the waist to reveal the narrow leather belt. "I'm sorry fer speakin' out. George says me tongue comes unhooked from me brain sometimes. I didn't stop ta think me words'd make ye jealous."

"I am not jealous," Jesse seethed. "Lord Alexander is naught to me but my enemy. Did he not tell you I am a Harcourt?"

Meggie's eyes widened. "A Harcourt with a Sommerville?" Everyone knew about the feud that had started with two Norman cousins who had come to conquer England with Duke William.

The duke had sent the pair to subdue Winchester Castle, promising they could share its bounty. Only when the Sommerville had laid eyes on the lady of the castle, he had not wanted to share her with anyone. A battle had ensued, and the duke had finally intervened, granting the lady and the earldom to the Sommerville, the castle and the wealth to the Harcourt. And so it had been ever since. The Sommervilles were possessive of their women; the greedy Harcourts craved the lost title.

"Alex is holding me prisoner." Jesse whispered, because he had the most infuriating habit of popping in on her. "If you would help me get word to my brother, I'd pay you well." Sending to Hugh was not the same as escaping, she assured herself.

"I couldn't go again' Lord Alex."

"He's threatened to harm me."

"Lord Alex wouldn't hurt a woman. He's buyin' ye clothes."

"'Tis part of his scheme to torture me," Jesse pointed out with as much patience as she could muster.

Meggie looked more perplexed. "It is? Always said the nobles had strange ways. Well, he's failed, then, 'cause I must say ye look that grand in these."

"That is not the point," Jesse muttered, but she knew she'd get no help from Meggie. Sighing, she glanced down at the despised garments. The fabric was fine and soft. Still, the clothes felt as confining as she'd recalled from the last time she'd been forced into a gown. "I prefer Ellis's hose and tunic."

Meggie's face fell. "I'm that sorry, m'lady. I did me best."

"It's not your fault," Jesse said sourly. It was Alex's, and she'd find a way to make him pay did it take her a lifetime.

"I—I wanted this ta be perfect. He's done so much fer George an' me. Lord Alex brought us together. When George lost his leg in an accident aboard *The Star,* the ship put in ta here lookin' fer a place where George could heal and work fer him ta do when he recovered 'cause he couldn't go back ta sea. Lord Alex remembered that I was savin' ta open a shop an' get out o' the trade. He offered me the coin I needed as a dowry if I'd wed George. Since George was handy wi' a needle—him bein' a sail maker 'n all—we opened this tailor shop."

"And I am certain Alex profited handsomely," Jesse snapped, well used to men's greedy ways.

Meggie looked shocked Jesse had suggested such a thing. "He's never taken a penny...even payed fer whot ye're wearin', but 'tis the only time he's ever asked o' us fer *anythin'*. I did so want ye ta like the clothes."

Oh, damn. Jesse didn't want to hear about his kindness, didn't want to know Alex could be anything but greedy and lecherous. "The clothes are fine." At a loss for words, Jesse ran a hand down her hip. "The...the fabric feels nice against my skin. The yellow reminds me of the sun and the green of the forest. More pleasing to the eye than Ellis's brown clothes."

Meggie brightened. "If ye're sure."

"Aye. I like them. Really I do," Jesse insisted.

"I'm so glad to hear that," Alex said as he entered.

"Do you never knock?" Jesse snapped.

He shrugged. "I find I learn much more when I do not." Still grinning, he crossed the room with that lithe, powerful stride of his that reminded Jesse of the sensual grace of the king's lion. He did not stop until he stood so close to her that the tips of his boots touched the hem of her surcoat. By then, her heart was thudding, her mouth unexpectedly dry.

His nearness, the heat from his body and the faint scent of the soap he'd used that morning teased her senses, made her insides draw tight. Fear? Nay, nor was it the hatred she wanted to feel. 'Twas anticipation that quickened her breathing, excitement that raised the fine hairs on her arms and neck. Why? Why him? Jesse fought the traitorous things shivering inside her. "I will wear these cursed garments back to your bloody ship because there is naught else, but I will tear them to shreds with my teeth and—"

"Then you will go naked," he said quietly yet firmly.

"M'lord!" Meggie gasped.

"Leave us a moment, lass." Over his shoulder he added, "And if you have another gown and a cloak, I will buy them, also."

"Nay," Jesse cried, but Meggie looked from one angry face to the other and fled.

"Will you take the clothes?" he asked when they were alone.

Jesse shook her head, determined to stand firm.

"For Meggie's sake. It would mean so much to her."

"You wretch! You put Meggie up to telling me that tale."

Alex spread his hands defensively. "'Tis no tale, but the truth, and I knew you would want to help her repay this debt she seems to feel she owes me," he added with a crooked smile.

"How did you know I'd pity her? I am a Harcourt."

And they were known more for their greed than their charity, yet increasingly he had trouble recalling she was a Harcourt. He waited for the remorse that should have spawned, felt only wonder at how things were changing between them.

"I remembered how gentle you were with the injured animals Gaby kept in the stables at Wilton," he said slowly, his eyes on her face, probing her thoughts. He saw a yearning that tugged at him. She craved approval, with no actual hope of getting it. Deep inside where the scars did not show, she was as wounded as the animals she'd cared for. He had not realized the need to heal her could flow so strongly within him. "You sat up all night with a hound of mine that had mangled his paw in a trap," he added, recalling the nearly forgotten incident.

"But I did not know then that I was Jesselynn Harcourt. Mayhap that made a difference in the way I acted."

So, she was determined to see herself in the worst light, and he did not truly know her well enough to refute her. But he wanted to—more with each passing moment. He changed tactics. "You did not come to Wilton to spy, then."

"Nay. I had truly lost my memory. But none of you Sommervilles believed me." 'Twas why Gaby had insisted on helping Jesse escape from Wilton when her memory returned.

"I believe you now . . . if it makes a difference."

It did. Almost as much as his belief that she was the kind of person who would be moved by Meggie's story. But Jesse would be damned before she'd tell him so. "I think you would say anything to get me to wear Meggie's clothes."

"Who, me?" He grinned like a saucy lad. She surprised them both by smiling. The curving of her lips was shy and fleeting. Grudging almost. He treasured it as the first of many. 'Twas a measure of how far under her spell he was falling.

Jesse forced her wayward lips back into a line, reminded herself that she was angry with him. "You are impossible."

"So I've been told. The tunic and surcoat truly do become you, though." His gaze fell from her face to the high swell of her breasts, the slender curve of her waist. Jesu, but she was beautiful. "I'd see you clad in silks and velvets," he murmured.

"I hate expensive things." She tossed her head, perversely glad he had shattered the moment. "And I'd see you in hell before I'd wear either." Green fire blazed in her eyes.

'Twould burn the man who got too close, but it would heat his blood beyond imagining. Alex had ever been one to dare what other men avoided. If only she was not a Harcourt, he might have given in to the craving to kiss the rage from her tautly held mouth and feel the flames build between them. Reminded of the feud, he stiffened and retreated behind the shield of mockery. "Alas, I am for Edinburgh, not hell, though some count that city and her dour Scots only a step above—"

"I do not want to go to Edinburgh."

"I thought you were anxious to rejoin your brother."

Her anger vanished like smoke. "Why would Hugh go there?"

"Now that we have momentarily thwarted his scheme, he likely seeks shelter with your Graham's kin."

"I'd not claim the Grahams as kin, but, aye, I'd see Hugh. When do we leave?"

"We have an hour before we must return to the ship. With all the wettings you've taken—" his eyes twinkled "—I thought you might enjoy a bath, so I asked George to heat some water. Meggie will return to assist you."

"I do not need a bath."

Alex shook his head. "Must your answer to everything be nay? You forego that which we both know you need and want, to spite me. Must I remind you of your pledge, again?"

"Oh, very well," she snapped, but something else niggled at her. "Why do you not hurry back to the ship to make ready?"

"They already know we sail for Edinburgh."

"How can they possibly?" She presumed either George or the men at the tavern had given him the news.

"I knew ere we left the ship. When you asked to accompany me ashore, I sent Bevan to conduct the search. He returned with news of their destination before you joined me on deck."

"Oh! You tricked me into that stupid pledge."

"Nay. I only found out after— Oof!"

Jesse's right foot connected with his left knee, drawing a satisfactory grunt of pain. But her triumph was short-lived, for he scooped her up in his arms and held her immobile.

"Give it up, Jesselynn," he murmured in her ear. "You'll only hurt yourself."

"I will kill you," she panted out. "I swear it."

"I know you would like to," he said, sounding almost sad. "But I am much larger and stronger than—"

"I may be only a woman, but I will find a way to best you."

Alex stood at the rail, watching the afternoon sun gild *The Star*'s wake as she slipped out of Blakeney's harbor.

"Has the lady settled down?" Bevan asked with a smirk.

Alex groaned. "I've not checked on her."

"She treated the laddies ta quite a spectacle." Bevan chuckled. Alex had never brought a woman aboard ship before, and the sight of one slung over his shoulder, thrashing and cursing, had packed the rails with spectators. When she had bitten him on the back, the sailors' gasps had mirrored Bevan's astonishment.

"You missed the opening act," Alex muttered, still not over the shock and embarrassment of having her suddenly turn on him in the middle of Blakeney's busiest street. "She kicked me and shouted at me for deceiving her with that pledge."

Bevan snorted. "'Tis what comes o' takin' a woman's vow."

"She said I had no honor," Alex added in disbelief.

Bevan knew there could be no crueler cut to a man like Alex, who had been weaned on the high principles all Sommervilles wore like a hair shirt. "What did ye do?"

"Threw her over my shoulder and kept walking." But the taunt had hurt the worse because he knew in his heart he had not played quite fairly with her. He leaned both hands on the rail, head bent. "I do not know what to do with her. She is like no woman I have ever met."

"Ye can hardly expect yer enemy's daughter ta fall at yer feet the way the rest o' the female population does," Bevan said with asperity. "And her yer prisoner besides."

"Fall at my feet! Hell, I think she has broken two of my toes." Lifting his left boot, he flexed it and winced. "She stomped on my foot when I set her down in my cabin."

"Well, ye could always beat her."

"Never." Alex's head whipped around, his fierce expression moving Bevan back a step. "Edmund beat her, and threw her into some dark prison." His grip on the wooden rail tightened until his knuckles popped out white as he listed the other abuses he suspected Edmund had heaped on his daughter.

"The poor mite," Bevan said gruffly.

"Call her that and she'll likely bite *you*," Alex grumbled. "She wants no one's pity." But pity her he did. Nay, 'twas more than that, he could not stand the idea of her being hurt.

"'Tis none o' yer affair, anyway. Once we find Hugh, ye'll be turnin' her o'er to him in exchange for his confession."

Alex drew in a lung full of tangy sea air and let it out slowly. It did not ease the knot in his gut. "'Tis what I must do, but I wish there was a way to protect her from Edmund. She is..." Is what? Contrary? Infuriating? Desirable? How could he explain what he did not fully understand yet himself? "She deserves far better than the life she has had with her father."

"Ye're babblin' nonsense 'cause she's comely, but ye've known dozens o' lasses more beautiful."

Had he? It was hard to think so when he regarded her fair face, expressive green eyes and gloriously wild hair.

"'Tis lust that ails ye, lad. Nothin' more."

Lust? Alex thought about the brave, rebellious spirit Edmund had not been able to subdue, recalled the mouth that was made to smile but seldom did. Aye, he feared she moved him in ways that had to do with desire but not with lust.

Bevan clapped Alex on the back. "What wi' rushin' ta Tyneham, ye weren't ashore long enough ta bed a woman after our voyage. Ye can hop into Lady Fiona's bed when we reach Edinburgh. A night there'll cure ye."

"Aye," Alex said absently. The idea did not stir him, the way Jesselynn could with her blazing eyes, stubborn chin and slender curves. 'Twas a potent combination. One he knew he must resist. He turned toward the prow, welcoming the cleansing breeze against his furrowed brow. "It worries me that Parlan told half of Blakeney he was bound for Edinburgh."

Bevan tugged at his lower lip. "Makes ye think he wanted us ta follow him. Could be he's layin' a trap in Edinburgh wi' his Graham kin ta back him. We'd best tread carefully, lad. The Grahams are accounted devious curs."

Alex nodded grimly. "It seems to me he's given us a chance to settle two scores at once...clear Papa and Gareth of treason and avenge Uncle James."

"What o' the lass? Will ye return her ta Hugh?"

Alex stared out over the dark, sparkling water but saw only duty. "I will use her to curb her brother." He could not afford to let anyone or anything stand in the way of saving his family. "I'd find a way to end this damned feud for all time."

"The feud's been goin' on fer three hundred years. How can ye think ta end it?"

"I have to." Steely determination edged Alex's deep voice as tension mounted. "We Sommervilles have ever lived with one eye cast over our shoulders to see if a Harcourt plot was hatching there. Two years ago Edmund tried to kill my father in battle. Now Hugh plots to frame Papa and Gareth for treason. Enough, I say!" He pounded the rail with his fist. "I will end this feud no matter what it costs."

"Aye, 'tis a worthy goal," Bevan soothed, "but how?"

"How indeed." Alex stared at the horizon, as distant and unreachable as ending the feud, and yet... "I have Edmund's daughter," he said slowly, thinking aloud. "Soon I may hold his son, as well. If rumor is true, and it seems to be, Edmund does not value either of them overly, but they are his only heirs."

"Ah. Ye'd ha' the means ta bend him ta yer will, but what guarantee that Edmund would leave yer family alone after ye'd released his bairns? Mayhap they'd ha' ta stay yer prisoners."

Alex's gut twisted as he recalled Jesselynn's aversion to imprisonment. "Nay. That is not the answer." Despite her earlier tirade, he'd hated locking her in his cabin. "Jesselynn may yet prove the key to ending the feud, but I am not certain how." He smiled faintly for the first time in hours. "If Gareth were here, he'd counsel patience. And Ruarke would say, 'Learn all you can about your opponent.' I think it's time to try both." 'Twas time to learn what secrets Jesselynn hid. "Ellis!" he called, turning and nearly tripping over the boy.

"You would not leave her locked up, would you, m'lord?"

So, she has gotten to you, too. "Nay. I was just about to ask you to prepare a small surprise for her on deck. Here is what I would like." Alex smiled at the quickness with which Ellis brightened on hearing what was planned.

Chapter Six

Dressed in Ellis's hose and a tunic, Jesse sat motionless on the window seat, her hands clasped in her lap. The relaxed pose was a sham. She was tense, tired from all she had done in the hours since their dramatic return to *The Star*, but too nervous even to pace. At last she heard heavy footfalls in the corridor. Her back straightened, her shoulders squared. This was it.

The key scraped in the lock and the door swung in, followed closely by Alex's face. The change in his features from wary, to puzzled as he saw what she had wrought, to appalled when the extent of the damage sank in was so funny Jesse nearly laughed. Nearly. She was brazen, not stupid.

"What . . . what have you done?" Alex croaked, eyes darting around his once-luxurious cabin, shorn now of velvet drape and Eastern carpet and wall hangings. All that remained was what had been nailed in place—bunk, desk and trunk. "What?" he repeated.

"I threw everything out the window," Jesse replied with a voice that shook in anticipation of the coming storm.

Alex eyed the open porthole. His body trembled with fury; his breath was harsh and quick as a winded horse's. At his sides, his fists clenched and unclenched, mute testimony to the battle he waged with his temper. Suddenly he yanked open the door, slamming it behind him so the walls shook as he left.

Jesse blinked. Waited for the lock to turn. Nothing. Mouth dry, palms slick, she crept over to the portal.

"Five six seven eight nine ten..." she heard growled through the solid oak planks. He was counting. By the time he reached twenty, he was going slower, sounding calmer. Jesse swalowed and scooted back to the window seat. Scarcely had she planted her bottom down when the door flew open again.

"Why?" he roared.

Jesse started as the hot word tore past her. Her heart pounded with apprehension, but she kept her head high. "Such richness offends me. I could not bear to be in here with these things bought with the sweat and blood of your sailors."

"You presume to judge me?" he bellowed. So much for the counting, Jesse thought smugly, oddly, stupidly pleased to have gotten to him. The door rocked on its hinges as it banged shut. Drawing himself up so he seemed to fill the room, he shouted, "I work beside my men and pay them a fair wage besides. You had no right!" Trembling with fury, he swore and kicked the trunk. "Thank God this was locked," he growled between his teeth.

Jesse smiled sweetly. "I picked your puny lock."

"What?" He whipped down on one knee, wrenched the trunk open so the lid smacked against the wall. His curses rang hollow in the empty box. "M-my books. You threw away the books my sire gave me." He shut the lid and sank down on the trunk. Tears glinted in the glance he shot her. She had forgotten how emotional Sommervilles were. "The rest I can replace, but books are not so easily come by, and one was copied in his own hand."

She had expected rage, mayhap even retaliation for ravaging his cabin and taking the costly garments and jewels from the trunk. That he would feel the loss of the books most keenly was a surprise. More surprising was the remorse she felt. She stifled it; revenge was never an easy dish to serve, and he had earned a generous slice. "You deceived me with your pledge."

"I understand 'tis revenge you seek for my trickery, but you go too far," he snapped. "My scheme wounded your pride, nothing more. For which you amply repaid me by causing a scene in town and another before my own men. Likely they'll not follow me again seeing I was bested by a slip of a girl," he grumbled.

Jesse had not known many small boys, but she imagined they looked so when defeated. Now that the danger of being beaten had passed, a smile lurked behind her lips. Ruthlessl‹ suppressing it, she asked, "Are you sorry you tricked me?"

"Of course I am," he muttered. "Did I not say so?"

"Not exactly." Jesse arched one brow. The pleasure o‹ having him in her power went to her head like strong wine. "‹ am more interested in hearing that you will not do it again."

"I will not." He raked a hand through his hair, exhaled an‹ looked at the floor. "I regretted the deed when I saw ho‹ kindly you treated Meggie. I felt the veriest wretch." 'Twas a‹ admission she suspected not many got from Alexander.

"I thought so, too." Oddly the sight of his bowed head mad‹ her want to go to him and hold him as she had Annie when th‹ girl cried. "Look beneath the bunk," she said softly.

Eyeing her skeptically, Alex opened the storage area an‹ found it crammed full. Not only were the things Meggie ha‹ made there, but his own clothes and the precious books. Al hissed through his teeth as he sat back on his haunches an‹ turned to look at her with new respect.

"You are a cleverly vengeful little vixen," he muttered. Tha‹ he understood best of all. The stubborn set of her chin and th‹ intelligence gleaming in the green eyes that watched him closel‹ struck a responsive chord inside him. "We are much alike, ‹ think," he mused, startled by the idea.

She liked it not at all, he saw by the way she stiffened. "W‹ are nothing alike."

"It explains why we clash." He ignored their obvious dif‹ ferences, intrigued by their similarities. The quick tempers tha‹ spoke of fiery passion, the keenness of wit, the loneliness eac‹ concealed, she with rebellion, he in roguery. Would they lov‹ as fiercely as they fought? he wondered. "Aye, we are muc‹ alike. 'Twas revenge for the knife wound you inflicted tha‹ drove me to extract that pledge from you," he pointed out‹ more certain of his footing now and heading back to his orig‹ inal plan. "And, too, I wanted to see you in a gown."

"What difference can my clothing possibly make to you?"‹

"Call it a whim," Alex said with a shrug. Mayhap she kne‹ it for a lie, because she looked more wary now than she ha‹ facing his fury. Standing, he set his smile to charm. "I ha‹ come to make amends. To offer you supper on deck, if tha‹ appeals."

So much so that she wanted to leap at the chance, he saw, but held herself back. "Would I have to wear a gown?"

Obviously she was used to conditions and restrictions, so he'd place as few as he could. "Nay, but you'd best wear the cloak we bought from Meggie. I won't have my men gawking at your legs in those tight hose."

"They will not. I'm skinny as a lad," Jesselynn added, bending to search beneath the bunk.

The sight of her shapely rear wiggling in the air did not improve the fit of Alex's hose. Nor did the knowledge that a single forward step would align him with that sweet slope. The familiar throbbing grew as he recalled how perfectly she had cradled against him the night before.

"Here 'tis." Jesse straightened and started for the door, nearly tripping over the cloak in her haste.

Alex steadied her with one hand, the other plucking the cloak from her as he leaned against the door. "A moment."

Jesse gasped and took a step back from the warmth in his eyes. "W-what do you want?"

"Only to save you from yourself." He deftly sorted out the cloak and swirled it about her shoulders. A tug on the ties brought her so close the toes of their boots met. "Is my cabin such a loathsome prison that you flee so heedlessly?"

"I—I do not like being confined." And his presence seemed to shrink the space even further, the heat radiating from his body making her mouth go dry.

"We will leave in a moment." His callused fingers brushed her throat as he tied the cloak, sending gooseflesh tingling across her skin, making her jump. "Easy," he murmured, stroking her neck, making the quivers worse. "Surely you do not fear me?"

"Nay, I—I am not used to being touched."

Alex smiled gently. He did not make the mistake of warning her that he planned to remedy that. "I am harmless."

Hah! And pigs fly. Wary of him, Jesse concentrated on looking over the ship as he led her from the cabin. It was not much larger than the great hall at Harte Court, shaped like an elongated bowl with the back end flattened off, and the other pointed to plow into the waves. It rolled and tossed like a bowl, too. The sight of land in the distance was reassuring. She shuddered to think of crossing the open sea in such a fragile, precarious craft. It must take great skill and courage.

"How do you make the ship go where you want?" she asked.

Pleased by her interest, Alex detoured long enough to show her the rudder with its system of cables and winches. That led to other questions about the sails.

Jesse was amazed that he took time not only to answer her, but to show her the thick ropes used to raise the canvas. His promise to take her aloft made her mouth gape open. He closed it with one finger and asked if she feared heights. *Not as much as she feared falling under his spell*. "Nay. I do not think so."

"Excellent. Ah. Here we are." Alex's sweeping gesture took in the blanket spread on the aftercastle's deck, the profusion of cushions strewn upon it and the two silver cups that flanked a napkin-covered tray from which arose the most mouth-watering smells. "Pray, sit, m'lady."

Feeling awkward suddenly, Jesse hugged her cloak close to her body and perched on the edge of one cushion. "I suppose I could try a bite." Her stomach rumbled loudly in agreement.

Alex grinned and plopped down beside her. "I am hungry, too." He whipped the linen off the tray, revealing roasted chicken, dark bread, cheese and a bowl of stewed apples still steaming and fragrant with cinnamon. "We do not usually eat so well on a long voyage, but Bevan picked up fresh supplies in Blakeney." Still she made no move to touch the food, so he selected a thick slab of bread, balanced a slice of roasted chicken atop it and held the lot out to her.

Jesse hesitated. "What of your men? Do they not eat?"

"'Tis the second time you've hinted my sailors are ill-used," he muttered. "Look to the deck below."

Craning her neck to see between the rails, Jesse found the men ranged across the sunny deck in small groups. Some laughed and talked, gesturing with a chicken leg or a slab of buttered bread, while others had their heads bent to the task of eating.

"They have the same food we do," she said in surprise.

"We have wine, while they prefer ale," Alex said slowly. "But otherwise 'tis the same. Did you think I'd starve them?"

"Well . . ."

"Is that what Edmund does?" he asked gently.

Jesse sucked in her lower lip and nodded.

"I see." Alex snagged a chicken leg and settled back among the cushions, watching Jesselynn as she finally tore into the food. She ate as though she expected the food to be snatched back at any moment. An ugly picture of mealtimes at Harte Court formed in his mind. When he had taken the edge off his own hunger, he asked, "Did he starve you?"

Jesse swallowed and looked away from the directness of his gaze. "Edmund does not believe in waste. Feeding peasants and servants more than what is necessary to keep them alive is a waste." Her voice was sharp, her eyes hard as green glass. "I found I could not eat whilst others went hungry."

The depths of her compassion pleased him. "You hunted for them and sneaked grain from Edmund's stores, did you not?"

She blinked. "How could you know that?"

"'Tis what I would have done." With his eyes, Alex willed her to believe him. He knew he had succeeded when some of the stiffness left her shoulders, shoulders that had borne a surprisingly heavy weight for all their slimness.

Jesse pleated the hem of her cloak. "You are not exactly as I remembered," she allowed. He counted that a victory of sorts.

"I have always treated my men well. My sire would have scalped me did I do otherwise, but at the time we met two years ago, I was not at my best." Alex smiled ruefully. "Emilie had just tossed me aside to wed Gareth. Losing a woman was not something I was used to. I fear I did not take it well."

"So I recall." Her smile was fleeting, but Alex counted it a victory, too. "You said she was dead?"

"Aye." 'Twas as though a black curtain fell over his eyes, shuttering all expression in the instant before he looked away. As the silence lengthened, his features drew tighter, sharpened by the anguish of some distant memory, then he shook it away and turned toward her again. "You might better ask about Gaby and Ruarke, 'tis a happier story."

Jesse burned to know why Emilie's death pained him. Did he still love the woman? "Gaby was very good to me," she said instead. "She interested me in herbs and in healing and in the welfare of the peasants. I have thought of her often."

"She's as much a tyrant as ever," he said fondly. "And she and Ruarke are so in love 'tis sickening to watch." His crooked grin said he found it anything but. "They have two girls—"

"No sons?" Jesse's faint smile faded. "Poor Gaby."

"Poor? Nay, you mistake the matter. Ruarke is well pleased with Cat and Philippa. And who could blame him. At two Cat is already a beauty, with Ruarke's fair hair and Gaby's violet eyes. Unfortunately she has my temper, I fear. Philippa is dark haired with the sweet disposition of an angel."

As he went on to describe the girls' antics, Jesse could easily see he was smitten with his tiny nieces. Odd, that a womanizer should like children so. The whole subject of children repulsed her. Not surprising, she supposed, considering Edmund had done naught but harp on getting an heir for as long as she could remember. When she could get a word in edgewise, she changed the subject. "What happens now? To me, I mean."

A good question. Alex chose his words carefully. "I'd call a truce between us at least until we reach Edinburgh."

Jesse sat up straighter. "A truce? Why?"

Alex picked up her hand, pleased when she did not snatch it away. "'Twould sadden me to lock you in my cabin for the voyage, but I'd do it rather than risk having you drown yourself trying to escape me on the high seas."

"What would I have to do?" she asked warily.

Alex repressed a sigh. He'd gotten women into his bed with less effort than this was taking. "Promise not to jump overboard if I leave the cabin unlocked and allow you on deck for meals."

Jesse could scarcely believe her luck, yet something inside made her push for more. "Only for meals?"

"You'd be underfoot when the men are about their duties."

"I'd sit in a corner for a chance at the fresh air."

With them, it was always a struggle for power, Alex thought, noting the gleam in her green eyes as she awaited his next move. This same battle had been going on between men and women for ages. He'd played the game before, but never with more relish or, he sensed, for higher stakes. He laced their fingers together, surprised at how small her hand felt nestled in his, shocked at the protective urge that surged through him. "You can remain on deck providing you go below if the weather is bad."

"I agree," she said, still looking skeptical.

Alex groaned. Jesu, she was a tough one to win over, but he was determined to succeed. The longer he was with her, the more convinced he became that through her he could somehow end the feud. "To bed, now. You look tired." He tugged her to her feet.

Jesse was surprised to find he had her hand. The wide, callused palm felt strange against hers, yet comforting. Overhead, the stars were beginning to pop out of a dark blue sky, but the idea of returning to the stuffy little cabin did not appeal. "I am not ti—" A yawn cut off her words.

"Stubborn," he murmured. But 'twas said fondly and with growing anticipation for the coming days.

"Ready?" Alex asked, head cocked, a light breeze ruffling his hair so the morning sun caught on the gold in it.

Jesse stared up, up, up the tall mast and gulped. She had not thought he'd actually let her do this. "Aye."

"Do not feel you have to," he replied smoothly. But they both knew that between his challenging grin and the circle of curious sailors looking on she'd not back down now.

Squaring her shoulders, she put one hand on the rough wooden pole. "Only tell me what I must do."

Brave little fox, Alex thought as he lifted her onto the mast's first rungs. "Climb slowly, make certain of your footing before you move up. Do not hurry. Do not look down, and remember, I am right behind you."

"I am counting on that," she said with a nervous laugh. That and the rope he had tied around her, the other end secured to his own waist. The climb was more difficult than she'd anticipated. She had to stretch to reach each rung, and the breeze seemed to have become a gale that tore at her hair and clothes. By the time her head poked up through the hole in the base of the crow's nest, her whole body was trembling.

"Sit down on the planking and scoot back out of the way," Alex said from below her. His calm gave her the courage to act. "All right?" he asked moments later as he hauled himself through the opening to sit beside her.

"Is this your revenge for what I did to your cabin?" she asked through chattering teeth.

His own gleamed white against his tanned face. "You were the one who wanted to try this," he reminded her. "Come. Admire the view." He tugged her to her feet, turned her to face outward, sheltering her between the chest-high walls and his hard body.

The world careened dizzily by miles below her. "Sweet Mary!" Jesse slumped back against him, senses reeling.

"Look out, toward the horizon," he ordered, one hand splayed across her rolling belly, his face tucked close to hers, breath warming her cheek. "Fill your lungs slowly, then let it out. I have you," he continued, arms tightening, "safe and sound."

Safe and sound. Jesse repeated that as her stomach settled and her pulse slowed to match the solid beats of Alex's heart against her back. Surprisingly she felt safer in his arms than she had in a long time, as though nothing could hurt her. "It is wonderful," she said moments later, uncertain whether she meant the exhilarating rush of wind in her hair, the glorious feeling she could touch the sky or the sensation of being protected.

"Aye. When she's calm, the sea's as beautiful as you are, but like you, when she is riled—" his chuckle vibrated in her ear "—she's pure hell to manage."

Light and free as sunlight, Jesse tossed her head and cast him a sidelong glance. "Some things are beyond your control."

His grin was pure magic. "That doesn't stop me from trying."

The truce lasted three days, until the morning Jesse came on deck and Alex told her they were within sight of Edinburgh.

"Please let me go," Jesse said in a rush.

"I can not. My family's welfare is at stake." The resolve in his narrowed gaze shattered the surface calm of the past few days. By unspoken agreement, they had not mentioned Hugh or the coins. Almost, as she had listened to Alex weave tales of his travels, she had forgotten they were enemies and this voyage not a pleasure trip but Alex's bid to capture her brother.

"I will go below till we land," she snapped, sick with guilt.

"Suit yourself." It angered him to have so quickly lost the ground he'd gained. The hell with her, then. "And wear one of the gowns Meggie made for you," he called after her.

"I will not," she shouted over her shoulder.

Damn her temper and his swiftly heating one. Counting to twenty chilled his voice. "Then you'll remain aboard."

She rounded on him, chest heaving, eyes angry green slits. "I'll throw myself into the sea and cheat you of your pawn."

He stood above her on the aftercastle, his big, lean body silhouetted against the morning sun, hands on hips, legs braced against the roll of the ship. He exuded power with the same casual ease the deck did the sun's heat. *Damn him.* "That threat wears thin. If 'twas what you wanted, you'd have jumped from the rigging when I took you up with me."

Wretch. He would remind her of that. The view from the perch had been dizzying, stimulating and a little unreal—like the time spent in Alex's company. Three wonderful days enjoying the freedom of the sea—the wind in her hair, the sun on her skin and beside her an engaging companion who had treated her like a person, not a weak, witless female. She had relaxed with him.

The descent to reality was as swift and crushing as falling from rigging to deck would have been. He was her enemy—no matter how much a small part of her might wish it otherwise. Guilt set its claws deeper. "The truce is over!" she cried before spinning about and fleeing the deck.

All the way to the cabin, the need to lash out, to exorcise those traitorous feelings rode her hard. By the time she slammed the door shut, a plan had crystallized. It took her only minutes to peel off her male garb and pull on the yellow tunic and green surcoat Meggie had made. Then she went to work with a vengeance. An apt turn of phrase, she mused as she applied her eating knife to his tunic, since revenge was her goal. By the time Ellis came scratching on the door, the deed was done.

"M'lord asked me to escort you up on deck while he dresses," Ellis said when she answered the door.

Jesse glanced at his clothes laid on the bunk and smiled. "Let us not keep him, then." She led the way onto the deck, her face averted lest Alex guess she was up to something. The man was uncanny when it came to reading her. He said it was because they were alike. She suspected he was in league with the devil.

"Ellis," she said when she'd taken up a spot at the rail that afforded her a clear view of the cabin door. "There is a favor I would ask of you."

"Aye, m'lady. Anything." Ellis was always helpful, eager and honest—so different from the poor servants at Harte Court who were thoroughly cowed by Edmund. One day, mayhap she could change their lot. "I must get a message to my brother."

"Alex will see to that," Ellis assured her.

Jesse shot a quick glance at the cabin door, knowing she had only moments. "Would you like to take service with me?"

"Leave Lord Alex?" Ellis looked appalled. "I could not."

Jesse groaned in frustration.

"I am ready," Alex called, snagging her attention. He wore the red surcoat, black tunic and hose she had laid out. As he turned to close the door, the surcoat's shoulder seam parted.

Jesse bit the inside of her lip to keep from smiling. She knew she should look away, but morbid fascination kept her gaze glued to Alex as he walked toward her, buckling on his sword. By the time he stopped before her, the seam running from his left armpit to the hem had likewise opened. *And he does not know.*

"Ellis, I'd have you stay aboard for the moment," Alex said. "I'll send a tailor to measure the cabin for hangings and such to replace what was...ruined." He pinned Jesse with a hard glance as he raked his hair back. Two seams opened in the under tunic, exposing his tanned left shoulder and arm.

Oh, 'twas too funny. Jesse coughed behind her hand, trembling so with suppressed laughter she dropped her cloak.

"What ails you this morn?" she heard Alex grumble. The next sound was that of threads popping as he bent for the cloak.

"M'lord!" Ellis gasped.

Alex straightened, the strangest look coming over his face as his clothes began to disintegrate. First the left sleeve of his tunic slithered off his arm and landed at her feet, then his surcoat came completely apart and flopped over his sword belt.

"What the hell!" he exclaimed. He looked down just as the front half of his tunic peeled away, baring his chest.

Jesse choked, tried to stuff the laugh back with both hands.

"You!" Alex bellowed. The rest of his words were buried under the sailors' startled exclamations and a few chuckles.

Jesse was pushed back as Bevan leaped between them. "Now Alex. Calm yerself," the old man cautioned.

"I am calm," he roared.

Peeking around Bevan's arm, her mouth went dry as dust. Alex looked every inch the infuriated lion, eyes blazing from narrowed slits. His bronzed skin rippled over flexing, clenching muscles, the golden pelt on his chest glistening in the sun. Around them, the crowd shifted nervously. Why had she not considered the blow to his pride when she'd snipped the seams?

Alex divided a smoldering look between the hanging tatters of his clothes and her white face. Well she should be afraid, he thought, but the spark in her eyes held something that appealed to him more than fear. Humor. It turned the tide of his rushing anger. He'd pulled enough pranks in his time to appreciate a good one—even at his own expense. Throwing back his head, Alex laughed. Tears welled, blurring her shocked expression, which made him laugh all the harder.

Mad, Jesse thought as Alex's rich laughter rolled across the deck and the sailors joined in. So lulled was she by his good humor, she did not object when he abruptly grabbed her hand and whisked her to the cabin. Once inside, he leaned his back to the closed door and put his arms loosely around her.

"Nay." Jesse braced her palms on his chest, trying to ignore the warmth of his naked skin.

"I have not asked for anything," he said huskily. The "yet" was clear. "The deed was cleverly done."

She felt cheated of her revenge. "Why are you not furious?"

Because he'd not give her a reason to hate him. 'Twas the opposite of what he was fast coming to want from her. "You are a handful, Jesselynn." She felt good in his arms, slender but strong. Tempted as he was to fit her curves to the ache in his body, he left the space she'd put between them. "I understand why you did it, and your defiance excites me," he murmured.

"You are mad," she whispered, not understanding *him* at all.

"Mayhap." His warm hands kneaded the bunched muscles along her spine and up to her nape. Fire danced across her shoulders, down her arms, making her pulse leap, her muscles quiver. Beneath her fingers, his heart picked up the beat. "Would you have me punish you?" His breath stirred the hair at her temple as he brushed his lips over her forehead.

She should move away, felt herself sliding instead, losing the ground she'd gained as his mouth drifted to her ear. "This is punishment," she croaked.

Aye. It was hell wanting to kiss her, knowing it was too soon. "I have been patient with you. Though God knows patience is not my long suit," he murmured, tasting the rim of her ear.

"Y-you were supposed to beat me. Oh!" Jesse moaned as his mouth sent shivers racing from her ear to her toes. "Please. I do not understand what's happening."

The sob she uttered had a sharp, panicky catch that brought Alex to his senses, made him remember her innocence, the men waiting on the other side of the door to row them ashore and the duty he could no longer put off. On a sigh of regret, he shifted his grip from her back to her arms. When she looked up, her eyes were dark with passion, bright with the determination to fight it. As must he. Though it damned near killed him.

Sitting her on the edge of the bunk, he briskly asked, "Did you pick the threads from all my clothes?"

She shook her head. "There was not time."

Thank God for that and the fact that she'd left his hose intact, Alex mused as he opened the trunk. Just now the inseams could not have stood any stress. Keeping his back to her, he stripped off the remnants of his clothes.

Even in the dim light, the bunching of his muscles as he unbuckled the sword belt and set it aside did strange things to Jesse's jumpy insides. What was happening? How had things gotten out of control? she wondered. And why had she never noticed the contrast between his wide shoulders and narrow hips?

"We will be going to my cousin's home," Alex said, his words muffled by the tunic he pulled over his head. "I would ask you not take your ire at me out on their home and furnishings."

Jesse stiffened. "Then do not rouse my anger."

"Easier said than done, I fear." Tugging his surcoat down to cover his loins, Alex turned to face her mutinous expression. "I have tried to deal fairly with you. Can you not meet me halfway?"

Jesse sighed. "I suppose. Most men would have beaten me for striking such a blow to their pride," she grudgingly allowed.

"You are welcome." Smiling, he offered his arm. Something flashed in his eyes when she turned up her nose at it, amusement or regret, she could not decide which.

Determination, she amended when Alex countered by placing his hand on the small of her back as he opened the door. Silence and many a sidelong glance greeted their appearance on deck.

Jesse ignored them. Color high, she kicked the hated skirts from her path with every step she took toward the rowboats.

"Stop pouting like that. It excites me, too," he whispered as he helped her down the rope ladders and into the boat.

"Everything excites you." She sucked in her lower lip and tried to ignore Alex all the way from ship to shore. Flustered, she scrambled from the boat the minute it touched the dock, barking her shins on the seats and tripping over her skirts as she climbed the steps to the dock.

"I'll hold the men aboard ship till we see whot Harcourt's up ta," Bevan said as he and Alex mounted the steps and stopped beside a towering stack of barrels.

"Hugh's here!" Jesse scanned the forest of masts but could not tell one from another. Her brother was here; rescue was at hand. No more gowns, no more of Alex's mocking humor, no more battles. She was happy. She was! So why did her insides feel so empty?

"Come. I will take you to my cousin's house in town." Alex took Jesse's arm and began to lead her past the barrels.

"Nay. I would go with you when you meet with Hugh."

His reply was drowned out by a loud rumble as the barrels suddenly shifted and started to fall.

"Look out!" Alex spun her around and shoved her clear. She went down on her knees with a cry of pain and rolled, the shouts of men and the thud of barrels hitting the dock ringing in her ears. Sitting up dizzily, she looked back, but Alex had been swallowed up by a mountain of barrels.

Chapter Seven

The fog rolling in from the firth that night combined with the darkness to turn Edinburgh's streets into murky tunnels. They suited Parlan Graham's purpose exactly as he and his kinsman stole through the city and into an alley across the way from the home of Laird Lionel Carmichael, Alexander's powerful cousin. "You are certain he came here?"

Guthrie Graham squinted at the imposing stone building through his single good eye. "Aye. Followed Sommerville here like ye said after—"

"After you bungled things at the docks this noon."

"Ain't my fault Sommerville's so quick." His scarred face mottled with anger. "Never seed the like o' the way he shoved the lass out o' the way wi' nary a thought ta savin' himself."

"Describe the girl to me again." Parlan was scowling blackly by the time Guthrie finished. "She sounds like my cousin, Jesselynn Harcourt, though I do not understand how she could be with Alexander Sommerville. You are certain she was not hurt by your failed attempt on Alexander?"

Guthrie's red-rimmed eye narrowed, and he spat into the mud, missing Parlan's shiny boot by a scant inch. "I always hit whot I aim fer. 'Twas a bloody miracle he's alive. And as fer the lass, she jumped up 'n' helped Sommerville's men dig him out, so I guess she weren't hurt. But if she's a Harcourt, why did she aid a Sommerville?"

"He has the devil's own way with women," Parlan snarled. Enraged, he turned away and studied the house with an intruder's eye. The upper stories and the roof rose above the eight-foot-high stone wall that surrounded the property. An iron portcullis and gate house guarded the entrance. "Getting in won't be easy."

Guthrie shrugged his massive shoulders. "I'll kill a guard and go in o'er the garden wall in the back."

"No mistakes this time."

"Ye're payin' me ta kill Sommerville and snatch the lass, and that's whot I'll do." He spat again, scoring a direct hit on the toe of Parlan's boot.

Jesse lay on her back in the center of the big bed, staring up at the canopy. She'd asked the maid to leave the bed curtains and the drapes open so the moonlight might filter in through the mullioned window and dispel the dark. 'Twas a wonder Alex had not ordered the chamber stripped of anything she might have ruined, but doubtless he'd had other things on his mind.

Like the accident. It was hours since their arrival at Alex's cousin's house, yet she still felt shaky inside each time she recalled how close Alex had come to being killed.

Bevan's shouts for help had brought men racing from every corner of the docks. They had sweated and cursed as they strained to lift the barrels. Jesse had worked beside them, her heart in her mouth, fearing that at any moment they might uncover Alex's still, crushed body. That she could not have borne. To have seen all that vital energy and keen intelligence snuffed out like a pinched candle.

Shuddering, Jesse pushed back the covers and climbed out of bed. Her fingers trembled as she pulled a borrowed bed robe over her shift. Her legs still felt weak as she walked to the window. Aye, weak. She'd never thought to admit that even to herself, but the incident had proved Edmund correct. Women were weak.

A man seeing his enemy buried beneath those barrels would have rejoiced and fled without a backward glance. She had immediately joined the fray, tugging at the barrels with all her strength until one had nearly rolled her down and Captain Bevan had ordered her to stand clear. Had she escaped then?

Nay, she had stayed, her eyes glued to the barrels, praying for Alex's safety like a foolish woman. Jesse pounded the stone sill with her fist and winced. 'Twas like striking Alex's chest.

Aye, his muscles were as hard. Her fingers splayed on the stone as her mind drifted back to that first morning in his cabin. He confused her, this man who was her enemy yet did not hurt her.

Nay, he had saved her life…for the second time. 'Twas only because she was useful to him, the voice of reason cried. But that did not explain why, when they'd finally freed Alex from the barrels, he had immediately sought her in the crowd.

Their eyes had met across the heads of smiling, triumphant men, his filled with an expression that shook her to the core. No one had ever looked at her with such longing, such naked need, as though she were a cup of water and he a man dying of thirst. At first she thought she'd imagined it, yet she had seen the look again, twice. Once when he'd given her into the care of a maid here to freshen up, and again when she'd entered the hall to eat the evening meal with Bevan and the other men.

Moaning softly, Jesse pressed her forehead to the cool glass and stared down at the garden beneath her window. Why had Alex's glances made her feel even more confused than ever? Confused and restless when she should have been plotting her escape.

Below, the moonbeams played tag among the shifting shadows of the lithe willow, darted down the rows of herbs and greens in the kitchen garden. There must be flowers, too, for she'd smelled them when she and Alex had arrived at the large, stately house, but the glass kept the scents at bay.

Suddenly she needed to smell them, needed to feel the breeze on her flushed face, needed to see the stars overhead. Freedom. Aye, that was what she craved, what made her feel restless.

Bevan stared at the fire in the hearth of Lionel Carmichael's paneled study, sorry the laird was not here to pound some sense into Alex. "Ye should be stayin' aboard *The Star*," the captain said for the tenth time that eve.

"There's more room here, and we are safe behind Lionel's stout walls, surrounded by his guards," Alex patiently replied.

"What happened at the docks was na an accident. That great hulkin' brute, Guthrie Graham, was seen near the barrels this morn. He's big enough ta ha' pushed them over by himself.''

"And he takes his orders from Parlan." Alex leaned his arm along the mantel and stared morosely into the fire struggling in the hearth. "Jesselynn could have been killed. How like a Harcourt to risk killing his own flesh and blood."

"The hell wi' the lass. Ye were buried alive. If ye had na wedged yerself in betwixt those two barrels...if we had na been so quick ta reach ye."

"You said she tried to help."

Bevan slammed his cup down on the oak sideboard, sloshing ale over the side and across the mellow wood. "I'd no ha' told ye that if I'd known ye were goin' ta carry on so about it."

Alex turned thoughtful eyes on his old friend. "She could have escaped, yet she did not."

"She's a woman," Bevan replied, as though that said it all.

But unlike any woman he had known. Sighing, Alex stared at the fluid shapes and vibrant colors of the dancing flames. He saw Jesselynn's stubbornness echoed in the tenacity with which the fire devoured the small pile of logs. That she had tried to save his life amazed him. The things he felt for her scared the hell out of him. What in sweet hell was he going to do with her?

"Ye best be rememberin' yon flame-haired lassie's yer enemy," Bevan was saying.

"So you keep reminding me every time I turn around."

"'Tis yer own good I'm thinkin' of," Bevan cried.

Alex exhaled sharply and dragged a weary hand through his hair, wincing as he touched scrapes and bruises—reminders of his close brush with death. "I thank you, Bevan...for your quick thinking on the docks and for caring enough to shriek at me like a fishwife." He grinned as a flush reddened the captain's weathered face. Sobering, he added, "I know Jesselynn is my enemy." It haunted him, mocked his growing obsession for her. "And a hellcat into the bargain."

"She's a feisty one, I'll grant ye that."

Aye. And the challenge of taming her was part of what drew him despite the warnings of his inbred caution and logical mind. Unfortunately, he was in too deep for caution or logic and suspected he had been since the first time he'd seen her.

Alex straightened, pushed her as far from his thoughts as he could. Crossing to the sideboard, he poured a cup of ale. "Have our men seen anything of Hugh and Parlan in the city?"

"Nay. 'Tis likely they're keepin' ta their ship." *Which you should do, too,* his frown said.

Alex turned the cup in his hands. "'Tis plain Hugh knows I am here, but I wonder if he yet realizes I have Jesselynn?"

"Hmm. If he's as keen ta get her back as ye think, it seems strange ye've not received a demand fer her return."

And thank God for that. Because I have not yet figured a way to keep her and capture Hugh. Alex drank deeply of his ale, but the strong brew did not wash the bitterness of dread from his mouth. "I've sent word to Cousin Lionel, and I'd wait until he comes with more men. Just in case Hugh and the Grahams decide to storm the house and take her."

"I'll be glad o' the extra men," Bevan said tightly.

"And you are hoping my cousin will help keep me in line."

"Well—"

"I will be careful, Bevan. Hell, you know I am always careful," Alex cajoled.

Bevan glanced at the bruise on Alex's temple and the scratch on his neck, and his scowl deepened. "Wi' a man as desperate as Hugh Harcourt, careful may not be enough. 'Tis more than a fine and a slap on the wrist he'll be gettin' if ye succeed in takin' him back ta England ta stand trial."

"He will come to me for the sake of his sister," Alex said wearily. Surely there must be a way to keep them both, only his usually nimble brain was dull with fatigue.

"Ye're tired, lad." Bevan downed his ale in a single swallow. "I'll go back ta *The Star.* I've left the twenty men-at-arms ye brought wi' ye from Ransford. They've spread their pallets in the hall below, in case ye've need o' them."

"I think we are safe enough here." Alex walked his old friend to the door. "Hugh and Parlan are likely aboard *The Salamander* plotting their next move." He kept a smile on his face until the door had closed behind Bevan, then he let out the breath he had been holding, and with it seemed to go the last of his strength. Jesu, but he was tired. His body hurt in a dozen different places, and his eyes were gritty with fatigue.

His steps slow as an old man's, he retrieved his cup from the sideboard and slumped in a high-backed chair, stretching his boots toward the crackling fire. Instantly Jesselynn's face materialized in the flames. He shut his eyes to close her out but saw her still. Worse, his mind raced with the question that had plagued him since this morning. Nay, it had begun the first night, when he'd found her lying on the floor of his cabin and learned of the abuses she'd suffered.

He'd been softening toward her since then. And this morn, when he'd lain on the rough plank docks, hemmed in by the barrels, not knowing whether he had pushed her away in time, fearing she lay nearby, crushed . . . Jesu, the agony of thinking he might never see her again had nearly driven him mad.

When the last barrel had been pulled away, he'd immediately looked for Jesselynn. Seeing her standing a few paces away, her face ashen with fear—for him—he'd known. Known that what he felt for her was love. Known, too, he could neither change those feelings nor escape them. He was a Sommerville and Sommervilles loved only once . . . deeply and irrevocably.

Disgusted with himself, Alex rose and paced to the window. In the garden below, a shadow moved among the trees, and Alex straightened, instantly alert. Could it be one of his men?

Or was it an intruder? Hugh, mayhap?

The air was cooler than Jesse had expected, but refreshing. The fog that crept over the garden walls added a mysterious quality to the night that appealed to her. Almost, she could believe all this was a dream. She was not really Alexander Sommerville's prisoner in far-off Edinburgh, but safe at Harte Court with Hugh. And Edmund was dead, never to trouble her or Hugh again. 'Twas blasphemy to wish him gone, she knew, but the relief at being free of him made sweet thinking.

Hugging her arms about her waist, Jesse tucked her hands inside her sleeves and leaned against the rough bark of a chestnut tree. Its branches spread over her like a canopy, the broad leaves blocking out all but a few moonbeams. 'Twas so quiet, she could hear the beating of her own heart.

Then the breeze picked up, rustling through the grass. Nay, something moved through the grass. Jesse turned toward the sound just as a dark shadow swooped in on her. Reflexively she fought back, but strong hands caught her about the waist; a huge weight trapped her against the tree. The impact jarred the air from her lungs and made her head ring like a bell. Over the peals she heard, "What the hell are you doing out here?" *Alex*.

"Let me go," she managed in a strangled voice.

"Jess." He eased back, but did not release her, his arms slipping around her so she was spared the roughness of the bark. "'Tis dangerous to walk in the garden alone at night, Jess," he rasped, his words warm on her cool cheeks.

Jess. She had not known her name could sound like that, soft and breathy and needful. "I—I felt restless." She tried to ignore the insidious way the warmth of his body stole into hers.

"I know the feeling. You were not meeting someone, then?"

Jesse blinked. "Who? No one knows I am in Edinburgh."

"That warm greeting at the docks was no accident."

"And you think Hugh...? Nay, he'd not risk harming me."

"Not even to eliminate me?"

"Nay. He loves me well." Even in the dimness beneath the tree, she caught the hint of wariness in Alex's eyes. "Hugh and I shared our mother's womb. It made us close, or mayhap it was because after she died no one wanted us. Whatever—we were all each other had. Hugh would not harm me."

Alex barely heard the last, his sympathy pricked by the dull acceptance in her voice. *No one wanted us*. He wanted her. So badly he shook with it. His arms tightened fractionally. "Why did you help free me?" He had to know.

"I...I am not certain."

Alex saw the rare sheen of tears in her eyes, heard the rawness in her voice. "Nay, you know," he murmured, staring intently into her eyes. "You feel it, do you not?"

"W-what?" she stammered.

"This thing that is between us," he said, low and quiet, his eyes glittering beneath lowered lids. "This wanting that fuels our battles, yet draws us closer together."

"Nay," Jesse whispered, but again she lied, for already his heat had kindled a tiny flame deep inside her. She tried to will it away. Failed. "I do not know what you mean."

"Liar. Sweet liar." The huskiness in his voice slid down her spine like hot honey. "We both desire what we should not—what we have no business even thinking about. Each other."

Jesse shivered and tried to look away from his dark eyes, but the sensual promise blazing there held her captive as surely as his steely muscles. She tried to remember he was her enemy, tried to dredge up the anger that fired their quarrels. Instead she thought of them standing together atop the ship, his arms wrapped around her, shielding, protecting. She had never felt more alive or more at ease than at that moment with the sun on her face, the world lying at her feet and this vital man embracing her. Aye, she knew too well what he meant. Her mouth went dry with it. Nervously she wet her lips.

"Ah, Jess." His gaze turned hungry, followed the path her tongue had taken. "I should not be here with you like this. Not feeling the way I do about you." Yet even as he spoke he lifted her off her feet, drawing her up so the planes and hollows of their bodies fit together. Male to female. Hard to soft.

"Trust me, Jess. I will not hurt you." He breathed the words across her mouth, making it tingle. "I have been wondering what you'd taste like. I think the time has come to find out."

Jesse's lips parted, but no sound came out. It seemed he required none. His tongue traced a feather-light trail across her lower lip, then reversed course, skimming the vulnerable inner side of her upper lip. *Good. So good.* Her eyes closed on a moan, and she opened her mouth a little further. Of its own accord, her tongue crept out to touch the tip of his.

An answering growl rumbled through Alex's body and into Jesse's seconds before his mouth clamped down on hers, kissing her with all the pent-up fury of a raging summer storm. Thunder echoed in her ears as her blood began to pound. Deep inside her something broke loose, something sweet and wild. It surged and built, shaking her like a tree in the teeth of a fierce gale. She welcomed the storm, craved its fierce sensual whirlwind.

Wrapping her arms around Alex's neck, she hung on with all her strength, following where he led, matching his movements as he tried to devour her mouth. Her whole body ached and pulsed to the rhythm of her straining body as she arched against him, struggling to get closer, needing to reach the heart of the storm and the secrets it held.

Jesselynn's frenzied response ripped away Alex's control and reason so swiftly his blood boiled with it. Desire had never been this raw, this fierce, this overwhelming. Never had a woman met him so perfectly. He ran his hands over her, stroking, caressing, deepening the kiss until he was deaf and blind to everything but the woman who had caught fire in his arms.

"Jess." He wrenched his mouth from the heaven of hers, gasping for breath. "I want you so badly it is killing me." He had to be inside her, filling her as she closed tightly around him. He felt strong and primitive and driven to possess the woman he loved. "I love you. Damn me, but I love you." He sank with her to his knees.

Jesse blinked as she felt the cool grass on her legs. "W-what?" Torn from her sensual haze, she stiffened in his arms.

"I love you." His eyes burned with raw intensity, and the muscles in his neck stood out like coils of rope. But it was the savage beauty of his face that struck her like a hard slap, jarring her back to reality. This was Alex Sommerville who held her, kissed her, made her feel things she had not known existed.

"N-nay. You . . . you can not."

Alex let the air hiss out between tautly held lips, trembling with the force of the effort required to pull back, to deny the desire clawing at him. "I know I should not, but—"

"'Tis impossible." She shook her head, trying to clear it.

"Nay. Nothing is impossible . . . not if you want it badly enough. And I do want you." His arms tightened around her again where moments ago he had given her room, space to breathe.

Desire. Aye, she could understand his wanting her. He was a rogue, a charmer. But love? 'Twas as much a fantasy as the mist swirling around them. "Nay." She pushed against his chest.

Alex eased his grip yet could not release her entirely. In the dimness, her eyes were dark pools in her ashen face. "I startled you. 'Twas too much, too soon. I apologize." He smiled ruefully. "I've been long without a woman, and feeling as I—"

Suddenly Alex was ripped away from her and swallowed up by a huge black shadow. The violent movement sent Jesse sprawling backward. When she struggled to her feet, she saw Alex battling with a mountain of a man. Grunts and curses filled the night air as the two writhed against each other in an uneven contest.

She wanted to run for help, yet feared to take her eyes from the fight for even an instant lest Alex be overpowered and killed by this monster. Fists clenched, she silently urged Alex on. For an instant, it seemed to work. Alex moved his opponent back with a series of lightning jabs to the midsection.

Then the attacker surged forward, roaring obscenities. With the backward swipe of one massive arm, he sent Alex flying out onto the moon-bright path. Over and over Alex rolled, and with him Jesse's thudding heart. The fog stirred and the ground shook as Alex's opponent rushed past Jesse.

"Stay clear," he spat. "I'd deliver ye ta Parlan unharmed."

Moonlight glinted off the wicked-looking knife he clutched, goading Jesse into action. She launched herself onto his broad back, sank her fingers into his throat. He stopped in his tracks and made a satisfying strangling noise, but his thick muscles prevented her from doing any real damage.

"Jess!" 'Twas Alex. "Leave off. Get away from there."

"Nay," she managed, panting with effort for the giant shook like a dog trying to rid itself of a pesky kitten, and her fingers were fast losing their grip on his sweaty neck.

"Don't hurt her, Guthrie!" Alex sounded near and desperate. "Jess. Jump. Now," he added. The crack of his fist meeting flesh punctuated his words, and the mountainous man shuddered.

"Hit him again," Jesse managed. Then Guthrie's beefy paw closed around her wrist and wrenched her loose. "Hellfire and damnation," she cried as she sailed through the air. Landing forced the air from her lungs. She rolled over in the wet grass, gasping for breath and pushing her tangled hair from her eyes.

Thanks be to Mary and Joseph, at least Alex was up. He even appeared fairly steady in his fighter's stance, fists at the ready, but the hulking Guthrie was strong enough to hurl oxen.

"Jess?" Alex called, slanting her a quick glance.

"I am fine. Jesu, look out. He charges." Jesse shivered as the scar-faced Guthrie ran at Alex, arms outstretched to crush every bone in Alex's body. "Alex, move, for the love of God."

He did. At the last possible instant. His actions so quick they blurred into a single line, he ducked Guthrie's clutches, spun about and gave the man a solid boot in the rear. Guthrie hurtled forward into a small tree. It cracked in two on impact.

Staggering back a step, Guthrie shook his head, then rounded on Alex. His eye narrowed; the scars that hatched his face stood out white in his red face. "Ye shouldna ha' done that. I've ways o' makin' the dyin' slow and painful," he said savagely.

"Alex," Jesse whimpered, starting forward.

He stilled her with a swift, hard look. "Go into the house and rouse the guard," he said harshly.

"Nay. They'd not arrive in time." Already Guthrie was moving, stalking with the deadly intent of an enraged bear.

"They only need pick up what I leave of Guthrie."

That got a roar out of Guthrie and quickened his step. He did not make the mistake of running at Alex this time, but halted a few paces away, then advanced slowly, fists swinging.

Instead of dodging, Alex leaped into the air and buried his foot in the man's stomach. Guthrie barely had time to grunt and swear before Alex pivoted smartly and struck again. A sickening crack split the air as the toe of Alex's boot connected with Guthrie's chin, snapping his head back.

Guthrie screamed, fell to his knees and wavered there, his mouth red with blood, then he slowly toppled backward to lie unmoving in the wet grass.

Jesse crept from the shadows. "Is . . . is he dead?"

Alex turned on her, and she stepped back a pace from the primitive fury in his face. "I told you to go inside."

"I—I thought you might need help." She looked down at the felled giant, then back at Alex. His hair was tangled and full of grass; his face glistened with sweat and a trickle of blood marred one corner of his taut mouth. Otherwise, he appeared unhurt. "How...how did you do that?"

"'Tis a style of fighting I learned in my travels to the East." A muscle jumped in his cheek as he flexed his jaw. "But never mind now, I hear the men coming." Jesse, too, caught the distant crunch of boots on gravel. "I want you to go up to your room and stay there. Is that clear?"

"Why are you angry with me?"

"Because you did not obey me and get to safety."

Ire chased the chill from her cheeks. "I do not take orders from you. Besides, you might have—"

"I do not need a woman to guard me." Alex snatched her elbow and shook her slightly. "Now come. I'd not have you found here nearly naked and mussed like some dockside whore after a tumble." His remark quelled her struggles, and she marched ahead of him to the house, head high. He saw the pain in her eyes and the sheen of unshed tears as she slipped in through the open door. Inside him, something twisted tight.

Damn. He had not meant to scold her, but the sight of her clinging to Guthrie's neck like a kitten on a mastiff had been more than he could take. Jesu, but 'twas time and past she learned obedience.

Sighing raggedly, Alex closed the door. Tomorrow would be soon enough for the lessoning, and after that he'd make amends for her wounded pride. He hurried back to the garden path and found his men milling around, torches high, swords drawn.

"Come," Alex called to them. "I've captured an intruder." But when they reached the chestnut tree, the spot where Alex had left Guthrie Graham was empty. Splotches of blood on the wet grass were the only sign he had ever lain there.

Chapter Eight

A slight sound jerked Jesse awake. Cautiously she lifted her lashes to the golden wash of sunlight and the sight of Alex slouched in a straight-backed chair beside the bed. As though she'd spoken his name, he started, eyes flying open.

Instantly alert, they darted once around the room before returning to search her face. "Are you all right?" His hair and clothes were rumpled, the shadows under his eyes as dark and gritty as his stubbled chin.

For some reason she smiled. "I feel better than you look."

"'Tis not much of a recommendation." His rueful grin became a grimace as he gingerly arched his back and stretched what had to be painful muscles judging from the way her less abused ones screamed when she hitched herself higher on the pillows.

Awkward suddenly under the soft gaze that had yet to leave her face, she asked, "Have you been here all night."

That she was nervous but not hostile pleased him, made the night in the chair worthwhile. "What was left of it."

Touched, she still asked, "Why?"

Alex's smile faded. "Guthrie was gone by the time my men and I returned. I did not want him making a surprise visit."

Jesse shivered. "You could have set a guard at the door."

"Nay. As precious to me as you are, I'd watch over you myself." Leaning close, he brushed a kiss across her forehead.

For once, her usually nimble mind went blank, her memories of last night suddenly too vivid. Shudders coursed through her; she stemmed them ruthlessly. "I—I can not be anything to you."

"You do not believe I love you?" He thought she wanted to. Jesse led with her chin. "I do not believe in love."

"Given your history I am not surprised," Alex said, hiding his pity. "But I will teach you—"

"Nay. I do not believe a greedy man like you could love just one woman," she said with a toss of her unbound hair.

The slur hurt. He itched to lie beside her, kiss her until she was as hot for him as she'd been in the garden last night. If only to prove to them both that he could, but that would frighten her, and unless he misread her totally, she was already afraid. "What do you mean, 'a greedy man like me'?"

"You are a rogue . . . greedy for women."

"Ah. So you think I fall in love with every woman I meet?" He put all the tenderness, all the desire he felt into a smile. "I have never said those words to anyone before."

Off balance, wanting to believe but afraid to, she retorted, "'Tis only because you have been long without a woman."

Alex started as his own words raked him. "That was meant to excuse the way I grabbed you and dragged you into the grass, not my declaration of love," he said quietly, intently.

Jesse bit her lip on a wash of longing so strong it brought tears to her eyes. *Do not care for him,* she warned herself, but 'twas too late. Alex had somehow taken root in her traitorous heart. His understanding, his acceptance, even the patience he had shown when she knew his own temper raged, had slipped under her defenses. And after last night . . .

Last night, he had showed her where even a taste of passion could lead. Alex's kisses had been as heady and intoxicating as the Spanish brandy Edmund swilled. One sip and she had craved the whole barrel. She hated herself for that weakness. "It does not matter whether you love me, because *I* do not love you."

What irony! Alex thought as pain lashed him. After waiting all his life for this, his words of love were flung back in his face. How his brothers would have laughed to see him brought low by the very reputation they'd often envied.

Restless, unable to sit still with the ache gnawing at his insides, Alex got up and paced to the window. When he turned, he caught the trembling of her lower lip, the sheen of tears in her eyes. *She cared, yet was afraid to.* Relief surged through him, hope soothed his taut nerves. Time. She just needed time.

Patience, he thought, wishing he had more. Conscious of her wary stare, he strode to the door and asked one of the guards to fetch them something to eat. She started when he flopped crosswise on the end of the bed. Smiling lazily, he propped his head on one hand. *Oh, you will be mine.*

She pleated the blanket hem. "You had men there, too?"

"I take no chances with the woman I love."

Mad. He was mad. "You do not love me," she said very slowly, as though to a dim-witted child. "We are enemies."

"Not any longer." A caressing note entered his voice, and his eyes moved slowly over her face, heating her cheeks. "You will have to get used to the notion of my loving you."

"Sweet Mary! You are mad," she muttered. "Nay, I will not get used to your crazed notions. I'll be going home with Hugh."

Alex supposed this was not the time to tell her he'd decided against returning her to her brother. And assuredly not the time to tell her he'd decided to wed her. Truth to tell, the idea was new to him, too. But pleasurable. That the state he had once despised should appeal so strongly convinced him marriage to Jesse was right for him—for them both. She fought his line like a shark, but he would prevail. Given time, and strong locks to keep his possessions from ruin, he added, glancing at her mutinous little chin and flashing eyes.

Jesu, she was beautiful. In the morning light, her hair was a blaze of glory against the white pillows, a tangled red halo. The mauve shadows under her eyes reminded him of her vulnerability. Inside Alex, the twin urges to protect and possess warred. "Do you have any idea how beautiful you are?"

Jesse choked on his words of praise. "I am not." Damn him. And damn the flush that heated her cheeks.

"You *are* beautiful."

His eyes strayed to the swell of her breasts, and she feared he could see her heart still in the valley between them, then leap and skitter wildly.

"You say that in hopes of getting into my bed."

"I am in your bed," he reminded her, eyes twinkling. And now was a good time to get her used to his touch. She shied away when he moved to sit beside her. "There is no reason to be tense. I will never harm you. Have I not already proved that?" He slid his fingers into her curly hair before she could turn away, gently massaging the skin at her temples.

How could he have known her head hurt? She wanted to resist, her head tipped back instead, lashes fluttering down.

"Good?" he murmured, kneading, soothing.

"Mmm. You are very skilled at this." She made a feeble effort to shift away, but he murmured reassurances, let his fingers glide over her scalp to the back of her neck. Of its own accord, it arched into his touch. She barely recognized the throaty little moans as her own.

"Jess," Alex whispered, brushing his mouth across hers, half-expecting her to bolt. Instead, her lips trembled, parted on a sigh. He felt it clear to his toes. Despite her anger, she was scarred, vulnerable. Vowing never to forget that, he wet the corner of her mouth with the tip of his tongue, let it smooth over the fullness of her lower lip, matching the caress with a sweep of his finger down her throat and up to frame her face. She opened for him like a flower seeking the sun. As he matched his mouth to hers, his senses filled with the sweet, wild scent of her skin and hair—warm, feminine, intoxicating.

Gentleness. How had he known that for all her flash and fire last night, she needed gentleness this morn? His tongue coaxed her lips to part, then darted away from hers, teasing, daring. 'Twas a lure she could not resist, with the heat curling low in her belly, she twined her arms around his neck and fenced with him until her breath was uneven, her pulse wild.

Alex had known he could make her want him, but not that she could send his own passion screaming for release with just a kiss. *Just a kiss.* That is as far as he'd planned to take this. Groaning, he lifted his head, gasping for air, struggling for control. "Jesu, you pack more punch than a gale."

Jesse's smile was pure delight in her newly discovered feminine power. Then she remembered where she was and with whom. "Oh." Her fingers flew to cover her wet mouth.

"Oh, indeed," Alex echoed, smiling tenderly. "Now you see that we belong together."

Distracted, Jesse shook her head. "Nay, there is nowhere I belong," she lamented, her tongue unguarded for once.

Ah. But she wanted to. "There is now. I think I have loved you since the first time we met."

"B-but we . . . we fought constantly."

"Love is the reverse side of hate, they say." He trailed one callused finger down her cheek. Strange how it made the breath catch in her throat, made her heart stop in the instant their gazes tangled, locked. "Both strong, passionate emotions. I think we will love as hotly as we once hated."

Sweet Mary! Jesse trembled, frightened by the intensity blazing in his eyes, confused by the answering spark in her.

"Easy," he murmured. "I will not make love with you until you love me, too."

"I can not love you," Jesse said by rote, but deep inside her, things stirred, wild things, soft things. Things that made her want to reach for him. She swayed—

A knock at the door saved her. "M'lord. Laird Lionel's just now riding into the courtyard," a voice called.

"Excellent." Alex sprang off the bed. "Get dressed and come down to the hall. I want to show you to my relatives."

As if she were a new hound. "I will not."

Vixen, he thought fondly, must everything be a struggle? "Good. I'll stay and help you dress."

Squealing, Jesse dove under the covers to avoid his outstretched hands. "Go away! I'll dress myself."

"If you're tempted to rip up your clothes, remember I've not yet paid you back for savaging mine. You'll find a double dose of my vengeance hard to swallow," was his parting shot.

She swore, found her boots on the floor and flung one against the closing door. The thud was drowned out by his laughter echoing in the corridor outside.

Sweet Mary, was there ever a more contrary man? But as she sagged against the pillows, her fingers wandered to her mouth, tender from his kisses. Where would this all lead?

"We've got ta stop these cursed Harcourts," Lionel Carmichael roared when Alex had explained Hugh's scheme. The older man's violet eyes blazed with unholy fury, and his face was bloodred to the roots of his long black mane.

Alex exchanged faint smiles with Ross, Lionel's son. The three of them had drawn apart from the rest of the clan in high-backed chairs drawn close to the hearth in the great hall. The clansman drinking and dicing at the other end of the long, cavernous room and the servants setting up the trestle tables for dinner took no note of their hot-tempered laird's outburst.

"I'm fer firin' Graham's ship and fryin' the lot o' them." Lionel slammed a meaty fist down on the arm of his chair.

"Now, Da. Ye know the Grahams would only complain ta the king," Ross said patiently. He had the Carmichael black hair and his sire's great height, but his lean build, blue eyes and the cool head he displayed even at two and twenty came from his mother, Lady Carina. Despite the difference in their ages, Alex counted Ross a friend and valued his judgment.

Lionel grunted. "Let'm. They'll no find *this* Carmichael unwillin' ta meet them in battle."

Alex winced as Lionel's gibe made Ross flush. Well Alex knew how a father's disapproval could burn. His own father had never understood why Alex wasted his intelligence and quick wits on the sea when there was work for him at court. True, Geoffrey would never have shamed Alex in front of others, but the breach between Ross and his father was very serious. The laird blamed Ross for the death of his eldest son, Lion, the year before.

"I'm no afraid ta fight the Grahams," Ross said tightly. "But I'd not see the Carmichaels outlawed by the king, as he swore he'd do after ye tried ta make war on the Sutherlands."

"I'd good reason ta make those curs pay fer Lion's death."

Ross sighed heavily. "'Twas a hunting accident."

"How would ye know? Ye werena even there ta guard yer brother's back." Lionel turned his face away.

Alex pitied them both, thinking of the guilt that had come between himself and Gareth. Raking his hair back, he said in a soothing tone, "We've no time to wage a war, and I'd just as well not attract King David's notice."

"'Tis obvious from the two attacks on ye that Harcourt and the Grahams know ye're here," Lionel snapped.

"Aye." Thinking of how close Jesse had come to injury drove Alex to his feet. "But Harcourt's scheme is not yet common knowledge, and I'd keep it that way until I can capture Hugh." Pacing, he added, "If King David hears we Sommervilles are suspected of treason, he may think to gain King Edward's favor and reduce his ransom by arresting me." Twelve years ago, David had been captured by Edward at Durham and had only been allowed to return to Scotland recently in exchange for a ruinous ransom.

"I say we storm the ship and kill Hugh," Lionel blustered.

Alex sighed. "I need Hugh's testimony to clear my family."

"Truth? From a Harcourt?" Lionel grunted. "Bah! The Harcourts are known for their lack o' honor."

Jesse had more than some men, Alex thought proudly. "Hugh loves his sister and will surrender to me for her sake."

"Fine," Lionel snapped. Draining his cup, he set it down with a bang that made the table jump. "I'm fer sending word that unless Hugh surrenders, we'll chop his sister into wee pieces."

"Da," Ross exclaimed. "We needna go that far."

Alex frowned, about to tell Lionel Jesse was not to be harmed when he heard a sound in the stairwell to his right. A gasp, he thought. Someone eavesdropped. "I agree with Ross," Alex said evenly. Motioning for his kin to remain seated, he soundlessly crossed to the opening, then whipped around the corner.

Jesse gasped in surprise and turned to flee up the stairs. Her foot caught in the hem of her surcoat, and she would have tumbled down the steps if Alex hadn't sprinted to her aid. "Cursed skirts!" she cried as he scooped her up. Embarrassed, she struggled to get away.

"Spying, Jess?"

The harshness of voice stilled her movements instantly. "Nay. Surely you do not think—"

Alex's nape prickled a warning. 'Twas entirely possible. She had been at Wilton two years ago, at Tyneham with Hugh, and now he had caught her listening in as he planned his strategy.

The lengthening silence, the grimness of Alex's expression alarmed Jesse. She put her hand on his chest in supplication.

The strong, angry thuds beneath her palm sounded counter-point to her own quick, scrambling heart. "You can not be-lieve—"

"What the hell is this?" a voice bellowed up the stairs.

Swiveling her head, Jesse saw two big, black-haired men blocking the stairwell. Beyond them, stood scores of other men, some with their dirks drawn, all with anxious, scowling faces. Jesse shuddered and reflexively shrank back against Alex.

"Caught her spyin'?" demanded the older of the two no-bles. He must be the one who had wanted to chop her into wee pieces. "We best put her in the dungeon."

"Alex," Jesse moaned, her hands knotted in the soft wool of his tunic. "Please do not let him lock me away."

"Lionel, you know I'd not treat a woman so." Alex's grip on her tightened as he walked down the few steps and into the hall, but he offered her no words of comfort.

"Alex. If this is your revenge on me for ruining your clothes, you have it," she whispered urgently, frightened.

Alex stopped walking, and some of the hideous coldness left his face. "You swear you were not spying?"

"Aye. On whatever you like. On Hugh's soul," she added, recalling the pledge made that first morn.

Alex's gaze traveled over her face before coming back to lock with hers, his eyes piercing in their intensity. "I believe you." He smiled, and it was like the sun blazing down on her, melting the ice that had clogged her veins. "If you had been spying, you'd have delighted in shouting it to the world, and to hell with the consequences."

"I…thank you." 'Twas humbling to be trusted so easily and understood so well by him. If she asked him why he believed in her, would he say because he loved her? Did she want him to?

The crowd of hard-faced men parted for Alex. Then appar-ently deciding a woman posed no threat, they drifted away toward the other end of the room. Jesse could not relax, for the two nobles fell in beside Alex. He carried her to the hearth where a trio of finely carved chairs sat before the small fire. He did not set her down, for which she was grateful. Her legs were too shaky to support her, her mind too dizzy with latent fear.

Until this moment, she had not realized how kindly Alex had treated her.

"Soft," grumbled Lionel, reminding Jesse of Edmund. "I ken ye Sommervilles are daft about women folk, but I'd not thought ta see the black day when ye'd risk yer family's safety ta coddle a treacherous Harcourt. Well, whot's ta be done wi' her?"

"Cousin," Alex said respectfully, but Jesse felt the tension in the muscular arms that held her. "She was not spying."

"I'm fer puttin' her in irons," Lionel grumbled as though Alex had not spoken, and Jesse felt afraid again.

"Irons, is it?" intruded a lilting female voice.

As Alex turned, Jesse saw a small woman advancing. Rings glittered on the slim hands that held the skirts of her yellow gown out of the way. As she drew nearer, Jesse saw threads of silver in the curly red hair covered by a thin veil and fine lines radiating out from the pursed mouth and angry blue eyes.

"Lionel Carmichael, what is this about puttin' the lass in chains?" the woman demanded. Hands on hips, head thrown back, she stared up at the glowering man.

Jesse winced, expecting Lionel to flatten the woman with the back of his massive hand. Instead he sighed deeply.

"Now, Carina. Ye best not judge till ye've heard the whole o' the sorry tale," he muttered. "She's a Harcourt."

Some of the anger left Carina's eyes, and her measuring glance made Jesse long again for a hole to crawl into. She hated it that her name was sullied, hated being judged by that alone.

"What has she done, then?" Carina asked.

Lionel's grizzled brows beetled. "Her brother is plottin' ta bring Geoffrey down, and Alex is holdin' her hostage ta force a confession from her brother." His jaw jutted out.

Carina met it coolly. "What happens if he doesna cooperate?"

"I'll not let anyone harm her, Cousin Carina," Alex said with such force it wrung a smile from Jesse. She had not known how much his unquestioning acceptance of her these past few days had meant until it had been withdrawn.

"Oh, Lionel wouldna really harm the lass, would ye?"

To Jesse's amazement, Lionel sighed and traced a circle in the rushes with his toe. "Ye ken I'd no hurt a woman, Carina."

"Of course ye wouldna, my love. But the lass doesna know ye as I do." The smile she gave him would have melted iron. It softened the hard edges of his face so he was almost handsome. Apparently satisfied, Carina turned a lesser smile on Jesse. "In case ye've no guessed by now, I am Lady Carina Carmichael."

Feeling decidedly awkward still caught up in Alex's grip, Jesse could only nod her head.

"Do put the lass down and stop cluckin' over her like a mother hen," the lady gently rebuked Alex.

When he did not immediately obey, glancing down at her instead with that measuring gaze of his, Jesse feared he'd changed his mind again. "I'd remind you not to try and escape," he said when he finally set her on her feet.

But Carina pulled her away and launched into belated introductions as though Jesse were a guest, not a Harcourt. Lionel grumbled something about talking with his men and stomped away without acknowledging Jesse, but Ross gave her a smile very like his mother's. Two girls Jesse had not noticed before stepped from behind their mother and curtsied as their names were called. Averly and Elspeth.

"As soon as I've seen Jess to her room and had a word with her, there's a plan I'd discuss with you," Alex said to Ross.

Plan? What kind of plan? Most certainly it involved Hugh, and Jesse was suddenly afraid—for Alex, as well as for her brother. "Take me with you," she whispered to Alex. "I will talk to Hugh. You will see you were mistaken about him."

"Nay, Gareth heard your brother speak openly of his scheme. I must see he does not succeed." Alex's eyes were shadowed with something that increased Jesse's fears. *Desperation.*

"'Tis not fittin' fer ye ta be in the lass's bedchamber," Lady Carina said. "She'll come above ta my solar."

Where was Alex? Jesse wondered, scanning the courtyard from the solar window. Supper had come and gone, and the servants were now lighting candles to chase the shadows from the cozy room, still there was no sign of either Alex or Ross. Laird Lionel had joined them for the meal, but he had merely grumbled something about hot-blooded lads sowing wild oats when Lady Carina had asked if he knew where the two were.

Though the food had been good, the Carmichaels pleasant and the congenial mood in the hall heaven compared to what she was used to at home, Jesse had been tense, her appetite scant. She had missed Alex's familiar presence. Worse, his absence preyed on her mind and her heart. Had he found Hugh?

"I am certain Alex is all right," Carina said, coming up beside Jesse. "He has many friends in Edinburgh."

Women friends. Jesse's stomach clenched. Which was worse, thinking of him lying with another or fighting with her brother?

"Ye ha' a care fer Alex, don't ye?"

"Nay, he is my enemy." The words sounded weak even to her.

Lady Carina smiled sympathetically. "'Tis those Sommerville eyes. I thought so when I met Geoffrey soon after he wed wi' Catherine. All three lads inherited his eyes, but there is somethin' especially bewitchin' about the way Alex uses his."

Well she knew that. Jesse swallowed hard, refusing to admit how deeply he affected her—even to herself.

"Come," Carina said after a moment. "Let us drink spiced wine and listen to Averly play the lute."

Her mind weary of being tied in knots, Jesse allowed herself to be led to a chair before the fire with a docility that would have startled Alex. Cup in hand, her eyes drifted over the swirl of activity in Carina's warm, cheery solar.

At one end of the large room, eleven-year-old Elspeth played with a group of girls who had been sent to Carina for training in the gentle arts. The children laughed and dashed about in a wild game of blindman's bluff. Elspeth resembled her father, especially in her strong chin and the condemnation in her eyes when they lit on Jesse.

Averly was two years older and already betrothed. It was easy to see why she had been snapped up, for she was her mother all over again. She played the lute with a skill Jesse envied, singing about a knight and his lady. Everyone, from the girls to the servants who attended them, smiled a great deal. 'Twas a far cry from the stifling atmosphere at Harte Court, where fear hung on the air instead of laughter.

"'Tis the first ye've smiled." Carina slipped into the chair beside Jesse's. "What has given you pleasure?"

"I thought it must be wonderful to be part of such a loving family," she said, oddly comfortable with this woman she'd known only a few hours. How different her life might have been had she been raised in such a household as this.

"A big family. I've had seven bairns. In addition to Ross and the girls ye've met, there's eight-year-old Margaret back at Carmichael Castle, two sons, Hunter and Boyd, fostered out to be raised by other lairds. And Lion—"

Jesse was shocked to see tears in Carina's eyes. "Lion?"

"M-my oldest son died a year ago."

"Oh, I am so sorry," Jesse said from the heart, thinking how devastated she'd be if aught happened to Hugh.

Carina sniffed. "'Tis selfish of me to weep when most women have lost several bairns and I've got six of my seven."

"You are fortunate not to have died in childbed." Jesse shivered. Imagine having seven children. "Lionel is very greedy for heirs," she added with a disapproving frown.

"Lionel? Nay, but he suffers more at the birthin' than I do, swears we'll never ha' another and has to be coaxed back to my bed." Seeing Jesse's dubious look, she added, "He loved me so much he kidnapped me in order to marry me."

Jesse gasped. Edmund's sire, Hugh The Cruel, had abducted the only daughter of a wealthy man, gotten her with child and forced her to wed him. Then the fiend had killed her father in order to inherit the man's property through his daughter. The vile tale was one of Edmund's favorites. "How dreadful."

"Not really." Carina smiled. "Lionel had no other choice. We first met at a gatherin' o' the clans. Da refused ta let Lionel court me because there was bad blood twixt our families, but Da didna reckon wi' Lionel's determination. Course 'twas no all milk an' honey wi' us at first." The lady tossed her head. "Even though I was drawn ta him, in my pride I wouldna wed him because he had taken me instead o' wooing me. Still, his patience and gentleness won me over in the end.''

"Laird Lionel is gentle and patient?'' Jesse blurted out.

"For me he was. 'Twas that and the fact he didna force me ta his bed or ta the altar until I loved him that convinced me he truly did care. Men hide much of what they feel,'' Carina added. "When a man shows ye his true self, ye can be sure 'tis love.''

Jesse nodded, suddenly realizing Alex was a man of many complex parts. Beneath his lazy quicksilver smile, he hid compassion, a razor-sharp intelligence and the strength to bring down a brute like Guthrie. But there was more to him even than that. Things that drew her...like a loneliness she sensed matched her own. And things that made her wary. "Did...were there many other women in Lionel's life?''

"Nay, but just because a man has been a rogue in his youth,'' Carina said, deciding it was foolish to mince words, "doesna mean he canna be faithful to the right woman once he finds her.''

Was she the right woman for Alex? Bah. She should not even be thinking such things. He could not really love her. Jesse turned away from Carina's assessing blue eyes. She grudgingly admitted to the desire that sizzled between her and Alex. 'Twas impossible not to. And there were many things she admired about him—when he was not making her furious. But love...

"Where is he?'' demanded a female voice. A stunning woman swept into the solar, her cowl thrown back from sleek blond hair, her billowing cape revealing a voluptuous figure garbed in peacock-blue silk oversewn with twinkling gems.

"Damn,'' Lady Carina muttered. "Fiona, what brings ye here?''

The lady flounced to a halt before Carina. "Where is Alex?''

"Lady Fiona Ramsey, I'd make known ta ye Lady Jess—''

"Pleasure,'' Fiona snapped, a scowl marring her beautiful face, her eyes dark with annoyance. "I have just heard that Alex is in town, and I must see him immediately.''

"I fear he isna here,'' Carina said shortly.

"I'm sure he'd want me ta wait here for his return. After all, we are nearly betrothed."

Betrothed! Jesse's hands curled into fists as she fought to stem the pain flooding through her. Fiend! Seducer! Betrayer!

Chapter Nine

The night watchman had just cried ten of the clock, and the bustling docks had long since settled down for the night. Even the weather suited Alex's purpose. High clouds hid the moon, and wisps of fog hung over the dark water of the Nor'Loch as he and Ross rowed out across the ship-clogged harbor.

"We should ha' brought more men," Ross grumbled.

"And alarm the watch Graham has surely set on deck *The Salamander?*" Alex hissed back, conscious of how the water magnified every sound. He and Ross had been aboard *The Star,* arguing strategy with Bevan, when word had come that Parlan had gone ashore with an armed escort. Of Hugh, there had been no sign. That, coupled with something Guthrie had said the night before, had sent Alex scrambling to put his plan into motion.

Bevan had protested, loudly. "'Tis daft ye are," he'd shouted as Alex ordered a boat made ready. "Graham's men'll clap ye in irons the moment ye step aboard his ship."

"They'll not recognize me." Alex had pawed through his trunk, unearthing an old tunic, coarse hose and a leather eye patch. A guise suitable for a messenger from Harte Court.

Bevan had ranted and raved all the while Alex dressed, but Alex had been undeterred. "There's something queer going on. The men we set to watching Graham's ship have seen no sign of Hugh, though Parlan's been out and about. And last night Guthrie specifically said he'd come to take Jesselynn to Parlan."

"After killin' ye," Bevan had snapped.

"To Parlan, not Hugh." Alex believed Jesse when she said her brother loved her. So why, after Guthrie's failure to free her last night, had Hugh not sent around a demand for his sister's release? Because he was not aboard *The Salamander?* That possibility had gnawed at Alex all day.

"Well, here we are," Ross whispered.

Alex looked up at the dark bulk of the ship towering over him, and his nape prickled as it always did just before he risked his neck—even if it was a calculated risk. He assumed that was God's way of reminding him that every man was mortal and he'd best watch his step.

A gulp of air and a swift, silent prayer eased the tingling. He lowered the eye patch and nodded to Ross, who smiled grimly.

"Ahoy *The Salamander*," Alex shouted in English.

After a brief spate of questions, the boarding ladder tumbled down the side of the ship. He climbed up it with a land-lubber's clumsiness that had the sailors on deck grinning by the time he hauled himself over the rail.

Alex swayed before them, seemingly off balance and out of his element, though his muscles were tensed, his senses alert for the slightest hint of danger. "I've come with a message from Lord Edmund Harcourt fer his son, Hugh."

It was the sailors who looked uncomfortable now. "He's no aboard, but we could take it fer him," offered one fellow.

"Nay. 'Tis fer his lordship's eyes only." Seemingly casual questions revealed that Hugh had been put ashore before the ship had reached Blakeney. The sudden scrambling of Alex's pulse was part fear, part relief. Hugh could be making more trouble for his family. On the other hand, the question of giving Jesse up could be postponed. The two thoughts warred in his mind.

"Ye could gi' the message ta Lord Hugh's cousin, Parlan Graham . . . he'll be back in a couple a' hours."

"I know Lord Parlan," Alex said sharply. *Only too well*. "Tell me where Lord Parlan has gone, and I will seek him out."

"He went ta Edinburgh Castle ta see the king. Somethin' about his cousin, Lady Jesselynn."

The sweat on Alex's body turned to ice. *Parlan meant to take Jesse from him*. "I will seek him there."

Alex left, chest aching with the need to see Jesse. The prospect of losing her made him frantic to touch her again. Stopping briefly at *The Star* to show Bevan he was unhurt and to send a messenger to Ransford warning the Sommervilles about Hugh, he and Ross rushed back to the Carmichaels.

"Do ye think Parlan means to accuse ye of counterfeiting?" Ross asked as they trotted through Edinburgh's dark streets.

"Nay, I think he will tell the king I've kidnapped Jess and demand she be returned to him. What think you the king will do?"

"David Bruce is a stranger even to his own people, havin' been imprisoned for long years in England," Ross said as they dismounted. "His fondness for fine things outstrips his purse. Ye might be able to keep her if ye offered him a rich bribe."

"Too risky," Alex muttered, gut tight with frustration. "I have little coin with me, and Parlan could better my offer."

"Ye could tell King David the lass came ta ye willingly."

Alex stopped on the stairs. "I doubt I'd get her to say that." She desired him, and after the time spent aboard ship mayhap even cared for him, but she did not yet trust him.

"Likely the king would not question her. If he did, what man would take a woman's word over another man's? Besides," Ross added, oblivious to Alex's pained expression, "ye're the man wi' the silver tongue where the lassies are concerned. Seduce her, if ye havena already, and she'll be too happy ta complain."

Anxiety over Jesse's reaction pushed Alex up the stairs. Not that he doubted his ability to seduce her, but when desire had cooled, she'd be furious. Eyeing the gleaming claymores displayed on the entryway walls, he decided she'd probably take one to that which he valued most, as she'd once threatened.

Ross rubbed his chin. "Why, this might even end the feud that's been plaguing yer family all these years. Only think, when Hugh is executed, and Edmund, too, if he was in this plot with his son, the Lady Jesselynn will be the last surviving Harcourt—and yer prisoner."

Alex had thought about that ... all too often since the notion had first occurred to him. With Hugh gone, Edmund's death, whether he hanged for counterfeiting or died of old age, would leave Jesse heir to the vast Harcourt estates. And as her husband, Alex would control her fortune. What would his prickly little vixen think of that? He exhaled sharply. The worst, likely, that he had wed her for her property, not herself.

"Alex!" Ross grabbed his arm, turning him around. "Many a problem's been settled by a marriage. If ye wed her, 'twould end the feud for good and all because there'd be no more Harcourts."

"Aye," Alex managed. His family's interests warred with his concern for Jesse. If she were less defensive, less skeptical of him, he would have laid the plan before her and begged her to marry him so their two families might live in peace. But with only her grudging desire to bind her to him, Alex did not dare.

"I admit there would be benefits," he said at length, feeling the weight of Ross's stare. Having Jesse to wife was the chief one in Alex's heart, if not his more logical mind.

Ross slapped him on the back. "It's settled, then, we'll find a priest whose willing to waive the reading of the banns and get ye wed without delay. Da's sure to object, of course."

"He's not the only one." Alex grimaced, thinking of Jesse's reaction. "I'll need time to convince her to marry me."

"Convince her? A man o' your reputation? Surely ye jest."

"My reputation is part of the problem," Alex muttered. "If she doesn't slash my clothes or throat to ribbons, she'll scream the kirk down at the very least."

"Gag her, then."

Alex stiffened, appalled. "Nay, I could not, would not treat her so." Pride kept him from mentioning that she did not return his love. Nay, he'd not flaunt his one failure for all to see. "I think it best if Jess and I sail from Edinburgh with all possible haste." They'd been happy aboard ship. Mayhap on the journey home he could get her to fall in love with him.

"Then what? Do ye continue on as before? I thought ye were set on ending the feud for all time."

"I am." Alex's hands clenched into fists. "I will marry her, but I'll do it in my own time." And with her willing.

"M'lord!" The steward galloped across the dim entryway and skidded to a halt in front of Alex. "Thank the Lord ye've returned. There's a messenger come from Laird Geoffrey."

* * *

For one who had learned to creep about Harte Court like a wraith, Jesse found eluding the net of soldiers Lionel Carmichael had set around his house and grounds easy. Though there were a lot of them. Apparently the laird was determined to have no repeat of last night's performance in the garden.

Mindful of Guthrie's attack, yet nearly more anxious to avoid meeting Alex, she skirted the garden and made for the large, square stables at the far side of the house.

Inside, 'twas dim, the only light coming from a single lantern. The sharp, familiar scents of straw and animals were oddly soothing after so many days in strange surroundings. She sighed, feeling better already. A wild gallop through the quiet city to the docks and Hugh was just what she needed to chase thoughts of Alex's betrayal from her mind and heart.

The beasts lifted their heads and nickered as she eased the door shut behind her. Shushing them softly, she took the lantern and went to the nearest stall. A long, curious nose was thrust into her palm; gentle brown eyes regarded her unblinkingly as she scratched it. A palfrey, steady and easy gaited enough for a woman to ride, or a man on a long journey. What Jesse needed was speed and stamina. A stallion, mayhap, though a war-horse would be too hard to handle for one of her slight weight.

Conscious of the passing time, she searched quickly through the rest of the stalls, grudgingly giving Lionel Carmichael high praise for his horseflesh. She had found the horse she wanted, a big bay with a white blaze and was dragging a heavy saddle towards its stall when she heard a soft whimpering.

The saddle plopped to the ground as she spun toward the sound. "W-who is there?" she whispered.

It came again from the back of the stables where the shadows were deepest. Low and pitiful. An animal in distress? She waited for someone else to respond to the cry, yet knowing she was the only person in the building. The third whimper proved too much. Turning her back on her escape horse, she picked up the lantern and walked toward the noise, with only her puny eating knife for defense, her heart thudding against her ribs.

She started when the light caught on the eyes of an enormous brown hound. It was wedged between two upright timbers so only its head and forequarters were visible. Panting loudly, it gazed at her forlornly, yellow eyes glazed with pain and fear.

Jesse forgot caution. Setting the lantern down, she knelt in the straw and extended her hand for approval. "Are you stuck?"

The poor thing whimpered and stretched out to sniff her, but some sort of convulsion shook it, making it strain and groan. Mayhap it was sick.

Wary now, Jesse backed up a few feet but could not make herself leave entirely. Head cocked, she watched the beast shudder in the throes of some terrible pain. When the shivering stopped, the dog whined and again cast her a piteous look.

"Bah. Sick or no, I can not stand to see you suffer." Crouching down, she approached its head again. This time the dog licked her hand. "Let me see what the trouble is." Crooning softly, she ran her hands over the dog's massive head, shoulders and front paws. "You are not cut, nor do I feel any bones broken." Half the dog was still hidden by the beams, but it did not seem to be stuck as she had first feared. "Are you afraid to come out for some reason?"

As if in reply, the dog tensed and shook all over, groaning and straining and panting so Jesse's heart lurched. Fists clenched helplessly in her lap, she whispered, "What is it? What ails you?" Sweet Mary, this was awful.

When the dog stopped shaking, Jesse grabbed hold of its thick leather collar. "At least come out so I can see the rest of you." She tugged with all her might, but the dog weighed at least as much as she did, and she could not budge it.

Jesse sat back in the straw, panting nearly as hard as the dog, heart aching with defeat. "I can not do this alone. We need help," she was forced to admit. Scrambling to her feet, she patted the dog's head. Its soft, reproachful whine brought tears of pity and frustration to her eyes.

"I am not leaving you," she said firmly, throwing her arms around its neck. Just then another shudder shook the poor animal, and Jesse hung on tighter, biting her lip to keep from crying. Never had she felt so useless. When the tremors had subsided, she stood. "I am going, but I will return."

Whirling, Jesse left at a run. She was halfway across the stables when the the stable door burst open and a tall figure streaked in. It darted from stall to stall, pausing only long enough to peek inside before hurtling on.

Alex. Jesse began inching back into an empty stall.

Too late. He stopped dead in his tracks when he spotted her, his mouth falling open before snapping shut. Even at half the length of the stable, Jesse saw murder in his eyes as he advanced on her.

"Jesselynn!" he roared from a foot away.

Much as she wanted to run, she thought about the dog and braced herself. "You can shout at me later. Now I need—"

"A spanking is what you need," he said though clenched teeth, then the anger drained from him on a long, ragged sigh. "Oh, Jess." He startled her so when he picked her up that she yelped. The yelp became a groan as he squeezed the air from her body. "God, I was so worried. So afraid something would happen to you out at night by yourself."

Jesse could have told him she had spent many a night out by herself, but all she could manage was a weak, "Alex."

"'Tis all right, love." He was petting her hair and kissing her neck. "I understand why you ran. Fiona was still here when I came in. I sent her and her lies packing. Then I went looking for you, knowing what you must have thought. When I found your room empty . . . God, my heart stopped beating then and only started again when I got my arms around you."

"Alex," Jesse whispered, dazed. She had not been hugged often, and never like this. As though he tried to absorb her into himself, as though he'd never let her go. Precious, she felt precious and a little dizzy from the relief pouring through her. "Fiona lied about the betrothal?"

"Lies. I never spoke to her of marriage. Never." The last was growled in her ear and accompanied by another squeeze.

"Alex. I can not breathe." He gave her an inch and took her mouth in a bruising kiss that tasted of desperation and homecoming. It soothed away any lingering doubts. "Alex," she managed when he lifted his head. "There is a dog I want—"

"You can have ten dogs. Tomorrow. Right now I am taking you inside. You are shivering." She could have told him that was because his protectiveness had moved her, but he was already sliding an arm under her legs and lifting her up.

"Wait." She put a hand on his muscular shoulder. "There is a dog in the back that is hurt and needs help.

He blinked, cocked his head. "I suspect I owe the dog my thanks. Likely you'd be gone had you not stopped to aid it." At her nod he sighed and shook his head. "Then I am doubly glad you are a compassionate woman," he added, setting her feet on the ground and taking her hand. "Lead on, my lady."

The dog was exactly where Jesse had left it, in the throes of another convulsion. To her surprise, Alex immediately knelt down, running capable hands over the animal "You picked a hell of a spot to birth your pups," he murmured, sitting back.

"She is having her pups here, by herself?"

"Aye. So it would seem."

Jesse had never actually seen anything born before. "Where is the father of her pups?"

Seeing her fierce frown, Alex suppressed a smile. "I doubt the male would be much help to her now."

"Typical," Jesse snapped, a protective arm around the dog.

Alex rolled his eyes and went to get a blanket and some water. Returning to find the dog in between birth pangs, he spread the blanket in the straw. "Move aside a moment, Jess, and I'll see if we can get her out of that corner." 'Twas easier said than done. The dog seemed to weigh nearly as much as Gareth's war-horse and was frightened besides. Swearing, straining and coaxing, Alex finally got her out into the open.

"Oh, Alex. Her belly is huge," Jesse exclaimed, eyes wide, her hands clasped tightly together as she watched him settle the dog into a more comfortable spot.

"Do not forget, she is a big dog." He ran his hands over the rippling mound. It should not be long now, he thought. "But 'tis good you *happened* along. She's looks to be a young dog, and this may be her first litter."

"Have you ever done this before?" Jesse asked anxiously.

Alex grinned. "I've not had any pups myself, but I assisted at a few birthings when I was younger."

His teasing brought a faint smile that vanished under the dog's groan. "Oh. What can we do to help her?"

Likely naught, but he'd not tell her that and have her think him cruel. "Fetch another blanket." By the time she returned, the first pup was out and being licked clean by the mother.

"I missed everything?" Jesse exclaimed, her disappointment clear as she sank down to observe the proceedings.

"There will be another one along shortly." And there was. They arrived in a steady stream, as though nature had been holding them back until the nervous mother had help. Alex kept Jesse busy drying off the pups and making certain they stayed warm while he and the mother attended to breaking the birth sacs on each new delivery.

Jesse was not surprised at the skill with which Alex handled the birthing. He was competent at everything he did. Nay, it was the gentleness with which he soothed the mother when the pains came that amazed her, petting and praising the dog. Even more amazing was the joy she found in their closeness. It seemed the world had narrowed down to this corner of the stable and the only two people in it were herself and this man who alternately infuriated her and fascinated her. The passion that blazed between them frightened as much as it excited; she was far more comfortable with this sharing.

Strange how things work out, Alex mused, aware of Jesse's soft smile and sidelong glances. He'd arrived at the stables fearing he'd lost her and ended up drawing her closer.

"Six," Jesse murmured, sitting back on her heels when it was done. Her smile deepened as she watched the tiny, sightless babes root around for their mother's milk. "Are they not wonderful?" Despite the shadows under her eyes, they glowed with a joy he hoped to put there often.

"Did you never see any newborn pups?"

"Nay. Birthings never interested me at all." She shrugged, but the gesture was not casual. "Mayhap because Edmund harped constantly on the subject of heirs."

This did not bode well for the children he wanted, but Alex kept his tone light when he said, "We should let her rest."

Jesse nodded. Her mind still on the puppies, she let Alex pull her to her feet. They borrowed the groom's soap and washed in a bucket of water. Alex draped his arm around her as they crossed the courtyard; somehow it felt right having it there.

"Tired but happy," Alex said, his voice low and soft as the night breeze that ruffled her hair. It was not a question, more a statement of how they both felt.

"Aye." Jesse leaned her head against his shoulder, found a spot there that fit her perfectly.

Alex chuckled, charmed by this new softness in her. Mayhap she had not even known she possessed it. Picking her up, he swung her in a slow circle, his eyes never leaving hers. "Every day I find something else to love about you. Today I found compassion, understanding and jealousy." His low voice, rough with emotion made her heart pound a little faster.

The orange of the torches blurred with the gray stone twirling by. All she saw was the love in Alex's eyes. Love for her. A strange, heady sensation washed over her, warming her in all the places where their bodies touched. "My jealousy pleased you?" she whispered through lips gone suddenly dry.

"Aye." The banked fires in his eyes blazed to life as they watched her tongue wet her lips. "It shows you care."

"I wanted to scratch Fiona's eyes out," she admitted.

"Fiona is someone I saw when I came to Edinburgh. She made more of our friendship than was there." Alex brushed his smile over her pout, drawing the corners up, making her want more.

'Twas a mark of how far they had come that night that she twined her arms around his neck and pulled his mouth back to hers. The kiss exploded through Alex with the savage fury of a storm at sea. It went beyond the lush pleasure of her untutored mouth moving on his, tasting, exploring, to the wonder that she desired him enough to turn aggressor.

"Jess," he groaned moments later, wrenching free before he drowned in her. His body shook with the effort it took to stop before he went too far. "With you, 'tis not only my temper I have a difficult time controlling," he rasped in a raw, needy voice that mirrored his internal struggle. Her smug, wholly feminine smile made him chuckle. Swinging her up, he made for the house. His stride was quick as he mounted the steps to the house. "'Tis past time you were in bed."

"Your bed?" Her wariness confirmed the need for restraint.

"Nay." His eyes were oddly gentle in the dimness of the entryway. "Not until you love me, as I do you."

They did not speak again until he asked her to unlatch the door to her chamber. Shouldering it open, he marched in and set her on the edge of the bed. The only light came from the single candle burning on the table by the window.

"You are very skilled at sweeping a woman off to bed."

Damn, but she was a handful. "Do you know how unfair it is for you to whip me for a reputation I earned before we met?" Alex asked, raking back his hair in weary annoyance.

"Aye." She looked at the floor. "All my life I have lived under the cloud of my family's greed."

"But you are not like Edmund, and I think you have learned that there is more to me than rumor suggests."

Jesse's head came up. "Aye. You have shown me so tonight."

"'Tis late. You should be abed for we sail early tomorrow."

"Sail? What about Hugh?" she cried, grabbing his sleeve.

Alex looked away. "Your brother is not in Scotland."

"What!" Jesse's hold on him tightened. "Where is he?"

"He is in England." Alex covered her hand to soften the blow and knelt beside her. He dared not tell her that Hugh was the Sommervilles' prisoner, according to the message just received from his father. "Guthrie's comment last night made me suspect Hugh was not aboard *The Salamander,* so I rowed out to the ship and learned that Hugh is not—"

"You what? You fool! Parlan could have captured you."

Alex smiled at her vehemence. "I thank you for your tender concern, but I knew Parlan was not aboard, and I went in the guise of a Harcourt messenger.

"Oh." She chastised herself for thinking first of Alex's safety instead of Hugh's. "Where is my brother?"

"According to the crew, he and Walter Beck were set ashore in England." Alex knew from his father's message that Gareth had captured Charles, the apprentice who had made the coins for Hugh. Obviously Hugh had wanted to prevent Charles from incriminating him. The two men had entered Ruarke's castle through the postern gate using the key Walter still had from his time as Wilton's steward—before Gabrielle and Ruarke discovered his dishonesty and had him tossed out on his ear.

Alex's jaw clenched as he recalled the rest of the message. When their presence had been discovered, the two men had taken Gaby and Arianna de Clerc prisoner. Gareth had saved them, but he had been wounded in a sword fight with Hugh. Both Hugh and the Becks were now in Ruarke's dungeon, awaiting the journey to London to stand trial. But if he told Jesse that tale, she'd be frantic with worry, thinking Hugh would not survive in his family's custody.

"There is more, isn't there?" Jesse asked, unable to pierce his shuttered expression but feeling the tension in his arm.

Alex decided part of the truth was better than a lie. "I have reason to believe that Parlan may go to the king and demand that I turn you over to him so he can take you back—"

"Sweet Mary, nay!" Jesse's face went white.

"What is it? Why do you fear him so?"

"Because I know what he is capable of," she said hoarsely, eyes haunted. "I was playing in the stable loft when he dragged the cook's young daughter and . . ." She choked on the rest.

"Shh." Hugging her close, he pressed her face into his shoulder and tried to absorb her shudders into his body.

"'Twas so sudden and so terrifying that I could not move," she murmured, not realizing she clung to Alex like a lifeline. "H-he . . . she had no chance to defend herself. Later, when I could, I crept down and helped her into the house. I complained to Edmund. He laughed, said it showed Parlan had backbone. It was not Parlan's backbone I wanted to take cook's axe to."

Her fierceness drew a faint smile from Alex. "I am sorry you saw that." Leaning away, he smoothed the springy wisps of hair back from her face. His thumb lingered to wipe a tear from her lashes. "Was that when you decided to take up the sword?"

"Aye." His perceptiveness no longer surprised, it warmed. 'Twas a relief not to have to explain or defend herself. "I did not want to be weak or vulnerable, so Hugh taught me."

"You learned your lessons well." He had the pink scar on his shoulder as proof. "Now, to bed." She looked up at him and nodded, her dazed eyes still reflecting a hint of fear that made him long to remain with her. But if he stayed he might be tempted to offer more than mere comfort, and, too, he had much to do if he was to keep Jesse from Parlan's clutches.

Alex roused the household at dawn the next morning, but the king's messenger caught him ere he rode out the gates. The words on the fine parchment invited the Carmichaels' two honored guests from England—Lord Alexander Sommerville and Lady Jesselynn Harcourt—to dine with King David that very day. Pretty and flowery though the phrases were, 'twas still a royal summons, and only a fool would disregard it.

Chapter Ten

The brilliance of the late-afternoon sun did not lighten Jesse's mood, nor did it dispel the aura of impending doom that seemed to cling to Edinburgh Castle. Perched atop a rocky cliff, it towered over the city, glowering down at the Carmichael party as they dismounted in the courtyard.

Jesse looked up at the black stone castle. The last rays of the sun bathed the mullioned windows a bloodred, making her shiver. Did Parlan watch her from behind them like a spider waiting for prey to wander into its web?

"I'll not let him take you, Jess," Alex assured her, placing her hand on his arm as he led her into the palace.

"And I'd not go. But he is my kin. What if the king . . . ?"

"No one can take you from me." He flashed her a grim smile, looking every inch the defending knight in a red surcoat that emphasized his muscular build. The tawny streaks in his hair were as shiny as the heavy gold links he wore around his neck and hips. Fortunately he ignored the current fashion for shoes with long, pointed toes, wearing soft black boots instead.

"Have I told you how beautiful you look today?" he asked.

Jesse surprised them both by blushing. "'Tis the green silk surcoat and cream tunic borrowed from Carina. Though I will likely trip over the hem and disgrace myself before the king," she grumbled, but his words had pleased her.

"Still can't admit you enjoy dressing as a woman?"

"I am not comfortable in costly things."

Alex accepted that as he'd come to so many things about her. Mayhap in time he'd help her change some. If not . . . well, he would love her as she was. "Stay close to me, and if King David should ask, tell him you came with me willingly."

"What?" Jesse stopped on the palace steps, ignoring the people who jostled her from behind. "I can not lie!"

"Not even to stay free of Parlan?" he muttered as he urged her to motion again.

Cornered, she bristled. "What reason could I give for being in the company of a Sommerville?" She stomped up the steps, her gown hiked above her ankles and damn them all.

"Tell his majesty a part of the truth—that you followed your brother and I rescued you from drowning."

"And why did I remain with you? I do not think either of us wishes to discuss this counterfeiting business with the king."

"I always said you had a quick mind."

"For a woman?"

He smiled ruefully but did not take the bait. They had reached the entryway, and he drew her from the flow of people to whisper, "Tell his majesty that you lost your memory again as you did that time you fell into the gorge and Gaby rescued you. Say you only recovered it when we arrived in Edinburgh."

Jesse frowned up into his tense face. "If I am quick of wit, you are even swifter at twisting words around. Does it never bother you to lie and shift people to your own purpose?"

"Not when I know my cause is just." Alex winced inwardly recalling the lie about Hugh. Not truly a lie—he'd just withheld the whole truth. To save her from worry, he rationalized, smoothing an errant curl from her forehead for the excuse to touch her. "Think of me as the lesser of two evils."

"You definitely are that." For all he was a Sommerville. Jesse nibbled on her lower lip, eyeing the fond look she could not quite believe was really for her. Working together last night had changed things between them, made it impossible for her to hate him. She sighed. "I will do as you say."

A fierce, unreadable expression flickered across his face. "You will not regret trusting me. If I could, I would wrap you in wool and tuck you in my pocket to keep you safe."

"Oh," was all Jesse could manage past her suddenly tight throat, unbearably moved by his concern.

"Come. Much as I would wish us elsewhere, 'tis time," Alex said gently, urging her forward. As they entered the great hall, Ross hurried over to them.

"King David has not yet arrived, but Parlan is here."

Scanning the room, Jesse spotted her cousin's blond head above the others. Though scores of people and the length of the richly appointed room separated them, she could feel his fury and determination. Unconsciously she shrank back against Alex.

Instantly his arm came around her like a shield. "Do not worry. I am right beside you," he murmured. The reassuring warmth of his body seeped into hers through the clothes separating them. "I will not let him take you."

Tipping her head up, she drew strength from his steady gaze. "I wish we were back aboard *The Star*."

"No more than I do." Jesu, when she looked at him like that, with trust instead of hostility, he believed he could do anything—even make her fall in love with him. "Just another hour or two and we will be on our way," he said, smiling softly.

"Thank you, Alex." The words were less rusty and welcome.

"I'd have you save your thanks until later...when we are private." He gave her a quick, playful wink that chased some of the worry lines from her forehead, then led her through the crowd to where Carina and Lionel waited.

In the gallery above, musicians played a familiar ballad and servants passed through the milling guests with trays of drink. Alex snagged a cup of wine for Jesse, but nothing for himself. Nay, he'd need his wits about him ere this business with Parlan was done. When Alex turned in an apparently casual survey of the room, he noted that Parlan had gone. But out of sight was not out of mind. Mentally he girded himself for battle.

The steady hum of conversations eddied around him—the burr of the men punctuated by high female laughter, but dark thoughts chased through Alex's mind. 'Twas easy enough to assure Jesse of his protection, but he had no army to back him should King David give her to Parlan. And he'd not endanger his kin by drawing them into a war with their sovereign. Nay, he was on his own.

At his side, Jesse chuckled over Carina's tale of a brawny Highlander who was reputed to have consumed an entire side of roasted beef in one sitting. When she smiled, her face soft, her eyes twinkling, something tightened in his chest, and his love for her grew. He'd never give her up, no matter what. Bending close, on the pretext of speaking to her, he inhaled the scent from her hair, touched his nose to her cheek. "Is this your first time at court?" There was much about her he did not know.

"I've been dragged to King Edward's court a time or two."

"How does the Scots court compare?"

She looked about the room, her nose wrinkling. The air hung heavy over the large, crowded room, smoke from a hundred candles vying with the aroma of food, sweaty bodies and the perfumes splashed on to counter that. "'Tis much the same, except in London I was ignored. Here everyone stares as though they know my business. It makes me edgy."

"'Tis because you are a beautiful woman, Jess."

She sighed. "I wish you would not keep saying that."

"'Tis the truth." His voice dropped lower. "You attract enough male attention here to rouse my Sommerville instincts."

"What instincts are those?"

"Possessiveness. All Sommerville males are supposedly born with it in abundance. I had thought myself lacking in that trait till now—till you. I'd keep you all to myself."

His raspy tone sent the words shivering down Jesse's spine. Sweet Mary, he was impossible to resist. Yet she felt disloyal to Hugh every time she moved closer to Alex.

A liveried servant bowed before them. "His majesty would meet wi' ye and the lady in his study."

Jesse's hand tightened on Alex's arm. She wanted to turn and run, though she knew they had no more choice in obeying the summons than they'd had in coming here today. Alex had made it clear that if they fled Edinburgh they'd have several Scots ships hot after them—Parlan's included—armed with a royal warrant. At least with Alex beside her she felt less weak.

Jesse nearly groaned aloud when they entered his majesty's study to find Parlan standing at the king's right, a triumphant smile curving his thin mouth.

King David wore purple velvet, a collar of diamonds and a look of intense irritation. "Lord Parlan tells me ye've kidnapped his young cousin," his majesty said bluntly.

Alex tugged Jesse's hand to remind her to curtsy while he swept the Scots king a low bow. "Nay, I did not kidnap her, your majesty." He told how he had saved Jesse from drowning. His voice was strong, confident, yet she felt the tension in the tightness of his hand wrapped securely around her smaller one. "Nor did I realize who she was until we were well underway for Edinburgh. I only recognized her because she had once spent time at Wilton Castle with my brother Ruarke and his lady wife."

"How came a Harcourt to live with a Sommerville?" King David asked suspiciously.

"A fall had stolen her memory from her then." Alex flashed his most winning smile. "The same thing happened when she tumbled into the sea."

"I do not believe it!" Parlan exclaimed. Fists clenched, face red to his blond roots, he took a step forward.

The king held up a hand to stay him. "What proof ha' ye that this is true? That ye didna capture her ta hold fer torture or ransom as Lord Parlan claims."

"I have demanded nothing for her, nor have I abused her— as I might have given the fact that our families are sworn enemies. Let the women of the court take her away, strip her clothes from her and look for bruises if you doubt my word." Alex squeezed his vixen's hand to stifle her gasp of indignation. "Do not make a scene," he muttered from the side of his mouth.

"Fiend," she whispered, shooting daggers at him.

Alex sighed. Damn, but she had a hot, quick temper. Taming her seemed to be an ongoing task. He just thought he had her calmed and she'd erupt again. If she was angry now, she'd be furious when she heard the other things he might have to say.

"I demand my cousin be returned to me!" Parlan shouted.

"Nay!" Jesse cried, drawing three shocked glances.

The king stared at her as though she had sprouted two heads. "Why would ye prefer ta stay wi' a Sommerville?"

Jesse blinked, struggling to come up with an answer for that bit of seeming stupidity, but Alex calmly raised her hand to his lips and kissed it. "I fear the Lady Jesselynn has fallen in love with me," he said simply and not at all humbly.

Parlan's bellow of outrage drowned out Jesse's yelp. "That canna be. She's promised to me," he roared, anger bringing out the burr he had worked hard to eliminate. "She's lost her mind."

"Do ye ken who ye are?" King David asked her sharply.

"Of course I do," Jesse snapped, forgetting to whom she spoke. "And I assure you I have not fallen—"

"Careful, Jess," Alex softly warned. "Think of Parlan."

Jesse glanced over to see her cousin watching her like a cat about to pounce on a mouse. Her stomach rolled. Once again 'twas fall in with Alex's scheme or find herself at Parlan's mercy. "I hate you for forcing me into this," she growled at Alex.

"I know." Sadly. "Later you can kick me."

"I get to choose the spot." She smiled grimly at his wince.

"He is influencing her," Parlan shouted.

"Alexander Sommerville's reputation with the ladies is well-known to us," the king muttered. "Well, what say ye, m'lady?"

The tension hung so heavy in the room Jesse nearly choked on it and the words Alex expected her to utter. 'Twas a matter of pride, but cling to it and she'd find herself at Parlan's mercy.

"Jess," Alex hissed. His panic pleased her. At least he was not completely sure of her. Irrelevant as it seemed at a time like this, 'twas an important part of the conflict that seemed constantly to churn between them. She did not entirely understand its source, but in the spirit of combat, she gave him a this-is-up-to-me smile and freed her hand.

The few feet to the king were the longest she had ever walked, and she was glad of the skirts that hid her knocking knees. Sinking low before his majesty in a swirl of green silk, she dipped her head, then raised carefully limpid eyes to the king. "I fear what Lord Alexander says is true." Her heart pounded so she could scarcely hear her own words but pressed on. "When I regained my memory I knew 'twas wrong to want a Sommerville." *There*. She had not said she loved him.

"Aye, women are weak creatures," King David commiserated, not realizing how she ground her teeth. She supposed kicking the king of Scotland was a poor idea, but she resolved that Alex would get two kicks from her.

"It matters not," Parlan interjected, coming to stand over Jesse like a vulture. "She was promised to me."

King David brightened, seeing a way out of this morass. "Ha' ye a betrothal contract?"

Parlan frowned. "Nay, but...but she is my kin, and I know Edmund would want me to stand by her."

"She must wed me. 'Twas my cabin she stayed in this past week," Alex said smoothly. "My bunk she slept in."

"Oh! Of all the nerve," Jesse gasped, surging to her feet and turning on Alex.

"She was promised to me," Parlan shouted, drawing his sword. "And I'll not give her up without a fight."

"With pleasure," Alex growled, one hand curving around the hilt of own blade as the other took Jesse's wrist and thrust her safely behind him.

"Hold, I say," King David commanded. "I'll not ha' two braw men risking death o'er so foolish a thing as a lass." He fingered the jewels at his neck as he looked from one man to the other. "I'll decide the matter myself, and ye'll both abide by my decision or I'll ha' ye in the castle dungeon."

"Let go of me, you snake," Jesse hissed the minute she and Alex were away from the royal presence. Snatching her arm from his grasp, she whirled and raised her leg to knee him. This time it was her skirts that hampered her, and the blow caught him in the thigh again instead.

"Ouch! Damn you. That spot's still tender." Alex rubbed his leg and glared at her before recapturing her arm and hustling her toward the hall.

"Serves you right," Jesse grumbled.

"For saving you from your cousin?"

"For... for ruining my reputation."

"I had not thought you cared for such things."

"You . . . you made it sound as though we had spent the entire time in . . . in bed," she cried, her cheeks red as his surcoat.

"'Twas necessary." Torches flickering from brackets in the stone walls sent shadows dancing over his face. But despite the harsh wash of light and dark, his expression was incredibly tender. "Only the implication that we had been . . . intimate together could counter Parlan's claim of kinship."

Too true. Jesse exhaled the hot, angry breath she had been holding. With it went most of her rage, leaving her hollow and scared inside. "I am sorry. I . . . I just felt cornered."

"And frightened." He framed her face with his hands, his thumbs whisking over her cheeks, soothing. "Ah, love, 'tis all right. I understand."

His empathy brought the sting of tears to her eyes. "Oh, Alex." Needing to stay strong, she resisted the urge to fling herself into his arms and weep. "What are we going to do?"

"I'll not give you to Parlan, no matter what the king says. We will make a run for it if we have to."

Her heart skipped a beat. "You would do that for me?"

"I should spank you for even having to ask." His quiet voice was at odds with his words, and his eyes were soft and dark with things that heightened her awareness of how close they stood in the deserted corridor, of how much she wanted to take the single step that would align her body with his. "You know I would do anything for you," he whispered. "Anything."

Jesse swayed, trembling with the realization that she was falling deeper and deeper under his spell. She dared not give in to the desire that even now warmed her blood and curled into an ache low in her abdomen. All her life she had seen women bent and sometimes broken by a man's will. She could not let him slip past her defenses. Worse, if she surrendered to Alex, how could she face Hugh when they landed in England? "I can not give you what you want in return for your help."

"Jess. What is it?" His gaze wandered over her face, making her skin tingle as though he had stroked her chin, her lips, her cheeks. "I have not asked for payment."

"Aye. You want me to love you, but I can not." Even if she believed in love, even if he were not a Sommerville, she could not afford to need him that much. Because when he grew restless and walked away, he would take too much of her with him.

Pain tightened the corners of his mouth, then he exhaled harshly. "Give it time, Jess."

"Alex! Just the man I was looking for," Ross called, striding toward them.

"Things went well wi' the king, I see," his cousin observed, taking in the intimacy of their posture.

Alex forced himself to step away from Jesse, but he kept her hand, needing the warmth of her skin as an antidote to the bitterness clawing at him. Why could she not love him?

"Alex?" Ross prompted.

"We are not yet certain of the outcome," Alex said woodenly.

"At least he listened," Ross said when Alex finished explaining what had transpired in the king's study. "While we're waiting for his majesty's decision, there is another messenger come from yer father. He said he had ridden without pause, stopping only to change mounts," Ross added ominously.

Jesse dutifully accompanied Ross into the hall while Alex went to speak with the messenger. Accepting a cup of wine she really did not want, Jesse stood at Ross's side, oblivious to the swirl of laughter around her. What more bad news had this messenger brought from England? Out of blind loyalty, she had protested her brother's innocence to Alex, but she knew Hugh and Parlan were up to something, and she feared the worst.

Her mood sank further when Fiona Ramsey's voice intruded. The woman stood nearby, complaining long and loudly to everyone within earshot of how cruelly Alex had treated her the night before. "Sent me away wi' a pat on the head—like a dog," Fiona grumbled. "And after all we've been ta each other."

Would that be her fate when Alex tired of her? Miserable, Jesse edged toward a window and finally slipped into the seat built beneath it. It was dark outside now, and a cool breeze streamed in through the open window. Grateful for the respite, she leaned her aching head against a section of paneled wood and closed her eyes. Would Alex really wed her if the king agreed they should? Did she want him to? A week ago, the answer would have been a resounding nay. Today she was not so certain.

Suddenly a hand reached in through the window and grabbed her arm. "Where is Alexander?" Parlan growled.

Jesse gasped and tried to stand, but his grip tightened, and he jerked her hard against the stone sill, hurting her as Alex had not even when she had struggled to escape him.

"Where is he?" Parlan demanded again.

"A-across the room." Jesse wildly searched the milling crowd for some sign of Ross or Laird Lionel in the smoky hall.

"Think you I did not look around the room for your lover before I came over here?" Parlan sneered. "Uncle Edmund will be furious when he learns you ran off with his enemy." Before she could cry out, Parlan snagged her other arm and dragged her backward through the window.

It was her worst nightmare come to life, Jesse thought as Parlan thrust her into his cabin a short time later. No one had tried to stop her cousin from leaving the castle with her held securely before him on his horse. She had looked about frantically for a familiar face, someone who would mark her going and report it to Alex. But with the celebration at the palace in full swing, the stables area had been deserted.

Parlan had moved swiftly, as though he had planned to kidnap her all along. A boat awaited them at the docks. Parlan's men had quickly rowed across the harbor to *The Salamander*. With every stroke of the oars, her hope of being rescued dwindled. Once on deck, Parlan had given curt orders to prepare to sail and hustled her into his dank, stuffy cabin.

Jesse surveyed the disorderly room with distaste. How different it was from Alex's neat cabin. Once she had despised the place, now she longed for it. And Alex.

"'Twill not take long for us to get under way," Parlan said. "Once we have cleared the harbor, I will return to you."

"Do not bother," Jesse retorted, hiding her fear from him behind a look of contempt.

A slow smile spread over his face, but his eyes remained cold and calculating. "I shall enjoy taming you, Jesse. You remember the little serf girl I tumbled in the stables?"

She winced but did not retreat. "You'll not take me as easily." If need be, she'd kill herself first.

"I hope not." Now his eyes were hot, avid. "The more you struggle, the better I'll like it. Think on that, sweet cousin."

Her skin crawled and panic clawed at her insides, but she returned his leer with loathing, raked her nails across his hand when he tried to touch her.

"Bitch." His hard slap sent her reeling back against the bunk, stars dancing before her eyes. She tensed to repel his next attack, but a voice outside called to him.

"I'll be back," Parlan warned, and stormed from the cabin.

Jesse sagged, the metallic taste of blood in her mouth. Her whole body shook with delayed reaction, but the ploy had been well worth it. Parlan had forgotten to lock the door.

"Oh, Alex. Please hurry. Please," she whispered. Odd how certain she was that he would come for her. But would he arrive in time? In case he did not, she'd best make plans of her own.

Scrambling off the bunk, Jesse ransacked the cabin for anything she might use to aid her. Under a pile of clothes atop Parlan's trunk, she found a small dirk. Her next thought was to get out of the encumbering gown.

Parlan's clothing swam on her. Worse, they stank of him, but needs must, she thought as she stripped off the tunic and surcoat Carina had fussed over only a few hours ago. The plain wool tunic covered her to the knees, but nothing else of his came close to fitting, so she left on her own hose and the leather shoes embroidered with tiny pearls. She doubtless looked a strange mix of male and female, but at the moment she cared even less about her appearance than usual.

As the motion of the ship increased, Jesse's hopes that Alex would reach her in time faded. He was probably still with the messenger from his father and did not even know she was gone.

Armed and dressed, ready as she'd ever be, Jesse hesitated at the door, recalling the layout of the ship. There was a short corridor outside, then another door that opened onto the deck.

She would be most vulnerable then. The hallway was dark, empty. So far, so good. Breath bated, she reached for the outer door.

It opened before she touched it, and a figure slipped within to join her in the pitch-black. Trapped! Jesse pressed her back into the wall, the dirk in front of her. Air eddied as the man moved, his clothes brushing lightly against her, making her skin crawl. She could not hear his footsteps over the pounding in her ears. Had he gone by?

"Jess?" Hoarsely whispered. Only one man called her that—

"Alex." She dropped the dirk as she fumbled for him in the darkness, hands greedy, tears streaming down her face. He caught her up, hugged her so tightly she could not breathe. It wasn't enough. She squirmed closer, wrapped her legs around his waist and clung, her whole body shaking with fear and relief.

"Shh. 'Tis all right," he murmured, rocking her gently. "It is all right, love. I have you now."

"Oh, Alex. Oh, Alex," she managed between sobs.

"We can not stay here," Alex whispered a moment later, wondering how in hell he was going to get off the ship with a hysterical woman clinging to him.

"Aye. Of course." She pulled herself together with astonishing speed. Unwinding first her legs, then her arms, she started to slip from his grasp. "Thank you, Alex." She kissed him, hard and quick and full on the mouth. He was the one left reeling while she searched the floor for her fallen knife. "What is our plan?" she asked.

Alex shook his head, first to clear it, then in wonder. Once again he had underestimated her. "You are quite a woman, Jess. 'Tis no wonder I love you."

"I . . . thank you." He heard the blush in her voice, marked it as another victory that she did not throw his words back at him.

He touched her face. "You are all right? He did not hurt you?"

"Nay. I am fine. Scared only and very glad to see you." Jesse belatedly realized he was wet. "Did you swim to the ship?"

"Partway—I've a boat tied to the stern. We must make our way there at once and climb down the rope." He laced his fingers with hers. "For once, I am glad of your male garb."

Jesse smiled. "I thought I should be ready when you came."

She believed in him. It tasted nearly as sweet as her kiss had. "I feared I'd not be in time." His raw words told her more clearly than any clever ones how much he cared. She could have hugged him again. "Stay close and do exactly as I say."

For once, Jesse did not even think of arguing. For once, she willingly placed herself in his care. They slunk out on deck without being challenged and crouched behind a pile of canvas and old rope, mute testimony to the ongoing repairs. A few torches had been lit against the night, and the deck teemed with sailors scurrying to get the ship under sail.

"Carry this and keep your head bent as low as possible," Alex whispered, handing Jesse a small coil of rope. He set a half-empty cask of nails onto his shoulder. Hugging the shadows, he led the way to the stern where he had tied his boat. He'd hoped it would go unnoticed in the confusion of setting sail.

Suddenly Parlan materialized from the gloom. "I am glad you were fool enough to attempt a rescue." His eyes burned savagely. Beside him Guthrie's battered face twisted into a grin of anticipation as he started forward, hands curved into claws.

Alex shoved Jesse behind him, tossed the keg of nails at the charging Guthrie. Guthrie's roar as he waded through the spilled nails with his bare feet nearly drowned out the sharp song of steel striking steel as Alex's blade countered Parlan's.

"Jess, get down that rope," Alex commanded without pausing to take his eyes from his opponent. But Jesse saw Guthrie had recovered and was coming on again despite the nails sticking from his bloody feet. Alex was holding his own against Parlan's lethal blows, but he'd be powerless to take on both men.

"Alex. Beware!" She threw her little knife at Guthrie. It struck him high on the chest. Not enough to seriously wound, but it did stop him midstride, bellowing in enraged astonishment.

Alex whipped his head around, saw Guthrie reach to pluck the blade from his flesh. Knowing the giant would be after

Jesse in a second did he not act, Alex snatched the knife from his belt. Left-handed, he hurled it at the mountainous man. It flew true, slitting Guthrie's throat as surely as it had the targets Alex had practiced on since youth, dropping him to the deck.

"Alex!" Jesse's cry switched Alex's attention back to Parlan barely in time to block a downward thrust that would have severed his own neck. Fury fueled Parlan's strokes as he went on the attack. Alex countered blow after blow, content to let Parlan expend energy while he saved his and looked for an opening. Then he saw it, a dip in Parlan's blade as weariness caused a momentary lapse.

Steel shrieked as Alex's sword slipped under Parlan's guard. Then it was Parlan bellowing, his silk surcoat split, a bloody line laid across his ribs. His sword fell as he grabbed his side.

Alex did not pause to savor his victory. Sheathing his sword, he swung Jesse onto his back. "Hang on," he ordered as he went over the rail. Hand over hand, he lowered them down the side, but the rope began jumping before they were halfway down.

Looking up, he spotted Parlan's face above them, his sword flashing as he sawed on the rope. The hemp gave. Jesse screamed. Down they plunged into the black water. Her arms were still locked around his neck when they surfaced.

"Loosen your hold," he rasped, "we're in no danger." To prove his point, he swam to the boat and hauled them into it.

Only when she felt something solid beneath her feet did Jesse relinquish her grip on him. Slumping in the bottom of the boat as he plied the oars, she pushed the wet hair from her eyes. "We made it," she gasped.

"Aye." He grinned at her. "Did you doubt we would?"

She returned his smile with such blinding certainty that Alex forgot about his wet clothes and the few nicks he had taken from Parlan's blade. "Nay. I trusted you to see me safe."

Trust. He had wanted her trust. Now he had it.

Oh, hollow victory.

Alex struggled to keep his smile in place, tried not to think about the terrible news in his father's latest message.

Hugh Harcourt was dead.

Chapter Eleven

Alex stood on *The Star*'s aftercastle and watched the sullen sun slip toward the cloud-crowded horizon as he searched for some sign of Parlan's ship. Though they had not sighted *The Salamander,* he knew Parlan would follow him to London to get Jesse back. He was counting on it. There Parlan would be arrested and stand trial for his part in Hugh's scheme.

But Parlan was not the main thing on Alex's mind.

Hugh's death was.

The urgent message from Alex's father had explained that the Sommervilles' troubles had not ended with Hugh's capture. True, the bastard had confessed his crimes to the Bishop of London, but while the Sommervilles had been busy celebrating Gareth's wedding to Arianna de Clerc, Hugh had hanged himself. The Sommervilles were certain to be blamed because their men had been guarding his cell at the time.

King Edward, fearing Edmund might use Hugh's death as an excuse to declare war on the Sommervilles, had agreed that the matter be kept quiet until Hugh's cohorts had been caught.

Walter and Charles were already under guard in the Tower of London. Charles had confessed to having made the coins for Hugh. Walter had likewise admitted his part in the scheme. Both men insisted Hugh had told them that the men behind the plan were Geoffrey and Gareth Sommerville. Hugh had even introduced them to a masked man who had claimed to be Gareth Sommerville.

'Twas most likely that man had been Parlan Graham. Alex's task was to bring him to London. 'Twas a duty he welcomed, nay cherished, especially after Parlan's kidnapping of Jesse.

Alex sighed, thinking of the girl asleep in his cabin below. It would break Jesse's heart to learn her beloved brother was dead, and she would blame his family. Raking a weary hand through his hair, Alex admitted he did not have the courage to tell her. The thought of seeing hatred in those green eyes that had lately looked on him with desire and trust did what slipping aboard *The Salamander* alone to rescue her had not—made his nape tighten with fear.

He stiffened, shaking it away. Surely there was no need to tell her just yet and give her days to grieve, he reasoned. What would it matter if she went on thinking her brother was alive, at least until they reached London?

None. He would use these few extra days to deepen her trust in him so that when the blow fell, she'd not turn away from him. She would need him then, for Edmund would surely demand the return of his daughter. Mayhap even wed her to Parlan.

Nay! Alex's hand clenched the rail in silent denial. Wedding her himself was the only way to put her beyond the reach of Edmund and Parlan. Given her reaction when he'd suggested it to King David, Alex did not see how he'd get his prickly little vixen to the altar without binding and gagging her as Ross had suggested. Telling her Hugh was dead would not aid his cause.

Alex remained at the rail as the night darkened, his thoughts as turbulent as the storm gathering all around them. They were just passing Holy Island, off the coast of Berwick-upon-Tweed when the wind picked up. The sea swelled from a chop to a stomach-lurching roll in moments. Lightning crackled over the island, and a light mist began to fall.

Bevan joined Alex at the rail. "We'd best make fer land."

Alex opened his mouth to agree.

"Fire!" screamed the lookout atop the mast, and everyone jumped, searching wildly for the flames. A fire at sea was the thing a sailor feared most. "There! To the east."

Indeed, a fire did burn but a mile away across the water, sending black smoke skyward. Nothing lay in that direction but the Farne Islands, small, inhospitable dots of rock and scrub. It must be a ship ablaze. "Piper! Battle stations," Alex cried.

He watched through the glass as they drew near the fire. The pirates who plied the Mediterranean ofttimes used the ruse of a burning ship to lure another vessel to its doom. He doubted these were pirates, did not think it could be Parlan. But the stern pointed away from him so he could not make out the name.

Men ran around on deck, their faces black with smoke. Their screams for help cut across the distance separating the ships, pricking Alex's conscience. No matter who they were, he could not refuse to render aid.

"Look sharp!" Alex shouted. "There may be men in the water."

"They were within fifty yards of the ship and closing when Alex heard a loud whoosh, looked up and saw the sky rained fire. Some fell short of *The Star,* hissing into the water, but one great glob landed on the deck with an angry splat. Flames spread out on impact, lapping at the wood like hungry orange tongues.

"'Tis Greek fire!" Alex screamed.

"Break out the casks o' vinegar!" Bevan bellowed, vaulting down the steps from the aftercastle and heading for the helm. "I'll bring us about at the double."

"Archers aloft!" Alex shouted through cupped hands, then he went to organize the fire fight while Bevan and the helmsmen struggled with the cables and pulleys that operated the tiller.

Another crew might not have known how to cope with this ancient weapon, but Alex's men were veterans of voyages to the East, where the terrifying mix of naphtha, sulphur and pitch was the favorite weapon of the pirates. Water would not quench it, only sand, vinegar or urine would do that. Bags of sand were always kept on deck. Until the vinegar arrived, the sailors made do with sand and the third retardant.

When he could, Alex spared a moment to find out who had done this monstrous thing. Chest heaving with impotent rage, his glass swept the avid faces of the men he had come to save, men who had lured *The Star* in, then turned on her. Alex was not surprised to find Parlan's face among them, his evil smile a white slash against his smoke-smudged skin.

Eyes fierce, red rimmed, Alex roared, "I'll see you in hell for this." Though he knew Parlan could not hear him.

"Alex!"

He spun around as Jesse lurched up the aftercastle's steps and fell into his arms. "What are you doing up here?"

"I—I heard the noise and smelled smoke." She trembled, her eyes wide, her nails digging into his flesh. "What happened?"

"Parlan lured us into a trap."

"Sweet Mary!" she whispered. "What can I do to help?"

How typical. "Nothing." He gave her a quick hug, then released her. "Get below where you will be safe."

"What if the ship...burns?"

Alex felt her fear and his own doubled. He forced himself to speak calmly. "It won't, but if there is any danger, I will come for you. Now go, so I can get to work."

"I will wait where it is safe," Jesse said, and he believed her. On the run, he hefted two bags of sand and disappeared into the smoke. He was not the only one who could twist words to suit himself, she thought as she sought shelter in a corner of the aftercastle. She would go mad confined to the cabin, wondering what was going on above, fearing they all might die.

Face pressed between the slots of the railing, she watched the men work. The first fire had been contained and pieces of burned wood thrown overboard but another raged in the ropes stored in the forecastle. Grit hung like a black curtain over the ship, shifting with the wind so she could hardly keep track of Alex as he came and went like a wraith, beating at the fire, shouting encouragement to his men in a hoarse voice.

They had drawn away from *The Salamander,* and the hail of arrows from the archers in the rigging deterred Parlan from closing in. But globs of liquid fire still reached *The Star*. Each new blaze seemed to take longer for her crew to put out. Her heart in her throat, Jesse watched them pour vinegar and sprinkle sand. Would their efforts be enough to save the ship?

It was her fault Parlan had lured Alex and his crew into this spot. Mayhap if she went to him and begged him to break off the attack... Nay, 'twas a stupid notion. Even supposing she could reach his ship, Parlan would not willingly let Alex go.

Suddenly a burning brand landed near the steps and lay there unnoticed by the men. Jesse rushed down the stairs and stomped on it, but the strange liquid fire stuck to her feet, singeing her leather boots and scorching her feet. She screamed and stomped harder, panicking as the fire squirted up her leg and ignited the edge of Parlan's tunic. "Alex! Help! I'm afire." She raced in frantic circles that only fanned the flames. "Water!" Scrambling to the rail, she launched herself over the side.

"Nay, Jess!" Alex made a grab for her, but his hands clenched empty air. "Jess!" He howled his anguish into the teeth of the wind. Far below, in the churning water he thought he saw her surface. Knowing she could not swim, realizing there was no time to order a line secured, he snatched up the nearest floatable object—a scorched hatch cover—and jumped overboard.

"Of all the cursed luck!" Parlan shook a fist at the heavens as they opened up and the rain began to fall in earnest.

"Capt'n." His lieutenant rushed up. "The sea grows so rough we must douse the fire pots or risk bein' set ablaze ourselves."

"Coward!" Parlan spat. Though the ship bucked beneath him like an unbroken stallion, all Parlan saw was *The Star* slipping away. A pall of smoke hung over her as she slithered down the side of a steep, watery trough, but the absence of the red glow on her decks meant the fires were out. Still, the sailors aboard her must be frightened and exhausted.

"We will go after them...press our advantage," he decided.

"B-but we are shorthanded, Capt'n. We've not replaced the men we lost in the last storm, and their archers are deadly."

"Cease your whining," Parlan snapped. "Our men are fresh—"

A scream of agony brought Parlan around to see a fire pot topple from a catapult, spilling molten flame across the deck. One man was engulfed by it. "Let him be," Parlan shouted as the sailors tried to beat the flames from his clothes. "Put out the fire on the deck first. Throw anything that burns over-board—including that man.''

''B-but Capt'n—!''

''The way he thrashes about he'll set the whole ship ablaze,'' Parlan growled. ''Do as I say, then order the men aloft to put on more canvas.''

''But the storm—''

''Devil take the storm. Nothing will stand in the way of my getting Alexander...and Jesselynn.'' Parlan scowled savagely. Aye, she'd rue the day she chose Alexander over himself.

Alex spotted Jesse's white face and flailing hands moments after surfacing, reached her in two strokes. ''Hold tight to me,'' he shouted into the wind-whipped water. Coughing, gasping, she latched onto his neck and clung like a monkey.

''Alex,'' Jesse rasped in his ear, her body trembling. ''You should not have come after me. Now we'll both be drowned.''

''Not without a fight, we won't,'' Alex replied with more confidence than he felt. When she nodded despondently and slumped in his embrace, he feared she had lost her will to live.

''Jess...hang on and try to stay awake,'' he pleaded. He thought she nodded again, and her arms tightened on his neck.

Maintaining a death grip on the piece of planking with one arm and Jesse with the other, Alex frantically searched for some sign of *The Star*. All around them he saw nothing but undulating walls of wild gray water. *God save us*, he prayed. Gritting his teeth against his fears and the salt water that clawed at the nicks and scrapes he'd gotten fighting the fire, Alex focused his energy on staying afloat.

As they crested one froth-capped wave, he thought he caught sight of the two ships separated by a wide expanse of water. Unless he had gotten hopelessly turned around, it seemed *The Salamander* now burned while *The Star* beat a hasty retreat. Nor could he blame Bevan for wanting to put distance between the crippled ship and Parlan's vicious madness.

Alex kicked out in the direction of the ship, knowing the effort was likely futile. Even had someone seen him and Jesse go overboard, darkness and the stormy sea made rescue nearly impossible. His hopes plunged further as their makeshift raft slid down the side of the wave and the ship was lost from sight.

Still the inbred urge to survive was strong in Alex, and he continued toward the spot where he'd last seen the ship. His struggles against the icy, turbulent water quickly sapped his strength, forcing him to rest often.

"Let me go," Jesse croaked. "I weigh you down."

"Nay. We are in this together," he whispered.

Finally Alex reached the point where he doubted they would survive. He was so weakened from the countless hours battling the cold water that he could no longer kick. Instead, he concentrated on keeping hold of the plank and Jesse and let the huge waves carry him where they would. If God was merciful, they might somehow wash ashore on one of the Farne Islands. If not . . .

A light.

He squeezed his salt-blurred eyes shut, then opened them quickly, scarcely daring to believe . . . aye, there it was—a dim light twinkling at him a short distance away. Hope stirred his aching muscles into motion. Shifting Jesse's limp body, he adjusted his grip on the wood and forced his legs to kick.

"Jess, 'tis land," he murmured when he was close enough to make out a dark mass rising from the roiling water.

"Where." She stirred, kicked feebly.

"That's it. Hang on a little longer," he crooned. "We will make it." She nodded weakly but soon slumped again.

Alex's words came back to haunt him a few moments later when the waves dashed them against a partially submerged rock. The impact ripped the piece of plank from his grip. Groaning, sputtering, Alex tightened his hold on the now-unconscious Jesse and scrambled to latch onto the rough rock, but a second wave sucked them up and spat them forward. Like a pea launched from a slingshot, they flew through the foam-flecked water on a collision course with a deadly pile of glistening wet rocks.

Teeth bared, Alex flipped Jesse onto his shoulder and turned so he would strike the stones feetfirst, knees bent to flex and absorb the worst of the impact. An agonized grunt was torn from his throat as he hit, his legs folding so far his knees brushed the rock. Ignoring the pain, he leaned forward and grabbed hold of the deeply convoluted rock with his free hand. In the momentary lull before the next wave struck, Alex pulled himself up the slick surface with Jesse still slung over his shoulder.

"Thanks be to God," he whispered. His limbs trembling with exhaustion, he got Jesse from his shoulder to his lap, then leaned his back against the rock. The most persistent of the waves still licked at his feet, but he was too weak and dizzy to crawl another step. And thirsty. Jesu, he was thirsty.

It still rained, and he tilted his head back, mouth opened to wash the salt from it as he silently gave thanks for their deliverance. A dull sort of lethargy settled over him as he lowered his head, yet he found the will to push the tangled hair from Jesse's face and purse her lips to receive the water.

When she did not respond, his heart contracted. "Jess," he whispered, chafing her cheeks with his numb fingers.

She whimpered and slowly licked her lips. Her lashes fluttered up. "Alex?" she said hoarsely.

"Aye." He hugged her. "We are safely on land."

She frowned and looked dazedly around. "How? Where?"

"'Twas surely God's will. I think we are on one of the Farne Islands, but 'tis inhabited," he added, recalling the light that had led him here. He hoped they were friendly. Jesu, but he was too tired to fight anyone else today. And cold, he added as a shiver shook Jesse and was echoed by his own aching body. Though the rain had slackened to a fine mist, the air had a nasty bite. "We had best be about seeking shelter."

"Aye," Jesse managed despite her raw throat. Tired as she was, he must be exhausted. Even in the dim light he appeared haggard, his eyes dull with fatigue. He had saved her life, nearly at the cost of his own. She felt the strangest urge to hug him to her breast and caress his head as a mother might an injured child. Instead, she reached up to stroke his jaw. "Alex. You saved my life." She smiled her thanks.

He kissed her. "Wait here while I climb to the top of the rock. Do not come up until I call you. Promise?" he added.

"I doubt I could move without help."

He started up the rocky cliff. His faint moans and groans made her wince, and she managed to turn so she could watch him. He moved as slowly as an ancient crab from one rock to the next.

Just as Alex reached the summit, a torch was thrust over the side, and a rough voice called, "Ah, I thought me light'd guide someone ta me beach." A large man, the folds in his fleshy face emphasized by the light's harsh glare, bent down, extending a hand to Alex. "Where's yer ship? Is it caught on the rocks?"

They were rescued. Joy giving her strength, Jesse struggled to her knees, but Alex's reply stopped her.

"I am alone," he said loudly, the words obviously meant to carry to her. "I was cast overboard during the storm, and my ship sailed on without me."

Why did he lie? Shivering, Jesse clung to the slippery rocks, her mind whirling. Did Alex mean to leave her here as punishment for landing them in this mess? Nay, she dismissed the idea as quickly as it had come. He had nearly died saving her.

The old man withdrew the hand he had offered and scratched at his mane of tangled white hair. His welcoming smile became a frown. "Think ye they'll come back lookin' fer ye?"

"I pray not," Alex replied in the hard voice he had used on Parlan. "Else your light will lure them onto the rocks."

"Figured me game, did ye?" The old man's cackle raised the hair on Jesse's nape. *He was a wrecker!* "Ah, well, seems 'twas a wasted night after all." From behind him he drew a sword and raised it over Alex's unprotected head.

Jesse's startled gasp was covered by Alex's cry of, "Nay, please do not kill me." He cringed into the rocks like a frightened lad. "My . . . my sire will pay well for my safe return."

"How much?" the old man exclaimed, lowering his sword.

"A—A hundred pounds . . . in gold," Alex stammered, but Jesse caught the slight movement as his right hand inched around his waist toward the sword still slung in its scabbard.

He needed a diversion!

Without further thought, Jesse raised her head and howled like a wolf on the prowl. The old man gave a startled cry. Alex leaped over the lip of the cliff and was lost from sight. She heard the muffled sounds of a scuffle, a thud, then a long, drawn-out scream as a body fell past her.

"Alex!" Jesse peered down at the shape wedged between the rocks, half-hidden in the foaming surf. "Alex?"

"Jess!" Hard hands grabbed her back from the edge, strong arms wrapped around her as they knelt on the stone ledge. "Jesu, but your cry was timely," he rasped, holding her close.

"Oh, Alex. I was so frightened." Tunneling her hands in his wet, tangled hair, Jesse captured his mouth and kissed him as he had taught her . . . fully, deeply and with all the desperation coursing through her trembling body. The frantic need to be close to him was tempered by the answering hunger in his own lips as they molded to hers. She tasted salt and knew it came in part from the tears running down her face. "Are we safe?" she asked moments later.

"Aye." He hugged her tighter. "But I must get you somewhere warm. No doubt the old bastard had a hut or cabin nearby."

"H-he was a wrecker?"

"And mad with it." Alex's eyes held hers steadily. "God alone knows what we will find here, for the old man was evil."

"Thank God you recognized the signs ere he captured us."

Alex nodded. "Much as I hate taking a life, I can not regret that he died before he could lay a hand on you."

He helped her to her feet, somehow managed to get them both up the slick face of the cliff. Flashes of lightning illuminated a path. Their arms around each other, they stumbled down it, drawn toward a tumble of rocks by a faint glow that seemed to come from within them. "A cave," Alex whispered. "Wait here whilst I look inside."

Jesse was only too glad to slump against a boulder while he drew his sword and slipped up to the gaping entrance. Much as she wanted to remain alert in case he needed help, her muscles had turned to jelly.

"'Tis empty," Alex announced, startling Jesse from a light sleep. Groaning, he picked her up and staggered the few feet into the cave. By the light of the single torch the old man had left burning, he undressed them both, rolled them up in the first blankets that came to hand and slept.

Tomorrow would be time enough to deal with the fact that he and Jesse were alive . . . and alone together on an island.

* * *

Jesse awoke to Alex's touch. "Do not shake me," she grumbled, opening one eye to glare at him.

"You slept so long I became worried." The stream of pale light coming in through the cave's opening emphasized the shadows under his eyes, the scrapes and bruises on his face.

"You look as bad as I feel." Indeed, every muscle in her body protested loudly as she straightened her legs. "Even knowing we are lucky to be alive does not lessen the pain."

"Food and a hot bath will make you feel better."

"Where would we get such things?" Her gaze narrowed. "Nay, 'tis a ploy to get me up to cook for you. Let me sleep."

"I have already seen to the cooking, and the hot water will do your aching muscles more good than the sleep." He swept her up in his arms, blanket and all, ignoring her groan of misery. "You will thank me for this later, my lazy little wench."

"I am not your wench," she protested as he carried her deeper into the caves. The mustiness and sour odor were stronger than in the main cavern, and she covered her nose. Torches burned in the walls, their flickering light revealing chests, barrels and piles of things she could not identify. Here and there the light caught on the shine of cups, swords and armor. Farther along, a dark tunnel cut off to the right. As they passed it, the sharp smell of decay made her eyes water.

"What is that terrible smell?" she asked.

"You do not want to know." He stooped through a stone doorway, straightening into a tiny round room with a hole in the ceiling. It let in sunlight and a patch of blue sky that was reflected in a pool of shimmering water that covered the floor.

"Oh," was all Jesse could say as he sat her down beside it. Extending one toe, she found the water was very warm.

Alex gave her an I-told-you-so grin. "'Tis a hot spring. If you will lie down on your back so your hair hangs into the water, I will wash it—then leave you to the rest."

Jesse looked around nervously, then up at the hole.

"We are alone here." His deep voice tickled her spine.

"B-but surely there are other people."

"Once, but now they are—gone." His eyes filled with a disgust she did not feel strong enough to question. "The island is small," he went on. "I searched the whole of it in less than an hour. We are alone. Does that thought frighten you?"

Fear was not the word she'd have chosen to explain her heart's sudden lurch. 'Twas more like anticipation, as though she stood poised on the threshold of some great new adventure. "I am not afraid." Her voice was steadier than her pulse.

He was. Afraid he could not control himself. Alex forced a rueful grin. "Nor would you admit it if you were, my stubborn little vixen." Picking up a piece of soap, he washed her hair with surprising gentleness. "You have beautiful hair."

"Nay. 'Tis impossibly curly and an awful shade of red."

"Like fire." His touch was almost reverent, his expression full of wonder as he wove his fingers through her hair.

Jesse's skin drew tight, her scalp tingled. Her stomach filled suddenly with dozens of butterflies.

"Are you cold?" he asked when she shivered.

"Nay." She was hot and trembly and dizzy. And the edge of that precipice loomed nearer. How could her mouth be so dry when she felt as if she were drowning?

"I could never hurt you, you know," he murmured.

She moistened her lips and nodded, waiting for his avowal of love, was oddly disappointed when it did not come.

The flick of her tongue had Alex's pulse scrambling, his body tensing. *Jesu,* he looked away, struggling to master his desire. It had been heaven and hell to awaken beside her this morn. The sight of her pale, sleep-softened features, the feel of her slender limbs tangled with his larger ones had inflamed him beyond belief. Even as he'd wrenched himself away from her, he'd vowed to keep his distance, avoid touching her, lest he do the unthinkable—force himself on her. Yet here he was washing her hair. Fool! Think of something else.

"Let me tell you what I have found thus far," he managed. Sounding as dry as the priest who'd lessoned him in his letters, Alex began reciting, "Armor and plate. Some gold and jewelry. Most of the salvage was household goods—chairs, beds and rolled-up rugs, chests of clothing, bolts of fabric and piles of leather goods. In the way of food we have casks of wine, barrels of salted meat and fish, wheels of hard cheese, sacks of herbs, spices and grain."

Jesse shuddered. "Think how many people the wrecker's lights lured to their deaths. If not for your quickness in realizing what the man was about, he might have killed us," she said, sitting up as Alex wrapped a second blanket around her wet head.

"Or worse," he said ominously.

"Worse? Explain."

Alex sighed and sat back on his haunches. "You recall the tunnel you asked about earlier? The one that stinks so. I found two small pens there and in them, the . . . the bones of two men."

Jesse's hand went to her throat. "D-did *he* kill them?"

"There was no sign of violence. Mayhap in his madness he forgot to feed them. I buried them."

"Sweet Mary! Why would he have penned them?"

"Mayhap he held them for ransom," Alex said in disgust.

Jesse closed her eyes briefly. "Edmund does that." The memory made her sick. She opened her eyes to Alex's face. Swimming in the shimmer of her tears, it mirrored the pain inside her. He understood. Unbearably moved, Jesse reached for him, wanting his arms around her to keep the gnawing at bay.

"Ah, Jess." Alex took her hand and squeezed it, knowing it was not enough, yet he dared not give her more with passion raging so close to the surface. In desperation, he changed the subject again. "The wrecker chose his home wisely. In addition to this hot pool, there was fresh water nearby. Some things are in good condition. Others have been ruined by salt water and careless storage. Later I will sort them out, find what we need to keep and throw away that which is spoiled."

Pride kept Jesse from throwing herself at him when he obviously wanted distance between them. Well, she had her wish, he no longer loved her. Pain rippled through her. In vain, she tried to think it did not matter. "I will help you," she said, the effort of controlling tears making her voice sound harsh.

"Very well." Damn. He'd hurt her. He shook with the effort it took to keep himself from reaching for her, knowing she was not ready for him yet. "I leave you to your bath." Without waiting for her reply, Alex rushed from the cave.

Bloody hell! She was driving him mad. He had to find a way off this island. He'd not last two days on this cursed island without doing something they would both regret.

Chapter Twelve

There was another storm brewing.

Holding aside the blanket that hung over the entrance to the cave, Jesse studied the sullen sky. The heaviness in the air, the brooding intensity of the thick clouds that blotted out the setting sun increased her edginess. But it was not only the weather that had her nerves jumping.

"Is it raining?" Alex inquired from within.

Ordinary words. Yet after four days alone with him, it took only the sound of Alex's husky timbre to make her skin feel tingly and a size too small. "Not now, but it will soon," she replied, her voice less steady than she wished. Aye, the storm was as inevitable as the impending explosion between Alex and herself. 'Twas only a matter of time till the rains came...only a matter of time till some spark ignited the fire that smoldered in Alex's dark eyes whenever he looked at her.

Jesse shivered. She was drawn to him—more with each passing day—but she was not ready to give him the words. Mayhap she never would be. Dropping the blanket, she turned. Her gaze slid carefully past Alex kneeling by the hearth, turning the fish he had caught. Yet she could not help but note the way his muscles bunched beneath his clothes, the way his hair, still wet from his bath, framed his chiseled features, his hot, dark eyes.

Jesse wrenched her head aside. "'Tis gloomy in here," she muttered. Nerves vibrating with awareness, she moved around the stone room, lighting the torches in the wall brackets, then the candles set in tall bronze pickets at either end of the oaken table where they took their meals. There were thick rugs on the

floors and walls to keep the damp at bay. The trunks stacked
in one corner held the clothing they had rescued after pawing
through hundreds of ruined garments.

Alex groaned, following the provocative sway of her hips
inside her hose and tunic. "Why do you not put on a cloak?"

Jesse swung around. "Why? It's hot in…" Her voice trailed
off as she saw the hunger gleaming in his eyes.

"Aye. It is." The cave suddenly got much warmer.

Flustered, Jesse turned away, forcing her thoughts down
other paths. The past four days she and Alex had slaved from
dawn to dark, making the wrecker's hovel into a home of
sorts, throwing out the old man's refuse, scrubbing the chamber and airing items to furnish it. She had found an odd satisfaction in working with him. He was strong and bold and
clever enough to perform seemingly impossible tasks, charming enough to make doing them fun. Aye, they had laughed
and cursed and sweated together. If not for one thing, Jesse
might have been content for the first time in memory.

Though they both tried hard to maintain the fiction that
they were companions, friends, struggling to survive, there was
no getting around reality.

They were a man and a woman alone on an island. A man
and a woman who had nearly burned down the garden with
one kiss.

"The fish is ready," Alex called out.

Jesse jumped, her gaze colliding with his for one brief,
charged second before she leaped into action. Watching her
dart about, setting out silver plates and cups for the wine, Alex
knew exactly what drove her to flit like a startled bird.

Desire. The air around them sizzled with it, ached with it.
Desire, forbidden by the feud that separated them, by her
stubborn resistance. She wanted him. They both knew it. But
at some level she still did not trust him enough to admit it.

"Did you say the fish was done?"

Alex brought his head up, found Jesse watching him, her
eyes soft, her hair tumbling wild about her shoulders. When
she looked at him like that, he could hardly keep from taking
what he wanted. Yet he knew he must or risk losing her forever. Still, a little push could not hurt. "Aye. I am ready," he
said in a husky drawl. He let his eyes drift down her body. By

the time they came back to her face she was flushed and breathing too quickly. *Good.* So was he. "The bulbs," he prompted.

Jesse swallowed hard, her hands a little unsteady as she grabbed up the forked stick and poked through the coals for the lily bulbs she had found beside the stream. The enticing smell of the herbs she had sprinkled on them filled the room as she dumped them into a bowl and dashed to the table.

Alex followed closely, pleased by his opening move. "Are you certain they are good to eat?"

"You do not have to eat them." Tossing her hair, she pulled her stool to the table. "I only suggested it because I have come across them in my rides before, and you said we needed greens in addition to the salted meat and cheese."

"A man learns a thing or two on a sea voyage," he allowed, "and one of them is that eating fruits and vegetables keep him from sickening." A man also learned to do without a woman, Alex mused, but celibacy had taken on a different, more painful meaning now that he lived under the same roof as Jesse.

Four long days working beside her, listening to her voice, smelling her hair, watching her face light with each discovery. Four even longer nights spent dreaming about doing more with her than looking and listening and aching were slowly driving him insane. 'Twas time her sails were trimmed.

Alex set the platter of fish on the table with a thump that made her jump, then he moved his stool from the end of the table to a spot that crowded her right side. She eyed the space nervously before he grinned wolfishly and swung in beside her.

"Alex?" she croaked.

"Jess," he countered.

Jesse knew little of this man-woman thing, but she did know the signs of a predator on the prowl. "What are you doing?"

Giving you a thing or two to think about tonight while you toss in your lonely bed. "Eating supper." He reached his spoon into the lily bulbs and sampled. "Mmm. Good. Try a' bite."

Jesse looked at the spoon he thrust in her direction with only a little less skepticism than she did the dark, too-knowing eyes glittering at her through lowered lashes. When she made no move to taste, he touched the tip of the spoon to her lower lip. Heat radiated out, making her mouth tingle, reminding her of his kisses. She shivered, wanting to move closer, struggling to remember why she should not.

"I would never force you, Jess." 'Twas more than the food he meant, she saw by the ghosts that briefly flickered across his face. "I love you. Trust me...just a little," he whispered.

Jesse knew how Eve had felt when confronted by temptation. Weak. Very slowly, her gaze locked on his, she opened her mouth. The bulbs tasted the way she remembered he did, hot and pungent and wild as the coming storm.

A clap of thunder reverberating through the caves jerked Jesse upright in bed. Hand over her thudding heart, she glanced around the shadow-draped room.

The candle on the chest by the bed had gone out, and the weak spill of light from the next room was not enough to calm her fears. Head tilted, she listened for some sound to confirm Alex's presence in the great room beyond. Nothing.

"Alex?" she whispered. The stone swallowed her voice. She was alone. Alone in the dark. Panic replaced fear. Throwing off the blanket, Jesse shrugged a bed robe on over her shift and dashed into the next chamber, Alex's name on her trembling lips.

The empty room brought her up short. Hastily she searched the gloom for him. The fire had burned down to coals, and a single candle flickered on the table. He was not within. Why had he left her? Hands shaking, she pushed aside the blanket in the doorway and stared warily into the night.

Thunder boomed again. A flash of lightning bathed the landscape in white-hot light. To the left stretched the path that led up through the black rocks to the cliffs where the wrecker had awaited them. Jesse shivered. 'Twas not a journey she wanted to make again, and certainly not tonight.

"Alex! Alex, where are you?" she cried, but a curtain of hot wind pushed the words back into her mouth.

She swiveled as another bolt crackled through the sky, illuminating the second path winding down to the grassy meadow that covered the spine of the island. Though the island was small, from here she could see only as far as the stand of saplings that rimmed the meadow. They writhed in the wind even as the tall grass bent before it, so she could plainly see the rocks that dotted the meadow. Alex had jokingly said they had been sprinkled on the land by the hand of a careless giant.

Oh, Alex. Jesse stifled a sob. She wanted him here. Now. She needed the strength of his arms around her, craved the beat of his heart against her own to steady it. What if something had happened to him? What if she never saw him again?

Her sob became a gasp as a dark figure emerged from the trees. Despite the distance separating them, she recognized Alex's wide shoulders, proud stance and long, purposeful stride. He wore breeches, nothing more, and she knew she would not feel safe until he hugged her close against his naked chest.

"Alex!" Jesse raced down the path, heedless of the stones cutting into her bare feet. He met her in the meadow, grasping her by the arms she so desperately wanted to fold around him.

"What is it? What's wrong?" he demanded, expression fierce, hair blown wild by the wind.

"I woke up and you were gone."

"Gone? You risked breaking a limb running—"

"Oh, Alex. Do not scold. Just hold me." She wrapped both arms around his neck. She had only a second to wait before he groaned and enfolded her in an embrace so satisfyingly ardent it drove the air from her lungs.

"What am I going to do with you?" he murmured into her ear.

"Hold me," she breathed. "Never let me go."

"Oh, Jess." Her heart gave an odd lurch at the sound of her name on his husky voice.

"Closer, Alex. Hold me closer."

He moaned and his hands slid down her back, lifting her so they fit together perfectly, moaning again in response to her sigh of pleasure. Her robe had fallen from her shoulders so only the thin shift kept her from the heat of his chest, from the thundering power of his heart echoing against hers.

"Oh, Alex. Why did you go?" she whispered into his neck.

A tremor shook his big body. "You know why."

"I am not afraid of you." She was more afraid he would release her. The wind tugged at her hair where it had come loose from her braid, twisting curly red around strands of sun-bleached brown. "Please, I do not want to be alone any longer."

Alex groaned. Images whipped through his mind, images as hot as the wind buffeting them. Images of rolling in the grass with her, of filling her, of emptying himself. Desire burst through him like wildfire, searing, tearing at his control. "But do you want me, Jess? Do you love me?" he rasped.

"I want to be with you, but I can not tell you I love you when I do not believe in it...do not even know what it means!" she exclaimed, willing him to understand.

Her unspoken cry for help tempered his passion as nothing else could have, gave him the patience she required. *Jess. My poor, unloved little Jess. I'll make it all up to you if you but give me the chance.* "You must trust me. 'Tis love, Jess," he said softly.

Love? Jesse tried the word out as a flash of light illuminated the meadow. *Love.* Tipping her head up as the last of the brightness faded away, she stared at him. His eyes were dark and mesmerizing as ever but unguarded, for once, all defenses lowered. She saw herself in them. Why had she not realized he was her other half? "I—I had not thought it would be like this."

"What did you expect?" He still held his breath.

"Confinement. A black, airless pit."

Alex nodded. "And?" he prompted.

"'Tis a lot like standing atop the mast. I feel dizzy, breathless and excited. But I am not afraid." Before she could change her mind, Jesse dragged his head down for a kiss. She tasted the surprise on his lips, felt the groan that ripped through him as his mouth opened to claim hers. A heady sense of power raced up her spine, calming any lingering doubts. She tunneled her fingers in his thick hair, glorying in the growl that rose from his throat.

Joy exploding through him, Alex took everything she offered, tempering her untutored haste with experience and a gentleness he had not known he possessed. Her passion, unfettered for the first time, nearly drove him wild. He wanted to rip off the few clothes that separated them and drive into her. Here where they stood, with the savage weather surging around them, echoing their own tempest. He wanted her body, her essence, her soul—everything she was he wanted to absorb into himself. He wanted, he craved, as never before.

Wrenching his lips from hers, Alex buried them in her hair and dragged great gulps of air and the subtle scent of woman. His woman. Aye, she was his. "God, how I love you."

"I . . . I love you, too." Shyly, but firmly.

"Ah, Jess, as God is my witness, I will love you and cherish you always." It struck him then how far they had come together, she from the belligerent hellcat who hated all men, he from the rogue who treated women lightly. Aye, 'twas a fitting match. "We will be married," he declared.

"What?" When he repeated himself, Jesse shook her head. "I am scarcely used to the idea of love and you want us to wed?"

"Aye. Now. This very moment."

Jesse could only gape at him, oblivious to the encroaching thunder and the rising wind. "There is no priest. No church."

"We will betroth ourselves," Alex said impulsively. "'Twill be as binding as wedding vows and keep us free of sin until we can find a priest to say the proper words over us."

"Since when are you worried about sin?"

"Why, since meeting you."

"I do not want to marry you," Jesse said louder and more slowly so the words would penetrate his thick skull.

The wretch had the gall to look hurt. "We love each other. 'Tis the sensible thing to do. I am accounted a good marriage prospect. There are many women who'd jump at the chance to—"

"Then wed with one of them," she said in a panic, "because I do not want to wed. All the married folk I know are miserable."

"Ruarke and Gaby are happy—as are Lionel and Carina, my mother and father and dozens of others in my family." He smiled crookedly, eyes dancing. "We Sommervilles make very good husbands."

Jesse stubbornly ignored the warmth his possessive gaze ignited inside her. "You are an arrogant beast!"

"But I am about to become *your* arrogant beast."

"Never—" His mouth cut off the rest of her words, moving over her lips with devastating thoroughness. The kiss was deep and wet and every bit as bold as he was. By the time he raised his head, she was clinging to him, her nails digging into his bare chest, her control in shambles, swamped by a tide of rising passion.

His smile was slow, supremely male. "I want you in every way there is for a man to want a woman, Jess," he growled. "We were meant to be together. Marry me, Jess. I swear you'll not regret it. We will love each other to the end of time." His husky drawl curled around her like a caress, soothing her doubts.

"Aye," she whispered.

Thank God. Alex set her down, his hands trembling as they cupped her face. "We'll wed here, in the open." Her sigh of approval confirmed his decision. The wind tossed her hair like a fiery banner. Overhead, thunder and lightning dueled. 'Twas a fit setting for the wedding of two such fierce spirits, Alex mused. Taking her right hand in his, he began, "I, Alexander Sommerville, do plight my troth to you, Jesselynn Harcourt, so help me God."

Jesse shivered and slowly pronounced her own vows, her whole being focused on the rugged face bent close to hers. His eyes were as black as the night sky, compelling, mesmerizing. One thought took root in her dazed brain. She did not have to live alone in the dark any longer. Alex would be there for her.

"'Tis done." Alex sealed their betrothal with a kiss so sweet, so gentle, tears welled in her eyes. "Now you are mine," he breathed into her mouth. "Mine to keep and protect."

Jesse stiffened. "I swore I'd belong to no man."

"And I said I'd never wed, yet here we are." He nipped the end of her nose. "I'd say it was an even trade, vixen. I have you. You have me, and I doubt we'll know a dull moment."

"You are impossible."

"So I've been told." Alex chuckled, thinking how Gareth would laugh to see him now. Jesu, somehow he had to figure a way off this island and back to his family. But that was tomorrow's problem. "Come, I've a craving to try out that fine bed."

Jesse's pulse leaped, but she hung back. "Nay."

"Are you afraid . . . of me?" He looked shocked and hurt.

"I want to stay here," she said quickly, before she lost her nerve. "In the open where we can feel the wind on our faces."

"We'll be feeling rain soon," Alex grumbled, practicality warring with cognition. "And I'd not have your first time—"

"It is *my* first time," Jesse reminded him, touched by his thoughtfulness but determined to have her way in this at least. Standing on tiptoe, she smoothed his frown with her fingertips, then slid them into his windblown hair, drawing his head down.

Alex wanted to take this slow and gentle, for her sake, but his good intentions nearly went up in flames when her mouth closed over his. She tasted of wine and love as her lips parted and she matched her tongue to the leading edge of his in a kiss that demanded as much as it gave. Desire had never built so swiftly, ached so rawly as it did now. Groaning, he swung her up, fusing their bodies together. Hard to soft. Drowning. He was drowning in her, Alex thought, struggling to remember she was a novice at this. He gasped, wrenching his mouth from hers.

"Aye," she echoed, breathing hard, staring into his midnight eyes. The wind keened, whipping her hair around them; thunder boomed closer, but the fury of the storm was nothing to the forces building inside her. "Alex!" she cried, digging her nails into his shoulders. "I need you."

On an answering groan, he sank with her to the ground, so her bed robe lay under them in the long, waving grass. "Jess. I have never wanted anyone as I do you," Alex murmured as he stretched out beside her. His mouth slanted across hers, hungry, demanding. He crushed her close, fitting the empty cradle of her hips to the full, throbbing strength of his.

Jesse shuddered, straining against him. This was what she had been missing all these years, but she wanted more. There had to be more. Impatient, she tugged at the shift that kept her from his heated flesh. He obliged her by stripping the garment away, leaving her skin bare to the wind for the instant it took him to fill his hands with her breasts.

"Beautiful," he murmured, drinking the little gasp from her mouth as his thumbs stroked her nipples, hardening them. His fingers tugged sensuously until the gasp became a low, throaty purr, drowned out by the crackle of lightning. "So beautiful." He raced over her collarbone and beyond, nipping and tasting, leaving a trail of moist, tingling skin from neck to breasts. She started when his tongue laved one sensitive peak, groaned as he drew it into his mouth, suckling hungrily.

She clutched at his hair, holding him close to her breast. "I want it all . . . everything."

He shuddered, groaning as her words nearly shattered his control. "All I have to give," he growled, his voice dark and smoky, rich with promises he set out to fulfill at once. With his mouth and hands he roused in her a fiery passion she had not known existed. Desire came in waves, crashing through her like those she could hear beating on the distant rocks. Yet she felt free, vividly alive for the first time in her life, her body straining to the rhythm his long, clever fingers set as they slipped inside her and sent her flying.

The sight of Jess coming apart in his arms, the sound of his name trembling on her lips, ripped away the last of Alex's restraint. Stripping off his breeches, he rose over her, parting her thighs with hands that trembled.

Lightning flashed, revealing Alex poised above her, face taut with passion, fierce with love. Moaning, she reached up and drew him to her. A groan of pure pleasure escaped her as she welcomed the hard, plunging edge of him to fill the void inside her, body and soul. He stretched her to the limits, and what pain there was was quick, fleeting. "Alex," she gasped as he set her afire, melting her from within.

"Now we are truly joined," Alex growled, and she felt such joy, such a sense of completeness as they moved together. Like two halves of one whole. She wanted to tell him, but one look at his dark eyes, tender yet shining with a love that went beyond their physical joining, and she knew words were not necessary.

"Take me deeper. Let me show you how good it can be," he whispered, cradling her bottom in his big hands, lifting her into the quick, sure strokes that carried them higher, higher. Into the light.

With each thrust of his hips she burned hotter until the core inside her shattered on a wave of ecstasy so beautiful, so right

t chased the darkness from every corner of her being. "Oh,
Alex!" Jesse cried out in ecstasy.

Rasping her name, Alex buried himself in the heart of the
explosion, utterly consumed by the flames, by the feel of her
body tightening around his, by the love he poured into her.
Release shuddered through him like a fire storm, leaving him
drained and gasping for breath.

Moments later, the first fat raindrop landed on his back.
'Jess," he groaned into her tangled hair. "We have to get up."

"Mmm. Can't."

"I know, but—" One raindrop became two, five, a dozen.
Groaning again, Alex levered himself onto his knees. Much as
he wanted to savor this moment and the sight of Jess sprawled
before him in naked abandon, her face soft with passion spent,
it was now raining in earnest. Wrapping her in the robe, he
stood, swung her into his arms and ran for the cave.

"What about our clothes?" Jesse asked.

"Tomorrow." He sprinted up the trail, ducked into the cave
as the rain came down in torrents. "Ah, just made it." He was
not even breathing hard, but he was grinning from ear to ear.

"You look like a lion home from a successful hunt."

He smile faded. "I should have been gentler."

"I did not want gentle." She touched the hard line of his
jaw. She nearly melted inside when he nuzzled her palm.

"But you deserve it." His embrace tightened in apology.
"We have to get you dried off." Stopping long enough to pluck
the candle from the table, he strode to her bedroom. He set her
on the edge of the bed, the candle on the trunk. "As God is my
witness, Jess, I meant to be gentle and tender, but—" He
dragged a hand through his hair, scattering rain. "But you do
the same thing to my passion that you do to my temper."

"Have you considered counting?" she teased.

He laughed. "That method has not a prayer of succeeding.
The way you make me burn, I can think of nothing else but
you."

Inordinately pleased despite the fact that the same was true
for her, Jesse looked down and realized he was naked. Beautifully naked. Her eyes roamed possessively over his muscular
bronzed body. The wide shoulders, broad chest tapering down
to a narrow waist and hips. She had never thought to want a

man, but she wanted him, again. As a lover, he had been ever
bit as forceful and vital as he was at everything else. Where sh
had expected to feel cornered, threatened, he had made her fee
alive. Free. And powerful. "Why did surrendering to yo
make me feel powerful?"

"Surrender? Hah!" he said, startling her with the realiza
tion that she had spoken aloud. "'Twas you who conquere
me, stripping me of every thread of control I ever had. Yo
loved every moment of it, little vixen, and unless I miss m
guess, you are about to unman me again."

Jesse flushed. "You want me to?"

His body stirred beneath her gaze. The smile he gave her wa
new and soft, stripped clean of mockery. "Again and again
my beautiful, new-made wife." Kneeling on the bed, he lai
her back and spread her wet hair on the pillow, combing hi
fingers through it, oh, so tenderly, his eyes never leaving hers

"This time we will go slowly," he murmured as he un
wrapped the bed robe and licked the raindrops from her skin

They did not, but again it was not his fault that her hunge
burned through his control.

Toward dawn, he awakened her and showed her the sweet
gentle side of love. When she cried with the wonder of it, h
kissed the tears from her cheeks and wrapped his arms aroun
her so they slept heart to heart.

Chapter Thirteen

Jesse ducked through the entrance to the cave and straightened, blinking at the bright morning sun.

"Ah. The air smells fresh and clean," Alex said as he joined her, stretching his arms wide as though to hug the world, naked but for skimpy linen drawers tied low on his hips.

"Aye." She smiled up at him, admiring the play of sunlight on bunching bronze muscles and his wide, engaging grin. "Small wonder, 'tis the first we've been out-of-doors in two days."

"That is your own fault."

"Mine!" she yelped, flushing.

He grabbed her before she could turn away, tucked her under his arm and whispered into her ear. "Have pity, lady, I am but a weak-willed man, and you are more woman than I have ever held."

High praise indeed from a man of his repute. Jesse wallowed in the melting warmth his words brought. "Are you certain 'tis not because you've been so long without a woman?"

"Very." His body hummed with joy at their teasing.

Tipping her head, Jesse smiled at him. "I love you," she said with a simplicity that shot clean to his heart.

"And I you, my lady, my life." Alex found the contrasts in her endearing. In bed and out she could be bold and bashful by turns. "When you look at me like that, you turn me inside out." As proof, he took her mouth in a scorching kiss, molding their bodies together so she could not doubt he desired her.

"I want you as much as I did on our wedding night," he murmured.

"You, sir, are a randy goat."

Alex sighed. Her words were only half-jesting. Despite the
many pleasurable hours spent in bed, he had yet to convince
her she was beautiful and more a woman than any he had
known. "What am I going to do with you?"

"Feed me, I hope. You promised we'd not sup on cheese and
moldy biscuits again this day."

Alex groaned and set her feet back on the ground. "Eaten
from your fingers, they tasted like ambrosia."

"You are too much the poet."

"And you too much the naysayer."

They frowned at each other for an instant, then Alex threw
back his head and laughed. "I can see our life will not be dull."
He planted a playful swat on her bottom and tugged her down
the path toward the meadow. "Come, wife, we've a meal to
find. The tide should be out, so I will dig for clams while you
see if there are any bird eggs in the nests among the rocks."

Jesse shook her head. 'Twas impossible to stay angry with
him. From the top of his long, sun-bleached hair to the tips of
his tanned feet, Alex exuded charm and confidence. Being with
him was like being sucked up into a whirlwind.

These past two days and nights had been a revelation. His
lovemaking had taken her to such heights, plumbed facets of
her inner self she had not known existed. Their mutual explo-
ration had taken them from raw passion to exquisite tenderness, and not once had she felt anything but cherished. She
easily saw why Alex was a success with women—he always
gave more than he took.

Lying secure in his embrace in the warm glow of sated desire, she had listened as he spoke of his youth, his travels, his
plans to enlarge the Sommerville trading fleet. He had coaxed
from her details of her own life that even Hugh was not privy
to. When the telling had brought tears, Alex had kissed them
away and promised to keep her from hurt.

Jesse believed he meant what he said, believed that Edmund no longer had the power to hurt her. Only Alex did, and
it worried her that she was not woman enough to hold him.

Here, where they were alone together, she stood a chance, but they found some way to return to the mainland—

"This afternoon I will begin work on the boat," Alex announced as they reached the meadow.

"B-boat? But what can you use to build one? The timber that the wrecker salvaged from the ships has been chopped into small pieces for the fire."

"True, but there should be enough saplings to fashion a small raft with sides."

Jesse looked to the slender trees and her heart lurched.

The island boasted one tiny beach ringed by tall, dark rocks. Because they had the warm pool inside the cave, Jesse and Alex did not swim here, but Alex had caught several fish in the makeshift nets he'd strung across the narrow cove.

The tide was just coming back in, Jesse saw as she climbed down the rocky path to the beach. And Alex still waded in the shallow water, his head bent to search for clams. Just the sight of him made her pulse race. She smiled to think how he'd welcome the surprise she held behind her back.

At the sound of her boots crunching on the coarse brown sand, Alex whirled about. Recognition brought a grin that made her blood sing. She could not doubt his love when he looked at her as though he had been starving for the sight of her.

"What did you find, love?" Coming ashore, he added a few hard-shell clams to the bucket on the sand.

"No eggs, but I gathered some—"

"I missed you." He wrapped a hand around the back of her neck and kissed her thoroughly.

"—dandelion greens," she finished weakly.

"And strawberries. I tasted them on your tongue." He craned to see over her shoulder. "Give them here."

Jesse grinned and backed up. "They are for dessert."

"*You* are my dessert."

"I had a thought," she said archly, "on how we might enjoy both together." She waggled a wicked brow at him, then went up on her toes to whisper in his ear.

"Jess!" he exclaimed, startled and intrigued at once by her suggestion. "I can see I've spawned a monster."

Jesse felt her face flame. "Am I too bold?"

"Never that," Alex said, cursing himself for having forgot ten her fragile feelings. "I am delighted that you find plea sure in our lovemaking. You heard no complaints from me thi morn, though you screamed loud enough to be heard on th mainland when I but—"

"Alex!" Jesse cried, but there was no heat, no anger in he as there would have been a week ago had he teased her.

He chuckled and kissed her flushed nose, enormousl pleased with the changes in her. Not that her temper had dis appeared, but rebellion was no longer her first response to challenge. She smiled often these days and seemed to enjoy lif despite their circumstances. Aye, beneath her prickly exterio he had found a lively, charming, witty woman. One who coul fire his passions in bed and captivate his interest out of it 'Twas a rare combination he guessed did not exist in man marriages. "I love you more than I did yesterday," he sai solemnly.

"You said that yesterday," Jesse replied, smiling foolishl feeling ridiculously happy and at peace with the world.

"Come, wife. Let us hurry with supper so we can have thi dessert you have planned. I can see I never gave proper thank to the people who had to grow or hunt down my food. It is full-time task," he grumbled as they started back.

Jesse started to nod, glancing at his bucket. "What are thos green things in with the clams?"

"More lily bulbs."

Jesse stopped and lifted one by its leaves. "I thought we ha agreed that you would stick to harvesting the sea."

"Aye. But I saw them on my way down here. They smelle of garlic when I plucked them, and I thought the flavor—"

"Garlic!" She noted the shiny leaves, dropped the bulb an wiped her hand on her tunic. "Tell me you did not taste them."

"Nay, I—"

She shook him, frightened and angry. "You swear? No with so much as the tip of your tongue?"

"Nay. Why? What is it?"

"Lily of the valley, I would guess. 'Tis deadly poisonous."

"Oh." Alex swallowed hard. "I—I did not know."

"You were supposed to leave the plants to me," she scolded. "I may know little of cooking," she admitted without apology, "but from Gaby I learned which plants were safe to eat, which dangerous. *Sweet Mary, what if she had lost him.*

Alex drew pleasure from her frantic hug. "I humbly beg your pardon," he murmured in her ear. "'Twas wrong of me to flaunt your orders." As Jesse leaned back to gape at him, mouth open in astonishment, he gave her a very sober look. "Though it happens seldom, I most willingly admit when I am wrong."

"You've a courtier's tongue," Jesse said crisply, wondering how he could charm her in so many ways.

"Aye, my sire saw to it I was trained as a courtier, but my heart belongs to you." He grinned crookedly.

She could not help returning it. "Rogue."

"Siren." He lightly pressed his smile to hers.

Laughing together, they linked arms and returned to the cave, mightily pleased with the day and each other. As was their custom, they prepared the meal together—cool pink clams still salty from the sea, hard biscuits made from their precious store of flour and a stew of dried beef, wild onions and red wine.

"Shall I teach you to play chess tonight?" Alex murmured over the rim of his cup as he finished the last of his wine.

"What about dessert?" The blaze in his eyes kindled a familiar heat deep inside her, warming her.

Alex smiled as passion softened her features, turned her eyes to smoky green. Wonder at the changes love had wrought in his little vixen made his heart swell. Cupping her chin, he kissed her thoroughly, possessively.

Jesse leaned into his kiss, her breasts melting against his chest as she wrapped her arms around his neck. She gloried in the groan that rippled from his body into hers as he dragged her off her stool and settled her in his lap. The urgent need mingling with the wine on his tongue gave her a dizzying sense of power. No matter how often they made love, he still kissed her as though he could not get enough.

They were both hot and flushed by the time Alex slid his mouth to her ear. "Jess, you are a siren."

"Mmm. I love you, too." She wiggled her bottom against the proof of his rising desire.

The air hissed through Alex's teeth as he struggled against what they both wanted. "The night is yet young, and you are new to this, love. I'd not wear out my welcome." He nuzzled her ear to ease the sting to her thin skin. "What say I teach you chess? 'Tis a game we can play with our children as my parents did with my brothers and me."

"Children?" Jesse felt the blood drain from her face.

"Aye. Children. I know 'tis not your favorite subject, but I have wanted some of my own since Gaby gave birth to baby Cat." And as hot as things were between them, babes were bound to come sooner rather than later, so she'd best get used to the idea.

"I had forgotten how greedy men are for sons," she said woodenly, pushing at his arms in an effort to get up.

But Alex was having none of that. Tightening his hold on her, he said, "'Tis a daughter I have my heart set on. A tiny red-haired snip I can spoil right along with her mama."

"Oh," was all Jesse could say.

Alex knew better than to push. He had planted the seed, so to speak, and told her he was not greedy for sons. Best to let her think on it a bit. "Mayhap I'd better not show you how to play chess, after all. 'Tis a man's game."

She rose to the bait faster than a starving trout, scowling up at him and demanding he get out the board and pieces he'd carved those first sleepless nights.

They sprawled on a pile of furs before the brazier, but the heat of competition kept them warmer than the fire. She caught on quickly, played with a wit and boldness that came as no surprise to Alex. He won the first two games handily, but by the third she had reached her stride and had his back to the rail.

"Jesu, are you certain you have not played this before?" he grumbled when she put his king in check.

"Who but yourself would teach a woman to play chess?" She smiled partly because she was winning, mostly because it was true. Hugh had grudgingly lessoned her in weaponry; Alex had willingly made her a partner in all they did here. Before that, aboard ship, he had let her climb the rigging and explore to her heart's content, treating her fairly. Fair. Aye. Alex was fair. Hot tempered. Arrogant and stubborn, too, but honorable.

While she was busy staring at his handsome profile and thinking about honor, he wriggled out from her clutches.

"You played well," he consoled as they packed the game pieces away, looking nearly as disappointed as she was.

"You could have thrown the game in my favor."

Alex snorted. "You'd accuse me of having no honor," he said as he stretched out beside her.

Jesse laid a hand on his arm. "Now I regret some of my hasty words, but I had been taught from earliest times to despise your family, and you especially made me so angry."

"As you did me." He picked up her hand, laced their fingers to keep thoughts of the feud at bay. "And, too, I desired you, which only added to my ire." His voice reflected none of the conflicting emotions that assaulted him whenever he thought about home and the problems awaiting them there.

"Mmm." Jesse rolled over onto her back and smiled when he took the hint, pulling her into the sheltering curve of his body. Her hair spilled across the fur like a molten river, glinting in the firelight that gilded her face. Seeing her like this chased the fear from his gut, made him think things would work out. They had to, because he was not giving her up. "Mmm," she murmured again as he freed his hands and threaded them through the curly mass, her mouth tipping up for his kiss.

"Happy?" he whispered across her waiting lips.

"Aye. Happier than I have ever been, ever expected to be." Her smile dimmed. "If only..." *If only I knew Hugh was safe I would never want to leave here.*

"If only?" Alex prompted, braced for the worst... a question about Hugh... the lie he'd have to give her in return.

"If only we could stay here always, just the two of us." *With no Hugh to disapprove of me, no Edmund to fight you over me, no other women to distract you.*

Alex's smile was just as wistful as hers. "Aye, but our supplies are bound to run out, and unless we want to try our hands at wrecking..."

"Nay." Jesse sighed regretfully, and because he hated to see her sad, Alex forced his own dark thoughts down.

"Where are the strawberries, wench?" he asked, his eyes bright with false devilry.

"Wench!" she huffed, stiffening in his arms.

"Wife," he amended, but she looked only slightly less displeased with that title. "Come, love." He pulled her to her feet, then swung her into his arms. "I've a mind to find out if the berries taste sweeter eaten from your skin."

A week later, Jesse found the boat.

She was alone at the time, gathering berries at the far end of the island, and hoping to escape the ring of Alex's sharp axe as he felled trees for his raft. He worked with a vengeance brought on by three days of inactivity—fierce rains that had forced them to remain inside the cave.

What time they had not spent in bed or chasing each other about the pool, they had passed sifting through the wrecker's loot. They had located more jewelry, but little food to add to their dwindling supply. When that had palled, they had turned to chess. Her first win had caused Alex to beam so proudly she became suspicious.

"Did you let me win?"

"Not me. I hate losing—and I'd not give a saucy wench like you anything more to crow about."

"I do not crow."

His expression turned warm and intimate. "You certainly seemed pleased with yourself this morn when you unmanned me with your clever little mouth."

"So." She had tossed her head, dancing on familiar soil.

"You'll hear no complaints from me." Reclining on a blanket before the fire, wearing nothing more than a swath of linen about his hips and a happy grin on his handsome face, he had looked every inch the lion, king of his domain.

And she was his queen.

She would not give him up!

Jesse scowled down at the wooden hull mostly buried under a tangle of thorny berry bushes. She would never have found the stupid thing had she not waded in to pluck the last remaining fruit and stubbed her toe on it. Better it had stayed hidden. Now she would have to tell Alex about it and...

Wait! The cursed thing probably did not even float. A sound boat would have been kept down on the shore, not hidden away in this gully. 'Twould be cruel to dash Alex's hopes by showing him the worthless thing.

Nay. Jesse sat down slowly. Recalling Alex's oft brooding expression when he gazed out over the sea, his nearly frantic drive to complete the raft, she knew she could not keep this from him. Everything she now held dear was here on the island, and she dreaded returning to the mainland. Not so Alex. He worried about his family and the crew of *The Star*.

Shoulders slumped, Jesse dragged herself back across the meadow. The ring of iron on wood grew louder and sharper as she approached the trees, like the ringing of a peal of doom. His back was to her, broad and sweaty, bronzed by the sun and covered with wood chips. She longed to throw herself on him and sob out her fears. "Alex!" she called.

He turned at once and something he saw in her made him throw the axe aside and run to her side. "What is it?" His dark eyes probed hers, intently searching, deeply concerned. Full of love.

Please do not ever stop loving me. "I've something to show you," she managed.

"Has someone come? A ship? You'd best wait here."

"Nay. It's safe enough." *I hope.* "Come. I will show you."

Shouldering the axe, he followed behind her across the meadow where they had made love in the sunshine. The lump in Jesse's throat grew. They passed the rocks where their cave was nestled. She could hardly breathe for the ache in her chest. They crested the hill where Jesse had gathered those strawberries the week before and tears filled her eyes. Sweet Mary, but she did not want to lose him.

"Jesu! Is that a boat I spy?" Alex dropped the axe, bounded down into the gully and thrashed into the bushes without a care for the bloody scratches on his arms. "It is a boat! Jess, you are a marvel." He tossed her a grin, then bent to examine her find. "I can not tell a bloody thing about her condition until I get her out of here. I'll need ropes... and some of the saplings on which to roll her up the hill."

Jesse turned her face into the wind and wiped her tears on the hem of her tunic.

Two strong arms came around her from behind, drawing her back to be rocked against Alex's hard chest. "Shh. I know you are afraid, my heart," he whispered, nuzzling her cheek.

"I am not afraid," she insisted with her former ire.

"Aye, you are." He curved his big body about her like a shield, his mouth warm on her chilled neck. "Only trust me a little. You are mine now, and I will not let anyone hurt you."

"What about Edmund," she sobbed, her fears pouring out in a rush of scalding tears.

"A pox on Edmund." He swung her up, ignoring her stiffness and feeble protests, to hold her high in his embrace, forcing her to meet his implacable gaze. "We belong to each other. You are a Sommerville, now. I will protect you."

Being called a Sommerville rankled somehow. Mayhap because she had been taught to hate the name. "I am afraid Edmund will make war on you. He has many men. He'll quash you like . . . a bug!"

Alex snorted. "Edmund Harcourt is a coward. And he does not value you as I do. You are my wife, and I will keep you safe from him. My brothers and I will vanquish any army he fields . . . providing he sends one, which I doubt." He smiled at Jesse, showing her only his confidence, hiding his one great fear.

'Twas not Edmund who threatened their newfound happiness, but rather Hugh's death that could come between them.

"Only trust me, love me," Alex repeated. She sighed and nodded, but he knew she was not convinced. "Come, let us see about this boat you have found."

It was in sorry shape, one side bashed in, its timbers badly rotted in places. Still, Alex declared he could make it safer than the raft he'd intended to build. It took him two days to wrestle the boat up the slope of the gully and across the meadow—using ropes to pull and the saplings as rollers—and down to the beach where he planned to repair it.

It was backbreaking work. Watching him strain in the hot sun, muscles bulging, face contorted with effort, Jesse marveled at his tenacity, determination and sheer capacity for hard work. Despite her dread of leaving the island, she could not stand to see him work alone. Surprisingly he allowed her to do what she could, as long as it was not dangerous. When the boat shifted on the saplings and bruised her shin, he swiftly ordered her aside, never mind his own welts, cuts and raw, scraped skin.

Men were contrary creatures, Jesse thought as Alex stood back on the sand to survey the dilapidated little boat, hands on hips, sweaty, grimy face split by a victorious grin. Yet in the next instant she added, *Sweet Mary. but he is wonderful.* Looking at him and realizing that of all the women he had known, he had chosen her to wed made her feel light and dizzy, as though she had swallowed a huge bubble of sweet summer air.

"Why are you beaming, wife?" he asked, throwing a hot arm about her shoulder and hugging her so she stuck to his wet side.

She clung there shamelessly, basking in the glow from his eyes, nearly black against his sunburned face. "I love you."

"And I you." He kissed her, quick and hard. "There were times when I thought we'd not get her down to the water."

Jesse smiled, content to let him think 'twas the boat that made her sparkle and not the heady sense of belonging. To him. "If you are done for the day, let us go back to the cave. I'll check on the gannet I left stewing while you take a bath."

"Is that your delicate, ladylike way of saying I stink?"

"Nothing I do is ladylike," she said woodenly.

Alex frowned. "What is all this?"

"Well, look at me," she commanded, her disgusted gaze taking in her burned, scratched arms and legs, left bare by the grimy shift she wore to work in. "And my hair feels like a rat's nest."

Alex was too wise in the ways of women to point out that she had wanted, nay begged, to help do the dirty work. "Jesu, Jess. You do not need to be dressed in silks to be a woman." He felt as fiercely protective of her as he'd been of his family when he'd defended them to her that first night aboard *The Star.* And why not? She was now the most important member of his family.

"You do not understand," she began unhappily.

"Nay, 'tis you who do not understand. What do you think a woman is? Some pale-faced beauty who sits on a velvet cushion, working on a tapestry with one hand, directing her household staff with the other and singing sonnets into the bargain while accompanying herself on a lute she picks with her toes?"

Jesse felt her lips twitching. "Well . . ."

"Women and men both come in many shapes and kinds. How dull 'twould be if we were all alike. And how would we survive without the skills of others to make up for those we lack ourselves? I am not the warrior Ruarke is, nor a man of the land like Gareth, but I do not count myself less a man than they. Nor should you degrade yourself because you do not measure up to some ideal of womankind foisted on you by your sire."

How sure of himself he is, Jesse thought, wishing she felt as secure. "It is not just what Edmund thinks," Jesse said, though it had started with him. "There is the way women are treated. The beatings, the abuses, the . . . the unfairness."

"There is truth in what you say. I can not change the way other men deal with their wives and daughters. But I promise that as my wife, you will be cherished and loved. And only beaten if you truly deserve it," he added with a teasing smile that seemed permanently to have replaced his mocking one.

Cherished. Aye, she was that. Jesse grinned, thinking of the pledge he had foisted on her. How far she had come since that day. How far they had both come—together. She cocked a brow at him and said archly, "And do you not leave this boat project a pace and take a rest you will be too tired to beat me."

"I am not a bit tired," he grumbled, turning back toward the boat. "And there is so much to do."

Men, Jesse huffed. Wise as they thought they were, they never knew when to quit. 'Twas up to her to save him from himself. "Well, I am exhausted," she said, wilting suddenly. "I guess I will drag myself up to the pool for a hot soak." She smothered a smile as he whipped around, scowling fiercely.

"I do not like you to bathe alone when you can not swim."

Jesse lowered her lashes and peered up at him through them. "I will wait for you then," she said wearily.

He swung her up so fast she gasped. "Dammit, Jess, I knew you were doing too much." He started up the path to the cave. "I never should have agreed to let you help," he fussed. His arms tightened about her when she agreed with him and settled further into his embrace. 'Twas a mark of how tired he was that he did not immediately suspect her unnatural docility, she mused, hiding her smirk in the curve of his shoulder.

The feel of the hot water closing over sore, aching muscles drew a long sigh from Alex as he lowered both of them into the pool, clothes and all. For a few moments he drifted there, his eyes closed, one hand on the rocky edge. She stood on tiptoe, the water at her chin. In the dim light, his features were drawn, his lashes emphasizing the circles under his eyes.

How hard he works on the boat, Jesse thought. Feeling a little guilty for not sharing his enthusiasm, she began to slowly knead the stiff cords in his neck and shoulders. "Feel good?" she asked when he groaned, letting his head fall back against the rim of the pool.

"Mmm. I always like it when you touch me."

Jesse smiled. He was too proud to admit she'd been right. They had that in common, among other things. She dipped her hands into a bowl of soft herbal soap and started lathering his face. Many's the time he had washed her, but 'twas the first time she'd had him at her mercy, and she planned to do a thorough job.

The wide forehead, the expressive brows, the high cheekbones, and lastly the square, cleft chin and firm jaw. Never had he seemed more precious to her or more vulnerable than he did now, lying still and unguarded beneath her hands. Some of his restlessness seemed to have settled, except for those times when he looked to the sea and she sensed he thought of home. Or did he long to be back aboard ship?

"Mmm." He sighed as she started on his chest.

"I wish my hands were big and strong like yours." Hers seemed woefully inadequate to the task of massaging the tightness from his thick muscles.

"I do not." Alex's husky voice ended on a groan.

"What?" Her hands stilled on his ribs. "Did I hurt you?"

"Not exactly," he managed. Her lithe, clever fingers were chasing the stiffness from his upper body, but every muscle below his waist was clenched in anticipation. He could not remember ever getting this hard this fast. Perversely, he wanted the sharp, grinding ache to last forever, so he forced his mind to something less pleasant. "We do have to go back."

"I know." Nibbling on her lower lip, Jesse returned to washing. "I know we have avoided speaking of Hugh, but when I think of his reaction to—" Alex shuddered so violently that her eyes flew to his face. The shadows could not hide his pained expression. "What is it?"

Damn. "'Twas naught. A cramp. You were saying?"

Jesse hesitated, then pressed on. "I fear Hugh will see me as disloyal for wedding you." There. She'd said it and felt better. A mark of her trust in Alex.

Tell her, his conscience urged. Nay, Jesse was happy, mayhap for the first time in her life. He'd not steal it from her with tragic news that could wait until they were back on the mainland. "You need not worry about Hugh's reaction."

She cocked her head. "How can you be so certain?"

"Because he would want your happiness above all else."

Jesse sighed. "I suppose you are right, and you have made me happy," she added, twirling a lock of his chest hair.

Alex's throat tightened. "I love you. Whatever I have done in the past—whatever I do in the future—has been to ensure your safety and our happiness. Remember that."

"I will," she murmured. "You must be tired, Alex, you are very solemn tonight." Reaching her arms around his neck, she drew his head down and ran her tongue across his lower lip.

Groaning, Alex opened his mouth over hers, his hands sliding up under her wet shift to her waist and drawing her close. His groan was echoed by Jesse's as she arched, fitting herself against the blatant proof of his arousal in silent invitation. He answered the call by rocking them together as he took the kiss deeper, demanding, then giving in return.

They were both breathless by the time he lifted his head.

"Where did that come from?" Jesse asked, wiggling her hips, eyes bright. "I touched naught but your neck and chest."

"A look from you is all it takes," he murmured, nuzzling her throat. He disposed of her shift, then lifted her so her breast met his mouth. The nipple peaked, hard and sensitive to the air he blew across it. "Beautiful, Jess," he whispered, gazing up her slick body to her eyes smoky with passion, her teeth clamped on her lip as anticipation spiraled through her. He felt it shake her in the instant his mouth closed over the tip, heard her groan, nails sinking into his shoulders as he suckled.

Waves of pleasure rippled through Jesse, the pressure building inside her until her hips were rocking with it, sending the water sluicing between them. Her head fell back; the cave filled with quick, uneven gasps that made Alex's blood churn fast and hot as the tide around them.

"Jess," he cried, ripping away his linen drawers as he lowered her. Her back bowed as he thrust into the wet, fiery core of her, welcoming him with a throaty groan and a tightening of her legs around his hips. "That's it . . . take what you need, love," he crooned, setting the pace, then racing to catch up when the fever inside her built to a frenzy. "Jess," he rasped, welding his mouth to hers as they reached the light together.

I am never giving her up, was his last coherent thought.

Chapter Fourteen

"Are you ready to go?" Alex asked.

"Aye." Reluctantly. Seated in the middle of the boat, Jesse curled her fingers around the seat and prayed for strength as Alex pushed their craft into the sea.

Three weeks it had taken them to repair the boat, rig a sail and make her seaworthy. Three weeks she had had to resign herself to the voyage, yet as time passed, she had felt weaker and queasier. The past few mornings her body had betrayed her totally, sending her racing for the slop bucket the minute she tried to get out of bed.

Gazing up at the crude piece of canvas flapping overhead, Jesse sent a brief prayer for their safety skyward. And it seemed God had heard her, for the light breeze filling the sail stirred only a mild chop on the blue water.

Alex looked very much in his element here, one hand on the tiller, the other on the rail, his deeply bronzed face lifted into the wind, his sun-streaked hair streaming out behind, bravely challenging the unpredictable seas. She understood a bit of what he felt, and wanted, with all the zeal of new love, to share it with him. "This is exciting." Yet she could not resist a last look at the island that held so many precious memories.

"Aye, 'twas a special place, a magical time." Alex stroked her calf with his leg. "If things were different, I would have stayed there with you and the rest of the world be damned."

Touched, Jesse fought the tears she had sworn not to shed. Swallowing hard, she changed the subject. "It seems strange to be wearing so many clothes." They both wore plain hose and tunics, and there were two other sets of clothes sealed inside a small chest with the wrecker's coin and jewelry. "'Twill seem stranger still to be back among people," she added.

Alex's jaw tightened. "Whatever awaits us in England, we will be together, Jess." Her quick nod tore at Alex's conscience. Damn but he was sorry Hugh had died.

"How long do you think it will take to reach land?"

"If I am right about this being one of the Farne Islands, we are at most six miles offshore. If the wind holds fair we should see land before dark—I hope."

"Aye. I do not relish spending the night at sea."

Alex cast a wary eye at the advancing line of clouds. If they covered the sun he would have no way to chart the boat's course. His insides churned with dread, yet no outward sign did he display. He set himself to lull her with cocky smiles and entertain her with funny stories. When the wool and wax he had rammed between the boat's planks to seal them leaked in places, he calmly set Jesse to bailing and kept up his chatter.

Time passed. Every muscle in his body strained, urging the boat. The sun was hours shy of kissing the horizon when he lost his battle and the clouds obliterated it.

"A-are we are c-close?" Jesse clutched the seat against the rise of the swells that she feared heralded another storm.

"We must be," Alex said with a confidence he was far from feeling. The slender mast behind Jesse wobbled precariously on the fastening rigged with pegs and rope. If they lost the sail he had only a single oar with which to pole the craft in rough, dangerous seas. The single thing in their favor was that the wind had switched to the east, blowing them toward land. 'Twould be a close thing indeed.

"Jess. I want you to take one end of that rope—the one I fastened to the metal bracket sunk into the side of the boat— and tie it around your waist." Her eyes went wide with fear, but she did as he had ordered. Not a moment too soon, either, for with a sharp crack the mast toppled over to the right. The boat rolled with it, yawing sharply.

Jesse screamed. Alex threw himself left to counteract the weight, but the drag of wet canvas threatened to swamp them. He had to cut the lines that still bound the mast to the boat.

"Take the tiller," he shouted, lifting her into his place. "Keep the bow headed into the waves as best you can." Leaping over her empty seat, he hacked at the ropes with his knife. Just as the mast slid free and into the water, a wave struck them.

Alex stumbled, nearly tumbled over the side, but the boat suddenly shifted again, rocking him back. He sprawled across the seat and cracked his skull on the rail. Stars dancing before his eyes, he sat up, shaking his head.

"Alex. Are you all right?" Jesse had shoved the tiller all the way over and was leaning with it. 'Twas what had saved him.

"Thanks to you I am. 'Twas quick thinking, love." He picked his way back to her, rubbing the knot on his head.

Eyes dark and frightened in a face gone white as sea foam, she scrambled onto the middle seat while he took the tiller. "Oh, Alex. I was so afraid for you."

"Come here, love." Despite the awkwardness, he took her on his lap, wrapping his free arm around her quaking body. "Shh. It is all right, Jess. You saved me." Both of them. His gut tightened, thinking she would likely have died alone in the boat. "'Twas a smart, braw thing to do."

"For a woman," Jesse said, falling back on an old argument.

Alex's smile faded, his jaw clenching, his eyes blazing. "I have met few men who could match you in loyalty, bravery or honor," he said in the tone usually reserved for speaking of Sommervilles. "I am sorry you resent being a woman, but I am glad of it." The respect that glittered in his eyes warmed her. "Yet first you are a *person*. A person I am proud to call companion, friend, lover and wife."

Jesse's lips curved beneath their film of salt. "Oh, Alex. I—" Her eyes widened at something she saw over his shoulder. She blinked, looked again, then jumped up, waving her arms.

"Jess! Sit down." He made a grab for her waist.

"Nay." She swatted his hands away. "'Tis a boat."

"Ahoy the ship!" called a deep voice. Alex swiveled around to see a fishing boat bearing down on them.

"Oh, ye look that beautiful, m'lady," cooed the bright-eyed maid the innkeeper had sent up with Jesse's bathwater.

"Thank you." Jesse felt herself flushing with pleasure. Well rested, bathed and dressed in a gown brought from the island, she had to admit she felt a good deal better than she had last night when she had sailed into Carr End's harbor in a fishing boat surrounded by piles of stinking herring. But beautiful? She truly wanted to be beautiful. For Alex. Because tonight they were getting married, again—this time before a priest.

"'Tis not necessary," Jesse had replied when Alex had awakened her this afternoon and told her what he had arranged while she had been sleeping the day away. "I could not feel more wed to you than I already do," she softly added.

Instead of the expected smile, he had scowled fiercely. "I will not give Edmund a chance to question my right to you."

"Your right to me?" she'd cried, contentment vanishing. "I am not a piece of land."

"Of course not. I only meant that unless we were legally wed by a priest, Edmund could take you from me."

Oh. Still, "How can you say you love me yet make it sound as though you are discussing a piece of property or a horse?"

"I mean no such thing," he had said gently, kissing the end of her nose. "You see a slight where none is intended."

She had scowled. "Well . . ."

"You know I love you. In your heart you trust me," he had said firmly. "Else you would have thrown something at my head. I must admit I'd rather have this peace and loving between us instead of useless battles." The tender sincerity in his smile had all but stolen her heart anew.

"Aye. I guess it is the strain of being back," she had said. Life had been so much simpler on the island. Now they faced more serious problems than gathering food. Edmund's wrath, Alex's family's censure, and those cursed false coins. By unspoken agreement, they had not mentioned the scheme that had brought them together. No matter who had fostered it, the plot pitted her brother against his and had the potential for disaster. If it blew up in their faces, could their love survive? She wished so desperately, but wishing might not be enough.

"Are ye all right, m'lady?" asked the maid.

Jesse blinked free of her memories and looked at the hovering girl. "Fine. I am fine. I was only worrying that . . . that I would trip on my hem."

The maid hastily assured her she'd not be so clumsy, but Jesse worried about it all the way down the inn's steep, narrow stairs. Not until she had nearly reached the bottom did she look up and realize Alex stood in the hallway below watching her.

"Jesu, but you are beautiful," Alex murmured. The dark green of her surcoat intensified the color of her eyes and made her sun-kissed skin glow. It fit close to her body, showing off the curves of her bust and hips, the slenderness of her waist. In time her flat belly would round with their child, but he knew the sight of her then would stir his senses as provocatively it did now. His woman. His wife.

He smiled possessively, letting desire burn in the gaze he had locked on hers. She blinked, tripped and would have fallen down the last two steps if he had not caught her. "Easy."

"Oh, hell. I knew I would do that," she muttered so bitterly he chuckled aloud.

"We'll order the maids to cut your gowns short in front."

I'll still hate them, she thought. But for compensation she had the gleam in Alex's eyes. "'Tis an idea." Kicking at her hem, she took Alex's arm and walked with him from the inn.

Jesse bending. Alex was so astonished he scarcely saw the houses they passed, his attention focused on the proud woman beside him. Optimism bubbling inside him, he thought about the messages he'd sent to his family letting them know he was safe. About Jesse and their marriage, he had said not a word.

Time enough to face that when they reached Wilton. He had decided Jesse would feel more at ease there than at Ransford. 'Twas not that Alex feared his father's reaction to the news they had a Harcourt in the family—exactly. But he'd welcome Ruarke's and Gaby's support. "We are here, love."

Jesse looked up to find herself at the door of the church with scant memory of having walked through the little seaside town. Inside, it was cool, dim, the only light the tiny circles cast by a brace of candles at either side of the altar. The air was redolent with incense, stinking of mystery and, aye, danger.

The hairs at Jesse's nape rose. As though aware of her urge to flee, Alex tightened his grip on her waist. Looking up, she met his compelling midnight gaze and thought, I love him, but will that be enough to hold him?

"Relax, Jess." His warm breath fanned across her prickly skin, soothing down the gooseflesh. The familiar scent of him wrapped around her, blocking out her anxieties.

"I fear I'll not make you a good wife." That was not all she feared, but she knew speaking of Hugh upset Alex.

"You are exactly the sort of wife I have always wanted," he said softly, his eyes drifting over her face. "I love you, Jesselynn Sommerville. Now come, the priest awaits us."

Jesse shuddered to hear herself called Sommerville. She hoped 'twould pass in time, but she could not shake the feeling that she was being disloyal to Hugh. If only she could speak with him, 'twould ease her. Mayhap she could send a note—

"Good eve," intoned the priest who met them at the altar. He was tall and skinny with disapproving brown eyes. "I understand that you spent a month alone on an island with Lord Alexander Sommerville. Is this true, my daughter?"

Jesse's cheeks flamed. "Aye, but—"

"Harrumph. 'Tis true, she is ruined, then," he said to Alex. "I agree to waive the posting of the banns." Pushing his face into hers, he added, "You are lucky Lord Alexander is an honorable knight who takes his vows seriously, else you would be fit for naught...not even the convent."

"Oh," Jesse gasped. Outraged that she should bear the stigma of their adventure just because she was female.

Alex grabbed the priest up by the front of his robes. "You will not speak to her so," he growled, ignoring the man's garbled words of protest. "I have already told you of our betrothal. We acted with honor...both of us. You will apologize to my lady for the slur you cast on her."

Jesse was so stunned by Alex's ardent defense of her she barely heard the priest's mumbled retraction. Truly he is wonderful, she thought, glancing sidelong at Alex.

Sensing her regard, he turned his head. His fierce expression softened as swiftly as Lionel Carmichael's had when he'd looked at his Carina. Whatever lingering doubts Jesse had harbored about whether this proud, forceful man truly loved her vanished in that instant.

"Are you all right?" he murmured. "We will wait and seek out a more godly man if you wish."

Jesse swallowed, shook her head. "You make me very happy."

"So will I slay all your dragons," he replied knowingly, though she doubted he could truly understand how much his defense meant to one long used to fighting her own battles.

"You may begin," Jesse told the priest in her best lady-of-the-manor voice.

With Alex's chuckle still tickling her ears, Jesse knelt beside him. She barely heard the priest read the marriage rites, so busy was she making pledges of her own. Their private ceremony on the island had seemed more fantasy than reality. Now she viewed her situation more realistically.

She was wedding in a strange place to a man whose family had fought with hers for generations. From this day forward her life would be different. She viewed the future with some trepidation, and a twinge of guilt. But what Alex had said was true. Hugh loved her and would want her happy. She could not imagine being happy anywhere but with Alex. He had taught her to laugh and to love. Best of all, he had taught her to appreciate herself.

Unbearably moved, Jesse stole a peek at Alex's profile. Calm yet uncompromising in the flicker of candlelight that could not shadow the intelligence gleaming in his dark eyes. Life with him would not always be peaceful. Their tempers were too fiery. But at least their arguments were open and honest, not treacherous like Edmund's. Besides, once the air had been cleared by their shouting, there was the pleasure of making up.

"You may arise, my lady, and kiss your new lord and master," the priest intoned.

"'Twill be a cold day in hell before any man is *my* master," Jesse grumbled as Alex helped her to her feet.

The priest gasped, but Alex only hugged her to his side, laughing. "Come, give us a kiss and we'll be on our way."

Jesse artfully dodged his lips, half playing, half wanting to exert control. The low growl as he accepted her challenge sensitized her skin and made her insides tremble. Giggling, she tried an evasive maneuver, but he had the homing instincts of a bird returning to its nest.

She expected hot and hungry when his mouth finally captured hers, but his kiss was sweet and searching. A vow more compelling than those they had just exchanged, it gave her confidence. "I love you," he whispered when he raised his head.

"And I you. With all my heart," she murmured softly.

The priest muttered something about hot-blooded youth, but fell silent under Alex's hard stare. "Come," he murmured to Jesse. "I have a surprise waiting back at the inn."

"I may have a few surprises of my own for you," Jesse purred, slanting him a burning look as they exited the church.

Alex missed a step and it was she who steadied him. "You are courting trouble, wife," he said huskily.

"Nothing I can not handle," Jesse assured him, drunk on the heady sensation of wielding power over her rogue of a mate.

He groaned. "Careful. 'Tis been three nights since we've made love. Hot as I am for you, I fear we'd burn down the bed."

"I am counting on it." Her eyes lit with sensual promise.

Alex swallowed. "What of the wedding supper?"

"I do not care if I ever eat again, so long as I am naked in your arms within the next five minutes," she purred in his ear.

"Jesu, Jess, you'll be the death of me." Her feet barely touched the ground as he bore her along the narrow crooked streets. "Where did you learn such seductive wiles?"

"From you."

They reached the inn in record time. His hand trembled slightly on the small of her back as they mounted the stairs. His breathing was as rushed as though he had run miles. "You are a witch, you know that?" he muttered as he opened their chamber door. The dulcet sounds of a lute cascaded through the opening.

Jesse spun about and looked...and looked. "Sweet Mary," she whispered. Green silk covered the walls, shimmering in the reflected firelight so the room resembled the inside of a jewel. The bed was gone and the floor strewn with large pillows. Before the hearth a cloth had been spread over a low table set with silver and candles. Flowers spilled from large urns in the corners—roses whose sweet scent reminded her of the ones that had grown wild on the island. "It looks like something from your tales of the East," she murmured, desire banked by wonder at his romantic gesture.

"I was hoping you would think so."

His quiet satisfaction was lost on Jesse, who was busy investigating—touching the silk, smelling the flowers, flitting here and there like an inquisitive bee. She lifted the covers on the silver dishes to see what he had ordered for supper, smiled her approval, then stopped short when she saw the bed tucked behind the door, its thick drapery replaced by sheer linen.

"It . . . it is beautiful." She was awed. All this, for her.

"*You* are beautiful." Alex basked in the glow of her green eyes, the warmth of her smile. She ducked her head shyly where only moments ago her boldness had more than matched his. He watched her closely, thinking how softly feminine she was beneath her tough exterior and how good it was to see her free and easy again. Passion would wait until he had indulged her other senses. He told the maid to serve the meal.

They ate sitting on fat cushions, the fare the most exotic a small town had to offer, because food was important to her. Roasted beef, chicken in mustard sauce, tiny green peas and savory, almond-studded rice. When their plates were full, their cups brimming with red Bordeaux wine, Alex dismissed the maid and the old man who played the lute.

"To us, my love," Alex proposed, lifting his cup. "May we have a long and fruitful marriage."

Fruitful. As in children? Jesse's fragile happiness blew away like a puff of dust. "Oh, Alex. I do not know—"

"Jess." He reached across the table and lifted her chin, his thumb whisking over her lower lip. "You must know that more than pleasure can come from the times we make love."

She wrenched her chin free, trembling. "I thought you were different," she cried. "I thought you understood, but scarcely are we wed and you are greedy for heirs."

Alex clenched his fist against the rising tide of hurt and anger. Neither would help. "I am not greedy, I simply wanted—"

"I know what you want." Sweet Mary, she had not known it would hurt so to crush his hopes, his dreams. "What if I am barren like Edmund's wives? He's always said I was unwomanly—"

Alex laughed. He couldn't help it. 'Twas so ridiculous. Then seeing the tears in her eyes, hastened to make amends. "Not only are you woman enough to bear children, I think you already are."

"Are what?"

"With child. With *my* child." The last rang with possessiveness as his eyes caressed her stomach.

Jesse looked down for confirmation, found her belly flat. "B-but I do not feel any different," she muttered, dazed.

"You've been sick these last mornings, and, too, we were a month on the island and not once did you have your monthly courses," he reasoned, ignoring her flush of embarrassment. "I would say my seed struck fertile ground."

"Must you put things so crudely and arrogantly."

"Arrogant?" Alex groaned. Pregnant, Jesse was going to be even harder to handle. 'Twas going to be a long eight months. "Aye, I do feel arrogant. And proud. And happy. I can not wait to hold our babe. This proof of our love that nestles beneath your heart. How would you have me say that? Tell me and I'll amend my speech."

Jesse burst into tears. "Oh, Alex, I am sorry." She made no protest when he rounded the table and gathered her onto his lap. "Edmund has driven five women to early graves trying to get his cursed heir," she sobbed into his chest.

Alex started. "Edmund killed them?"

"My mother died in childbed. Two women killed themselves. One took a fall down the tower stairs, and the last died of a choking sickness." She shuddered, leaning back so she could see him. "Rumor has it the last two were helped from this life."

"Jesu." *That monster,* Alex thought, tightening his grip on her. He had been right to see she did not return to Edmund's house. "Small wonder the subject disgusts you."

"I am not disgusted to be having our babe." Sniffing, Jesse dried her tears on the trailing sleeve of her surcoat, then looked down and ran her fingertips over her flat stomach. "It hardly seems possible.'' The smile she gave him when she raised her head was shy and sweet. "Do you really hope 'tis a girl?''

"Aye.'' He kissed her very gently, hiding his own fears. Her mother had died in childbed. "I love you, Jess.''

"And I you.'' The black velvet that fit his broad shoulders and chest like a second skin was a perfect foil for his tanned skin and dark eyes. He looked unbearably handsome, smiling at her in the firelight that brought out the gold in his hair. Behind him the silken wall hanging billowed in the air coming in through the open window, reminding her of all he had done to make this evening special—and seductive. Make no mistake, even wedded he was still a rogue. But he was her rogue, and she'd scratch out the eyes of any woman who tried to take him.

"Will you drink to us now, Jess?'' he asked cautiously.

Mayhap even rogues were sometimes insecure. Spirits buoyed by the thought, Jesse grinned at her twice-wed husband. "Aye. To our love and to our babe,'' she said easily, earnestly.

Alex released a pent-up breath. "I adore you.'' His laughter and the lingering kiss he gave her set the tone for the evening. Lighthearted, with an undercurrent of passion carefully banked, yet waiting for the right moment to flare into full flame.

They fed each other bits of food, enjoying things they'd been denied on the island. Alex growled with mock ferocity as he tore a hunk from the buttered piece of bread she offered him, then slowly licked the butter from her fingers. Moaning, Jesse shifted around to recline beside him on the cushions. His lips were slick and warm on hers, his tongue provocative.

"Oh, Alex,'' she murmured when he raised his head. "Thank you for this. It has been like a dream, a fantasy.''

"We have only just begun.'' He kissed her again, starving for the feel of her mouth melting under his, then demolished the braids the maid had pinned in wheels above Jesse's ears. Once freed, he streaked his hands through her hair, fanning it out from her face so it streamed across the pillows. The red lights in her hair leaped and sizzled, burning him even as her passion did. "Your hair is like fire.'' It crackled and twined about his fingers. "Bright and wild and beautiful as you are.''

"It's a lot of bother. I should cut it short.''

"Nay." He raised a fistful to his lips. "I forbid it."

Now it was her eyes that crackled. "You are not my master."

"Your slave, then." Grinning, he wrapped her hair around his neck. "Bound by silken chains. Do not cut it lest you cast me adrift." His lids lowered, eyes glittering with sensual promise. "I'd be lost without you."

Jesse shivered, caught in the threads he wove about her: compassion, laughter, passion. Invisible to the eye, more permanent than the tendrils looped about his throat. Irresistible, because she had craved them all her life. "Oh, Alex . . . I love you so. Never leave me."

Alex smiled. She loved and trusted him. "Fear not, we Sommervilles are possessive where our women are concerned."

"Good." With a daring that was second nature to her after a month together, Jesse took his mouth in a blistering kiss.

Alex groaned, meeting her sensual forays as he had her sword strokes when they had played at sword fighting on the island. His control slipped further and . . . nay. He pulled up short of madness, fought for sanity and found it by releasing her mouth and seeking the sleek column of her throat, bathing it in wet kisses. "Aye, show me everything you feel," he crooned as Jesse's head fell back to give him greater access. He wanted this night to last, wanted to brand her so thoroughly she'd not look him in the eye without remembering and burning anew.

Jesse was spinning through an unrelenting storm with Alex her only anchor, and he was driving her wild. She had not realized such sweet torture existed, had not known she could want so badly her whole body was aflame with need. His hands and mouth were everywhere, touching, stroking, tantalizing. Suddenly even the thin barrier of silk between them was too much, and she began to tear at her clothes.

"Easy, love. Let me." He divested her of her things with consummate skill and devastating leisure, stoking the flames higher as he dragged the sensuous silk across her sensitive nipples, her trembling thighs. When she thought she could stand it no longer he stretched out beside her, drawing her heated flesh against his, smooth to rough, soft to hard.

His callused fingers caressed her from hip to shoulder, lingering at her breasts to shape and mold, to gently pluck the sensitized nipples. She moved restlessly, searching for more, finding it and arching up off the pillow with a glad cry as his mouth replaced his fingers, suckling gently, as though he knew how tender her breasts had been of late.

"Let me show you what you mean to me," Alex rasped, his mouth sliding down her slick skin to reverently kiss her belly. The silky flesh trembled at his touch, and he fancied it was their babe approving its sire's salute. "Dear God. I never thought to love anyone as I do you," he whispered. Then he was moving lower, kissing and nipping and nuzzling, lingering in those spots that wrung sharp cries from her, her fingers buried in his hair as though she'd never let him go.

Desire raced and vaulted, shooting through her like a star across the heavens. She strained toward the pleasure he promised her without words, finding it as his subtle caress drew her over the final crest. She cried out, frightened of the dark, but Alex was there, wrapping her in light, surging into her, filling the aching emptiness deep inside.

Alex wanted to pause, to savor her incredible beauty, her pleasure-dazed eyes, dark and hot as green smoke, her flushed cheeks, but the wildness in him demanded fulfillment. He struggled to temper it, trembling with the force of the battle he waged between the urge to protect and the need to conquer.

"Come to me, my love," Jesse whispered. Her hands were greedy as she reached for him, her hips needy as they shifted forward and stole his reason. She met him on equal terms, matching his hunger with her own brand of aggression, and they taught each other that it mattered not who led or followed, as long as they sailed together, higher and faster.

With Jesse's cry of completion ringing in his ears and his heart, Alex felt himself shoot over the edge with her.

Moments later, hours later, Alex's mind rejoined his sated body. He and Jesse lay tangled together in a welter of arms, legs and wrinkled silk. Content though he would be to lie here the rest of his natural days, they had a ship to catch come morning.

She barely stirred when he sorted them out and carried her to the bed. The coolness of the sheets drew a murmur of protest, then she curled into his side like a contented cat. If only they could always remain as close as they were now, Alex thought. But he doubted even God could keep Hugh's death a secret for the span of their lifetimes.

Chapter Fifteen

"**W**ake up, my love. We are here." Alex touched Jesse's cheek as Wilton's drawbridge settled to earth.

Jesse hastily rubbed the sleep from her eyes and sat up as their horses thudded over the wooden bridge. She rode in Alex's arms at his insistence. Typically she had balked. He had calmly pointed out that she'd been seasick and needed the rest.

"Feeling better?" he asked neutrally.

"Aye." Grudgingly. "But uneasy about my welcome."

"Gaby will be happy to see you," he assured her.

She sighed. "What of Ruarke? And your parents?"

"They will accept you as my wife," he replied, but the tensing of his body made her queasy stomach churn anew.

The thunderous roar that went up as they rode into the inner bailey made speech impossible. Peering out from the shelter of his arms, Jesse saw the road through the grassy field was lined with Wilton's people screaming Alex's name and waving wildly.

Jesse caught the sheen in Alex's eyes and knew how glad he was to be home. She wished she had a place and people that meant as much to her. "Alex, where will we live?"

Again he tensed. "I have not given it much thought." His gaze avoided hers, and she sensed he withheld something.

"Alex!" The great bellow that rose above the chaos could only belong to Ruarke. Jesse spotted the big warrior vaulting down the steps of the castle, followed by a horde of people. "Make way for my brother," the lord roared, waving away the swirling crowd and yapping hounds.

Eager hands reached to steady Alex's horse. He swung a leg over the saddle and slid to the ground with Jesse in his arms. "Brace yourself," he muttered seconds before the human tidal wave engulfed them. They were patted and hugged and kissed until Jesse could scarcely breathe, but she enjoyed it.

"Jesselynn?" inquired a familiar voice, and Jesse found herself face-to-face with a much-surprised Gaby.

"Good day, Lady Gabrielle," Jesse said hesitantly.

Gaby looked from Jesse to Alex and back. Her violet eyes rounded with questions, and her fine brows all but disappeared beneath the edge of the linen caul that covered her black braids. "Now this is a story I'd give much to hear. Do put her down, Alex and we'll go inside."

"Aye. This calls for a celebration!" Ruarke boomed, sending the servants flying with a dozen orders at once.

Alex began walking toward the castle, still carrying Jesse in his arms. "She has been ill and is in need of sleep."

"I just woke up," Jesse insisted, wriggling futilely.

Gaby watched with interest as the pair argued the matter— Jesse prickly, Alex protective. Well she knew this scene, for had not she and Ruarke played it hundreds of times in their short married life? Alexander Sommerville and Jesselynn Harcourt were in love. Astounding. Disastrous.

"I will see to the lady myself," Gabrielle said, shooing her women from the best guest chamber as soon as they had deposited the warm wash water and refreshments she had ordered. Closing the door behind them, Gaby watched her guest for a moment, Alex's parting words burning in her brain. "Say naught of Hugh, I beg you," he had whispered anxiously for her ears alone.

Hollow eyed and covered with travel dust, Jesselynn moved from the open window to the empty hearth, her shoulders slumped, her too-large cape trailing dejectedly after her. Obviously she was as nervous as Alex.

"I am surprised you are still with Alex," Gaby said evenly.

Jesse stopped at a chair set before the hearth. Her hands clenched the back of it for support, her mouth dry. "S-so am I." Damn, why was this difficult? Gaby had been her friend.

Still was, apparently, because instead of pressing for answers, the petite beauty set about making Jesse comfortable.

Moments later, relieved of her cloak and the film of dust that had coated her hands and face, Jesse settled into one of the chairs while Gaby took the other and set the tray of refreshments on a low table between them. The sweet wine cut through the tightness in Jesse's throat; the bread, cheese and cold fowl eased the gnawing in her belly.

Replete, Jesse sighed and leaned back in the chair; yet conscious of Gaby's gaze she could not relax completely. "No doubt you are wondering how I come to be with Alex."

"Given the fact that when you lived here the two of you went at each other like a pair of fighting cocks, I am curious." She frowned suddenly. "Do not tell me Alex has done something foolish, like kidnap you in hopes of ending this feud he hates."

"Even more foolish, I fear." Jesse toyed with the stem of her cup. "He has wed me."

A clap of thunder could not have made Gaby start quicker. "I—I am . . . shocked," she managed at length.

"No more so than I." Her heart ached and she longed for Alex's support. If Gaby, with whom she had once been close, looked so disapproving, what would Alex's parents think?

Jesse had met Lord Geoffrey and Lady Catherine on only a few occasions. They were handsome people who spent a great deal of time at court. The lord was a big man like his sons, a scholarly man. Soft, Edmund had called Lord Geoffrey, always carrying on about improving the lot of the people. But then, Edmund cared for no one but himself. Most of all, though, Jesse remembered how devoted the Sommervilles were to one another. They would not be pleased with their middle son's choice of wife.

"I...we had always assumed Alex was wedded to the sea," Gaby said slowly. "And after what happened with Emilie—"

"Alex said she was dead." But no more than that, she suddenly realized.

"Aye, she is. Which proves there is some justice in this world. She took too much of a potion meant to rid her of the child she carried—a child she claimed was not Gareth's, but Alex's."

"Sweet Mary!" Jesse moaned. "Surely Alex did not—"

"Nay. Even if Alex had loved her—which he did not—he has too much honor to lie with his brother's wife. But her words caused Gareth to go after Alex with a sword and cut his neck."

"Oh, my God." Jesse felt sick, remembering how she'd taunted Alex, asked him if he'd gotten the scar on his throat from a jealous husband. Small wonder he had looked so stricken. She vowed to beg his forgiveness the moment she saw him. Shivering, she took a sip of wine to settle her stomach. "'Tis a wonder either of them could bring himself to trust a woman again."

"Apparently it was just a matter of finding the right women." Gaby's cheek dimpled. "Gareth wed Arianna de Clerc a month ago. They are expecting a babe in the spring."

Jesse mentally counted back on her fingers and decided that all the Sommerville men must have potent seed.

"And here are you and Alex married . . . when?"

Jesse sighed and reluctantly began the tale of how she had fallen into Alex's hands in the first place. Under Gaby's sympathetic gaze and gently put questions, she found it easier going than she had feared. News of the babe, Jesse kept to herself. 'Twas early days, yet, and it might not prove true.

"You love him very much, do you not?" Gaby asked when the story had unfolded.

"Aye." Pleating her skirt with trembling fingers, she sighed raggedly. How could she put a lifetime of insecurities into words? "I fear I'll not be able to hold him," she mumbled. "I do not have the court polish of the ladies he has known. I hate wearing gowns and stitching tapestries. And . . . and I am only one woman. He is used to many."

Gaby shook her head. "A Sommerville will not stray from the woman he loves, and I am certain from the way Alex looks at you that he loves you. Only see how he treats you."

"He treats me very well," Jesse said defensively. Then she noticed the twinkle in Gaby's eyes and smiled. "He does have a terrible temper and is *the most arrogant*—"

"Not *the* most," Gaby interjected, laughing. "Surely Ruarke has equal claim to that title. Though I suspect that when Ari arrives she will say Gareth is the most arrogant." She reached over to give Jesse's hand a companionable squeeze. "Years ago, when Ruarke and I were first married and locking horns with each other—as two strong-willed people are apt to do—Lady Catherine said 'twas not easy being wed to a Sommerville, but 'twas worth the effort involved in taming the proud beast. Truly there is no man more loving. Have you not found there are compensations?"

Jesse choked on her wine.

"Just so." Gaby's cheeks were as pink as Jesse's felt. "I had wondered how love would affect Alex. I see he is every bit as overpossessive and protective as Ruarke and Gareth."

"Possessive, aye," Jesse allowed. "But he usually encourages me to do things on my own—thank God, because I could not stand to be stifled. Since he has decided I am with child, though—"

"You are! Oh, Jesse. This is wonderful news."

As the warmth of Gaby's delight seeped through her, Jesse stopped cursing her hasty tongue. "It's only been a month, and I do not know how he can be so certain," she cautioned.

"It must be another Sommerville trait. Gareth claimed to know Ari was pregnant at two weeks." She chuckled. "Be prepared to be smothered. Ruarke would have wrapped me in fleece and kept me in a trunk for the entire nine months had I let him."

Jesse grimaced. "I foresee eight months of battling." She linked her fingers with Gaby's. "I have missed you."

"And I have oft wondered how you fared after you left us. I was wrong to send you away that day you regained your memory. I know we did so because we feared the Sommervilles might use you as a hostage against your father, but that was not their intent, as I learned *after* I had helped you escape."

"Were they terribly angry?"

Gaby's eyes darkened at the memory. "Furious."

"Ruarke did not beat you?" Jesse asked anxiously.

"Nay, but my lack of trust hurt him, which was worse than taking a beating myself."

Jesse nodded, understanding. "Trust is important to Alex, too." She finished her wine, then set the cup aside. "Alex calls me prickly and a vixen, which is no more than the truth. I do not want to bite at every turn, but trusting *anyone* is hard for me," she said, her gaze focused on her painful past.

"I remember you were not pleased when you realized you were a Harcourt," Gaby said sympathetically.

"Nay. I *hate* what Edmund has made of our name," she said vehemently. "Ever since I returned home I have worked in secret to better the lives of our villeins, and now I can not continue with that." She sighed, nibbling on her lip. "So much has happened so quickly that my whole world has turned upside down. I have fallen in love with a man I once thought I despised, wed into the family mine has feuded with for centuries. I do not care if I never see Edmund again, but I love Hugh. Deep down I worry this will end in a confrontation between Alex and Hugh." Raising troubled eyes to Gaby, she said, "I would die if aught happened to either of them."

Gaby quivered as though a great pain speared her, and her hand trembled in Jesse's.

Jesse tightened her grip. "Gaby. What is it?"

"'Tis naught. I but thought on your words. Truly you have had a most harrowing five weeks. And now there is a babe coming." Gaby stood abruptly. "Alex will have my head if you do not get a rest before dinner." She began to bustle about the room, turning down the bed and fluffing the pillows. "Come. Slip out of those clothes and crawl between the sheets."

Jesse hesitated. "Are you sure nothing is wrong?"

"Only that you look tired and thin. Alex said you were sick on the voyage. I want you healthy and rested when the rest of the family descends on us."

Now it was Jesse's turn to tremble. "When?"

"I am not certain when to expect Geoffrey and Catherine, since I do not know where Alex's messenger may find them, but Gareth and Ari should arrive from Ransford by dinnertime."

Jesse lay down as Gaby had bid, but her nerves were strung as tight as a condemned man who faces the gallows come sunset.

"Married?" Ruarke thundered, and the windows in his study shook. "Married to that Harcourt b—"

"Careful," Alex said sharply. "'Tis my wife you slander."

Ruarke grumbled something under his breath. Though two years Alex's junior, he stood a few inches taller and was more heavily muscled from years of wielding his heavy sword. His dark blond hair was cut close, the better to fit under his helmet. "Why?"

"Because I love her."

They glared at each other from identical sable eyes. "Her cursed sire has been plotting to get Papa's title for years, and you went and married the wench."

"She is not a wench." Alex smiled ruefully, thinking of a similar conversation he'd had with Gareth a month past, only then the shoe had been on the other foot.

Ruarke slammed his cup down. "Stop grinning. 'Tis likely she seduced you as part of some scheme to infiltrate our camp."

Nay. He'd done the seducing, and the lying, Alex thought on a pang of guilt—and apprehension. "She was drowning when I pulled her out of the water in Tyneham Bay," Alex said tightly.

"See. She was there!" Ruarke crowed.

"She had followed her brother to see what he was about."

"So she said," Ruarke sneered.

Alex gritted his teeth. Ruarke saw everything through a warrior's eyes. A person was either good or evil, but if he could convince his brother that Jesse was good, she could have no more staunch champion, besides himself. "Ruarke—"

"She'll murder you in your bed."

Alex raked both hands into his hair to keep from strangling his brother. "She saved my life twice this past month."

Ruarke grunted, some of his rage fading.

'Twas the opening Alex had been hoping for. He told the tale from beginning to end without pausing to let Ruarke get a word in edgewise. "Once I've seen Gareth and spoken to Mama and Papa I plan to hire a ship and go after Parlan."

"No need for that. I hear his ship sits in London harbor."

Alex started. "Who told you?"

"Bevan MacLean when he came to report you drowned."

"*The Star* survived. Dear God, I did not dare hope." Alex sat down, his legs suddenly weak with relief.

"Bevan was consumed with guilt at not being able to find you two. Because of the dark and the fire 'twas some time before he realized you were even missing. He went back to look, then limped home to tell us what had happened."

"Bevan and the crew are safe," Alex murmured. He wallowed in the joy for a moment, then polished off his wine. "I've still a score or two to settle with Parlan. He twice tried to have me killed and he kidnapped Jess."

Ruarke crossed his arms over his massive chest and rocked back on his heels. "That may be easier than you think. Edmund has found out about Hugh's death."

Alex's hackles rose. "What does Edmund intend to do?"

"He swore vengeance, of course, then scurried back to Harte Court with Parlan at his side." Ruarke's disgust was plain.

"Was aught said about Jess?"

"They assumed she died at sea with you, since that was the word Bevan put out when he landed."

Alex smiled for the first time in hours. "Let us see if we can't keep news of my survival quiet for a while."

"Aye." Ruarke brightened suddenly. "With Hugh gone, she is Edmund's heir—unless by some miracle his latest wife produces a son." He clapped Alex on the back, nearly sending his brother sprawling. "I am sorry I doubted you, Alex. 'Twas a stroke of genius tying her to our family."

"Is that why you wed her?" Gaby asked. She stood in the doorway holding a tray, a dark scowl on her face.

Alex went to her immediately. "Nay, it was not like that—"

"You always were one to spot the main chance and seize it," Ruarke crowed. "Harcourt's only living child. I can not wait to tell Gareth and Papa what you've done." Without giving Alex a chance to speak, Ruarke added, "This good news has given me a monstrous appetite. What have you brought us to eat?"

"Hold a moment," Alex said anxiously. "Ruarke. Gaby. Sit down, both of you." They looked surprised at Alex's grim tone and even grimmer expression, but they sat at once. Alex stood before them, one arm resting on the mantelpiece, his brooding gaze on the cold, empty hearth. Without Jesse, this is what his life would be like. Bleak. Cheerless. Dark. "I do not want Jess to find out that Hugh is dead, not until I have figured out a way to break it to her gently and with a minimum of . . . fuss."

"Why?" Gaby went stiff with disapproval. "Do you not think she deserves to know her beloved brother is dead?"

A muscle jumped in Alex's cheek. "Hearing that Hugh is dead will upset her, and she has already been through so much. I'd wait until she is stronger." Until I am sure she will not bolt.

Gaby relented fractionally. "She *is* tired and much too thin, but how do you suggest we keep the news from her now that it is common knowledge? 'Twill be on the lips of every servant and every traveler who stops here." She paused before adding, "I suppose I could drug her food for a few—"

"Nay!" both brothers exclaimed at once.

"I have told you before that you can not go about drugging people to suit yourself," Ruarke chastised.

"I'd do nothing to harm the child she is carrying," Alex said in a quiet voice that had more impact than Ruarke's roar. "'Twould seem my babe will be born a few weeks after Gareth's."

"Jesse has already let the news slip," Gaby said. "I am happy for you both."

Ruarke's gaze narrowed speculatively. "This is the end of the Harcourts, then. Your wife is Edmund's heir, and her child will be heir to her property. If aught should happen to Jess—"

"Do not say it," Alex warned. God, his blood ran cold at the thought of something happening to his Jesse.

"I but stated the obvious. If something should happen—"

"Ruarke Sommerville! Stop saying that at once," Gaby demanded, hands on hips. "Nothing is going to happen to Jesse."

The door burst open and Gareth catapulted in at a dead run. "Alex! I could scarce believe it when Ruarke's message came." There were tears in his eyes as he launched himself at Alex. Alex's own eyes were far from dry as they hugged and thumped each other's backs. Unable to contain himself, Ruarke joined in.

The disagreement of a few moments ago forgotten, Gaby stood back and watched, smiling mistily.

"I sometimes forget how sentimental Sommervilles can be," Arianna said, hurrying into the room, her blond hair wind-blown, her cheeks pink below faintly moist blue eyes.

Gaby did not expect Ari to cry. The woman was terminally cheerful. "'Tis one of their more endearing qualities." She gave her sprite of a sister-by-marriage a quick hug. "I did not expect you for an hour or so."

"We would have been here earlier only Gareth slowed his pace so the babe and I would not be jostled."

"Thoughtful as ever," Gaby said.

"Stiflingly so," Ari agreed, beaming at her husband.

"Alex!" Gareth exclaimed again, disentangling himself to stare into his brother's face. "When I thought I would never see you again, never be able to redeem myself for having hurt you—"

"He hid out in the forest for a week," Ari supplied. "And carried on so he drove away all the game."

"Aye." Grinning, Gareth went to Ari and wrapped one arm around her. She barely reached his breastbone. "Ari had to—"

"Lure him from the wood with my womanly wiles." She batted her lashes outrageously and the pair dissolved into laughter.

"Do not mind Ari," Gareth said, seeing Alex's stunned expression. "She has a talent for reading my thoughts."

Alex blinked. What had happened to the morose man he had parted company with at Tyneham? Now he seemed as lighthearted as a lad. Judging from his own recent experience, Alex decided it must be Arianna. Alex had spoken with her briefly before leaving Tyneham and worried that she would hurt his brother as Emilie had. Obviously he had been wrong. Gareth had never looked merrier. So would he be, were it not for Hugh's death hanging over him like a black cloud. He wanted peace for Jesse and himself almost as badly as an end to the feud. Or mayhap more.

"I wish you would put this business with Emilie behind you." Alex clasped his shoulder. "I know now that I would have felt exactly as you did if I thought my wife had been unfaithful.''

"Your what?" Gareth exclaimed. His mouth dropped open as Alex's tale unfolded, but he took the news more calmly than Ruarke had. "Jesselynn is now Harcourt's heir," he said at once.

"If you say my child will inherit the Harcourt estates does something happen to Jess, I will strangle you," Alex growled.

"Easy." Ruarke held up a placating hand. "We have enemies aplenty to fight as it is."

Alex nodded, his fists slowly unclenching. "Aye. I am determined to make Parlan pay for kidnapping Jess."

"On that, we all agree," Ruarke grumbled. "And Edmund Harcourt with him. I've set men in a ring around Harte Court with orders to let me know the moment anything or anyone stirs."

"How many men have we?" Alex wanted to know.

"Several thousand," Ruarke replied. "Not as many as Edmund can field, but ours are battle trained, loyal and eager to fight. He has a few hundred mercenaries that will put up stiff resistance, but the bulk of his army is made up of his poor, underfed vassals. They will answer his call to arms because they must, but their hearts won't be in the fight."

"What fight?" asked a voice Alex knew all too well. His heart sank as he turned and saw her standing uneasily in the doorway.

His first thought was to send her upstairs until he'd told Gareth and Arianna to keep Hugh's death secret. But she looked so forlorn he went to her instead. Dropping a kiss on her lips, he murmured, "I had hoped you would sleep longer."

"I—I could not rest easy."

Alex grazed her cheek with a finger. "I'll go up with you."

"If you do, neither of us will rest." The wry smile took the sting from her words.

Alex fought a surge of desire. It had been four days since their wedding, four long nights spent holding her and nothing more out of concern for her illness. "You still look tired." And so fragile it tore at him. "I will sit in a chair while you—"

"Nay, I am too . . . too nervous about my reception here."

Alex leaned closer. "Gaby did not welcome you?"

"As an old friend. 'Twas as though we'd not been separated these two years, as though I wasn't a Harcourt."

"You are a Sommerville now," Alex reminded her.

"Aye." That made Jesse more uneasy somehow.

Ah, hell. Better to get this over with. Nerves sizzling with apprehension, Alex turned to face his family. One look at Gareth and he knew Ruarke had told him to say nothing of Hugh's death. Relieved, confident, Alex drew Jesse forward to meet Arianna.

"Hello," the little blonde mumbled, staring at her riding boots. 'Twas so unlike the bubbling girl he had met moments ago that Alex looked to Gareth for an explanation.

His brother's guarded expression caused Alex to belatedly remember what Gareth had said about Ari when they were at Tyneham. "My Ari could not tell a lie to save her soul."

Doomed, Alex thought. How long were his brother and wife staying? And how could he keep Arianna from speaking to Jesse?

"Make haste, you dolts," Parlan shouted at the soldiers manning Harte Court's main gate. The moment the drawbridge clattered to earth, he kicked his weary mount across it, tearing down the road through the grassy outer bailey, scattering other travelers from his path with no regard for their rank or safety.

He smiled for the first time since the night Alex had taken Jesselynn. The dream he had mourned when he had limped into London and learned that Jesselynn had perished at sea, was alive and well again, because she was.

Parlan abandoned his winded horse in the bailey and bounded up the castle steps. "Where is Lord Edmund?" he asked a maid.

The woman cried out, one hand raised defensively. She'd have been pretty had not her face been bruised, her eye swollen shut. Dimly he recalled having bedded her, then beaten her in a fit of temper because she was alive and Jesselynn was dead.

"I've not time for you," he snapped. "Where is Lord Edmund?"

"In the vault, but he'll not want ye disturbin' him."

"He'll welcome me and call me son." And heir. Edmund allowed no one but himself inside the vault beneath the castle, but Parlan thought his news would gain him entry.

"Go away," Edmund replied to Parlan's knock.

"I have news," Parlan shouted. Pressing his ear to the thick iron-banded door, he heard the grating sounds of not one, but three, bars being lifted. His palms itched greedily.

Edmund opened the door a crack and scowled warily at Parlan. "This had best be good."

"It is." Over Edmund's shoulder, Parlan saw the glitter of gold, and his heart raced. "Jesselynn is alive."

"What? How? Where is she?"

Parlan darted a glance at the corridor behind him. "I do not wish to keep you standing here with the door open. . . ."

Edmund let him in. While Parlan told him what the Harcourt scout lurking near Wilton had learned, he glanced about the room. Gold coins were stacked neatly beside Edmund's tally sticks and a ledger. What intrigued Parlan most were the chests stacked along one wall. Were they full of gold? Or gems?

"Who said she'd wed a Sommerville?" Edmund roared.

"'Twas rumored in Wilton village."

"I'll kill her!"

"And deprive yourself of your only blood heir?" Parlan asked softly. "Why not petition to have the marriage annulled?"

Edmund's gaze narrowed. "Aye. But I'd punish her, too."

Recalling his cousin's reaction to him, Parlan said, "Oh, I think Jesselynn will view marriage to me as a punishment."

"Will she?" That made Edmund smile. "Then I'll hurry to London and get the church working on an annulment."

Chapter Sixteen

Jesse greeted the ringing of the dinner bell that evening with a heartfelt groan. She had been staring at the trees swaying in the torch-lit garden below their chamber window for an eternity, wishing they were back on the island. "I am really not very hungry," she mumbled.

"Then we will not go down."

"But—" Jesse whirled, frowning at Alex, who sat by the fire writing messages to Bevan and his other captains. It amazed her that so active a man could find pleasure putting words to parchment. He had taught her the rudiments of reading, but she did not enjoy it as much as he did. "Gaby and her women have been working all afternoon on a special dinner for you."

Alex set the quill aside and leaned back, stretching his legs beneath the writing table as he gauged her mood. Only slightly less nervous than he was and not hiding it as well. He wanted to be with his family, but his stomach knotted every time he thought about what he stood to lose when she learned Hugh was dead. "A special dinner for us." When she shrugged his amendment aside, he asked, "Is it the babe?"

I am scared to death. "The sickness comes only in the morn. Gaby says it is a sign the babe is well planted." His cocky grin made her long to recall the words, but she could not suppress a shiver of desire as he rose and strolled toward her. He had already dressed for dinner in a blue surcoat that turned his skin to burnished gold. The plain wool gown she'd insisted on wearing seemed dull by comparison.

Poor little fox, Alex thought. So much more at home in the wild. "Come here, love." He opened his arms, and she came into them with a ragged sigh that tore at his heart. "My family will not bite you," he murmured, stroking her back.

"Your brothers hate me because I am a Harcourt."

"You are a Sommerville now," he reminded her, wishing she did not start each time he said that. "Nay, they are merely wary, concerned for my welfare."

So am I. Thinking of Edmund's rage when he learned of her marriage, she hugged Alex tighter. "Where will we live?"

"Where would you like to live?"

Jesse leaned back so she could see his face, tender above her in the candlelight. "In the woods."

"Just any woods?" he asked, eyes twinkling. "Or the woods near Harte Court with your merry band of thieving peasants?"

If there had been any reproof in him she would have pulled away, angry and hurt, but his support never wavered. She relaxed into the strength of his embrace and smiled. "Well—"

"I would need my luxuries . . . my soft bed and hot meals."

"A hut could be every bit as comfortable as your cabin."

"That is what I am afraid of," he teased, kissing the tip of her nose. "Now that I am getting on in years and happily married, I've a yearning to settle into a comfortable home with big beds, warm fires and a cook at least as good as Gaby's."

Breath bated, Jesse rested her hand over the steady thud of his heart. "You will not be going back to sea?"

So, the Sommervilles were not her only worry. "There is salt water in my veins, so 'tis likely I'll take short voyages from time to time, but a ship is no place to raise a child or pen up a wife who likes to ride." His arms tightened around her, his eyes darker, more intent. "I will never leave you, Jess."

She leaned her forehead into his chest, lids burning with tears. Until this moment she had not admitted to herself how much the idea of his going had frightened her. "I love you."

"Not half as much as I love you." He set to work demolishing the braids the maid had coiled above Jesse's ears.

"Alex. You are mussing my hair." She struggled; he held her close with one hand, the other scattered pins in all directions.

"What does it matter if we are staying here?"

Jesse went still. "We can not disappoint Gaby."

"Mmm." Alex slid his fingers along her scalp, massaging the dents from the pins. The delicious sense of freedom had her moaning softly, then she realized her hair was not the only thing he had liberated. Somehow he had undone her laces and his hands were inside her clothes, caressing, tantalizing.

"Alex! What are you doing?" she gasped, trying to wiggle away despite the warmth spilling through her.

"If you have to ask—" He swept her up, laid her tenderly on the bed and followed her down. "I am doing something wrong."

"Is this your answer to everything?" she chided, her arms twining about his neck to take the sting from her words.

The soft smile he gave her as he gently smoothed the hair back from her face and kissed her temples was so at odds with the hunger blazing in his eyes that it stole her breath away. "'Tis not the only answer, but surely the most pleasurable. Here there are no worries, no fears, nothing but the two of us." His voice dropped to a sensual purr. "Like it was on the island."

"Aye. Take me there, Alex. Love me," she whispered, low and urgent. Home, the thought spilled through her like warm wine as he gathered her against the hard planes of his body, her lips parting for the hot, avid thrust of his kiss. This was where she belonged. Arching into him, she told him so without words, unleashing all the love, all the longing pent up inside her.

"Jess," he gasped, shuddering. "I want to go slowly, but you are turning me inside out." He peeled her clothes away, his mouth racing to explore every inch his hands uncovered. There was a fierceness to his kisses that sent her pulse soaring, an urgency to his lovemaking as though he sought to bind her to him forever. Yet when they merged, it was she who cried in triumph as his groan of surrender filled her with a sense of power.

Rising about him with a throaty laugh, she brought new meaning to the tender skills he had shown her, her hair flowing over them like a curtain of fire. His name trembled on her lips as ecstasy rippled through her and drove him over the edge.

"You will be the death of me, woman," he growled, cuddling her close in the sweet aftermath. She was a constant challenge, yet brought him a deep contentment he had never thought to find.

"Mmm." Pleased with herself and with him, she stretched sensuously and nipped at his slick shoulder. "Just so I am the only one killing you."

Alex groaned. "I have not the interest or the strength to ever look at another," he said carefully, knowing she was only half teasing. "And you are too damned handy with a knife for a man's peace of mind."

"Will we stay here forever?"

He chuckled, nuzzling her silky hair. "Here in bed?" He felt her smile into his shoulder.

"Nay. Though 'tis a good idea for we never quarrel in bed. I meant here at Wilton."

"We can stay for a time, if you like."

She toyed with his chest hair while she thought that over, then, "Nay. I think we should have a place of our own."

A place where she fit in. 'Twas a familiar theme. He only wished he had a solution to her questions . . . the spoken and unspoken ones. In truth, he was as anxious as she to be off by themselves where the chances of her learning about Hugh would be reduced. "I'd stay here until I speak with my parents." The shudder that stiffened her made his stomach clench tighter.

"They will not be pleased," Jesse said unhappily.

Alex moved so he could see her face, wanting to take the sting away. "If they forgave Gareth, who is the heir, wedding a burgher, they will not mind about us," he said, even knowing things would be . . . delicate at first. "Besides, we Sommervilles have always wed for love. When they see how much we love each other, they will readily give their blessing." He hoped.

She smiled faintly. "I am a little frightened."

He was very frightened—of losing her. Lying to her was tearing him apart, but . . . would she still lie so trustingly in his arms when she knew Hugh was dead? He shuddered.

"Alex?" She gently touched his cheek. "What is it?"

A brisk knock at the door sent Jesse scrambling to get under the blanket. "Go away," Alex called, reaching for his hose.

Ruarke stuck his head around the door, grinning. "The guest of honor was missing, and Gaby sent me to delicately inquire—"

"No one would send you to do anything delicate," Alex said.

"Nay, but the two of you once interrupted Gaby and me." His massive shoulders shrugged. "So it seemed a fair turnabout."

"Out," Alex shouted, advancing on the door and slamming it.

"Shall I tell Gaby you two are on your way down?" Ruarke demanded from the other side of the thick oak planks.

Alex looked to Jesse, peering out from the blankets like a ruffled red owl, her eyes dark and wary. "Aye," she said with a conviction that surprised them both.

"You do not have to," Alex assured her, coming to the bed.

"I know," Jesse said softly. And somehow that made all the difference in the world.

Jesse stopped in the doorway of the great hall, blinking against the blaze of hundreds of candles. The castle folk packed the trestle tables like herring in a barrel, all laughing and chattering. As though sensing her presence, they suddenly stopped talking and turned to gawk.

Jesse fought the urge to bolt. "I should have braided my hair," she muttered. "Everyone knows what delayed us."

'Twas her sparkling eyes and flushed cheeks that gave them away, not her flowing hair, but wise in the ways of women, Alex mentioned neither. "I could announce that it is my preference."

"Nay, I—"

"Alex! Jesse!" Ruarke bellowed from the dais at the far end of the room. "Hurry. I am like to starve waiting on you."

"Nay, you could live on your fat for a week," Alex replied, grateful to have the tension broken. Everyone laughed. There was not a bit of fat on Ruarke's warrior body, but his appetite was legendary. "See, all will be well," he murmured, guiding

Jesse between the tables and solicitously seating her on the dais.

Jesse nodded, eyes sweeping the room as he slipped into the chair beside hers. Though the hall was not as lavishly furnished as Harte Court's, the costly tapestries on the wall, the richly carved furniture, the fine clothes worn by the Sommervilles and their knights grated on her.

"Wine, love?" Alex held out the beautiful silver cup the page had filled for them to share.

A small sip was all Jesse could get past the lump in her throat. 'Twas partly apprehension, partly the feeling of being smothered by the richness. "I can not be comfortable here."

"Look around you," Alex urged. "Tell me what you see." When she started to decry the splendor of the room, he said, "Nay, not the material things, though I know for a fact they were not bought at the expense of Wilton's villeins. Listen to the laughter on the air, look at the smiling faces of the people."

"Aye," Jesse said as her gaze roamed the tables. She could feel the happiness . . . the love. Though the surroundings had been rougher, Alex's sailors had likewise been content. "Wherever we live, I would have it be like this."

"On that we agree," Alex said from the heart.

"What are you two whispering about?" Gareth asked.

Jesse turned, her smile faltering as she became aware who sat at her other side. She did not know Gareth even as well as she did Ruarke. And it was he Hugh had sought to frame with those cursed coins.

"I hope you had a good rest." Gareth's deep voice, so much like Alex's, immediately soothed her nerves. "When the meal is over, Ari and I—"

"Would take you to the stables to see the foal we helped deliver," the blonde put in, leaning around her big husband.

"While we were in Scotland, Alex and I helped birth a litter of pups," Jesse said, turning to him for confirmation. 'Twas quick in coming, his smile as warm as the hand lingering on her back as she described the incident. "Alex knew just what to do."

"I am not surprised, he has the healing touch," Gareth said, and Jesse knew it could be her cure he spoke about, too.

"Aye, he does," she said softly. *And I love him so.* Sweet Mary, this seemed like a dream, sitting here in this bright room with so many happy people, accepted by them though she wore no jewels and the simplest clothes Gaby had to lend. Mayhap it really was going to be all right, she cautiously mused.

The meal progressed so pleasantly after that that Jesse wondered why she had been nervous. Alex's earlier comment about Gaby's cook was borne out by the delicious smells that filled the hall as the first course was carried in. Still, old habits died hard, and Alex caught her looking around to see what the common folk at the tables were being served.

"You will find naught amiss on that score, either," he assured her. "Now eat, you have—"

"A babe to nourish. I know."

Hearing the tiny bit of pique in her tone, he smiled and tucked a lock of hair behind her ear. "Of course we want a healthy babe, but firstly 'tis you I worry about."

"Alex. If you do not stop mooning over her she'll get naught to eat," Gaby scolded.

"I fear she will have to get used to eating—and doing a great many other things—while I stare," Alex replied, his dark gaze steadily holding Jesse's, soft as velvet.

"Oh, Alex," Jesse said a trifle breathlessly.

"Look at me like that and I will have you back upstairs so fast your head will spin," he whispered as he plucked her eating knife from her waist and held it out to her.

"You will just have to get used to it," she shot back. Taking the knife, she turned her attention to the food he had been distractedly selecting from the passing platters and placing on her end of the manchet bread trencher they shared. Choice morsels of roasted game, chicken in wine and sauced pork. "Delicious," she murmured, the first bite melting in her mouth.

"Aye." Alex speared something with his own blade, though he scarcely tasted it, so wrapped up in her happiness the rest of the room seemed to fade away.

"I never thought to see him like this," Gareth ventured over their bent heads.

"'Tis good to know he is no more immune to love than we are," Ruarke observed around a mouthful of chicken.

"I think it is wonderful." Gaby beamed at the pair.

"I hope Mama and Papa will think so, too," Ruarke added ominously, his voice so quiet for once only she heard.

When Gaby had remodeled Wilton, she had had the old so-lar divided into a bedchamber for Ruarke and herself and a small sitting room where the family could gather in private. 'Twas there she directed the servants to serve the fruit, nuts and sweet wines after dinner.

"Ari designed this tapestry for us," Gaby confided, show-ing Jesse the sketch and the unfinished piece stretched on a frame in a corner of the room.

Though she had no talent for it herself, Jesse recognized the skill that had gone into drawing the scene of life at Wilton. The castle formed a backdrop for Ruarke astride his war-horse, with Gaby and the girls in a field of flowers in the fore. Young Cat chased a butterfly, but baby Philippa lying on a pillow drew Jesse's eye. "'Tis beautiful." Her finger touched the threads of the babe's hair. What would theirs look like?

"I am green with envy that she can create such wondrous things," Gaby said wistfully.

"You made a beautiful home at Wilton where there was only a pile of rubble when you came here," Jesse pointed out.

"Running my castle is practical, something I just do. 'Tis not the same as having a gift like Ari's."

"It is wondrous to someone like me who has no idea how to manage a castle," Ari put in, taking Gaby's hand.

"Does Lady Catherine run Ransford, then?" Jesse asked.

"Nay, Mama is much in London with Papa," the girl an-swered. The ease with which she spoke of the earl and count-ess after being wed to Gareth for such a short time surprised Jesse, made her a bit envious. She found herself hoping they would accept her as readily as Ruarke and Gareth seemed to have done.

"Why are you not running the castle?" Jesse blurted out.

Rather than taking offense, Ari smiled ruefully. "I have no housewifely skills and no interest in learning them."

Scandalous. "Gareth does not object?"

Ari laughed softly. "I fear he spoils me."

As Alex did her. Would he understand that she did not wish to spend her day running their home? Jesse glanced at the three tall men standing by the hearth. Ruarke listened to something Gareth was saying, but Alex watched her closely. She smiled to let him know she was fine, but he still looked worried.

"Ari is a goldsmith," Gaby said, giggling when Jesse spun back around, eyes wide.

"They let you join the guild?" Jesse asked, astonished.

"Regrettably not." Ari's smile dimmed briefly. "But it no longer bothers me, because I am thinking of starting my own guild just for women," she confided in a whisper.

Jesse joined her laughter to Gaby's, feeling more at home with these two women by the minute. "I . . . I can scarcely believe everyone has made me welcome," she blurted out.

"I liked you even before you were Alex's wife," Gaby replied, linking arms with her. "For Ruarke and Gareth, the fact that their brother loves you is enough."

"I have always wished for a sister, now I have two." Ari took Jesse's other arm and they strolled back toward the fire where the poker was heating for spiced wine.

Jesse sighed. The only thing she lacked was the courage to ask for Alex's help in contacting her brother. Mayhap tomorrow.

Conscious of little but his tautly held breath and the smile on her face, Alex watched Jesse approach. So far Ari had not spilled his secret, yet he'd not rest easy until he and Jesse were alone in their room again. And tomorrow it would be the same, and the day after that. Jesu, he wished—

Wine hissed and boiled as Ruarke plunged the hot poker into the pitcher, filling the room with the fragrance of the cloves and cinnamon Gaby had added from her spice chest.

"Toast," Gareth called as he handed around the cups of steaming liquid. "To our wives." They all drank deep, then he added, "Ari does more than smith. She and Papa are working to give land to some of our villeins."

"Most of them need more than just the land. They must be taught how to think for themselves," Jesse put in. Her hand tightened around the cup as they frowned. She had never spoken out before, except in anger, would have fallen silent were it not for the warm reassurance of Alex's arm around her waist

and the conviction she at last had something to contribute.
"For the past two years, I have been helping the peasants steal
grain from Edmund." Their gasps of surprise gave her courage. "I told them to eat some and save the rest to plant. Alas,
they ate it all. 'Twas plain they needed guidance. We were
building a hut in the woods to lock up the planting seed
when—"

"I think you have experience Ari and Papa lack," Alex
smoothly interjected, though the hair at his nape prickled. She
had been about to mention leaving home to follow Parlan and
her brother. Hugh's name would have shattered this pleasant
gathering like a blast of black powder, mayhap taking their
transient happiness with it. "They have not worked side by side
with the villeins as you have."

"You could help us," Ari said quickly, eyes alight.

Alex groaned, thinking he had made things worse, but Jesse
seized on Ari's suggestion that they work together like a hungry fish snapping up a fly. She needed this, he thought. Resigned, he offered his services, too, for the chance to keep the
conversation away from dangerous ground. "Tomorrow will
be soon enough to begin," he added, seeing Jesse's drooping
lashes. When she reluctantly agreed, he herded her toward the
door.

Hurried footsteps in the corridor were the only warning he
had before the door swung open and his parents rushed in.

"Alex!" His father grabbed him around the neck; his
mother latched onto his right side, both of them laughing and
crying at the same time. Gareth and Ruarke scrambled to join
in.

Jesse found herself shoved aside, but before she could feel
left out, Gaby put an arm around her waist. "I was seldom
hugged as a child, either, and I found that Sommervilles took
some getting used to."

"But they mean well." Ari took Jesse's hand and squeezed.

"I like the hugging," Jesse said, moved to tears by the sight
of Alex and his parents. But it seemed strange to be happy here
with people she'd been reared to hate. She studied them a moment. The earl had more silver in his golden hair than when
last she'd seen him, but he was still as vigorous as his sons.
Worry lines bracketed Lady Catherine's fine features and her

amethyst eyes ran with tears, but she looked younger than her years. "I fear they won't want me here," she whispered.

Lady Catherine looked up just then, disengaged herself from her son's side and walked toward Jesse. "Jesselynn," she murmured, stopping a few feet away. "Bevan told us how you came to be with Alex. I am glad you were rescued."

"Alex saved my life." Jesse was confused by the deep sorrow in the countess's eyes at what should be a happy time.

"Mama," Alex exclaimed, reaching for Jesse's hand. "Jess and I were on our way to bed."

"To bed?" His mother looked first bewildered, then affronted. "There will be none of that," she said stiffly.

"Alex?" his father questioned, backing up his wife.

"'Tis all right, I assure you," Alex said hastily, a shade desperately, dividing a pleading glance between them. *Just let me get her away from here before someone says something.* "I will escort her to, er, her chamber and return to explain."

He was ashamed of her. Jesse tried to free her hand, found herself pulled from Gaby's sisterly embrace to his fierce one. "Let me go. I can find my own way."

"Jess," he growled, panic warring with the urge to protect. What he really wanted to toss her over his shoulder and run. It was all unraveling around him, he could feel it as surely as he felt the angry pulse hammering in her wrists.

"At least let me offer her my sympathy before you drag her away," Catherine said, frowning at her son.

"Sympathy?" Jesse looked first to Alex. For once he avoided her gaze, but he shuddered as though a blade had pierced him.

"For your brother," the lady said kindly.

Alex groaned, his arms tightening around her.

"Hugh was arrested?" Jesse told herself she should have been expecting it, still tears filled her eyes so the white faces of the Sommervilles swam before her. Nay, what she saw in their expressions went beyond imprisonment. "Alex?" she whispered, eyes wide with dawning horror. "Nay, it is not true. He can not be . . ." Gray dots danced before her eyes, merging together in one swirling mass that sucked her down a long black tunnel.

* * *

"Jess. If you would listen to me," Alex said, his voice low and charged with emotion.

Jesse looked up at him from the bed where they had made love so joyously just hours ago. The joy lay like ashes in her mouth, the burned remains of their once-glorious love. "Is it true?"

Alex dropped his gaze from the pain in hers. Damn. He'd known this would be hard, but he'd not known it would hurt him so to see her suffer. And 'twas only the beginning. She did not yet know the worst. Jesu, what should he do? For once his facile mind offered no clever words, no quick way to turn defeat into victory. There would be no easy way out of this—for either of them. "Jess." He reached out to comfort her, stifling a groan of despair when she shied away as though his touch revolted her. "Aye, Hugh is . . . dead," he said as gently as he knew how.

"Dead?" she echoed dumbly, shivering. Cold. So cold. She wrapped her arms around her waist and huddled into herself as she'd done so many times before to escape cruelty and betrayal, but she found no comfort. "W-when?" she managed.

"A month ago. I am sorry, Jess. As God is my witness, though your brother was my enemy, I am sorrier than you can know that he is gone . . . because you loved him."

She heard his words, but not the ache behind them, sunk too deep in her own personal hell. Hugh was dead. She accepted it, mayhap had been expecting it from the moment she'd heard him plotting with Parlan. Dimly she recalled the times she had mentioned Hugh to Alex and his now violent-seeming reaction. "You knew before we left Edinburgh."

"Aye, but—"

"You lied to me," she whispered hoarsely. "All those days on the island, you knew and said nothing.

"I did not want to upset you with something you could do nothing about," he said in the gentle voice she'd heard him use with Ruarke and Gaby's two small girls. How good he'd been with them, how surprised she'd been to see him playing with them, and how moved, thinking he'd make a good father. Far better than Edmund. Wrong. Alex was just like Edmund.

Cruel. Greedy. Her mind got that far before her belly revolted.

When she gagged, Alex grabbed the pot from under the bed and lifted her. But she refused to give in. The tremors that shook her as she struggled to conquer her sickness ripped him apart.

Jesse swallowed one last time and lay back, shoving Alex's arm aside. "I do not need you," she grated out, savoring this one small victory in the wasted landscape of her life.

"Jess. I love you so much this is killing me, too. I did not tell you about Hugh's death because I thought—"

"You could use my ignorance to your advantage."

"What do you mean?" He cocked his head, the intensity of his gaze palpable. Searching for a weakness he might exploit, she thought in disgust, the crack in her heart widening.

"You are a very canny man. Shrewd enough to seize the advantage, charming enough to make me enjoy being used."

"Jess! You can not really believe that."

The pain in his voice tore at her. She fought to stay strong, to stay clear of the web of his charm. "You would do anything to end the feud. I think you planned to use me from the start. Worse," she went on, her voice dripping with the venom roiling inside her, "you'd make your own child a pawn in this."

Grief ravaged his handsome features. "How can you think that?" He took her hand, gripped it almost painfully when she tried to snatch it back. "You know I love you and our babe."

"I know only what you have told me. Lies."

"Lies!" he growled. "I never lied to you. My only sin was withholding the news of Hugh's imprisonment and death." When she did not answer, merely stared at him, her loathing and mistrust plain, he raked a hand through his hair. "How can you look at me like that? After what we have been through, the hardships, the triumphs, the loving . . . how can you forget how it was between us? Jesu, but we near burned down the night."

Jesse trembled in memory of their shared passion, but held her ground. "I grant you are a skilled lover," she said coldly.

"Skilled?" he shouted, incredulous. "I love you."

"You saw me as a means to end the feud."

"This can not be happening." He groaned and squeezed his eyes shut. "I love you," he hoarsely repeated.

He did not deny her accusation about the feud. "You used me, and for that I hate you." Jesse turned her face away from him.

Alex shuddered. They'd come full circle, from hate to love to hate again. How could something as beautiful as their love have ended in such ugliness? "I'll find a way to convince you."

Jesse felt his shudder echo inside her, or was it the crumbling of her heart. She'd find a way to leave him.

"Married! I can not believe you married her," Geoffrey exclaimed, turning from sullenly contemplating the rain that beat against the solar window.

Alex sighed, drained from the encounter with Jesse, whom he had left sleeping behind a locked door with a maid to watch over her, yet knowing his parents deserved an explanation. He gave them the only one he had. "I love her."

"Jesu, Alex," the earl grumbled, shoving a hand through his hair. "Of all the women you have known, why a Harcourt?"

"Her name is Sommerville now," Alex reminded him, "and she is nothing like them, as you'll see when you come to know her."

"Nay, she is not greedy. She has been helping the peasants defy her father," Gareth interjected, leaning against one side of the mantel while Ruarke held up the other.

Geoffrey silenced his eldest son with a glare that included Gaby and Ari in their high-back wooden chairs and Alex who stood with his legs spread, his arms folded across his chest.

"Gently, Geoff," Catherine murmured, coming up to softly cup his rigid chin in her palm. The shadows beneath his wife's pale violet eyes betrayed the strain of believing Alex lost to them this past month.

Her warning reminded him that their middle son could easily erupt and storm off if cornered. Geoffrey sighed. Jesu, he was glad Alex was alive, but this marriage... "What do you think Edmund Harcourt will do when he learns Jesselynn is alive and wed to you?" he asked, striving for calm.

Alex stiffened defensively. "He has abused her all her life. Made it plain he does not value her."

"At worst, he will start a war."

"He'll find us ready," Ruarke growled. "I've sent men to watch Harte Court."

"And no doubt he has set spies on us," Geoffrey said wearily. "He will likely petition the Church for an annulment."

"Nay!" Alex drew himself up to face the challenge, fists clenched, eyes defiant. "I will not give her up."

"I never thought to agree with a Harcourt, but I have no wish to mingle my blood with theirs. An annulment would—"

"Too late," Alex snapped. "She carries my child."

"Jesse is Edmund's heir," Gareth slipped in. "When he dies, Alex would control his wife's—" His words died at Alex's growl.

"Hmm." Geoffrey rubbed his stubbled chin, black eyes narrowed in thought. "You may have a point, Gareth."

"This is my wife and child we are discussing," Alex ground out.

"I will grant she is comely, but—"

"I love her," Alex wailed with such anguish that Geoffrey exchanged worried glances with his wife.

"Oh, Alex." Catherine went to her son immediately and embraced him. Reaching up to brush the hair from his forehead as she used to when he was young. "If you truly love her—"

"I do, Mama. I will never love anyone else."

"We will welcome her, then," Catherine said at once. "And warmly, won't we, Geoff?"

The earl sighed, knowing he was beaten. The Sommerville men loved fiercely. Did he turn his back on the girl, he'd lose his son in the process. "Aye."

Alex heaved a sigh of relief. Another hurdle crossed. Now all he needed was time to win back Jesse's trust and love.

"Lord Alex!" The maid who'd been with Jesse streaked into the room. "Lady Jesselynn tied me up and ran off."

"We'll search the grounds," Ruarke bellowed.

"She told me she used to sneak out of Harte Court disguised as a page." Alex ran up to their chamber to search for clues.

The stench of burning hair met him at the door. Even before he looked in the hearth, he knew what he'd find. Still it wounded him deeply to see the smoldering ashes that had once been the crowning glory she'd promised not to cut and realize she hated him enough to revert back to her old, vengeful ways.

Feeling as though a huge chunk of himself had been hacked off with her hair, he found a strand that had escaped the flames. Straightening, he rubbed it between his fingers before tucking it inside his tunic. 'Twas all he had of her beside his memories, but he would get her back, that he vowed.

"Where would she go?" his father asked as Alex ran back through the hall on his way to the stables.

"To the woods between London and Harte Court."

Sweet Mary but she felt wretched. Wet, cold and tired.

Jesse wiped the rain from her eyes with her sleeve and squinted at the road ahead through the darkness. She longed to rest, but dared not linger for fear of bandits. Besides, London could not be more than an hour distant. Thoughts of hot food, dry clothes and a warm bed at a convent she knew of near the city had her setting her heels to her horse's mud-caked sides.

Alex had surely discovered her missing by now. What had been his first reaction? Rage at discovering his prize gone? His face swam before her, bleak and haunted as he had tried to convince her he loved her. Nay! Memory twisted like a knife inside her.

Jesse heard a shout behind her and turned to see a band of men bearing down on her. Alex? Her heart soared like a bird, then fell as quickly as if it had been shot. She kicked at her weary mount, but that moment's hesitation had cost her the race. A horse edged ahead of hers, forcing her to turn and stop.

"I will not go back, Alex," Jesse warned, bracing herself to battle his charm as she turned her head. "Edmund!" she whispered, surprise and fear chasing every other thought from her head.

"Jesselynn." He sat still, his breath billowing like dragon smoke in the misty air, his eyes burning hell bright from within the metal eye sockets of his helm. Around them milled twenty of his mercenaries. "I could scare believe it when my men brought word you'd forsaken Wilton's hospitality," he growled.

Sweet Mary, aid me! It took every bit of courage she possessed to keep her spine straight, her voice steady as she bravely said, "I am on my way to London."

"Aye. And thence to Harte Court," Edmund allowed.

She raised her chin higher. "I wish to remain in London."

Edmund spat into the mud. "Your wishes never concerned me before. They are less than nothing now that you've allied yourself with a Sommerville. You disrupted my plans."

Good. She hoped to disrupt them permanently.

"Riders approach, m'lord," growled one of Edmund's men.

Jesse looked over her shoulder as a troop of men materialized from the fog, riding hard, brandishing swords over their heads and screaming at the top of their voices.

"Curse the luck. Sommervilles," Edmund spat. He made a grab for her mount's reins.

Jesse eluded him but had no time to flee before the Sommervilles thundered up to face Edmund's force across the muddy road. Heavily armed, they outnumbered Edmund's men two to one. In the fore sat Alex, hard eyed, grim faced, flanked by his equally stern brothers.

"What do you want?" Edmund demanded angrily.

"My wife." Alex wore no armor and his head was bare, rain-slicked hair plastered to his skull. His sword lay across his thighs where she had ridden on the trip from the coast to Wilton. It seemed it had happened in another lifetime, to another woman. A happy woman. Jesse did not expect to ever be happy again. "Jess," he ground out. "Are you all right?"

"Aye." Her lower lip quivered with something that could not be longing. Nay, she had torn him from her heart, yet tears clouded her vision so it seemed the two of them were alone.

"You cut your hair."

"Aye." She heard the suffering behind his words. She'd meant for him to suffer, but the victory seemed hollow somehow.

"Come home with me, Jess." Such anguish. Such pain. His. Hers. But the sting of betrayal was too fresh, ran too deep, mingling with old fears. Hands braced against the pommel for support, she shook her head.

"Jess. For the love of God. At least give me a chance."

She raised her eyes, recoiled from the torment in his, but held firm. "There can be no chance for us as long as I am a Harcourt and you a Sommerville."

"Cut the bastard down," Edmund hissed.

Jesse gaped in stunned horror as an arrow whizzed past her. Whipping her head to follow its path, she saw Alex's attention was fixed on her. "Alex! Beware!" she screamed.

Alex started, but it was Gareth who saved him, leaning to shove Alex from the saddle at the exact moment the singing length of wood and metal shot toward Alex's heart.

Gareth's grunt of pain as the arrow entered his shoulder shattered the frozen tableau.

Edmund caught Jesse from behind, dragged her from her mount to his lap. "Back," he bellowed as Alex leaped up from the mud and started toward them, sword raised. "Come any closer and I'll prick her." His knife flirted with the curve of her throat.

Alex stopped. "You'd not kill your own daughter."

"Not unless you force me to," Edmund snarled. "She's as good as dead to me as your wife."

Jesse's last glimpse of Alex as Edmund carried her off was of him standing in the rain, sword up, head high, defiance in every line of his proud body.

Small good it would do either one of them.

Chapter Seventeen

'The weather has cleared,'' Gareth said, turning from the window. ''We should start back for Wilton.'' 'Twas noon of the fourth day since their encounter with Edmund Harcourt.

Ruarke tore the last bit of flesh from a chicken bone and tossed it to the hound that sat at his feet. Gaby would have scolded him for such slovenliness, but she was not here. Jesu, but he wished she was. Between Gareth's wound and Alex's madness, Ruarke did not know which way to turn.

Ruarke had worried when Alex had gotten drunk and stayed that way for a week after Emilie tossed him aside for Gareth. But this was worse, far worse. Alex had gone wild when Ruarke had refused to let him go after Jesse. Telling Alex he'd be committing suicide had not deterred him one bit. ''Better a quick death than dying a little each day knowing those bastards have her,'' Alex had raged, fighting the four men who held him.

''Does it seem warm in here to you?'' Gareth asked, drawing Ruarke's attention back to the present and another worry.

Eyeing his brother's flushed face, Ruarke swore. ''Jesu, but I wish Gaby were here. I think that wound of yours is festered.''

Gareth flexed his bandaged shoulder and winced. ''The king's physician tended it himself. Mayhap I should have let him bleed me as he wanted to.''

''I am going to send for her,'' Ruarke decided. ''She can treat your wound and try to pound some sense into Alex's hard head.''

"If you are going to talk about me, at least do it behind my back so I can't hear," complained a hard voice from the bed.

Ruarke sighed and turned to the figure sprawled there, bound hand and foot to the four bedposts with heavy rope. "Alex, if you would only be reasonable," he said wearily.

"Going after my wife is reasonable," Alex spat, tugging the ropes. "I'd like to see anyone try to keep you from Gaby was she in trouble. In fact, I remember you riding to her rescue—by yourself—and ending up in Bryan Carmichael's dungeon."

"We are only thinking of you," Gareth put in, coming to lean against one of the bedposts, his face drawn, slick with sweat.

"Jesu, Gareth, you look worse than I feel," Alex grumbled. "You should not have lunged in front of that arrow."

"'Twas worth it," Gareth muttered, rubbing his shoulder. "I saved your life and at last eased my conscience."

Alex nodded. If not for Gareth taking that arrow, he would be of no use to Jesse. That Gareth now felt absolved of guilt was the other good thing to come of this sorry mess. "If you want to do me another favor, you'll cut these ropes so I can—"

"Nay!" both brothers shouted together.

Alex swore at them, and went on swearing until Ruarke put his hands over his ears. "I am going to send for Gaby—"

"Saints above! What has happened to Alex?" Gaby demanded, advancing on them like a whirlwind, travel dust still clinging to her boots and cloak.

"Gaby. You should not be here," Ruarke exclaimed, going to her at once. "I gave strict orders for you to remain—"

"You just said you were sending for me." She elbowed past the two gawking men and stared at Alex. "What in the world?"

"They're holding me prisoner here," he said forlornly.

"Ruarke?" Gaby demanded, rounding on her husband.

"He's gone mad." Quickly Ruarke told the tale, ending with the reason they had Alex tied to the bed.

"Surely you see that I have to go after Jess," Alex growled

"What I see is that Gareth's wound needs immediate attention." She led Gareth to a chair, then went below for hot water and her medicine chest.

Alex sighed and closed his eyes. Furious as he was at his brothers, he'd been worried about Gareth. It would be unbearable to lose him just when they had made peace between them.

"I should beat her more often," Ruarke grumbled.

"You do not beat her any more than I do...Arianna!" Gareth started at the sight of his wife standing in the doorway. "By all that's holy! What—"

"Oh, Gareth." She was kneeling beside him in an instant, touching his face, his shoulder, eyes dark with fear. "I just knew something was wrong. I told Gaby that we needed to come. I...I felt you reaching out to me, calling for help."

"Why are you all standing about?" Gaby snapped, busting in with a flock of servants hurrying in her wake. "Get Gareth's tunic off." She cracked out orders with a military precision that chased away Alex's fears for Gareth.

He watched from the bed, reminded of how Jesse had taken charge of turning their island caves into a home. She had surprised even herself by enjoying the tasks, he thought. Especially herself. When it came time to set up their household, he knew she'd do a wonderful job. He only hoped they'd get the chance to try. Jesu, he was worried about her.

Every time he thought about what Edmund and Parlan might be doing to his Jesse, he went a little mad. So he tried not to think about that. Instead, he concentrated on how he'd rescue her. He had all the details planned, all he needed was to get out from under Ruarke's damned sharp eye.

Alex saw the glimmer of a chance when Gaby finished cleaning and treating Gareth's wound. After sending Ari off to put Gareth to bed in one of the other chambers, she approached the bed.

"Ruarke. Surely you do not intend to keep Alex tied up here forever." She looked at her husband with large, pleading eyes.

"He'll run off and do something foolish is he not watched," Ruarke grumbled, giving Alex a knowing look.

Alex snorted. "Stop acting so damned superior. Gaby
rescue would be your first priority were our situations r
versed."

Ruarke had the grace to flush but not to give in. "Har
Court is nigh impregnable, built to withstand a lengthy sieg
There isn't an army large enough in all England to take it."

Alex had not been thinking about attack, but subterfug
Gaby played right into his hands.

"Alex is smart enough to know that," she assured Ruark
"Mayhap the king could help Alex get Jesse back. She is h
wife, after all. Now, why don't you untie Alex and the two
you can begin thinking of ways to get Jesse free."

"He'll run the moment our backs are turned," Ruarke sai
with the insight of a man who'd do the same thing himself.

Alex bit back a smile of triumph, keeping his face bland
a glowering Ruarke reluctantly untied him. For hours, Ale
played the part of a docile man who'd seen the error of h
ways. He visited the garderobe and returned. He drank win
ate the meal Gaby pressed on him. He even talked of possib
plans to free Jesse, knowing none of them were the one he ha
worked out in his head. The only one with a chance of su
ceeding.

All the while, he thought of Jesse inside Harte Court, an
seethed and chafed and waited for his chance. The momer
Ruarke's back was turned, he bolted, taking no one with hin
He would not risk the life of even one of his brothers in th
desperate scheme. This was something he must do alone.

Alone. Dear God, had she ever felt so alone?

Jesse slowly paced the confines of the small room lodge
high in the oldest of Harte Court's four towers. She had bee
here a week and was heartily sick of the place. 'Twas wors
even than the days she had spent locked in Alex's cabin aboar
The Star. Then, at least, she had the prospect of sparring wit
him to keep her mind alert and her senses sizzling.

Now she had nothing, nothing but bleak memories of be
trayal and too much time to think. During the day, she ruth
lessly kept thoughts of Alex at bay, but he haunted her nigh
so she slept poorly and dreamed when she did.

They were vivid, sensual dreams from which she awoke sweaty, aroused and disappointed to discover 'twas the twisted blankets wrapped around her, not Alex's strong arms. Then she would remember why he was not with her and the tears would come, hot, bitter tears. She cried for Hugh, she cried for her unborn child, but she never cried for herself. She had been stupid to believe in a man like him. Now she must pay the consequences.

Jesse pressed her hands to her mouth to keep back the sobs that filled her throat. Sweet Mary. She must not dwell on this or she would go mad. She braced her hand against the stonework of the arrow slit and dragged in cool night air. Had it not been for the babe, she might have fashioned a rope from the sheets and risked the five-story drop to the courtyard below.

The growing darkness outside fed her fears, and she hurried to light a brace of candles. Their illumination chased the shadows into the corners, revealing a mean cell with a bed, chair and table. In the hearth a tiny fire struggled to stay alive. Edmund used to lock his wives in here when they displeased him. Two of them had died within these damp stone walls. Would she be the tower's next victim?

Better that than Parlan's wife.

Jesse shivered, wrapping both arms around her for support.

After leaving Alex on the road, Edmund had ridden hard for Harte Court. He had turned on her the moment they'd gained the hall, slapping her face and calling her whore for wedding their enemy—son of the man responsible for Hugh's death. Learning that the Sommervilles had killed her brother had been worse than Edmund's blows or Parlan's lurking presence.

Even though Alex had not been present when Hugh had died, Jesse felt soiled by his touch, as though her brother's blood had somehow been on his hands when he had held her, made love to her. Even her memories of their sweet interlude on the island were tainted now. Deep in her own private hell, she had barely heard Edmund when he had announced his plans to have her marriage annulled and wed her to Parlan.

"I shall enjoy taming you once we are wed," Parlan ha murmured. The malicious intent in his eyes had turned h stomach. Far worse had been Edmund's laughter.

"Aye, she'll not be so high and mighty when she's be broken to the saddle by a *man*." And Edmund had made plain he did not mourn the loss of Hugh. "I am satisfied make Parlan my heir. The estates will still be controlled by m blood when they pass to the children you will bear Parlan."

A bubble of hysterical laughter had risen in Jesse's throa If Parlan wed her soon he might not realize that the child sl bore was Alexander Sommerville's. The irony of that ha buoyed her spirits, given her the courage to endure Parlan's h stares and Edmund's taunting ones. She had lost Alex, but sl still had his child.

Spine stiff, she had headed for the sanctuary of her roon but that had been denied her, along with the services of the o maid who had shown her compassion in the past. 'Tw. Blanche who brought her food and water to wash and em tied the slop bucket. Poor, broken Blanche.

The scraping sound as the guard outside lifted the bar fro the door heralded Blanche's arrival with the evening mea There was a limp to her step that had not been there at noo She kept her head averted, hiding her face behind tangle blond hair.

"What is wrong?" Jesse asked. "Did Edmund beat you?

"Aye," the girl mumbled. They were the first words she ha spoken all week, and Jesse took advantage of the opport nity.

"I was not certain he was here. Neither he nor Parlan hav come to gloat over my imprisonment."

"Parlan is busy hunting down the villeins who ran awa from one of the farms," Blanche muttered.

Jesse gasped, stomach clenching. Damn. 'Twas likely h men. And here she was unable to aid them . . . or herself.

"Edmund has forbidden Parlan to visit you because he'd b after you like a stallion at stud. He's to wait until you hav your monthly courses. Edmund wants to make certain you d not carry a Sommerville babe ere he lets Parlan breed one o you."

So much for her plans. Jesse splayed a hand over her belly. When Edmund discovered she carried Alex's child, he would either order her doused with herbs to abort it or have it killed at birth. Any ambivalence she had felt about bearing a Sommerville fled on a fierce wave of maternal protectiveness. She had to escape before anyone harmed her precious babe. But how? The door was guarded at all times, and she saw no one but Blanche.

Jesse eyed Blanche's bruises. Could the girl somehow help her? Damn, but she was as bad as Alex to even consider using Blanche. Yet Jesse's situation was desperate, her child's life at stake. Swallowing her distaste for the project, Jesse asked, "Does Edmund keep a close watch on you?"

"Aye," Blanche whispered through cracked lips. "I am not allowed past the bailey gates without his permission."

"God curse all men. If you help me find a way out of here, I will take you with me," Jesse said, and her conscience eased.

Blanche looked at Jesse as though she had offered her the moon, and Jesse winced. "He's expecting you to try and escape disguised as a page as you used to. His men have orders to strip and search anyone who tries to leave Harte Court."

"When we go, we shall stay clear of the gates," Jesse assured her. There was another way out of Harte Court that Jesse doubted Edmund even knew about. An ancient system of tunnels built by the first lord as a means of supply or escape in case of siege. Hugh and Jesse had stumbled upon the entrance many years ago while exploring the storerooms beneath the castle and kept the secret to themselves.

The bolt hole was located beneath a section of shelving in the room next to the vault where the Harcourts stored their portable wealth. Convenient for the departing lord who wanted to scoop up his treasure before dashing to freedom through the tunnels to the woods beyond. 'Twould be tricky getting out of her cell and across the open courtyard to the castle keep without being seen, but it seemed the only way.

"You must get me a sword," she told Blanche.

"Me?" Blanche squeaked. "Where?"

"They are kept in the armory, but your presence there would be questioned," Jesse said slowly. "There should be any number lying about in the great hall—especially at night when the men-at-arms sit around drinking and dicing. They'd be preoccupied and the dimness would cover the theft."

Blanche trembled so her teeth chattered. "H-how could I carry it all the way up here."

Jesse gritted *her* teeth. "You could conceal it under your clothes," she said, but she feared to push too hard. "Do not worry about it tonight. Only look about and see if there is one to be had when needed."

Blanche looked vastly relieved.

"Serve 'er the bloody supper an' be done wi' it," called the guard. "I can't eat me own meal till the door's closed."

Blanche scurried away. She was a frail vessel to house Jesse's hopes. Jesse recalled seeing serfs at Wilton who looked happier than Lady Blanche Harcourt. Of course, the Sommervilles were kind people, loving overlords.

Alex's face swam in the tears that blurred Jesse's vision. If only he had truly loved her.

A commotion at the far end of the great hall raised Edmund's head from the joint of mutton he had been devouring with noisy relish. Squinting against the candle smoke that hung on the humid summer air, he spotted Parlan advancing into the room with the commanding stride of the conqueror. "You had success?"

"Aye." Covered with dirt, stinking of horse and sweat, Parlan mounted the dais and threw himself into the chair at Edmund's left. Without acknowledging Blanche, the only other person at the head table, he demanded wine of the hovering page. "I overtook the wretched serfs yesterday, dragged them back to the farm and hanged them in the yard as a lesson—"

"How dare you dispose of my property?" Edmund roared.

Parlan blinked. "Why, to teach the rest of the folk that we do not tolerate runaways, of course."

"The lesson could have been made as well with a beating and a hamstringing so they'd not run again," Edmund grumbled. "Then *I* would not be out three men when there is a shortage of labor. You'll make no decisions regarding my people or property without express orders from me."

Parlan's whole body vibrated with the urge to strike his uncle down and take what had been promised him. But he was not yet wed to Jesselynn, and until then must stay his hand, no matter how it rankled. "Of course, Uncle Edmund," he said smoothly. "I am sorry if I erred."

Edmund grunted and soundly backhanded his page. The boy stumbled off the dais and scurried back to the kitchens. "See, *you,* too, remember who is lord here," Edmund growled, scowling at Parlan.

"Oh," Blanche said faintly. "I—I am going to be sick."

"Are you breeding?" Edmund demanded, turning on her.

"N-nay." Blanche flinched and colored.

"Worthless bitch," Edmund snapped. "Leave us, then." When she had quit the room, he snarled for the steward to bring more wine. "I received some interesting news from London."

"About the false coins?" Parlan asked warily. The subject had been dropped after Hugh's death, but when Edmund had approached the king about an annulment for Jesselynn, his majesty had hinted that the Sommervilles might have proof Parlan had been involved in the counterfeiting scheme.

"Nay. About the Sommervilles. Their woman—Lady Gabrielle and that upstart merchant Gareth wed—left London today."

"I did not know the women were in London."

"Neither did I. Someone will pay when I find out how they managed to leave Wilton without my knowledge."

"What of the Sommerville men?"

"There was a commotion at their house last night. My spies saw Geoffrey, Ruarke, and Gareth tear out of London town as though they chased someone, but there was no one else with them when they later returned. Of Alexander there's been no sign."

"Mayhap he is dead," Parlan said hopefully.

"Nay. There's been no rumor of a funeral." Edmund took a gulp of his wine and leaned forward, eyes glittering with excitement. "Something is afoot, though, for messengers come and go from their house like ants from a busy hill. 'Tis my guess they plan some sort of foray to free Jesselynn."

"Why would they do that?"

"Mayhap Alexander desires his wife back. Sommervilles are possessive bastards." Edmund smiled slyly. "'Tis a failing I intend to use to my advantage. I have sent out one hundred of my mercenaries and fifty men-at-arms to intercept the women."

Parlan's eyes widened. "You have?"

"Aye. Ruarke and Gareth would sell their souls to ransom their ladies. I have no interest in their souls, but I will let Geoffrey have the women back does he sign over his title to me."

"Brilliant," Parlan breathed. Imagine, he would one day be Earl of Winchester.

Jesse was still awake, pacing back and forth in an effort to work off some of her nervous energy, when she heard voices at her chamber door. One she recognized all to clearly, even through the thick wood. *Edmund.*

Her immediate reaction was to look around for something she might use as a weapon, but there was only the tray that held the crumbs left from her supper. Besides, bitter experience had taught her that physical resistance was useless against a man as large and strong as Edmund.

She moved to stand behind the chair, her hands gripping the back for support as the bar was lifted and the door swung open. Sweet Mary, grant me strength, she thought as he stepped inside.

"Ah, Jesselynn. Still up, I see," Edmund drawled with a hint of disappointment. It had been a favorite ploy of his to rouse her from sleep and harass her when her defenses were low.

"What is it you want?" she asked with feigned calm.

"I came to see how you fared." His scathing glance raked her from the short curls that framed her face to the tips of her slippers. "Blanche's clothes swim on a scrawny thing like ye."

Not scrawny for long, Jesse mused, smiling faintly. "I prefer my gowns loose," she replied, absently stroking the blue velvet surcoat that concealed her still-flat belly.

He frowned, irritated that she had not risen to the usual bait. "With yer hair cut you are even homelier than your cursed dam."

Jesse bristled, ready to lash back, but Edmund's smug expression stopped her. He wanted her to lose her temper and with it her perspective. Not this time. Fists clenched, she began to count silently. She knew the way to twenty, having heard it often enough from Alex. By the time she got there, her anger had cooled, and a new thought intruded. In her mind's eye, she saw Alex's dark eyes, hot with approval and desire as he undressed her in their warm pool. His love might have proved false, but his passion had burned beyond question. "I have it on good authority that I am beautiful."

Edmund gawked at her as though she had sprouted two heads. "So Alexander Sommerville said?" he sputtered, face flushing.

Jesse's smile widened. She was actually enjoying this. "He *is* rumored to be something of an authority on women."

"He's . . . he's a damned lecher. He'll . . . he'll bed anything in skirts, so you need not think you're so bloody special."

Special. Aye, Alex had made her feel special. For a week she had hated him for withholding news of Hugh's death and marrying her for profit, but just now, remembering the things he had taught her about herself gave her strength. She was not an ugly misfit, a weak woman. She was strong and brave and, for a wonderful, magical month, she had been cherished. 'Twas that she clung to as she raised her chin to counter Edmund. "But I am a special person," she said with quiet force. "You do not like me—because I remind you of my mother, whom you were forced to wed. But that is your problem."

"You'll not be so cocky when you're wed to Parlan."

Jesse shrugged. The thought of enduring Parlan's embraces after knowing heaven in Alex's made her belly cramp and her thighs press close together, but for the first time in her life she was able to hide her fear. Because she knew that having survived Alex's betrayal, she could survive anything. Nothing Parlan did could touch her inner self. "'Tis true I do not wish to wed Parlan, but I can deal with him."

"I thought you were afraid of him."

"Afraid? Of a mere man?" Dizzy drunk on her success thus far, Jesse forced a small chuckle and tried her hand at bravado. "Do tell him to mind his manners when he comes to my bed. If he thinks to play rough with me he'll not awaken come morn.''

Edmund seemed to shrink before her very eyes. In the harsh wash of candlelight his skin took on an ashen tone as his jowls sagged. Oh, happy moment, he looked a little sick at being robbed of one of his favorite amusements. ''Mayhap there is more of me in you than I thought,'' he muttered.

''Sweet Mary, I hope not!''

He frowned, his eyes shrewd and watchful. '''Tis a pity you were not born male instead of Hugh. You've more fire in one finger than he had in his whole body. I respect that.''

Once even such slim praise might have warmed her, but those days were long gone. The only place where she had truly belonged was in the arms of her enemy. Until he had betrayed her trust. Damn you, Alex. Damn you and your false love, she thought angrily. She had been right not to believe in love. What she had felt for Alex had been desire, nothing more. And his desire for her had been tainted with greed.

''You and Parlan will breed sons worthy of possessing the fortune I have amassed,'' Edmund continued.

Jesu, did men think of nothing but sons? Except Alex, of course, who said he wanted a daughter. Bah, likely he had lied about that, too. ''The Harcourts have not been lucky in the matter of heirs,'' she reminded Edmund, teeth clenched. ''Only one son in each generation has been born to carry the name. And Hugh is gone.''

''Parlan makes me a better heir.''

Was there ever a more unnatural parent? Jesse thought. Her lips twitched with loathing. ''I may well escape ere the marriage takes place,'' she warned with icy contempt.

She'd startled him, and it was a moment before he spoke. ''I would not put it past you to try, but I have brought two friends to share your chamber. Rest assured, I will not hesitate to turn them over to my men should you try anything.'' Stepping to the door, he pulled it open and shouted, ''Bring them up.''

Two men ducked through the doorway, each with a blanket-wrapped burden draped over his shoulder. As they slung their bundles onto the rumpled bed, Jesse schooled her features to betray no emotion, no matter what—

"Sweet Mary!" Jesse gasped as the men stepped back to reveal Gaby and Arianna. Trussed hand and foot, their fear-widened eyes gaped at her over filthy cloth gags.

Chapter Eighteen

*W*here the hell was Jesse?

Stomach tight with dread, Alex leaned against Harte Court's darkened kitchen building and considered his next move. It was nearly midnight of the second night since he'd sneaked away from his family. He had been inside Edmund's stronghold since dawn, still he had no idea where Jesse was.

Shuddering against the despair that swept him, he rubbed a weary hand over his grimy face. He was hungry, cold and bone weary, but he'd not rest until he had found Jesse. Searching an enclave as vast as Harte Court had proved to be slow, dangerous work, despite his disguise.

Jesu, where was she? His chin sank to his chest as he reviewed the places he had looked, the places he had yet to look. Asking questions was not possible. He had sidled up to a kitchen maid this morn and asked after Lady Jesselynn. The woman had gasped, crossed herself and fled. Alex had spent the next hour ducking into shadows every time he saw a knight or soldier.

Alex raised his head as a mounted troop rode into the courtyard. 'Twas late for a visit. But in his short time at Harte Court, he had seen all manner of goings-on.

The servants were little more than terrified sticks who scurried about their tasks with bleak faces and lowered eyes as though they feared to see too much. Who could blame them? The dungeons below the castle were filled with pathetic creatures who had run afoul of Harcourt. There, starving and torture seemed the order of things.

Locked in several of the chambers in the main castle were more noble prisoners, being held for ransom, Alex assumed. Their lot was likely better, for if they died, Edmund lost his profit. Though Alex had not coveted Edmund's estate, only sought to best him in order to free Jesse and end the feud, he began to think long and often about the changes he would make here when Edmund was gone. He itched to free all and sundry now, but was afraid to tip his hand until he had located Jesse.

Sighing, Alex raked a hand through his hair. The grease he had smeared there to darken it clung to his fingers, and he scowled. Gaining entry to the stronghold had been far easier than locating one small woman.

After escaping from Ruarke, Alex had headed for the market section of London to seek out a disguise. He had ended up a tanner, buying the cart, horse, hides, tools and even the man's clothes. Tannery was a noisome trade, what with the applications of animal dung used to soften the hides and the acid mixture of fermented bran necessary to remove the dung from the finished skins. The guards at Harte Court's gates had spent as little time as possible poking through Alex's cart before motioning for him to enter the outer bailey.

With that first wall breached, he had slipped through the gate to the inner bailey with a group of servants bound for the castle. Since then, he had spent every darkened hour—and a few more dangerous daylight ones—looking for Jesse. She had not been in the dungeons, thank God, nor was she in the castle keep. Already tonight he had searched the south tower and was trying to decide which of the other three to investigate. The presence of the men in the courtyard stopped him momentarily; he dared not cross it while they were there.

In the harsh pools of light cast by the torches, Alex saw the grim-faced men wore Harcourt's colors. Not visitors, then, but his henchmen back from performing some evil deed, he thought as they dismounted. 'Twas obvious they had been in a battle, because several were wounded. Two of the mounts carried double, though whether the blanket-wrapped figures were injured men or prisoners he was not sure until Parlan came out of the castle.

Alex's nostrils flared like a wolf scenting the enemy. Parlan had been away when Alex had arrived at Harte Court, but Alex had made locating Graham's chamber his first priority. He had feared finding Jesse's broken body in his enemy's bed, but there had been no sign she had ever been there, thank God.

For an instant, Alex regretted coming alone. With Ruarke beside him to deal with the soldiers who were constantly with Edmund no matter where he went, Alex would have ambushed him and found out where Jesse was being kept.

"Did you get both women?" Parlan called down from the steps of the castle, holding a torch aloft.

"Aye," replied a tall knight, dismounting and dragging one of the cloaked figures after him.

Parlan's grin shone across the courtyard. "And their guard?"

"Dead to a man . . . just as m'lord ordered."

Alex started. What fresh villainy was this? Was Parlan so desperate for women that he sent his men to kidnap them?

"Lord Edmund is in the old north tower. He wants them lodged there with the Lady Jesselynn."

Alex practically jumped from his skin. It was all he could do to keep himself from running across the courtyard and tearing into the stone building the pair of men were now entering, each with a woman slung over his shoulder.

When they disappeared from sight, Alex leaned against the kitchen building, barely feeling the cold stone at his back as his gaze devoured what he could see of the tower in the gloom.

Jesse was alive! Alive and in this tower. Relief made him dizzy. Most of the windows were dark, but a faint spill of light shone from the topmost one. 'Twas too far up and too narrow for him to have entered. He concentrated on watching the door, trying to gauge how many guarded the place.

A few minutes later, Edmund exited the tower and swaggered across the courtyard like a man who ground the world beneath his boot heel. *Enjoy your victory,* Alex thought, gaze narrowed as he watched Edmund enter the castle, *because before the new day dawns I'll have Jess free and you in irons.*

Alex waited with barely leashed patience for the soldiers to follow, waited for Harte Court to settle so he could sneak inside the tower and look for Jesse. Frustration replaced elation when the soldiers did not leave. Creeping closer to the tower, Alex peered inside and saw they had spread their pallets on the floor of the entry hall and bedded down for the night.

Bloody hell! Twice he circled the tower looking for another door or window. Nothing. Once he ventured to the door and pushed it open a crack. Muted voices greeted him, and he realized there were too many men within for him to overpower by himself.

Alex's nerves stretched tighter and tighter as the night dragged by on leaden feet. When the sky began to lighten, he was forced to move further away from the tower. In the loft above the stables, he took up a post and settled down to watch. Come nightfall, he was going in—no matter what.

The weak gray light of dawn crept into the tower room to find Gaby and Jesse huddled by the tiny fire.

"Blanche should be here soon," Jesse said wearily.

Gaby cast a worried glance at Arianna's still figure. She lay on the bed under every blanket and cloak they had between them, her face as white as marble. "Hopefully the guard will let Blanche fetch the things we need."

"Do you think she'll lose the babe?"

Gaby sighed and shrugged. "There was only a bit of bleeding, and the cramping stopped hours ago. I'd say there was hope."

Hope was something Jesse had nearly ceased to have. "I pray you are right."

"While we are on the subject of hope," Gaby said anxiously. "I hope Ruarke and Gareth do not do something foolish when they discover we have been taken—like try to storm the castle."

"Aye," Jesse said in a small voice. Despite her efforts to wrench him from her heart and mind, she could not help but ask, "Do you really think Alex is coming here to free me?" She winced at Gaby's quick nod, picturing Alex lying broken and bleeding in the dungeons, stretched on the rack for Edmund's pleasure. Perversely she could not forget the good times they had shared, in spite of the bad that had followed. "Why did he come alone against so many?" she wailed softly.

"He is afraid for you. He loves you."

Jesse shook her head, partly to chase out the yearning that it might be so. "He used me." Sweet Mary, would the pain never dim? Would she feel this same gut-wrenching sorrow in a week? A year? A lifetime? "He is greedy, like all men." Like Edmund. "He wed me to end the feud and gain my property."

Gaby sighed. "I know he did want to end the feud, but—"

"Then he should have said so instead of telling me he loved me," Jesse said, looking down at her hands. "He brags about how honorable he is, yet he shows me none."

"That would not have made a very romantic marriage proposal," said practical Gaby. "And our Alex is a romantic." She smiled faintly. "Too bad Ruarke did not inherit a bit of that." Then she collected herself to add, "Alex himself told me you were brave and beautiful and the only woman he ever loved."

Jesse made a noncommittal sound, her emotions churning as forcefully as the sea Alex sailed. She could not deny that she missed the closeness they'd shared, but neither could she forgive him for using her and their poor babe to place the Harcourt estates under Sommerville rule.

"I agree that he should have told you about Hugh's death," Gaby murmured. "But men are such cowards when it comes to discussing anything unpleasant. Ruarke tries to shout problems into submission. Alex looks for ways around them."

"He manages people. I hate that," Jesse said fiercely.

"'Tis not done out of meanness. In his arrogance, Alex always thinks he knows what is best for people."

"I do not like being pushed about." Though Jesse tried to cling to her hatred, the image that haunted her was of Alex standing in the road in the rain, looking as though he would move heaven and earth to follow her. *Oh, Alex.* Inside her, the longing to know he was all right coiled tighter and tighter.

"All the Sommervilles are domineering," Ari said softly from the bed. "'Tis their least pleasing quality."

They were beside her in an instant, Jesse grateful for the diversion from her own black thoughts.

"How do you feel, Ari?" Gaby asked anxiously.

"Better than you two look, I'll wager," Ari chirped. She started to sit, but Gaby would not allow it.

"You had best stay quiet until we are certain the babe is still well lodged inside you."

Ari settled back at once. "Is there aught to drink?"

"Blanche should come soon with food and wash water," Jesse said, holding a cup of watered wine to Ari's lips. "We will ask her to fetch Gaby's chest of medicines and fresh clothes." The guard had refused to disturb Lord Edmund's sleep to ask permission for the things to be brought.

"Do you have any of that sleeping powder in your chest," Ari eagerly asked, blue eyes glowing.

"Aye," Gaby said slowly. "But why would you want—"

"For the guard," Ari amended. "I was thinking how well that powder aided us the last time we were in danger."

Gaby smiled in understanding. "Aye, I have enough powder to put the guard to sleep, you clever minx."

"What a good idea," Jesse said, surprised little Ari had thought of such a thing. "Could we really do it?"

"Aye. You should have seen how well that worked on Walter Beck," Ari said. "He and Hugh Harcourt had sneaked into Wilton bent on rescuing Walter's brother. Charles was my grandfather's apprentice—" she scowled fiercely "—the one who made the counterfeit coins for Hugh." Jesse gasped at this, but Ari seemed not to notice. "Anyway, those two trapped Gaby and me in my chamber. When Walter hit Gaby and knocked her unconscious—"

"Ari saved my life by putting a sleeping potion in Walter's wine," Gaby interjected swiftly, seeing how painful this was for Jesse. "I do not have enough to drug everyone in Harte Court, however, but it might help get us out of this tower at least."

"Then what?" Ari asked.

Jesse swallowed the lump Hugh's name had brought to her throat. "There is a secret escape route." Her friends nodded eagerly as she explained about the bolt hole. "But we'd need to get across the courtyard and down into the bowels of the castle undetected." Clearly Ari's frailty was a problem. Even together, Jesse and Gaby were not strong enough to carry her. "If only we could put everyone to sleep for a time."

Gaby shook her head, mouth tight with disappointment. "'Tis a good idea, but as I said, I do not have enough powder."

The three fell silent, trying to think of something else that might work, then Jesse said, "What about a purgative? If I recall, there is hazelwort in the castle gardens."

"The very thing," Gaby exclaimed, chuckling. "The guards will find it difficult to stop us if they are fighting to get into the garderobe," she explained to the puzzled Ari.

"I am sorry Edmund took you captive," Jesse said a moment later. "But since he did, I am glad he was so stupid as to put us all together in one room."

"Typical male thinking," Gaby said, smile broadening. "They assume all females are weak, helpless creatures."

"We will show them." Ari extended her hand and the three of them knotted their fingers together in one fist. It was still small enough to fit inside the palm of any male hand, yet there was hidden strength in those pale, slender fingers. Together they would triumph. They had to.

Jesse's throat tightened. Here were no simpering females at the mercy of men. Partially, she thought it was because the men they had married took pride in their wives' strength, encouraged it. Alex had the right of it, Sommervilles did make good husbands. Oh, Alex. Why could she not stop thinking about him and what might have been?

She sighed raggedly and thrust her sorrow aside. "We had best make plans before Blanche arrives."

"How will we get permission for Gaby to go to the gardens?" Ari wanted to know.

Jesse paced to the arrow slit. Outside, the air hung heavy and still as a wet blanket, as though even nature knew of the danger threatening them. "We could say that in order to help Ari you needed fresh herbs besides those you had in your chest."

"Why should Lord Edmund want to help me?"

"Because, when the Sommervilles come to demand your release, Lord Geoffrey will insist on seeing you are both healthy before he gives in to Edmund and signs away his title," Jesse reasoned.

"For myself, I do not care about the earldom, but I resent seeing Geoffrey lose it this way," Ari said hotly.

"I resent everything Edmund has done," Jesse echoed. "My life and the lives of others have been ruined by his greed. If I can get away from here, I am never coming back—no matter what."

"You can live with us," Ari offered.

"So long as you are Alex's wife, the Sommervilles can protect you under law," Gaby reminded her.

Jesse tossed her head. "I would rather live alone."

"You know that is not possible," her friend said gently. "A young, marriageable heiress is—"

"Naught but a pawn in the games men play for wealth and power. Sweet Mary, but I hate such injustice," Jesse gritted.

"Aye," Gaby agreed. "Luckily we are married to Sommervilles, who value their women and deal fairly with them."

"Alex did not deal fairly with me," Jesse snapped.

Gaby sighed. "He thought to save you from Edmund."

"And to end the feud by wedding the last of the Harcourts." Inside Jesse the yearning to be free hardened into a knot of determination. "Let us go over our plan one more time."

They put thought into practice when Blanche arrived with the morning meal. She had a hollow-eyed maid and a gangly boy with her to carry the extra things, but once the trays and water buckets had been set down, Blanche shooed the two servants from the room. "Are you all right?" the girl asked, plucking at Jesse's sleeve. "Edmund told me about capturing the other ladies. I longed to come to you, but did not dare."

Jesse patted Blanche's icy hand and introduced her to Gaby, who sat by the fire looking weak and Ari, who lay in bed, still and pale as a soon-to-be-corpse. Because she did not trust Blanche's ability to keep silent under Edmund's questioning, Jesse dared not tell her what they were about. "I fear for Lady Arianna's life. To save her and the child, we require Lady Gabrielle's chest of medicines."

Blanche hurried away but returned moments later, eyes brimming with tears. "Edmund says he does not care what happens to her and her brat."

Jesse had been expecting this. "His black heart will cost him dearly when Lord Geoffrey demands to see his two daughters-in-law and one of them is dead of the miscarriage."

The baggage arrived a quarter of an hour after Blanche left to deliver Jesse's message. The women let some minutes drag by before Jesse pounded on the door and shouted to the guard that the Lady Gabrielle required fresh herbs from the garden. Permission was quickly forthcoming.

Jesse smothered a smile at the sight Gaby made as she left with the guard, her head averted, her manner timid. Did Edmund happen to spy on her, he would see exactly what he expected—a cowed, frightened woman.

Gaby and Jesse spent the afternoon hunched over the table, squeezing juice from the hazelwort leaves into a bowl with the backs of their spoons. 'Twas nearly supper time when Gaby announced they had enough.

"Sweet Mary, I am glad that is done." Jesse arched her aching back and wandered over to the narrow window. Dusk approached, draping the courtyard below in long, dark shadows, which suited her purpose exactly. "Blanche should be here soon."

Her stepmother had agreed to bring their food an hour before the evening meal was due to be served in the hall.

"I still think I should go with you," Gaby muttered.

Jesse shook her head. "'Twill be easier for one to creep about unnoticed," she said absently, her eyes on the courtyard.

"What is it?" Gaby asked, joining her at the window.

Jesse groaned, her head falling forward as she massaged the bridge of her nose. "I can not stop worrying about Alex."

"'Tis only natural."

"Nay, I should hate him." There was no hatred in Jesse's soft voice, nor in the prayers she sent aloft for Alex's safety. "I look below and wonder if he is down there somewhere, mayhap in danger because he came here for me."

"You love him still," Gaby said, stroking her back.

"Nay. Yet I do care what happens to him," Jesse said in a voice that trembled with confusion, "even though I know he has come here only to regain his . . . his pawn."

"Oh, Jesse. He does not see you as a pawn. Sommerville men are different," Gaby said, a faraway look in her eyes. "Oh, they are overbearing and possessive to the point of obsession, but there is no man more loyal and caring. If you look into your heart, I am sure you will find that is true of Alex, too."

Was it? Jesse's mind churned with conflicting thoughts. She thought about the island, how they had worked there side by side, whether they were fixing a meal or fixing the boat. In vain she searched her memories for a time when he had reviled her for being weak or womanish, and found none. True, he had taken on the hardest tasks himself, but even she had to admit they were things she could not have done.

Nay, he had gloried in her as a woman and a companion and encouraged her to do the same. He had taught her chess and archery, indulged her liking for swordplay and listened to what she had to say on any subject. In all things, he had treated her well. She smiled softly, remembering. Alex had been her husband, her lover, her friend—closer to her even than Hugh.

Thoughts of her brother ripped open scars barely healed. Jesse's smile died. "I can not forget that he wed me knowing Hugh was dead, leaving me Edmund's sole heir." 'Twas the only reason a virile, handsome man like Alex would have chosen to wed someone as unaccomplished and unwomanly as her. "Nor can I forget 'twas his family who killed my brother." Ari and Gaby both started, and Jesse quickly added, "I do not blame the two of you for Hugh's death. Only the *men*."

"You do not know the whole truth," Ari said, drawing Jesse back to the bed. "Hugh tried to kill me."

"Hugh would not do such a thing," Jesse insisted, shocked.

Ari's little chin jutted out. "He did. After I had drugged Walter's wine, Hugh panicked. He forced me to flee with him to the tower room above. It had been damaged years before and there were great holes in the walls." She shivered, her eyes dazed with memories. "'Twas empty except for the timbers the workmen were using to repair it. Gareth followed us. He promised to spare Hugh's life, but Hugh wanted to die then and there."

"'Twas because he did not trust Gareth to keep his word," Jesse said, her throat tight, aching with tears and denial.

"Nay." Ari reached out to cover Jesse's knotted fingers with her own. "Death was preferable to the thought of standing trial in London. He babbled about his father's contempt, your pain." Her voice grew gentler still. "Gareth refused to fight him. I—I have tried many times since to imagine how Hugh must have felt—frightened, cornered. He went a little mad, I think. He screamed that Gareth would fight him, and to give Gareth a reason—Hugh pushed me through one of the holes in the wall."

Jesse gasped. "B-but you are alive."

"Fortunately the stonemason's scaffold was some four feet below. Landing knocked the breath from me, but did no other damage to me or the babe I was carrying."

"I can see why the Sommervilles wanted him dead," Jesse said after a moment. "But I still can not forgive—"

Gaby put an arm around her shoulder. "Gareth did not kill Hugh. Your brother was captured and imprisoned. Later, he confessed to the Bishop of London—under no duress, I can assure you, for the cleric is well-known for his honesty."

Jesse nodded glumly, having heard the same. Yet her in-bred stubbornness would not let her give in. "How did he die, then?"

Gaby sighed and looked away. "Hugh hanged himself."

"That is not true." Jesse wanted to flee from the words, from the truth shining on her friends' faces, but her knees were too weak, her head too dizzy. She sank down onto the bed.

"Our men wanted Hugh alive to tell his story in open court," Gaby went on gently. "The Sommervilles' only crime was in underestimating Hugh's desperation."

Jesse groaned. It was true. Hugh had killed himself. She could almost hear him saying he feared facing Edmund's scorn, feared causing her pain, yet did not want to believe Hugh guilty of any of this. "Why did Hugh undertake such a mad scheme? Why did Alex not tell me how my brother died?"

"He knew you'd blame yourself." Gaby put an arm around her.

"Mayhap you should lie down," Ari suggested.

Jesse shook her head, hands clenched in the struggle to hold herself together. She could not collapse now. She could not.

"Men," Gaby scoffed. "They can be so stupid some-times. If only Alex had been honest with you from the be-ginning, you would have believed in his love."

"I do not believe in love," Jesse blurted out.

Gaby and Ari both gasped as though she'd said there was no such thing as God or heaven. "My sire was a cruel man," Gaby said slowly. "So I know how hard it is to be-lieve in love when you were raised with none. But love is all around you. Ari and I love you in one way, Alex in an-other. He can not quench the flames in his eyes when they follow you around the room."

"Lust," Jesse said succinctly.

"And happy you should be he desires you, for that is a most pleasurable part of love," Gaby quickly added. "But love is also caring more for another's happiness and safety than your own, and I think Alex has proved himself on that score."

"He would regain his pawn," Jesse said tightly.

"Stubborn girl. I can not force you to believe in Alex's love." Gaby sighed. "Only think on what I have said."

Jesse did not want to think. She wanted . . . she wanted peace, for herself and her babe. When they escaped, she was going to the woods to live with the peasants. Better a life of hardship than the misery plenty had brought her. The sound of the bar being lifted catapulted her from the bed. "'Tis Blanche. Time to put our plans into action."

Alex lurked in the shadows near the old tower, nerves so tense from waiting they screamed. The better to blend in, he had exchanged his tanner's garb and eye patch for the clothes of a soldier he had overpowered. He had a brace of knives tucked into his belt and one in his boot. For his purposes, the knife was preferable to the sword, deadly and silent.

Moments later, the Lady Blanche and a maid left the tower, having brought Jesse her meal. The quickness of their steps as they crossed to the castle suited Alex's craving for haste. Close on their heels, most of the guards trooped over to the hall for their own supper. Stepping from hiding, Alex moved toward the tower with the confident stride of a man who had every right to be there.

A single torch had been lit and stuck in a holder in the wall. Three men crouched over a dice game in the pool of light it cast. "Who are ye?" one growled, climbing stiffly to his feet.

"I've come ta relieve the guard upstairs," Alex replied in coarse English. The hair at his nape stood on end as the trio scrutinized him, but he maintained a calm facade.

The soldier frowned. "I don't remember seein' ye afore. Toss back yer cowl and let us ha' a look at yer face."

"Aye." In the few seconds it took him to cross the entry hall, Alex worked out the pattern of moves he'd make.

Under cover of pulling back the hood of his cloak, he struck the standing man in the neck with the side of his hand. As his stunned companions watched the guard crumple, Alex leaped the space separating him from the remaining soldiers, planted his right foot in one man's face, whirled and knocked the last man out with a blow to the head.

Breathing hard, Alex straightened and raked a hand through his hair, still wet from the washing he'd given himself earlier so none would connect the smell of the soldier with that of the tanner. All three were unconscious but unlikely to remain so for long.

He quickly bound and gagged the trio. Taking the torch, he mounted the stairs slowly, a knife at the ready. His heart in his mouth, fairly bursting with the need to find Jesse, he forced himself to check each floor he passed on his way to the top one.

The rooms on the second floor were used for storage. Two of the chambers on the third were occupied, one by an elderly cleric, another by two young boys who huddled together when he looked in through the metal grate that covered the window in the door. Though he dared not stop now, Alex clenched his teeth in rage and vowed to come back for all three.

At the top floor, a guard halted him before a door secured with three iron bars. "Who's there?"

"I've come to replace ye."

Unfortunately the soldier did not believe Alex, either. While the man was reaching for his sword, Alex felled him with a lightning quick fist to the jaw. After easing the body onto the step, Alex tied this man up, too. A glance over his shoulder showed the stairs below were still empty. Alex lost no time in lifting off the three bars that kept him from Jesse.

"Jesse?" whispered a soft female voice as he eased the door open. Gaby peeked around the portal. She recoiled when she saw him, then checked, eyes blinking rapidly. "Alex!"

"What are you doing here?"

"We were attacked on the way back to Wilton and brought here by Edmund's men. He'd force Geoffrey into relinquishing his earldom in exchange for our lives."

Alex's frown became a growl of rage. "Kidnapping women! Damn. Does Edmund's greed and perfidy know no end? Come, let us make haste to get away from here before Papa or my brothers come pounding at the gates trying to free you." He moved past her, taking in the small room at a single glance. Ari sat on the bed, her eyes round with wonder. "Where is Jess?"

"Gone."

"Gone!" Alex's knees threatened to buckle.

"Nay, not dead," Gaby said in a rush, grabbing hold of his arm to shore him up. "She went down to the hall to pour a potion into the ale."

"What potion? Why?" Alex's heart was pounding so loudly he could barely hear her answer.

"We are putting a purgative into the ale so we can disable the soldiers and escape through the tunnel."

"Oh, Lord," Alex moaned.

Chapter Nineteen

"I wish I had thought of this idea years ago." Edmund rubbed his hands in glee as he sat down to the table. "Of course the sons were not wed then, but I could have captured Geoffrey's wife. Aye, the lovely Catherine would have made pleasant sport whilst I waited for Geoffrey to sign over his title to me."

Parlan smiled and accepted a cup of wine from his page.

"To tomorrow," Edmund proposed. "The day which could well bring Geoffrey Sommerville to my gate on bended knee, offering all he has in return for his loved ones' lives."

"To tomorrow," Parlan echoed, lifting his cup to drink.

Standing in the shadows at the edge of the great hall, her face shielded by her cowl, Jesse groaned softly. Most of the knights and men-at-arms who packed the tables in the hall that night were noisily swilling their tainted ale. She had saved some hazelwort for the wine destined for the head table, but Parlan's page had taken the flagon into the hall before she could get to it. "Now what shall I do?" she whispered.

"You will come with me to a place of safety," a deep voice muttered into her ear.

"Alex?" Jesse croaked. Before she could look around, he had her arm and was hustling her to the back corner of the hall farthest from the dais and Edmund's watchful eye.

"Little fool," he grumbled, giving her a small shake.

Jesse swallowed the curse that rose to her lips. Sweet Mary, but he looked terrible, his cheeks pale and gaunt beneath the dark stubble of his beard, his eyes burning in their shadowed sockets. The sight of him brought tears to her eyes. Tears of relief and—damn him—concern. She fought hard to resist the urge to fling herself into his arms.

"Y-you should not have put yourself in such danger by coming here," she said weakly.

He stiffened. "How could you think I would stay away knowing you were in trouble?" he rasped. Though she wanted to deny it, the harsh intensity of his words warmed her to her toes. "You are all right? No one harmed you? Parlan did not . . . touch you."

"I am all right," she managed, still stunned. He *had* come for her. Risked falling into Edmund's hands to rescue her after she had run from him, rejected his love.

"It grieves me that you cut your hair." His raw tone as he gently touched the shorn locks sent a shiver of regret racing through her. "But I understand, and I forgive you."

"*You* forgive *me*!" she exclaimed, her voice drowned out by the minstrels playing in the gallery above the hall and by the din of Edmund's men noisily consuming their meal. "'Twas your lies and maneuverings that drove me away."

"I never lied to you. I married you because I love you and want to protect you," Alex growled, desperate to somehow make her believe him, make her see he loved her for herself. "There will be time to speak of this later, when I have you safely away from here." He sighed and brushed his hand across her belly, making her muscles flutter beneath the coarse servant's gown she wore. "I am glad you and the child were not harmed."

"The child...always the child." She pushed his hand away. "Can you think of nothing but your scheme to end the feud?"

"Ah, Jess." He gritted his teeth, struggling to remember that her scars went deep. Her trust in him had been too fragile, too new to withstand this blow. But if he was patient and gentle with her, mayhap. . . "'Twas not the feud that plagued me these last hellish days. I suffered the torture of the damned thinking what Edmund and Parlan might have done to you." He dragged in a ragged breath. "If we had lost our babe, I would have mourned, but if aught had happened to you—" He shuddered, his eyes squeezed shut. Opening, they glittered with the depths of his emotions. "I would not have wanted to live myself."

Jesse trembled, too, shaken by his words, the anguish in his expression. Sweet Mary, she wanted to trust him, but—

He smiled in gentle understanding. "Think on my words—'tis all I ask . . . for now." So much for humble, Jesse thought wryly. "Now, I need one thing—directions to this bolt hole so I can get you, Gaby and Ari there as soon as the guards are disabled. 'Twas a clever plan," he added, grinning. "Was it yours?"

"The hazelwort was my idea, but Ari used a similar ploy to disable Walter Beck when he and . . . and Hugh got into Wilton."

His hand found hers clenched in her skirt and squeezed it. "My family did not kill your brother."

"I know. Gaby and Ari told me all about it." Jesse's gaze dropped from his to the toes of her boots. It hurt to admit Hugh had been guilty. "Doomed for all eternity," she mumbled. "And 'twas partially my fault. If he had not feared my reaction—"

"You are not to blame yourself," he ordered, gathering her into his hard embrace.

The noise and smoke of the crowded hall receded, his warmth and strength soothing as a healing balm. If only things had been different, she thought, her chest tight and aching with suppressed feelings. If only their names had not been Harcourt and Sommerville, they might have found happiness together.

"Ah, Jess," he breathed into her hair. "I'd stay here and hold you for all eternity, but we dare not linger. I must get you three ladies to safety and then return."

"Return? For Edmund?" At his grim nod, her eyes rounded and she clutched at his arm. "You can not. 'Tis too risky. He and Parlan have not drunk of the ale."

Alex fingered the hilt of his knife. "I can deal with them."

"What if his guards are not affected by our potion? Are you so anxious for Edmund's death that you would throw away your own life?" she asked, aghast. Desperation flickered in the depths of his eyes, and her blood ran cold despite the heat of the hall. "Oh, Alex," she whispered.

"I do not seek Edmund's death or my own," Alex said quickly. "I would take him prisoner and see he pays for his crimes—especially for taking you, Gaby and Ari."

"Prisoner? But I thought surely you'd want him dead." 'Twas a mark of Edmund's evil that his own daughter could discuss his death, Jesse thought a little wildly, for this whole conversation seemed unreal. Hugh had often said the world would be better off without Edmund.

"True my family can not rest easy till Edmund is gone, but he'll not die by my hand," Alex vowed, his eyes locked on hers, "and confirm your fear that 'twas his estates I hungered after."

"B-but you could be killed," she whispered.

"I'd not be that careless," Alex assured her. "Not while I have a wife who loves me and a child on the way."

Damn. How skillfully he had hemmed her in. If she denied loving him 'twould be akin to telling him to sacrifice his life. She clenched her teeth over a groan of despair. *Do not care,* she warned herself. But it was too late, probably had been since that first morning aboard *The Star* when he could have hurt her and had not. Even if they never settled the trouble between them, even if they never lived together as man and wife, Alex was too fine a man to die. "Do not do this."

"I will take care. Come, now, I must get you to safety," Alex said, but before they could move, the doors to the great hall swung open and the steward bustled in. He was a short man, nearly bald, whose belly and chins jiggled with every step. The hall fell silent as he reached the dais.

"Lord Edmund." Harry bowed low. "Four monks have come seeking aid for one of them who is ill."

Edmund's lip curled. "Monks. A sniveling, greedy lot. Always looking for a handout. Turn them away."

"Nay, m'lord, I pray you do not." A monk entered and approached Edmund. "One of our number was injured in a fall."

Alex's eyes rounded at the sound of that familiar voice. "Jesu, 'tis Gareth." His brother wore an ill-fitting black robe with the hood drawn forward to hide the upper part of his face. Damn, his wound was barely healed.

"What can he be thinking?" Jesse muttered.

"Of rescuing his wife, damn him," Alex said unhappily. "And I imagine this 'sick monk' is Ruarke."

"How can they walk into their enemy's fortress—"

"I could not stay away when I knew you were here." Alex groaned. "If only they had waited until your potion had taken effect."

"If only they had not come at all. Now there are four more people who must be gotten out of here."

"But there are also four more swords to fight any of Edmund's men who are well enough to resist," Alex reminded her.

"'Twill be five of you against hundreds if the men from the barracks in the lower bailey are summoned here," Jesse shot back. "Nay, but you will all be killed."

Her concern warmed him, gave him hope. "Ruarke would not have come alone. You can rest assured his men are close by."

"We could not possibly get to the gates and open them."

"Not the main gate, but I could let a few in at a time through this bolt hole," Alex reasoned. "First I must get Gareth out of the hall before Parlan or Edmund realizes who he is."

Someone moaned, and Alex started, fearing Edmund had pierced Gareth's disguise, but 'twas a man at a nearby trestle table. White faced, lips contorted, the soldier rose and staggered from the hall, clutching his belly with both hands.

"It has begun," Jesse whispered.

Sure enough, others grimaced and shifted uneasily. A serving maid clapped a hand over her mouth and fled back into the buttery; two more soldiers followed the path the first had taken. If not for Gareth's presence here, Alex would have left the hall. Apprehensive, he looked toward the dais.

Edmund was glaring at the monk. "Very well, I will offer you shelter, but my lady wife tends to another matter just now. You must wait for her to look at your comrade."

"Blanche was to return to the tower and wait with Ari and Gaby," Jesse whispered. "I promised to take her with us."

Alex nodded, one eye on the tableau near the dais, the other on the increasing number of people leaving the hall. "Clutch your belly as though it ached and we will quit this place. When we get outside go directly to the tower and wait for me. I will waylay Gareth when he comes out and find Ruarke.''

The hall was beginning to empty by the time they reached the door. A maid fell to her knees before them and cried out.

"What is this?" Edmund shouted, surging to his feet.

Gareth whirled toward the door, reaching beneath his robe for his sword. As he turned, his cowl fell back, baring his face to the merciless glow of the candles.

"By God! 'Tis Gareth Sommerville," Parlan shouted.

"Seize him!" Edmund bellowed. Several soldiers got to their feet, but their faces were white, their movements slow. The entire hall seemed frozen in place. "What ails you cowards?" Edmund shrieked. "After him!"

Parlan screamed an oath and leaped from the dais, shoving men out of the way. "Come with me," he shouted, drawing his sword. A few other men rallied to his cause.

As the soldiers started down the aisle between the tables, Alex lifted Jesse over the fallen maid and shoved her out the door. "Get to the tower." Spinning about, he grabbed a torch from an iron wall bracket and tossed it into the rushes. Dry as tinder, greasy from the spillage of a hundred meals, the marsh grass immediately caught fire. Hungry yellow flames licked their way across the floor, forming a barrier between hall and door.

The first person to breach the curtain of thick black smoke was Gareth, his expression fierce, his sword held aloft. The descending blade hesitated as he recognized Alex, and relief lightened his face. "Jesu, I am glad to see you."

"Come," Alex shouted, smiling broadly. Together they dashed through the double doors, each closing one behind them. Alex kept the doors closed while Gareth grabbed a bench. Between them they wedged it in place across the doors. "You should not be here," Alex ground out, noting his brother's pallor.

"Neither should you," Gareth retorted. "But we both have just cause." Men began to pound on the other side of the door, and the two brothers hustled out of the entryway. "Where are Ari and Gaby?" Gareth asked on their way down the castle steps.

"In yon tower." Alex pointed across the torch-lit courtyard with the tip of his sword. "I have disposed of the guards in the tower, and Jesse has gone to fetch the women. She knows of a way out of the castle. How did you prevent Papa from coming, too?"

"We told him aught of Ari's and Gaby's capture." At Alex's grunt of approval, Gareth gestured toward the few sick souls who sat about on the ground, moaning and clutching their bellies. "They'll not try to stop us from freeing our women and leaving."

"Nay, but—" Alex glanced over his shoulder at the flames shooting from the windows of the hall. "Edmund and Parlan have surely escaped through one of the other doors and will try to rally what men they can. We had best gather our women and be gone. Where did you leave Ruarke?"

"In the stables—"

Three black-clad monks dashed around the corner of the castle, pursued by six Harcourt soldiers. Without a word being spoken, Gareth and Alex entered the fray. The clash of steel on steel played against a backdrop of crackling fire as the three brothers made short work of the enemy.

"Where is Gaby?" Ruarke demanded, wiping the blood from his sword. "Is she all right?"

"She is fine." Alex sheathed his sword and started toward the tower. "Jesse should be bringing them down any moment."

A grin split Ruarke's grimy face. "By God, these Harcourts are a sorry lot," he muttered. "Is it fear of fighting us Sommervilles that has them emptying their bellies?"

On the run, Alex told him about the hazelwort.

Ruarke grunted. "I saw little hope of opening the main gates, so I bade William de Lacy wait with my men in the woods near the postern gate. I thought it likely we might be able to get that opened at least."

Alex paused at the entrance to the tower. "I worry Edmund may send for reinforcements from the barracks in the lower bailey. Those men will be fit and ready to fight."

"Aye. 'Tis likely," Ruarke allowed. Bellowing orders over his shoulder, he sent the other two "monks" to open the postern gate and let in his army. "Tell William he must first take the gate that commands the inner bailey. He is to prevent any one from leaving or entering."

The three brothers pounded up the narrow, winding tower steps two and three at a time. Halfway up, they met the ladies coming down.

Ruarke seized Gaby around the waist. The stones of the old tower shook as he roared her name. Gareth welcomed Anmore quietly, but with no less enthusiasm. When he heard that she had not been well, he swept her up in his arms, his face bleak.

Jesse paused a few steps above the embracing couples, Blanche attached to her side like a burr. Jesse scarcely felt the thin fingers wrapped around her wrist. All her attention was focused on Alex waiting below.

He stood still as a statue, yet his eyes reached up to her, warming her so the cool, nearly dark stairwell seemed as hot and bright as the noon sun in summer. His gaze yearned, it implored, it begged for things she could not give him: love, trust and forgiveness. Sucking in her lip to still its trembling, Jesse shook her head, and the spell was broken.

Grimness replaced Alex's usual smile as he tapped Ruarke on the shoulder. "We must be going."

Back in the courtyard, Alex saw things had changed little in the few moments they had been inside the tower, except the smoke was thicker now, blocking out more of the light from the torches that ringed the courtyard. A few sick people lolled here and there, the soldiers among them seeming to pose little threat, but figures flickered through the shifting murk of night and smoke. Were they servants or Edmund's men searching for them? "The postern gate is a ways away," he began.

"And reaching it encumbered by our ladies is too risky until we control the inner bailey," Ruarke finished for him. "We must get them to safety now." Though he was the youngest, Alex bowed to his superior battle experience. "Alex, if you and Gareth will guide the women through this tunnel, I will join my men."

Gaby paled, but stood on tiptoe and kissed her husband's tanned cheek. "Be careful," she whispered.

Ruarke folded her close, kissed her thoroughly. "Off with you, now," he growled when she let him up for air.

Watching the two of them, Alex hurt anew for what he had had with Jesse and lost. When this was all over he would win her back. He had to believe that or go mad. "Jesse will show you where the bolt hole is," Alex said tightly as Ruarke disappeared from sight around the corner of the tower.

"Where will you be?" Gareth wanted to know.

"I have to capture Edmund."

Jesse and Ari gasped; Gareth grabbed Alex's shoulder and spun him around. "I do not like the sound of that, Alex." His jaw tightened as he beheld Alex's determined expression. "You have too much to live for to endanger your life like this."

"So I told Jess," Alex said evenly, avoiding her gaze. "But we must put a stop to Edmund's schemes against us."

"The risk is too great."

Alex shook his head. "No risk is too great if it frees us from Edmund's threat—but I will be very careful." His gaze was cool, determined as he turned toward Jesse. "Take them through the tunnel and wait in the woods until Ruarke comes for you." He sighed, lowered his voice. "And remember . . . I love you."

Jesse did not say anything as he turned and walked away, disappearing into the smoke that drifted across the courtyard from the castle windows. She could not have spoken. Her throat was clogged with tears, her heart ached beyond belief.

Edmund was not in his lavish bedchamber, but the strong-box lying empty on the floor, the clothes tossed about in hasty disarray were mute testimony to his brief visit here. 'Twas obvious he had taken what he could and fled into the night.

Alex stood in the middle of the room, his eyes smarting from the smoke. He had taken time to free the prisoners held on the floor below and probably missed his quarry for the delay. Recalling the gratitude of the men who would have perished in the fire, he could not regret the act.

So, where did he go from here?

His sword still clenched in one grimy fist, his knuckles seared by the flames he'd battled to get Edmund's prisoners out, Alex circled to the window. From this vantage point he could look out over the smoke to the wall and gate house that separated the inner bailey from the outer. Ruarke's banner swayed over a knot of men that writhed together in combat a few yards from the gate. Obviously some of Edmund's men were well enough to put up a fight. Did Edmund lead them?

Nay. A man of Harcourt's stamp would not have risked his neck or lingered to be taken prisoner by his enemies. Yet he was assured enough of his escape to tarry whilst he changed his clothes and took his seal and jewels from the chest.

Which meant that Edmund knew a way out of Harte Court. *The bolt hole?*

Bile rose in Alex's throat as he thought of the people precious to him who were likely already in that tunnel, unsuspecting that it held any danger. He left Edmund's chamber at a dead run, praying he was not too late.

"I thought I might find you here."

Edmund snatched up his sword and turned to find Parlan in the doorway of the vault. His face was sooty, his clothes filthy and torn, and behind him drifted curls of hot smoke. Edmund's gaze narrowed. "Why are you not defending my castle?"

"Because I, like you, see the hopelessness of the situation at present." Parlan glanced quickly into the dark corridor, then closed and bolted the door. "We would not want to be disturbed."

Edmund eyed him warily. "My men outnumber theirs."

"The only ones not retching are in the outer bailey, and Ruarke Sommerville will soon command the bailey gates."

"Not for long." Edmund hoisted the leather sack he'd filled with coins. "I'll go to the front gates and order my men to commence a siege on the inner bailey."

"Lugging your wealth with you?"

"I'd not want the Sommervilles getting their hands on it."

"Nor would I. 'Tis too bad Guthrie is dead. He'd have been strong enough to carry the lot himself. Another score I have to settle with Alexander. What of Jesselynn?"

"What of her? Even if they discover her whereabouts, the Sommervilles won't harm her. When my men retake the castle, she'll be returned to me."

To me, Uncle, Parlan amended. Men died in battle, and he'd decided this would be Edmund's last one. "With my help, you could carry more."

Edmund weighed the greed in Parlan's eyes against the gold he knew he could not hope to take out alone. His own greed won. "You're right, of course." Best let Parlan think he trusted him.

"How are we going to get away from here with the courtyard full of Sommervilles?"

"Fortunately the ancestor who built Harte Court did not want to fall victim to the perilous times in which he lived. He had constructed a little back door to his castle."

"The postern gate?"

"Nothing so obvious." Edmund chuckled. "Tunnels—leading from a room just down the way to the safety of the woods."

Better and better. "How clever of him."

Edmund cocked his head. "Did you hear voices without?"

Frowning, Parlan went and pressed his ear against the door. "I can hear nothing over the sounds of the fire raging above. Does anyone else know about these tunnels?"

"Nay. The secret is handed down from father to heir, but I did not share it with Hugh. And if someone should try to follow us—" Edmund's smile turned evil "—I've an ingenious way of eliminating unwanted pursuit. Near the exit from the passageway there is a lever concealed in a pipe. Depressing it opens a drain that floods the tunnels with water from the moat."

Parlan's smile matched Edmund's exactly.

Chapter Twenty

Sweet Mary, but she hated the dark!

The torch shook in Jesse's hand as she led her silent little flock through the tunnels. The circle of light was nearly swallowed up by the black that pressed around her like a stifling blanket. The wall was cold and slick with moss beneath her hand as she felt along it for the nails that marked the way through the maze of tunnels.

Added to her worries, Jesse feared Alex would not remember she had told him about the nails and thus lose his way. What if he never reached the tunnel at all? What if Parlan or Edmund killed him and she never saw him again?

Jesse stopped so suddenly that Gareth, following directly behind with Ari in his arms, bumped into her. "What is it?" he whispered. "Have we reached the end?"

"N-not quite," Jesse stammered. She forced her shaky legs to move, but her mind refused to release its grip on the horror that something might happen to Alex. Oh, was there ever a more contrary heart than hers? A heart given to a man she should never have come to care for in the first place. Jesse forced herself to face facts. She could no more cut Alex from her heart than she could forget the fact that she had been born a Harcourt . . . and he a Sommerville. What would become of them?

Jesse stopped in front of the stone wall that blocked the passageway. "This is it." Handing the torch to Gaby, she bent to locate the lever that moved the stone slab aside. It was so rusted that Gareth had to set Ari down and work it himself.

After much grunting and straining on his part, the mechanism finally made a loud grating noise and the stone swung outward, letting in a rush of cold night air.

"Wait here whilst I check outside." Gareth sounded so much like Alex that Jesse had to bite her lip to keep from crying. When he returned to pronounce the way clear, he said. "The rocks that conceal this entrance seem far enough inside the woods to hide us from view, but I think it best we remain nearby. If someone comes, I can close the stone and seal us within."

Gaby and Blanche bustled about setting up camp. They had brought candles, flint, blankets, a skin of watered wine and a loaf of bread to see them through until Ruarke came either to take them back inside Harte Court or whisk them to safety, depending on which way the battle went.

Jesse drank a bit of the wine but refused the bread. "I am going back down the tunnel a ways," she whispered in Gaby's ear while Gareth was fussing over Ari.

"Why?" asked Gaby, alert and wary.

"I am afraid Alex will miss the markers and become lost."

"I will come with you," Gaby said at once.

Much as she hated the thought of going into the dark passageway alone, Jesse shook her head. "Ari might need you." Indeed, the girl did look pale and exhausted despite having been carried. When Gaby nodded in reluctant agreement, Jesse released the breath she had been holding. "I'll not be long." She hoped.

Walking into the dark, alone, with only a flickering candle to light the way was one of the hardest things Jesse had ever done, nearly as hard as trying to deny her love for Alex. Perversely, it was thoughts of Alex that kept her sane during the terrible journey through the tunnels.

Still, anxiety lent wings to her feet, and she made the trip back in half the time. She was nearly at the other end; the door that led into the castle was in sight, and she was just passing the second of two tunnels that forked off from the main one—traps intended to confuse a pursuing enemy—when she heard a sound behind her. In the act of whirling around, strong arms seized her, a wide hand muffled the shriek that rose in her throat. The candle slipped from her nerveless fingers, plunging her into total darkness.

She felt the hot breath of her captor on her neck, smelled smoke and sweat on the hair that brushed her cheek as the man retrieved the candle and dragged her into the side tunnel. Nay, she would not give in to him. Determination lent strength to her flagging muscles. She kicked and thrashed like a wild thing. If she could reach the knife at her waist, she'd—

"Jess! 'Tis me," Alex hissed in her ear.

The fight drained out of Jesse on a sigh of relief. Sweet Mary, what relief! He was alive and here with her. She slumped against him, certain she could not move again. His next words had all her muscles snapping to attention.

"Not a sound," he breathed. "Parlan and Edmund are on the other side of the door ready to enter the tunnel.

Jesse's grunt of surprise did not make it past Alex's hand. Just as well, because the door creaked open and a wedge of light spilled in. The angle of the passageway kept her and Alex in shadows, but Jesse could see first Edmund, then Parlan enter. Both wore armor and carried heavy burdens. Parlan had a chest under one arm and a sack thrown over his shoulder.

Edmund's thick shoulders were bowed beneath the dozens of gold chains he had hung around his neck. He dragged a leather bag in one hand, held aloft a torch in the other beringed hand. The green emerald on his thumb glittered cold and bright as Edmund's eyes as they swept the interior of the tunnel.

"Ah, now where are those markers?" He moved closer to the wall, inspected it minutely, then nodded. "'Tis as I remembered, but you'll have to carry the bag so I can feel my way along."

"We should have brought a pack animal," Parlan grumbled.

"I thought you volunteered for that task."

Parlan grunted, then bent to repack their loot. The clank of shifting coins echoed down the stone corridors.

Jesse pried Alex's hand from her mouth and whispered, "I did not think Edmund knew about the tunnels."

"Obviously he does. I was just entering the storeroom when a door nearby opened and these two came out," Alex murmured. "I ducked down the bolt hole and had just doused my candle when you appeared. Why did you not stay with Gareth and the others?" There was anger in his voice as his arms tightened around her, and a concern that lent strength to her flagging spirits.

"I was afraid you would get lost in the tunnel."

"Nay, you feared I'd kill Edmund," he whispered reprovingly. "But I found his chamber empty by the time I had finished freeing his prisoners."

Jesse let the remark about Edmund pass. Now was not the time to argue that she worried more for Alex's safety than Edmund's. "You stopped to let those people out?"

"Of course. And the poor wretches in the dungeon, too." He sounded hurt that she had thought otherwise. "In all honor, I could not leave them to the fire that rages through the castle."

In all honor. Despite her resolve to distance herself from him, Alex's deed touched her. Most men would have satisfied their hunger for vengeance instead. 'Twas proof Alex was not greedy. The hard knot inside her eased fractionally.

Alex smiled in the dark as he felt her relax in his embrace. She loved him still. With time and patience he would make her admit it—first to herself, then to him. When this was over...

"Hurry with that, Parlan," Edmund snapped.

Jesse stiffened, recalling where they were and why. "Edmund and Parlan must think Ruarke's army will prevail," she murmured, "so they are making off with what they can."

Alex grunted. "But I do not think he'll leave. Were I Edmund, I'd get in through the main gate, rally my men and lay siege to the castle." Jesse did not need to see his face to know he was determined to see Edmund fail in that. "Does this tunnel we stand in lead out?" he asked.

"Nay. There is only one way out of the maze," she whispered. "It is marked by the nails I mentioned."

"We will withdraw as far down this branch as we can and let them get ahead of us... for the moment."

That last sent alarm skittering down Jesse's spine. She wanted to cling to him and beg him not to do anything that would endanger his life, but haste was crucial. They felt their way along the slick walls with their hands, going as quickly as they could in the pitch-dark until they had rounded a bend in the stone corridor.

"Crouch down behind me." Alex tucked her close to his body and drew his knife, pulling his cloak around both of them. The shivers that shook Jesse tore into him. "Easy," he whispered, hugging her tighter.

Jesse's heart pounded so loudly she thought Edmund would hear. Oddly it now seemed the most natural thing in the world to cling to Alex's coiled muscles and give herself into his keeping. An eternity seemed to pass before he stirred and pulled her up to stand beside him.

"They have gone on by."

"We can not let them reach the other end of the tunnel. Gareth and the others are camped in the exit," Jesse whispered.

Swearing under his breath, Alex felt his way back to the point where the branch joined the main tunnel. He peered around the corner, saw the two men a short distance away, their shapes backlit by the flickering torch. Their steps were slowed by their burdens. "How far is it to the other end?" he asked Jesse.

"Hugh judged it to be nearly half a mile."

"I have a little time, then," Alex muttered. And he'd need it to devise a plan. "Stay here, and—"

"Nay. I'd go with you."

His hand unerringly found the curve of her jaw, cupped it gently. It was too dark to see his concern, but she felt it in the way his fingers trembled as they stroked her cool skin, warming it. "I know how you hate the dark, little fox, and I'd not willingly leave you here, but—"

"Take me with you," she begged, willing to let him think 'twas only fear for herself that made her voice fray. "I know of a place where the tunnel curves. There you might sneak up close behind them without them seeing you."

"All right." Grudgingly. "But you must stay well back and out of trouble. Let me handle this alone."

Oh, Alex! she thought fondly, yet in exasperation. He worried about her, yet he was the one who took impossible chances. "Aye," she replied, though she meant to stay near and help if she could. Surely a lie given in hopes of saving another was not really a lie. It occurred to her his bad habit was rubbing off on her. Almost, she understood why he had acted as he had. Almost.

Alex brushed her hand with a kiss. "I love you, very much." She surprised him by tightening her grip on his hand.

"Alex. I want your promise that you will not risk your life. On the soul of our unborn child," she added, steel biting through her soft voice.

"You do not play fairly, my lady." Then, "Why do you care?"

"I . . . I do not know."

Alex drew hope from the fact that she had not denied caring. "Come." He gave her hand a gentle tug.

Typically she balked. "Swear."

"I will be careful," Alex vowed.

She sighed, then started ahead. Alex followed, pride swelling his heart. Most women would have run for safety, but not his Jesse. Nay, but she was brave. "For a woman," she'd have said had he told her so. And therein lay part of the problem.

Truly she was an exceptional woman, yet to her mind, she was unworthy of love. Not just his love, but anyone's. During their time together on the island, he had made a start at coaxing her from her cocoon, but her wings had still been so new, so fragile that the first ill wind to come along had crushed them, forcing her to retreat back behind the old barricades of anger and defiance. He desperately wanted a chance to help her fly again.

With a fierce effort of will, Alex forced his attention from the woman he loved to the two men who threatened her and everyone else he held dear. Sorely he was tempted to plant a knife in each of the backs marching ahead of him. Unfortunately he needed them alive—Parlan to stand trial, Edmund because he was Jesse's sire. If he died, Alex inherited a fortune yet stood to lose the woman he valued more than all the Harcourt gold.

His nerves wound tighter and tighter as he slunk along the dark tunnels. If only he could somehow get word to Gareth, between the two of them they might succeed.

Jesse tugged on his sleeve. When he leaned close, she whispered, "We are nearly to the spot I mentioned." As she spoke, Edmund and Parlan disappeared around a bend.

"Wait here." Alex fairly sprinted to the corner. Reaching it, he drew his sword and looked around the wall . . .

And down a length of tempered steel to Parlan's gloating smile. *Run, Jess,* his mind screamed even before he thought about the danger to himself.

"Do not move a muscle," Parlan ordered. "You were right, someone was following us," he called over his shoulder.

Edmund propped the torch against the wall and sauntered over, his gaze glittering to rival the gems on his clenched fists. "Are you alone?" he demanded.

Alex's eyes narrowed as he studied his opponents. The sword burned in his hand. All he needed was an opening.

It was Parlan's blade that moved . . . up to stroke Alex's vulnerable throat. "Drop your weapons and answer my uncle."

Ignoring the blood flowing wetly down his neck to run beneath his tunic, Alex reluctantly let go his sword and knives.

The clatter of metal on stone rang like a death knell, echoing hollowly down the corridors. The odds had been bad before, now they were terrible. He only hoped Jesse would have the sense to turn around and go back to the castle.

Set on brazening this out, goading them into making a mistake if possible, Alex straightened, dividing a contemptuous smile between the two men who faced him in the harsh wash of torchlight, their faces twisted with unholy glee. "I am alone. I need no help to deal with you two," he said calmly.

"Ha! I'll cut you down as easily as I did your uncle," Parlan boasted.

Alex growled deep in his throat, the hunger for revenge painting a red mist before his eyes. He started forward, was brought up short by the burning in his neck as Parlan's sword pricked him yet again. "Aye, you Grahams are such cowardly curs you can only kill a man from ambush or when he is unarmed."

Parlan's head reared back. "Pick up your sword, then."

"Hold," Edmund snarled, a hand on Parlan's sword arm to [st]ay him. "He's of more use to us as a hostage. Ruarke'll re[tu]rn my castle to me do we but show him we have his brother."

"You'd let him go free?" Parlan exclaimed.

"I am not so stupid," Edmund snapped, momentarily [d]rawing Parlan's attention to him.

'Twas the opening Alex had sought. Leaning away from [P]arlan's sword tip, he kicked out with his right foot and caught [th]e man in the kneecap.

Parlan bellowed in rage and pain, doubling over but not re[le]asing his sword. Hampered by the close quarters, Alex man[a]ged to swing and bring his other foot down on Parlan's sword [a]rm. Parlan's guttural groan rang out, and his weapon joined [A]lex's on the ground an instant before Alex's fist connected [w]ith Parlan's jaw, sent him sprawling back, unconscious.

The dance took only seconds, but mindful of Edmund, Alex [w]hipped the knife from his boot as he came up out of the [c]rouch and whirled. Too late. This time 'twas Edmund's blade [th]at stopped him cold.

"I should run you through for all the trouble you've given [m]e," Edmund grated. Hatred glinted from beneath his low[e]red eyelids, his face draped in hellish black and red relief by [th]e torch. "Drop the dirk."

Alex let the hilt slip through his fingers.

"Nay!" Jesse's scream echoed off the walls as she burst onto [th]e scene, a knife clenched in her fist.

Alex's heart lurched. God! This could not be happening. "Jess, get out of here," he shouted. He started for her, but [E]dmund's blade nicked his chest, keeping him at bay.

Jesse stopped a few yards from Edmund. "Drop your [s]word."

He laughed at her. "I could kill your lover and then you [b]efore you got close to me with that puny weapon."

Her chin came up. "Lover. Aye, Alex is that to me and [m]ore," she said proudly, feeling Alex's concern move over her [li]ke a warm wave, wanting to look at him and assure him she [c]ould handle this but afraid to take her eyes from Edmund for [e]ven an instant. "And as for this puny weapon, he taught me [t]o split apples with it as skillfully as a trained knife thrower [h]ired for your after-dinner pleasure. Drop your sword, or you

will find this puny weapon sticking from your Adam's ap
ple.''

"Jess!'' she heard Alex gasp, knew he warned her against
goading Edmund with empty threats. Doubtless he thought she
could not kill her own father. Mayhap she couldn't, but Ed
mund was not the sort of man who practiced such niceties, and
'twas what *he* believed that counted at the moment.

"Traitoress!'' Edmund roared.

Jesse shuddered, but her gaze never faltered from the cold
green eyes so like her own it pained her. "Drop the sword.''

"Your precious brother must be spinning in his grave to see
you defend a Sommerville.'' Edmund spat, cornered but still
knowing what would hurt her the most.

Damn him, Jesse thought, her heart reeling. But she could
not falter. Lives as dear to her as Hugh's memory were at stake
here. "'Twas pursuit of the hollow prize of your regard that
drove Hugh to that early grave,'' she replied. "The sword.''

Grudging respect flickered briefly in Edmund's face. "I said
you had more spine than a woman should,'' he grumbled.
"But you've not the stomach to kill your own father.'' Still
holding the sword, he began to back away from Alex.

Jesse tensed, raised her arm to throw the knife. She could
not just let him leave. Nay, he would find the others at the
mouth of the tunnel and take them by surprise. Mayhap kill
one of the women before Gareth could overpower him.
But...but... Sweet Mary, she could not do it. Her whole body
trembled, and she looked to Alex for help.

"Jess, come here,'' he rasped, swaying slightly, so Jesse
feared he might fall. Blood. So much blood on his throat she
saw when she rushed to his side, but the arm he wrapped
around her was as steely as ever.

"I—I could not do it,'' she whimpered into his shoulder.

"'Tis all right,'' he murmured, stroking her hair. "He is still
your sire, no matter what else he has done.''

"But we have to stop him.''

"I will,'' Alex replied, his attention on Edmund, who had
paused by the torch. In the instant Edmund stooped to pick it
up, Alex took the knife from Jesse.

Edmund's eyes widened when he straightened and saw the
blade raised to throw, then they turned cool and sly. "You

onor will not allow you to kill me, either, Sommerville. Only
ink how Jesselynn will feel to know you wed her so you
ould inherit my estates.'' His perception surprised Alex even
s he cursed it.

"I need not kill you to stop you from leaving," Alex said.

Edmund snorted and picked up the largest bag of loot. "My
rmor will repel your knife. The only vulnerable spot is my
roat. Strike there, and you kill me.''

Parlan chose that moment to stir. Groaning, he sat up and
oked around dazedly. "W-what has happened?"

"Jesselynn and Alexander have both found they've not the
tomach for murder," Edmund said, laughing nastily.

Alex surreptitiously retrieved his sword and whispered,
Jess, what lies up ahead?''

"There is one more bend." She frowned. "A slender pipe
omes out from the wall. Hugh and I could never figure out its
urpose. Then the passageway runs straight to the steps lead-
ng up to the exit.''

"Y-you can not leave me here," Parlan said suddenly. He
ried to get up, but his knee refused to hold him.

"You're of no use to me with that leg," Edmund snapped.

"But what about our plans?" Parlan whined.

"Your plans for me, you mean? I'd say the tables were
eatly turned." Parlan began babbling protests, but Edmund
gnored him. "Stay back," he warned Alex, waving his sword
s Alex advanced a step. The gleam in his eyes, part malice,
art madness, made Alex's blood run cold as the steel that
hreatened him.

"You will not get out of here," Alex said with forced calm.
I will follow you—"

"It matters not," Edmund said cryptically before backing
own the corridor. He took the torch with him, had one heavy
ag slung over his shoulder.

As the light receded, Alex stalked after him, but Parlan's
arsh cry cut through the rapidly encroaching darkness.

"Stop him! He's going to flood the tunnel."

Alex did not wait to hear more; already his nimble mind had
guessed the purpose of the odd duct Jess had mentioned. His
eart in his mouth, he raced blindly down the tunnel and

around the next bend. He skidded to a halt when he saw Edmund.

The torch lay on the ground. Edmund had one hand on the opening of a pipe a foot across at most. Too small to crawl into, but if Alex's suspicions were correct, it could bring enough water to flood the tunnel in seconds, drowning any unlucky enough to be trapped within.

Edmund looked away from the gaping black tube, triumph blazing clearly. "Too late," he said as he put his hand inside.

"Forgive me, Jess," Alex murmured. He hefted the knife, sent it hurling toward the fleshy folds of Edmund's exposed neck.

Edmund shuddered as the blade struck true. His mouth moved, but all that came out was a soft groan. A tremor shook him; his eyes rolled back and he crashed to earth with the force of a felled oak. His beringed hand opened, fingers grasping greedily for purchase on the stone floor, then went still.

Alex stood frozen to the spot, swamped by warring emotions. His family's enemy lay dead at his feet. The feud was over.

Alex should have been elated. But Edmund's death brought him no peace. Only more problems.

"I must leave you for a time." For all his cool tone, Alex might have been a stranger instead of her twice-wedded husband. The white linen wrapped around his throat was a reminder of how close she had come to losing him.

"Aye, you have what you wanted . . . the feud is ended, the Harcourts are no more." Trembling, she drew herself further into the recesses of the window seat, her eyes locked on the blackened ruin of the castle across the courtyard. Men bustled about like busy ants, clearing out debris, shoring up walls, yet she scarcely saw the work that Alex had put into motion two days ago after Edmund's burial.

"'Tis your love I want," he said quietly, yet with such torment she swung back to look at him. His eyes searched hers, as unrelenting as the light streaming into the room. "I love you, Jess. But I can not make you believe in my love." The groan he uttered when she shook her head seemed torn from him. His pain sliced into her, shaking her fragile defenses. '

ever thought to find a woman I could love as I do you," he
went on, "and still it is not enough. You said once my plot-
ings would come back to bite me." He grimaced where once
he might have given her a rueful smile. "You were right, and
he wound is almost more than I can bear. I wish I knew what
words to use to convince you that I wed you for love, not for
ny other reason."

Part of Jesse wished it, too, but she dared not let herself
trust him even a little bit. It had been like this ever since Edmund's death. Her relief that they were all safe, Edmund's
men routed and the fire extinguished had quickly turned to
apprehension as she awaited Alex's next move now that Harte
Court and the wealth of the Harcourts was his.

Blanche had had rooms prepared for all of them in the undamaged south tower, but Alex had not joined Jesse in her bed
that night or the one just past. Each night she had lain awake
waiting for him to come and exert his authority over her. Now
he said he was leaving and she did not want him to. She must
be going mad. *Stay strong,* she warned herself. "There are no
words," she forced past tautly held lips.

Sighing, Alex bowed his head. "I have asked Ruarke for the
loan of William de Lacy," he managed past the tightness in his
throat. Jesu, he wanted to go to her, put his arms around her
and tell her again and again he had not wed her for profit. But
he was right . . . no mere *words* could heal the breach he had
caused. 'Twould require action—and a plan as desperate as he
was. He only hoped it would work. "William will remain here
as captain until we see which of Edmund's men will serve
you."

Which men would serve him, he meant. Jesse tried to sum-
mon the anger that should have sparked, but she felt too
numb, too tired to care. What good would it do? In the end,
he would win. Because he was a man and she a woman. Even
that did not kindle her rage. Everything inside her had turned
to ice.

"I bid you good day, then," Alex said through teeth that
hurt from clenching them. She nodded, then turned away.

Gaby stopped him at the door. "You will take care of yourself. That wound to your throat should be cleaned and dressed
twice daily." She fussed unnecessarily with the linen bandage,

then stood on tiptoe to kiss his cool cheek. "I will stay here awhile to be with Jesse." That got a reaction.

Alex swallowed hard, his eyes shining with what Gaby could have sworn were tears. "I would appreciate that," he said in a raw voice before fleeing down the stairs as though all hell snapped at his heels.

"So much for peace following the end of the feud," Gaby grumbled as she walked over to the window seat

Jesse started. "What did you say?"

"I said there is much work to do."

"Aye." Listlessly.

Gaby frowned. "Where would you have your workers begin?"

"*His* workers," Jesse said succinctly. "And you had best ask Alex ere he leaves. Now that Harte Court is secured to him he wants no part of me or his poor babe. Nay, he'll not show his face around here again except to collect his rents. I knew this was all he wanted. I knew, but—" She could not go on for the pain and burst into tears, Alex's betrayal crushing her as years of Edmund's cruelty had not been able to.

"Hush, my dear." Gaby pressed Jesse's wet face to her shoulder. "Alex did not wed you to get Harte Court."

"'Tis true," Jesse said, recovering after a moment. Sitting back, she wiped her wet cheeks with her hands. "He's run off to London to . . . to romp with his whores."

"Alex did not look like a man anticipating a romp," Gaby said slowly. "He looked miserable."

"I hope he is." Because she certainly was. Jesse's mood remained low, despite Gaby's efforts to cheer her and Blanche's efforts to tempt her with tasty dishes from the kitchen. All around Jesse, the castle folk went about their duties with lighter steps, happy to be out from under Edmund Harcourt's heavy thumb, but their joy did not reach inside the shell Jesse was building to shield her shattered feelings.

The arrival of the stonemason changed that.

Master Robert Appleton came from Shelby town a week after Edmund's death, a few hours after Gaby had returned home to her castle and babies. Jesse reluctantly told Blanche to bring the man up to her temporary hall in the south tower. She regretted the impulse when she heard why he was there.

"I have not decided whether to rebuild or haul away the debris and start anew," she told him. In truth, the place held too many bad memories.

The gaunt old man scowled. "If I see no structural damage, we'll rebuild," he announced. "'Tis the best way."

Men! His arrogance pierced Jesse's numbness, reminded her of another high-handed man. "I know naught of your work."

Master Robert's grizzled hair fairly stood on end. "I did all the stonework at Wilton, including the oriel windows Lady Gaby says you much admired," he huffed.

Jesse abruptly swallowed the rest of her objections. Well she recalled Wilton's beauty. The man was a genius with wood and stone. "'Twas kind of Lady Gaby to send you here."

"Didn't. Lord Alexander is the one who approached me. Said I was to set things to rights before the cold weather came."

Jesse's remaining gloom flew out the window on a rush of rage. "Oh, he did, did he?" she seethed. *Arrogant ass.* Already busy spending *her* coin, repairing *her* castle. "What orders did he give you concerning the refurbishment?" Probably something extravagant, she thought, recalling his love of luxury.

"Well, he said—"

"Never mind what he said. *I* am lady here." Jesse drew herself up proudly, deciding then and there that *she* would rebuild her castle, raise her babe and run her estates herself. And to hell with Alexander Sommerville—wherever he was.

Chapter Twenty-one

'Twas Michaelmas, the twenty-ninth day of September Settlement Day. Already the vassals had arrived to settle their accounts with the Lady of Harte Court. The bright hues of their feast-day clothing turned the courtyard below Jesse's window in the south tower into a patchwork of color and movement. Their laughter and shouted greetings drifted up to her through the open window of her chamber, mingling with the warm morning air.

Jesse smiled to see her people so content and easy. How different today was from other Michaelmases at Harte Court, she thought. Then men had crept in on leaded feet, not knowing if they would displease Edmund and pay with their heads before the day was over. Yet her smile faded as she remembered the ceremonies due to begin shortly. "Sweet Mary, but I am nervous."

Blanche left off supervising the maids, who were packing Jesse's things for the move into the master chamber of the newly completed castle, and joined Jesse. "All will be well," she said cheerily, the plump, companionable arm she laid around Jesse's shoulders another mark of how things at Harte Court had changed.

"I hope so." Jesse sighed. Her dealings with the peasants had gone well, but now 'twas time to face the knights who held her keeps, to ask for their rents and their pledges of fealty. She should have summoned them for the swearing right after Edmund's death, but there had been so much to see to, and, too, she had been unsure of their support. "Suppose they deny me?"

"They'd not dare," Blanche said fiercely. "They love you."

"Hardly that." She still did not believe in love. "I will be content to have their respect and cooperation."

"You have it already. And why not? Though their work is still hard, now they are well fed, properly clothed and get to keep more of what they earn. Truly, this must seem like coming to heaven after years in hell. I know it seems so to me."

Sighing, Jesse put an arm around the woman who had become her friend. "There was much for me to learn and do—and the task is far from complete, but I could not have come even this far had you not taken over running the household."

Blanche's blue eyes sparkled to rival the sun glinting off Master Robert's fine windows in the castle across the way. "'Tis I who am grateful to you for letting me remain here instead of returning me to my parents to be sold into marriage again."

"Aye. 'Twould seem marriage is not for either of us," Jesse muttered. Alex had not returned once in the past three months. 'Twas plain he did not care for her, but he might have shown some concern for their babe. Her hand strayed reflexively to the hard mound of her stomach, clearly visible beneath her green silk surcoat though she was only four months along.

A boy, Gaby had predicted on one of her frequent visits to Harte Court. Another Sommerville. Jesse had cried herself to sleep that night, thinking of Hugh—the last of the Harcourts.

"Lord Alexander is not a bad husband," Blanche ventured. On this subject alone, she and Jesse did not see eye to eye. "He may not come to Harte Court, but he has not forgotten you."

Jesse growled, thinking of the things, and people, Alex had sent her way. "I would he had kept his help to himself."

"But Master Robert was a godsend."

"Aye." Grudgingly.

"And Master Simon, the carpenter, showed up with his apprentices just as you were wondering where on earth we were going to get all the furniture to replace what had burned. And their work is fine," Blanche added as Jesse's frown deepened.

"Aye." Even more grudgingly. "But sending George and Meggie here was a low blow." The pair had arrived with both children and a wagon load of fabric bolts, enough for bed curtains, window drapes, sheets—everything a castle needed—even to a new wardrobe for Jesse's rapidly burgeoning figure

"But they are very glad of the work," Blanche said. "And with all there is to do here, they'll be staying for a long time Meggie was so pleased to have their income insured and a bet ter place to raise their children in."

"I told you he was a fiend," Jesse snapped. "He knew would not turn them away, and he knew they'd remind me—" Her voice caught on the memory of that day…and the others that had followed. Tears filled her eyes, blurring the bright September morn and the glistening castle across the way that was all she had ever hoped for. Well, almost all. *Damn* Why could she not forget him as he had obviously forgotten her?

"Remind you of what?" Blanche asked.

Jesse blinked back her tears. She had vowed she would no shed another one over him, and she *would not*. Lifting her chin, she turned to Blanche. "'Tis just as well Alexander Sommerville has not come here, else I might have scratched ou his eyes."

"Mayhap he knows and that is why he has stayed away," Blanche mumbled.

"Probably. He seems to know everything else that goes on here." Aye, that was what rubbed. Alex was not even here, yet he seemed to anticipate her needs, and Harte Court's, as easily and thoroughly as he had when they been on the island, working side by side for every bite of food they put into their mouths.

That memory hurt worse than any other, haunted her dreams, for she now saw in it the promise of what life could have been like for her and Alex here at Harte Court, if only—

A scratching at the chamber door mercifully diverted Jesse's thoughts from wandering any further down that bleak yet oft-traveled path.

"'Tis Ellis, my lady," said the maid who had answered the door. "He says the ceremony's about to start."

Ellis. Another of Alex's gifts. "Lord Alex said the mistress of so great a castle as Harte Court should have a squire to see to her horse and protect her person," the boy had stated when she'd asked why he'd come.

"We both know Lord Alex owns Harte Court," she had snapped. Even though he had not deemed to live there.

Flushing under her angry gaze, Ellis had stammered, "I—I do not think Lord Alex sees things that way, my lady. He sent me hither, and I can not return to his service because I do not know where he is. If you turn me out—" He had let the sentence dangle dramatically, his eyes pleading as an orphaned pup's. Obviously the lad had learned more than swordplay at his master's knee. Naturally he had remained, too.

For a time, Jesse had suspected Ellis of passing information to Alex, but the people she had set to watch him had declared him as innocent of the deed as the others she tried to paint with that black brush—George, Meggie, Master Robert, even Master Simon had fallen under her jaundiced eye, yet nothing could she prove. Mayhap Alex really was in league with the devil. 'Twould explain why she had not been able to cast off the spell he'd woven over her, no matter how hard she'd tried.

Jesse stopped in the doorway of the great hall. She'd avoided this room all during the reconstruction, but it seemed her fears had been for naught. The dark, suffocating room that had been the stage for so many humiliating scenes in her childhood was no more. Though 'twas not lavishly furnished, the new hall fairly gleamed, from the mellow wood of Master Robert's beams far overhead, draped with vivid silk banners, to the freshly whitewashed walls hung with Blanche's cheery tapestries.

The greatest change was in the people seated at the trestle tables where they would dine after the settlement had been made. Their clothes were clean and sturdy, their faces pink and healthy, but it was the light, the happiness, shining in eyes once dull with despair that touched her heart.

Expectation, not fear, filled her as she entered. Crisp rushes crackled underfoot as she took her first step toward the raised dais. The scent of rosemary and new grass rose around her to mingle with that of hot tallow and the yeast from the bread waiting in the buttery behind the carved wooden screen.

Pride. That was what Jesse felt as she stepped up and took her place behind the high table. Pride in what she and her

people had accomplished here. Her hands might not have
wielded the saw or the stone chisel that built the hall, nor plied
the needle that made the banners, but it had been her vision
that had led them. Her hand that had steadied them, given
them direction after Edmund's death.

Once startled out of her numbness by Master Robert's arrival, she had been quick to act, sending messages to the towns,
farms and keeps under her control. She informed them of the
change in leadership, but fearing some men might not not welcome being ruled by a woman, she had made mention of her
large army under William de Lacy's command. "If you are
attacked, send to me at once for protection," she had told her
vassals. Implied had been the message that this same army
could also reach out to quash any who rebelled against their
new overlord.

Each day since then had been a challenge. She had made
decisions on everything from the harvesting of crops to her
vassals' marriage partners, settled disputes over property, in-
heritance and water rights. At first, she'd felt woefully inadequate to the task, but from somewhere deep inside her had
seemed to come the means to handle each crisis. Occasionally
she sent to Gaby or Ari for advice, but more often she found
herself thinking, "What would Alex have done about this?"
'Twas as though he stood at her shoulder, whispering in her
ear.

The first time that had happened, she had done the opposite of what that voice whispered, with disastrous consequences. Over time, it had become easier to rely on that inner
voice and think of it as hers. She had been grateful her days
were long and busy, though, because when her mind was idle
it too soon focused on the one thing that was missing from her
life. Alex.

Jesse groaned softly, the ache of his leaving still fresh. Surely
she was cursed. The longer he was away the more Alex seemed
to prey on her mind. Sometimes a face glimpsed in the courtyard—a taunting smile, a brow raised just so—would remind
her of Alex. Too many morns she awoke early, her mind
clouded with sleep, a dream of their time on the island lingering on her mind, and swear his scent lingered on the air, as
well.

"M'lady. Are you ready?" inquired a voice at her side.

Jesse started, turning to the new steward. Clive was a thin, capable man of middle years with earnest brown eyes and a bald spot he constantly massaged as though to encourage the hair to grow again. "Of course. Please begin." She scolded herself for daydreaming. And about Alex, of all people. As she sat down in her high-backed chair a grimy man two tables away winked at her. She blinked in surprise, then frowned. His clothes were patched and rumpled, his face streaked with black to match the patch that covered one eye. The other stared at her boldly.

"Is aught wrong?" asked Clive, all concern.

Her eyes drifted back, lit on the man's single piercing one and skittered away. "Who is that man with the eye patch?"

Clive looked, shrugged. "The tanner, m'lady."

Jesse's nose wrinkled as the word conjured up the terrible smells associated with that trade, but no whiff of dung reached her. A fleeting glance showed the folk sitting next to him seemed unoffended. Mayhap he *had* washed. She tried to look at him without seeming to, but it was hard to miss that knowing smile. Jesse flushed. "Has he been at Harte Court long?"

Clive blinked, clearly not understanding what had upset her. "Since I arrived two months ago. Does he offend you?"

"Of course he does," Jesse snapped. "Only see how he lounges there, all tattered and...and insolent." A blight on her first ceremony as lady here, a goad to her already nervous stomach.

"Shall I have him removed?"

"Nay." Much as the thought of tossing the cocky tanner out on his ear appealed, such treatment belonged in Edmund's era, not hers. She put a hand to her queasy belly and pressed. Something fluttered back. The babe? Wonder washed over her, but when she raised her head, 'twas the tanner's dark eye that locked on hers, sharing the moment, shattering it. "Pray begin," she told Clive in a voice that shook.

At a sign from Clive her vassals began lining up in the back of the hall. Jesse kept her attention rigidly fixed on them until Father Francis slipped into the chair beside her.

"Good morn, m'lady." Smiling, he opened the ledger where he would record the vassals' payments. He was the first priest to live at Harte Court in twenty years. Young, energetic and a balm to the souls of her people already. That the burr in his speech and the blue eyes so like his Uncle Bevan MacLean's reminded her of Alex, Jesse had learned to accept because once again Alex had sent Harte Court, and her, just what they needed.

"Do ye still intend ta return part o' the rent monies?"

"Aye. To those who must repair their homes and such, but 'tis important to first collect the rents." She knew from her experience working with the peasants that her people needed the discipline and guidance . . . at least for the time being.

"Sir Ralph Thurlow approaches," the priest whispered.

Jesse looked up to find her chief vassal standing before her. 'Twas the moment she had dreaded. The knight who held Ravenshead of the Harcourts was big and loud and had always carried out Edmund's orders. Would he swear to her? Or think her a weak woman, unsuitable to lead?

That the other men would follow Sir Ralph's lead was clear from the way they hung back, watching the tableau at the head table. Tension swept through the hall, silencing the voices until 'twas so quiet all Jesse could hear was the pounding of her heart. Curling her fingers inward until the nails creased her palms, she fought the urge to cringe.

Sweet Mary, what was she doing here? Out of the corner of her eye, she saw the tanner smile encouragement. No matter the source, 'twas all Jesse needed. "Sir Ralph, you are well come." For a wonder, her voice sounded fairly firm.

"Lady Jesselynn," the knight boomed. "'Tis passing strange to recall that gangly lass who used to play with the hounds under my feet." *Here it comes,* Jesse thought, bracing for the blow. "Yet here ye are all grown-up and lady here." A smile creased his large face, his dark eyes shone beneath grizzled brows as they swept the hall. "And what a wonder ye've wrought here. I never thought the day would come when I'd enter Harte Court Castle with an easy mind and a joyful heart."

Her eyes widened in surprise as he bowed low before her. "Gladly do I render the payment that's due ye." The coins in the sack he carried jingled as he plunked it down on the table.

)efore her. Turning, he raised both thick arms over his head
ınd roared. "God love and keep our Lady Jesse."

As one man, the others in the hall rose, shouting her name
ıntil the rafters rang with "God love our lady."

The strangest feeling moved over Jesse . . . warm and gentle
ıs the breeze from the open windows, chasing out fear and
doubt and even unworthiness. Was this love? she thought,
lazed. It gave her the most wonderful sense of belonging. Alex
ıad made her feel like this when they were on the island. Had
she loved him after all? Suddenly she realized she was crying
ınd fumbled at her waist for the linen square Blanche had
tucked there.

Of the rest of the ceremony, she remembered little but smiling faces and words of praise from her vassals as they settled
what they owed and pledged their fealty. The last man was
bowing before her when Clive ran up to whisper in her ear.

"The Sommervilles are come, Lady Jesse."

Jesse sat abruptly as her knees failed her. Alex? Alex was
here? Sure enough, a wedge of Sommervilles were advancing
into the hall, the candlelight gleaming off bright silks and
polished gems, Lord Geoffrey himself in the lead with Catherine on his arm. Behind him came Ruarke, Gabrielle and
Gareth. No Alex.

Somehow Jesse got down off the dais by the time they
reached it. Uncertain of herself, she started to curtsy, found
herself swept up on a tide of hugs and kisses. Her newly sensitized feelings soaked up the warmth of their greeting. Why,
it almost seemed as though they . . . they loved her.

"It is good to see you looking so well, my dear," Catherine
said, holding both of Jesse's hands in hers and smiling with
such loving approval Jesse felt the tears well anew, but the light
kiss the earl brushed over her forehead meant even more.

"You've wrought wonders here," he said in that deep, stirring voice. "And your people sing your praises. Ari tells me
there is much we could learn from you."

"Th-thank you," Jesse stammered, touched beyond words.

"Your gown is beautiful. I am pleased to see you in silks,"
Gaby said lightly as the earl and countess moved away.

Jesse grinned. "Blanche insisted, and really 'tis not so bad.
The skirt is short in the front so I need not worry about trip-

ping on my hem." Another of Alex's suggestions, she thought, shoving aside the pang that brought. "I am so pleased and surprised to see you all," she added breathlessly.

"Alex asked us to come." Gaby looked around for him.

"H-he is not here," Jesse managed past the pain that twisted inside her. Suddenly it was all too much. She wanted to run away and lick her wounds in private, but Gareth tugged at her sleeve.

"Ari wanted to come but she is not traveling these days." His grimace said a battle had preceded that decision. "She made you these." He thrust two silver cups into her hands. They were beautifully made, the stems fashioned from a pair of dolphins intertwined. "The pattern is like the one her grandsire used for the candlesticks he presented his wife at their wedding."

Wedding. The word slashed at her, mocked her. "Very nice," Jesse said numbly, setting the cups on the table.

"Weddin'!" Father Francis slammed shut the ledger and jumped up. "Wi' all the excitement I near forgot I've a weddin' to perform." He pulled a prayer book from his vestments and began thumbing through it.

"Whose wedding?" Jesse wanted to know. As lady here no one wed without her permission and she'd given no one—

"Ours." 'Twas the tanner sauntering toward her, but his height, the way he carried himself with such pride yet moved with fluid grace left her in no doubt as to who it was.

"Alex?" she gasped.

He stopped a pace away from her. "Jess," was all he said, but that single word shook her with the force of a storm. The unsmiling mouth was not like him, but she should have known the firm cleft chin, the strong jaw, the eye—

"Oh, Sweet Mary. Your eye." She had sworn not to touch him, but her fingers reached up, trembled over the patch of leather.

"Part of my disguise." He whipped it off and blinked at her.

"You fiend!" With the hand so recently set to soothe, she slapped his deceitful face.

"I think Jess and I need to talk, first," he said to the group at large. Before she could protest, he had her out through the buttery door and into the kitchen garden. "Either your hand got harder or I got softer." He rubbed his reddened jaw.

Jesse crossed her arms over her chest. "Much has changed ere, and I begin to see now 'twas your doing, not mine." Joy, victory, pride, all lay bitter as gall on her tongue.

"I had no hand in the things you accomplished here."

"Liar!" She fairly vibrated with outrage. "You sent Master Robert and Master Simon, and...and everything. You did t all." She was close to tears, struggling to master them.

Alex ached to close the gap between them and hold her but knew it was too soon. Much yet remained to be said. "I but provided you with the materials, the people. You did the rest."

"You were here," she accused, eyes hot and hostile.

"Aye. Think you I would leave my wife alone and unprotected?" he demanded stiffly. "I watched over you—even whilst you slept."

Jesse blinked. "You came to my chamber?" That explained why she had often awakened with the feeling he'd been with her.

"'Twas heaven and hell to see you sleeping there, so near yet forbidden to me." He sighed. "Many's the night I spent counting—not to cool my anger, but to keep from reaching for you. Still I accepted it as my penance and stayed close by except for those times I rode out to your other holdings."

"You went to them?" Contentment fled. "You told them to follow my lead? Likely you even coerced Sir Ralph into blessing me today—" She choked. A sham. It had all been a sham. "Now you are here to take everything I have worked so hard or."

Alex went to her then, took her by the shoulders because he feared she'd fly apart. "I am here to take nothing. All is yours. You have earned it. Nor did your vassals I visited know I was any but an itinerant tanner. Ask any in the hall today. My only purpose was to look and listen, to make certain none of your people plotted against you. Please believe me."

Jesse closed her eyes briefly, battling doubt. She could no more hate him than she could the babe who shared his blood. But trust? "Then why? Why did you keep yourself hidden?"

Alex exhaled softly, his grip gentling as he kneaded her tense muscles. At least she was listening. "Because I wanted you to see that I was not greedy for control of your lands or your wealth. And, too, there were things you needed to prove, to

your people, but most importantly, to yourself. You have come
into your own, my lady, and I am very, very proud of you.''

With tears stinging her eyes, Jesse looked up, expecting to
see the passion that edged his voice. Instead, she saw love,
sweet and tender. His eyes were dark wells of love so deep they
seemed endless. The love had been there all along, Jesse realized, mingling with his passion for her. Had she been too
blinded by her own insecurities to see it? Or was it because
until today, when she had seen her people's love for her, she
had not truly realized that love went beyond desire.

''No matter what heights our lovemaking reached, you were
not ready before to accept the rest of my love,'' Alex said as
though in answer to her question. ''Now you are.''

''Aye,'' she said softly, wondering at the feelings that bub-
bled up inside her. Happiness. Contentment. And belonging.
Aye. She belonged to him and he to her. Suddenly she wanted
to feel his arms around her, wanted to kiss him with the sun on
their faces. ''I—I love you.''

''Thank God.'' The fierceness of the joy and relief that
flooded his features made her feel light as air, but instead of
smiling and snatching her up, as she saw he wanted to, he
shuddered. ''Ah, Jess, I want to take you off somewhere private and show you how much I love you.''

''Aye.'' She took a step toward him, wanting, needing.

Alex shook his head, his fists clenching with the effort it
took not to reach for her. ''I've a debt of honor to settle with
you first. 'Tis why I chose Settlement Day. But before that, I'd
tell you that Parlan has confessed. 'Twas he who hatched the
plot to mint the false coins and frame my father, not Hugh. He
who first planted the idea of killing himself in Hugh's mind.''

''Oh.'' She clasped both hands over her heart, her eyes filling with tears of gratitude. ''Thank you, Alex. It eases my guilt
and my memories of Hugh to know that.'' Her fingers slid
down to her belly, and he could almost hear the ''but'' forming in her mind. She loved him, yet a tract of sadness remained.

He would ease that, too, Alex thought, reaching for her, his
fingers lightly stroking the mound of their child. ''She moved
just before the ceremony started.''

''Aye.'' Jess smiled through her tears. ''It may be a boy.''

Alex nodded. For himself, he had wanted a girl, but a boy ould suit his new plans better. Gauging her mood, he de- ided the time was ripe. "I'd have us wed again."

She started. "Again? But why?"

"'Tis a matter of that debt of honor."

Her frown deepened. "The marriage at Carr End wasn't le- al?"

So, she did harbor a niggle of distrust. Healing that and her adness were his final goals. "It was legal, but what I owe you an only be settled if we wed again." He extended his hand to er, palm up. "I hope that by staying away these three months have shown you I am not greedy or untrustworthy. Please ave enough faith in me, and in my love to wed with me again. 'Tis very important to me . . . to us."

'Twas the least she owed him, Jesse thought. "Very well." esse placed her hand in his, yet her curiosity grew as she went vith him back inside the hall where Father Francis and the thers waited. All the way to the chapel, Jesse tried to catch iaby's eye to see if she knew what was going on, but the crowd f laughing, cheering people—many of whom had already een into the wine and ale—kept getting in the way.

Inside the chapel, the sweet scent of late-blooming flowers illed the air, mingling with the voices of her people and his amily. Yet her third wedding was as strange as the other two, esse thought as she knelt beside her unsmiling bridegroom- usband, her palms sweaty as a virgin bride's. He loved her; he loved him. She even trusted him again, but would love be nough to keep her from remembering she was the last of the Iarcourts?

As Father Francis began to speak, Jesse cast a sidelong lance at Alex. His eyes were full on her, gleaming in the can- llelight, stripped bare of mockery, open to her as they had een on the island, letting her see clear down to his soul. In- ide her something stirred, unfurled. 'Twas her soul reaching ut to his. Vision blurring, she turned her hand and laced her ingers with his. Like to like. Two halves of one whole.

"Lady Jesselynn," Father Francis prompted.

She started, blushed as she wrenched her attention from Alex. "I did not hear you, Father."

"I asked if you would have Alexander Harcourt f
your—"

"Alexander *Harcourt!*" Jesse exclaimed, looking to Alex
He smiled then, slowly, sweetly, nearly blinding her with h
love. "Alexander Harcourt," he confirmed. "I knew me
words could not buy your forgiveness, but I hoped a deed fro
the heart would. I had my name changed to prove to you I di
not covet what is yours for the Sommervilles. God willing," I
went on softly, his free hand coming to rest on the curve whe
their child slept, "your brother was not the last of that nam
And together with our children, we will make it stand for e
erything that is good and honorable."

"Nay, you can not be serious," she whispered, heart swel
ing with the magnitude of what he would give up for her. Wha
of his family? His father? She turned, her gaze skimming th
happy, tear-streaked faces of the other Sommervilles to rest o
the earl's proud features. The smile of approval Geoffrey gav
her went a long way toward soothing her doubts.

"It weighed heavily on Papa's conscience that he did no
somehow prevent Hugh's death," Alex said, drawing her bac
around to him. "We can not bring Hugh back, but—"

"Oh, Alex. What can I say?"

"'I do' would be most welcome. I've a yearning to try ou
our new bed," he drawled, giving her a broad wink.

"You, sir, are a rogue. My rogue," she softly added, alon
with a loud, heartfelt "I do."

Epilogue

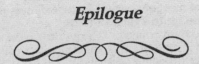

News that Arianna had been safely delivered of a son reached arte Court just ahead of a snowstorm the last week of February. Alex read the message to Jesse as she lay amid the pillows in their bed.

"They've named him Richard, after Ari's father," Alex id.

"Oh, I am so happy for them. They both came through it all ght?" Jesse asked with a hint of fear for her new sister.

"Ari and Richard are fine, but Gareth is still shaking so dly I can barely read his scrawl," Alex said with a smile that uld not conceal his own worries as he eyed the enormous ound Jesse's stomach made beneath the covers.

"Will you comb my hair?" Jesse asked.

He set the parchment aside, took an ivory comb from the ble beside the bed and started stroking it through her now aist-length curls, spreading them on the pillow.

Watching the contentment and adoration soften his features, she teased, "I think you wed me for my hair."

"Aye." He grinned. "And the clever brain beneath it." He ssed her forehead. "And the bright eyes." His lips deended.

"Comb," she ordered, giggling. As she had ripened with eir child, so their marriage had grown richer and fuller. Not at they did not quarrel. She was still stubborn, he still liked manage people, but they learned to share more and from the aring came understanding, compromise and a deeper love.

"I'll be glad when our babe is born," Jesse said, shifting ositions. "I've forgotten what my feet look like."

"Is he kicking up a fuss?" Alex now said he'd be glad of[a] son to carry on the Harcourt name.

"Nay, but my back aches." She rubbed at the annoyi[ng] pain.

"Ah, I thought there had to be a reason why you gave in s[o] readily when I suggested you lie down and rest."

"You did not mention a nap," Jesse said, eyes narrowin[g.] "You challenged me to a game of chess."

Alex shrugged and grinned. "The results are the same. Yo[u] are lying down instead of tiring yourself with working on th[e] ledgers." He set the comb aside and kissed her. "Sleep no[w.] I'll play chess with you when I get back from Alfred's farm.["]

"You are going out in this weather?" Jesse did not like th[e] sound of the snow beating against the window.

"He has a mare I wanted to look at."

And she sensed Alex's restlessness. Alfred's farm was n[ot] far, but Jesse wanted him near for some reason she could n[ot] identify. "I am not sleepy, but a game of chess might take m[y] mind off my back," she said slyly.

"Vixen." Fondly.

"I have had a good teacher." Jesse had not only learned [to] live with Alex's penchant for managing things, she'd eve[n] adapted it to her own uses. She helped him set up the che[ss] pieces, but her mind strayed. "Will you find enough to o[c-]cupy you here on land?" she blurted out.

The piece Alex had just picked up hung suspended. "Ha[s] that been bothering you all along and you never told me?"

"I've wondered about it a time or two," she hedged.

He snorted. "And not told me? I thought we'd agreed to b[e] completely honest with each other, Jess Harcourt."

Nothing was guaranteed to touch her quicker than the re[-]minder of what he had sacrificed for her happiness. He ha[d] realized even before she fully had how much she had wante[d] to make her family name shine again. "Speaking of honest[y,] your father still has a hard time calling you Harcourt."

Alex smiled, thinking of another surprise he had for he[r.] "Well, he'll have to get used to it because—"

"Oh, Alex— Oh!" She gasped and grabbed her belly.

"What is it?"

"I . . . I think the babe is coming," she said when she coul[d]

"Oh, my God!" For one instant her strong, capable hus-and panicked. Her second pain jolted him into action. He left ong enough to shout down the stairs for Blanche to fetch the nidwife, then sprinted back to her side. The wave of women ere not long in following, rushing about with hot water and lean clothes. It took the large, elderly midwife to restore or-er, but even she could not convince Alex to leave.

"We do everything together," he told the woman. Then he tripped off his boots, climbed into bed and knelt behind Jesse o she reclined in the vee of his legs, her back against the hard all of his chest. "I'll push with you," Alex told her with more heer than he felt. Jesu, he was scared. And things got worse efore they got better. He had never realized how much work nd pain was involved in birthing one tiny infant.

Hours went by, they were both wet with sweat, shaking from xhaustion and still the babe refused to deliver. Alex's arms ere raw from Jesse's nails, his legs and back muscles creaming from the cramped position, yet none of it pierced is concern for Jesse. "Rest, love," he crooned in between ontractions.

"There's the head," crowed the midwife.

Jesse slumped against Alex, panting. "Thank God."

"Amen," Alex echoed. One more push, one more tortured roan from both their throats and the midwife was holding a crap of wailing humanity aloft. "Our babe," he murmured everently as the child was laid on the bed, quickly washed and waddled.

"You have a son." Blanche was beaming.

Jesse looked up at Alex, saw by the flicker of disappoint-ent that crossed his face that he really had wanted a daugh-er. "Mayhap next time we'll get your girl."

"Next time!" He stared at her as though she had suggested e walk through fire. "You are not going through this again."

Jesse smiled . . . just before another pain ripped her apart.

"Twins!" Blanche and the midwife shrieked together.

The second babe slid into the world with little fuss. The nidwife presently handed a dazed Alex his second son.

Exhausted but exhilarated, Jesse fell asleep. When she woke, the late-afternoon sun slanted into the room. Alex tood at the window, bathed in golden light that turned his hair

to tawny fire. His head was thrown back, giving him the lo[ok]
of a proud and haughty lion.

"Alex?" she whispered.

He turned and she saw he held a blanketed cub in the cro[ok]
of each arm. "We have been waiting for you to waken. A[re]
you all right?" he asked gruffly.

Jesse read perfectly the darkening of his eyes before they sl[id]
away from hers. Blamed himself, did he. Well, she'd fix tha[t].
"I am fine. What do you think of your sons?"

Your sons. Though he had wanted a daughter, Alex felt h[is]
heart swell as he divided a glance between the babes. "They a[re]
perfect, Jess, only wait till you see." He was at the bed in tw[o]
strides, kneeling to lay them down beside her. "I think th[ey]
have my eyes."

"And your hair," Jesse said, sharing his excitement as [she]
unwrapped the two bundles for her inspection.

"They are identical," he marveled, looking from one ti[ny]
face to the other. His hands felt huge, clumsy as he hesitant[ly]
stroked the matching heads of gold down. They did not cr[y,]
just waved their arms and legs and stared at him from da[rk]
eyes so like his own the loving hurt. "Only the oldest is a lit[tle]
bigger and the younger has a mole on his flank just like I do[."]

"I remember that mark." Jesse wondered if someday [a]
woman would think it as fascinating as she did Alex's. "Bu[t I]
see nothing in them of me. 'Tis a bit disappointing after I d[id]
all, well, most, of the work."

Alex was very disappointed, too, but he'd not tell her so a[f-]
ter all she went through. "You shall name them both."

"Sommer for the older. Sommerville Harcourt," she e[x-]
plained, rewrapping the babes lest they take a chill. "A livi[ng]
symbol of the peace between the families."

Alex nodded his approval. "And Hugh for the younger?["]

"I'd like that," Jesse said softly. "Put them in their crad[le]
there by the fire and come lie beside me." The first he d[id]
willingly and skillfully, nuzzling their baby necks and mu[r-]
muring love words before tucking them in. But he balked [at]
joining her, as she'd half expected him to do. "I'm cold, Ale[x,]
and you know I won't sleep well without your arms arou[nd]
me." She smiled when he reluctantly crawled under the co[v-]
ers.

"Thank you for my sons," Alex murmured, holding her as though she were made of spun glass. "I have a gift for you, but 'll have to get a second one now."

Jesse turned so she could see his face in the wash of morning light. "I love presents, but you have already given me two. The Harcourts have never had two male heirs in one generation before. I can not wait until tomorrow and the next day to watch them grow."

"Aye, 'twill be something to watch. We will raise them both with love and honor." As you were not, he thought sadly, but he intended to spend the rest of their lives spoiling her to make up for that lack. Already he had Gareth looking for a horse for Jesse to ride come spring. And Meggie was fashioning a split-skirted gown he hoped would keep Jesse from going back to the revealing men's hose when she was up and about again.

"You will find enough to keep you busy on land?"

"Aye. I am going to court with Papa to help with the labor laws." Her squeal of delight ended in a hug that left him hungry for more. "Mayhap I'd best go to sea, Jess," he said, putting distance between them. "I do not want you bearing a babe every year, but I love you too much to leave you alone."

"I love you," Jesse said, putting all she felt into the look she gave him, glorying in the answering spark that lit his eyes. "There are herbs I can use to see we don't get too many babes."

"Really?" He looked skeptical, but tucked her into the curve of his body. "Good. I would rather not be further away from you than the few hours' ride to London."

"Nor would I. You were right, Sommervilles do make good husbands." But even as she snuggled close to Alex, the warm, syrupy feeling of belonging stealing through her, she was planning for that little red-haired girl he wanted. Mayhap in June of next year, when the strawberries came in season, they'd sail to the island, just the two of them and see....

"Harcourt," Alex reminded her, kissing the top of her head. "My name is Harcourt now, but I'll still be the best husband...."

"Aye. That you are." Jesse sighed. It did not matter whether they had a dozen children or just the two God had already

given them. Peace and love. Those were the things tha
counted.

Never in her wildest dreams had she thought to find either
Yet here she was, mistress of Harte Court, wife to a man wh
valued her for herself and mother to a whole new generatio
of Harcourts who would grow up to live in harmony with thei
Sommerville cousins.

Jesse drifted off to sleep with a smile of contentment on he
face, thinking she was the happiest woman in the kingdom.

*   *   *   *   *